"Kiss me."

She was vaguely aware that she was begging but didn't care. "Or I shall kiss you."

He swallowed and opened his mouth, probably to object. She had to do something fast, so she reached up and tugged at the white ribbon in her hair, pulling it inch by inch until it was free. Then she dropped it onto James's lap. While he stared down at the length of silk, she removed a few pins, letting her curls bounce down her back.

"Jesus, Olivia." With that, James took her face between his palms and hauled her toward him. Their desire exploded in a kiss that was fierce, hungry, raw. His tongue, hot and insistent, thrust into her mouth, as though he were claiming her for his own. He speared his fingers through her hair and grabbed a fistful like he was afraid she might pull away and end the kiss.

Not likely. She'd been waiting years for James to unleash the full force of his passion. She'd known it was there, simmering just beneath the surface, like lava waiting to erupt. And now it had. Every time her tongue tangled with his, he moaned. He breathed heavily, like he was starving for air—and for her. Never had she seen him so stripped of control, and it thrilled her.

"Olivia," he gasped. "I want you so badly that I forget who I am and what is right."

"I know who you are," she murmured. "And this feels very right to me."

Scandalous Summer Nights

ANNE BARTON

FOREVER

NEW YORK   BOSTON

Copyright © 2014 by Anne Barton

Excerpt from *One Wild Winter's Eve* © 2014 by Anne Barton

All rights reserved. In accordance with the U.S. Copyright Act of 1976, the scanning, uploading, and electronic sharing of any part of this book without the permission of the publisher constitute unlawful piracy and theft of the author's intellectual property. If you would like to use material from the book (other than for review purposes), prior written permission must be obtained by contacting the publisher at permissions@hbgusa.com. Thank you for your support of the author's rights.

Forever

Hachette Book Group

1290 Avenue of the Americas

New York, NY 10104

www.HachetteBookGroup.com

Printed in the United States of America

First Edition: October 2014

10 9 8 7 6 5 4 3 2 1

OPM

Forever is an imprint of Grand Central Publishing.
The Forever name and logo are trademarks of Hachette Book Group, Inc.

The Hachette Speakers Bureau provides a wide range of authors for speaking events. To find out more, go to www.hachettespeakersbureau.com or call (866) 376-6591.

The publisher is not responsible for websites (or their content) that are not owned by the publisher.

For my beautiful sister, Janis—
the kind of friend every girl should have.

Scandalous Summer Nights

Chapter One

Authentic: (1) Referring to an antiquity or artifact that is genuine;
not a fake or forgery. (2) True and real, as in
Her feelings for the dashing solicitor were authentic—
and, vexingly, unreciprocated.

London, 1817

 Any girl with a smidgen of good sense would have
given up on James Averill years ago.

Olivia Sherbourne's problem was not so much a lack
of good sense as it was an abundance of stubbornness.
She'd pined after James for ten long years. No matter that
he gave her scarce little encouragement; her patience was
born out of a love that was deep, abiding, and true.

Also, she'd once seen his naked chest.

It was magnificent. And it had sustained her for the
better part of a decade.

Even now, as Olivia surreptitiously watched him from
across Lady Easton's brilliantly lit ballroom, she could

well imagine what lay beneath his finely tailored jacket. Warm, sun-browned skin, sinewy muscle, and a sculpted abdomen to rival Apollo's.

Indeed, she could imagine all sorts of things. And she often did.

At the moment, as she spied him talking with her brother, Owen, the Duke of Huntford, she couldn't help thinking about how she'd love to slide her hands beneath James's lapels and up his chest, nudge his jacket off his impossibly broad shoulders, and spear her fingers through his short brown curls.

Normally, Olivia was more given to action than fantasy. She spoke her mind freely—her brother might say *too* freely—and did what she thought was right, even if polite society disagreed. She unapologetically pursued the things she wanted: an education that extended beyond music and French; some semblance of control over her future; and meaningful, if unconventional, friendships. She was not shy about chasing her desires.

Except when it came to James.

Because he mattered more than everything.

She'd loved him, her brother's childhood friend, from afar for so long that some might think her rather, well, pathetic. But he'd given signs of noticing her of late— distracted glances and puzzled frowns. Granted, they weren't the most encouraging of signs, but who knew? Perhaps tonight would be the night he finally asked her to waltz. A girl could dream.

And she was willing to wait for his feelings to catch up with hers. In fact, she would have been content to stand there, on the perimeter of the dance floor, catching glimpses of him here and there all evening. She easily spotted him in the throng. His athletic physique and easy smile turned her bones to jelly, and a soft sigh escaped her lips.

A throat cleared, and she wrested her gaze away from James, focusing it on the classically handsome face of the man standing before her. "My apologies, Lord Dixon. I fear I was woolgathering." Her cheeks warmed.

"It is I who should apologize, for startling you." The young marquess smiled reassuringly. "And I must confess I find your ability to daydream amid the chaos of a ball impressive. Not to mention charming," he added, blue eyes twinkling.

"You are most kind." Lord Dixon was just the sort of gentleman Owen would like her to marry: well respected, titled, rich, and unfailingly proper. Olivia herself could find only one flaw with him—he wasn't James.

The marquess smoothed a hand down the front of his waistcoat and cleared his throat once more. "Lady Olivia, would you care to—"

"Ah, there you are." Rose, Olivia's younger sister, rushed to her side, breathless and uncharacteristically agitated. "Good evening, Lord Dixon." She half curtsied. "I hope I'm not interrupting."

"Not at all. We were just about to—"

"I wondered if I might have a word with you, Olivia." She cast an apologetic glance at the marquess. "In private."

Rose's normally serene expression was marred by worry lines on her forehead. A chill slithered up Olivia's spine. Her sister wouldn't dream of impolitely whisking her away unless the matter were truly urgent.

"Of course." Lord Dixon bowed graciously. "Don't let

me delay you. We may resume our conversation later, if it pleases you."

"I shall look forward to it," Olivia said. "Thank you for your understanding."

"Yes, thank you," Rose echoed, even as she began tugging Olivia by the arm. She led her to a secluded spot between two potted palms and wrung her hands.

"You're frightening me, Rose. What's happened?"

"I've just learned some news. And I wanted to tell you before you heard it from someone else. I'm afraid you'll find it...distressing."

Olivia's fingers went numb. "Is someone ill? Anabelle's mother? Or the baby?"

"No, no. They're fine. It's nothing like that."

"Then what?"

Rose's eyes shone with compassion. "It concerns Mr. Averill."

"James?" Olivia's knees wobbled, and she grasped the edge of a pot for support. "Is he"—dear God, she could barely bring herself to utter the word—"engaged?" Her voice cracked.

Rose shook her head emphatically. "No."

Olivia took a gulp of air and nodded. "That's good." If James was neither engaged nor dead, the news could not be that devastating. Could it?

"He just made an announcement. It seems that he's preparing to travel to Egypt."

The ballroom tilted. "Egypt?"

"Yes, where he'll participate in an archaeological dig—for two years."

Olivia blinked. "Did you say *two years*?"

"I'm afraid so."

Olivia swallowed the painful lump in her throat. "When? That is, when will he leave?"

"At the end of the summer. I'm so sorry, Olivia."

"It's all right," she lied. "I knew he was fond of antiquities, of course. I just never imagined..." *A future without James in it.*

"Would you like to leave the ball? I could tell Owen that you have a headache and we could return home."

"No. No need to spoil your night."

"I don't mind—"

"I know." Olivia smoothed a few stray locks behind her ears as though composing herself were just that easy. "Summer's end. That's only, what, eight weeks away?"

"Yes." Rose looked as distraught as Olivia felt.

"Then that's all the time I have."

"For what?"

"To make him fall in love with me." Of course, she would first have to make him notice her. And treat her as something other than a piece of furniture that one avoided so as not to stub a toe.

Rose's brow furrowed with empathy. "I'm not certain it's possible to *make* someone fall in love." As always, Rose was the voice of logic and reason. But certainly there was also a time for passion. Olivia decided that time was now.

"You are right, as usual. Still, I must try."

"How?"

"I wish I knew." She'd already tried daring gowns, turned ankles, and moving bits of poetry. "None of my more subtle tacks has succeeded in capturing his attention."

"You must remember," Rose said sympathetically, "that Mr. Averill is a close friend of Owen's. Our brother can be terribly intimidating."

Olivia loved Rose for suggesting their brother might be the cause of James's apparent lack of interest, but she knew better. "James isn't afraid of Owen—or anyone." Though James looked a perfect gentleman, he was arguably the best boxer in all of London.

"True. But Mr. Averill is an honorable gentleman and, as such, would respect Owen's wishes with regard to you. A boxing match is one thing. Sisters are quite another."

"This is one aspect of my life that I refuse to let Owen dictate. And given tonight's news, I think I must resort to drastic measures."

Rose paled. "Your impulsive nature is one of the things I love best about you...," she began.

"But...?"

"You must think carefully about what you will say to Mr. Averill tonight. Your actions could have serious and lasting consequences—for both of you."

"I know." Olivia swallowed, sobered by her sister's words. "Wish me luck?"

Rose hugged her. "You know I do. Just...be careful. I don't want to see you hurt."

Olivia smiled weakly. "Neither do I." But she knew heartbreak was a distinct possibility.

Her unrequited love must seem ridiculous to her family and friends. Indeed, she questioned her own good sense on a daily basis. But this was no fleeting infatuation. She had a connection with James, understood him. She was charmed by the way his lips moved when he was deep in thought—as though he were talking himself through a difficult problem. She loved the way his eyes lit up when he recounted the latest additions to the British Museum. She even adored his tendency to become distracted by a rare plant when she endeavored to show off a smart new pair of slippers.

Still, she'd never stoop to snaring James in a marriage trap. She didn't want to trick him into taking her as his wife.

What she wanted—what she'd dreamed of every single night for the last ten years—was his complete and utter adoration. She wanted to wake up beside him and have cozy conversations over breakfast. She wanted to ride with him all afternoon and then find a shady spot where they could eat sliced chicken, crusty bread, and strawberries. She wanted him to pick wildflowers and tuck one behind her ear and look at her as though he couldn't believe how fortunate he was that he'd found her.

Although, in actuality, *she* had found *him*. But she loved him too much to quibble over such trifling matters.

And that's why the thought of confessing her feelings to James terrified her.

After tonight, she wouldn't be able to delude herself with platitudes like *He simply isn't aware you hold him in such high regard* or *He must believe his attentions would be unwelcome.*

She had to face the very real and terrifying possibility that he did not return her affections.

A shiver stole through her limbs, but she shook it off. Ten years of dreaming and two and one-half seasons of waiting could *not* be for naught.

Their fairy-tale romance would begin tonight.

Olivia simply refused to believe anything different.

James Averill could be forgiven if he arrived at the Easton ball slightly foxed.

He was celebrating, damn it.

In a couple months he'd be on a ship headed to the land of archaeological wonders.

It had taken years of meticulous planning, but he'd finally realized his dream. He'd saved enough money to ensure his mother and brother would be comfortable. He'd taken on a partner so that his clients wouldn't be left in a lurch.

In just eight weeks, he'd leave behind his office, complete with stacks of mind-numbing contracts and sleep-inducing law books, and set off for the adventure of a lifetime.

Which called for another drink.

He swept his gaze around the already bustling ballroom. Huntford and Foxburn were a head taller than most of the other guests and easy to spot in the crowd.

James smiled and nodded politely to a viscount and several older ladies as he meandered toward his friends. Thanks to his finely tailored coat and practiced manners, he blended into this privileged world rather well. Like certain species of lizards in the desert, he was capable of mimicking the landscape. However, at times such as this, he was acutely aware that ballrooms were *not* his natural environment.

He was a solicitor, someone who worked. For his living. Huntford and Foxburn didn't hold that against him, but then, they both knew he could kick their asses from London to Edinburgh and back again.

"Good evening, gentlemen." James had to admit that marriage agreed with both the duke and the earl. Huntford still brooded, but James suspected it was mostly for show. Foxburn now smiled with startling frequency.

"Averill," Huntford replied, welcoming him with a slap on the shoulder. Foxburn signaled to a passing waiter and James deduced that his drink was on its way.

The duke leaned his large frame toward James and lowered his voice. "There's a matter I need to discuss with you."

"Business?" James hoped it was nothing terribly complex. His mind was not at its sharpest.

Huntford frowned. "Of a sort. Can we meet at your office tomorrow?"

James raised a brow. "Of course."

"Very good. We will deal with it then." The duke pinched the bridge of his nose and shook his head, as if to clear his mind of troubling thoughts.

Foxburn idly tapped the foot of his cane on the parquet floor. "I understand congratulations are in order, Averill."

"Yes. Everything's been arranged. I leave for my expedition at the end of the summer."

"Egypt." Foxburn seemed to consider this as he took a large swig of his drink. "You're giving up all this"—he waved his cane in an arc to indicate the sparkling ballroom—"to ride camels?"

"And unwrap mummies," Huntford added.

"And sleep in a tent." Foxburn was really enjoying himself now. "Be careful you don't get sand in your drawers."

All three men squirmed at the thought.

"The discomfort will be worth it," James said confidently, "if I unearth one ancient artifact—one clue to the civilizations that came before us."

"What might that be?" Huntford asked, skeptical. "A bit of broken pottery? Something that *might* have been the tip of a spear but is more likely a plain old rock?"

"Well, yes." Actually, he hoped to discover something with pictures or writing—a unique piece that had never been seen before—but explaining himself to these two seemed a waste of breath. "If I find some old pottery or rocks, I'll consider the trip a success."

Huntford and Foxburn stared at him as though he should be carted off to Bedlam.

James was about to say the devil could take them both when the waiter returned with his drink. He took a long draw and found his mood improved almost immediately.

As the strains of a waltz carried through the ballroom, the duke and earl craned their necks in search of their wives. The duchess and countess were sisters, and although they didn't resemble each other, each was beautiful in her own right.

"You'd better hurry to your wives' sides," James advised. "There are half a dozen rogues here hoping to claim them for a dance."

Huntford growled. "Anabelle and Daphne are more than capable of fending off advances, aren't they, Foxburn?"

The earl snorted. "I feel sorry for the poor bastards."

James had no reason to doubt his friends, but he noticed they practically plowed through the crowd in order to join their lovely wives.

He smiled to himself and looked about for an inconspicuous spot in which to finish his drink and select a couple of beautiful young ladies to later seek out as dance partners.

It was a fine plan, and the evening promised to be pleasant.

Until Olivia Sherbourne waylaid him.

Waylaid was actually too benign a word; what Olivia did could best be described as *hunting him to ground.*

Appearing out of nowhere was an alarming habit of hers. One minute he was relaxed and pondering dance partners; the next he was toe to toe with a brown-haired, doe-eyed force of nature. A hurricane in a pretty blue frock.

"There you are!" she announced. "You must follow me."

No greeting, no niceties, just "You must follow me." Must he? *Really?* Because he'd been rather content standing there with his drink.

But Olivia was already striding toward the French doors at the back of the room, assuming he was following along at her heels like a well-trained pup. She was Huntford's sister, for God's sake. He couldn't *not* follow her.

Bloody hell.

She disappeared briefly behind a trio of matrons before slipping out the doors. James ducked out after her, determined to steer her back into the ballroom as quickly as possible.

He stepped onto the terrace, which spanned the considerable width of the house and was softly illuminated by a few lanterns and the moon, hanging in a cloudless sky.

"Over here," she called in a loud whisper. She stood at the corner of the patio, her white gloves waving him over like a beacon on the rocky shore.

Instinct told him he shouldn't do her bidding. Instinct was practically *shouting* at him, in fact, and his feet remained rooted to the flagstone.

Olivia seemed to sense his hesitation and doubled back toward him. "We haven't much time," she explained, dragging him unceremoniously along by his free arm. At least she hadn't made him spill his drink.

"Where are we going?" He thought it a fair question and desperately hoped the answer wasn't, oh, Gretna Green.

"Right here." She stopped before a stone bench.

"Why?"

She sat and pulled him down beside her. Her expression was impossible to decipher, but her chest rose and fell as though she were frightened. Her white teeth nibbled at her lower lip. Now that she had him here, she seemed at a loss for words.

That *never* happened with Olivia.

"Are you in some sort of trouble?"

"No," she said quickly. "Er, not that I know of."

He grinned. "How refreshing. Even as a girl, you always seemed to find trouble. Remember the time you managed to climb into the stable with the foals and couldn't get—"

"Don't," she snapped.

"Don't *what*?" He'd been trying to put her at ease so she could say whatever it was she needed to say. She seemed less than grateful.

"Don't treat me like Owen's little sister."

Holy hell. James drained his glass in one gulp and set it on the bench.

"If you don't want to be treated like a child," he said slowly, "stop acting like one. Start by telling me why you brought me out here."

Olivia moistened her lips with the tip of her tongue. It didn't help. Her mouth was as dry as a dust rag. "I needed to speak with you privately."

James's mossy-green eyes flashed a challenge. "I'm listening."

Her pulse raced madly. This exchange was not going at all as she'd hoped. James was supposed to have detected the tremor in her voice and taken her hands in his, smoothing the pads of his thumbs over the backs of her gloves. By now, he should be gazing at her with concern and a healthy dose of appreciation for the revealing neckline of her gown.

But his strong arms were crossed and his normally full lips were pressed together in a thin line. He had the look of someone who had requested tea an hour ago and was still waiting. Not thirsty so much as...exasperated.

Panicked, she considered making up an excuse for her behavior. She could say she wanted to buy a gift for Owen and Anabelle's new baby and was considering a puppy. Surely James must have an opinion on that—

"Olivia." The impatience gave an edge to his voice, but she also heard a hint of compassion, and it propelled her forward.

There would be no dipping her toe in the water. The only way to proceed was to hurl herself in—even if it was way over her head.

She swallowed hard and looked directly into his beautiful eyes. "I love you."

James blinked once. He wore the disoriented expression of someone who'd been woken in the middle of the night—and was not happy about it. "What do you mean?"

Olivia took a deep breath. "It happened in the summer of 1807, when you visited my brother at Huntford Manor. Owen preferred to spend summers with his friends, but Father insisted he spend at least one week with us, and he always brought you. I was eleven years old that summer, and one day I wanted to fish with you and Owen but he said I couldn't because I would only scare the fish and annoy him. I refused to leave—"

"Of course you did," James mumbled.

"So you remember that day?"

"No. Please, go on." He picked up the glass beside him and looked at the bottom forlornly.

"Owen threatened to throw me in the river if I didn't return to the house."

"Let me guess." James dragged a hand through his hair, leaving it charmingly mussed. "I championed your cause—bloodied your brother's nose so you could have your way."

"No. Even better. You gave me a chance to prove myself. You said that if I could bait my own hook with a live worm—without squealing—I should be allowed to stay and fish. Otherwise, I had to go."

"And how did you fare?"

"I succeeded. Well, Owen tried to say that it didn't count because of the retching—"

James cringed. "You didn't."

"A little. But you said that retching had not been prohibited by the agreement, so I must be permitted to stay and fish."

"I see." He looked over his shoulder toward the terrace. "So, I gather you wanted to express your gratitude, and now you have. Excellent. Shall we return to the ballroom?"

With a boldness that was shocking, even for her, she placed her hand on his leg. More precisely, his very hard and muscular thigh. "I haven't told you everything."

His gaze flew to her hand and remained there as he said, "I'm not certain we have time for the entire story, Olivia. We've been out here for a quarter of an hour and you're still in 1807."

She angled her head so that he was forced to look into her eyes. "I've waited ten years to tell you how I feel. Please, let me finish."

James placed a palm over her hand—the one still on his leg—and a delicious warmth traveled up Olivia's arm and throughout her body, leaving her breathless and tingling all over.

"If someone discovers us alone out here," he said softly, "your reputation will be shattered. Also, your brother will skewer me on the spot. If you feel that there's more you must say, we can arrange another—"

"This won't take long." She could feel him retreating and doubled her resolve. "I didn't fall in love with you that day, but I started to. Every summer I learned more about you, and you always made me feel important—like I was more than Owen's bothersome little sister. I lived for the moments I would see you again."

"You were young," James said. "It was infatuation."

Angry tears sprang to her eyes. "Then why have I waited for you? Why am I devastated at the thought of you leaving for Egypt? Why do I dream of you every single night?"

James stood and dragged his hands down his face. "You don't know what you're saying."

Olivia leaped off the bench and stood before him. "Look at me, James. I'm not a little girl." She put her hands on her hips for emphasis. "This is not a schoolgirl crush—not anymore."

"Have you been drinking?"

She heaved a sigh—he *would* have to ask that. "I may have nicked a few sips of Owen's brandy earlier today. But that was hours ago."

"You are incorrigible. Do you know that?"

She fingered the long curl that had been artfully arranged to fall over her right shoulder. "I can see that I have shocked you for the second time this evening, and I'm glad."

He clenched his jaw, and she longed to touch the faint shadow of stubble along his chin.

"I have half a mind to march into that ballroom"—he pointed behind her—"and inform your brother that he needs to find you a chaperone and tether her to you for the remainder of the season." His broad shoulders strained at the confines of his jacket each time he waved his arm for emphasis.

Olivia inched closer to him, so that only a breath separated her chest and his torso. The one she had seen in all its naked glory. He smelled like leather and ink and pure male.

"You won't do that," she said.

A feral smile lit his face. "Oh yes, I will."

Her heartbeat thundered in her chest. She knew what she must do.

Before she could lose her nerve, she threw her arms around his neck and stood on tiptoe.

And she kissed him.

Chapter Two

$\mathcal{J}$ ames inhaled sharply as Olivia's body collided with his. Her hands locked behind his head and she pressed her lips to his.

He grabbed her by the elbows and ducked out of her embrace. "What the hell are you doing?"

She took two steps back and pressed one hand over her mouth, the other over her belly.

"This is madness," he muttered, more to himself than to her.

His blood was boiling—and not from desire. How dare Olivia spoil their friendship? Things would never be the same between them now. No more playful banter, no more gentle teasing. She'd ruined *everything*. Including his lifelong friendship with her brother.

And if there was one thing he didn't need right now, it was a scandal. Or melodrama of any sort. Nothing that would interfere with his plans to travel and explore.

"I'm going to pretend that you didn't do that," he said carefully. "In fact, it never happened."

Her chest heaved above the neckline of her gown, which was much too revealing now that he thought on it. He was shocked that Huntford let her out of the house in that pitiful excuse for a dress. She looked as though she might cry. And she still hadn't spoken a word since he pushed her away.

He counted to ten in his head and let the anger seep out of him. Somehow, Olivia had gotten the wrong idea. The gentlemanly thing to do would be to firmly but kindly inform her that while he was flattered, he was in no way able to return her affections.

Above all else, he had to quickly escort her back to her brother's side.

He let out a long breath, grabbed her by the hand, and pulled her back to the bench. "Let's sit."

For once, she did as he asked. She was slightly more composed, but her lower lip trembled and her chin was puckered like a strawberry. He felt as big as a snail.

"I'm sorry for the way I reacted. You caught me off guard."

"I understand." She gazed at her hands in her lap.

James hated seeing her so defeated. Where was the spunk he'd always admired?

"I ... ah ... am very flattered that you would—"

"Brazenly launch myself at you?" The tiniest, most reluctant smile escaped her lips.

He chuckled, and the tightness in his chest eased. "As brazen launches go, it was impressive."

She giggled. "Thank you. If you were any less sturdy, we might both have landed feet-up in the hedges over there."

Ah, she was a good sport, but the hurt still showed in the tightness around her mouth.

James slipped an arm around her shoulders. "I am truly sorry. Most men would welcome the attention of a beautiful young lady, but I—"

"You think I'm beautiful?"

Had he said that?

She sat up straighter, as though his answer were very important.

"Of course you are." It was true. "And you deserve to be properly courted by the right kind of gentleman."

Olivia laughed, a throaty, lusty sound. "Alas, I've yet to be properly courted by *anyone*. Maybe because I've been blind to anyone but you."

He rested his chin on the top of her head and inhaled the sweet scent of wildflowers.

"I don't deserve that kind of devotion, and I certainly cannot return it. I'm leaving for Egypt at the end of the summer, you know. I'll be gone for a couple years."

She tilted back her head and looked at him. "That's precisely the reason I had to tell you how I felt. You've no idea how much I'll miss you. I can't even imagine going so long without seeing you."

Warmth bloomed in James's chest. It was nice to know *someone* would miss him—and not just because he was a damned fine solicitor or a good boxing partner or because he paid the bills. He supposed his mother and brother might miss him a little, but he'd been saving up for years to make sure they'd have all they needed in his absence. Now that he thought on it, they seemed more than happy to see him go.

"You know, I believe I shall miss you, too." He hadn't realized it until just then.

"Would you mind if I wrote to you occasionally?" Olivia asked. "I promise I won't flood you with letters, and you don't have to write me back if you're too busy with your artifacts and such. I just want to make sure that... that..." Her eyes welled.

"What?"

"That you don't forget me."

Before he knew what he was doing, he took her chin in his hand and smoothed his thumb over her bottom lip. Her mouth opened slightly; he was mesmerized.

Odd, he'd never noticed the perfect bow of her lips or the lovely slope of her nose. He'd never appreciated the way her eyes positively shined with emotion when she looked at him—like she was trying to show him all the things she felt inside.

And now, here they were. Sitting in the moonlight and touching each other. Alone.

A single chestnut curl dangled seductively over her bare shoulder, fluttering softly in the evening breeze. She leaned closer, giving him a glorious view of her round, high breasts and the crease where they squeezed together in the middle.

Blood rushed to his cock, leaving him pleasantly light-headed.

"Kiss me," she murmured against his thumb. "Just once."

He shouldn't. He knew it. But she was melting into him, a soft, silk-clad breast brushing against his arm.

"Please," she whispered as her heavy eyelids drifted shut.

One brief kiss couldn't hurt, he reasoned. One kiss, to say good-bye.

He slid his hand behind her head and pulled her toward him, heard her sigh.

For a heartbeat, their noses touched and their breath mingled—warm, forbidden, irresistible. Then his mouth was on hers.

He intended it to be the lightest and briefest of kisses, and it started out in just that way. He brushed his lips across hers, a mere whisper of a touch. But she tasted so sweet that he kissed her again.

Olivia ignited instantly, splaying a hand over his waistcoat and increasing the pressure of her mouth.

Whatever control James had pretended to wield slipped through his hands like a rope without a knot. The kiss went from tepid to searing in three seconds flat.

He speared his fingers through her silky hair and eased her lips apart with his tongue. She gasped, but then met each thrust with a passion that made his heart pound and his cock go as hard as sarsen stone. Bloody hell.

His fingers itched to caress the expanse of skin above her gown, to tease her nipples to tight buds beneath the blue silk. He imagined how beautiful she would look if he loosened the laces at her back and freed her breasts from her corset, baring them to the evening air.

But the croak of a bullfrog snapped him out of his lust-driven haze. The insistent bass reminded him of the time he'd dared Olivia to hold a frog while he counted to twenty.

Of course she had.

Abruptly, he pulled away and stood. "I did as you asked." He tried to sound unaffected, cool, but succeeded only in sounding like a prig. "Now we both need to return to the ball. Would you like to go first, or do you need a moment to compose yourself?"

Olivia remained seated on the bench. With a dazed

stare, she touched a gloved fingertip to her swollen lips.
A few more locks of her hair had sprung free. James was
about to repeat the question when she blinked as though
waking from a trance. "I'll go first."

Guilt niggled at his gut like rats chewing through a
sack. "If your brother should ask where you've been..."

She rose in one fluid motion, shook out her skirts, and
smoothed the hair at her temples. "I can handle Owen."

"I know. But we shouldn't have...*I* shouldn't have..."

A languorous, sated glow lit her face. "I'm glad we did.
And do you want to know something else? I can't wait till
we do it again."

Before he could utter a protest—they most certainly
were *not* going to do it again—she swept past him, cast-
ing a saucy grin over her bare shoulder.

As James watched her glide through the shadows
toward the house, dread settled over him. He had the
same awful feeling one gets after blindly stepping in four
inches of mud.

But there was one thing he knew for certain—nothing
in this world would keep him from going on his expedition. Nothing. And, more importantly, no *one*.

Olivia slept extremely late the next day—till a quarter
past two. Kissing was apparently quite exhausting.

She didn't ring for her maid but donned a green-striped
morning dress, twisted her hair into a knot at her nape,
and scurried next door to Rose's bedchamber. There'd
been no opportunity last night to tell her sister about the
kiss.

Close to bursting with excitement, Olivia tapped at the
door.

"Come in." Rose sat in a chair by the window with her feet curled under her and a book in her lap. "At last, you're awake," she said with a warm smile.

Olivia leaped onto the bed, flopping flat onto her back. Gazing at the ceiling, she said, "What a glorious morning—er, afternoon."

"You're rather jubilant. Things went well with Mr. Averill?"

Olivia faced Rose and grinned. "I think you should start calling him 'James.' He's going to be your brother-in-law, after all." Of course, she was only jesting about that. Perhaps. But not really.

Rose's eyes widened. "The meeting must have gone very well indeed."

"It was an excellent start. Almost better than I'd hoped. He kissed me, Rose. Not a chaste or brotherly kiss, but one full of passion." How could she even begin to explain such a knee-weakening kiss to her sister?

"What did you do?"

"I kissed him back. I would have kissed him all night if he hadn't insisted on protecting my reputation."

"I think that was very wise of him," Rose said diplomatically.

Olivia sighed. "Gallant, too."

"Have his plans changed, then?"

Oh right—Egypt. "There wasn't much time to discuss his trip, but the important thing is that he now knows how I feel about him, and I could tell by the way he kissed me that he *must* feel something for me, too."

"Love?"

Olivia sat up and swung her legs over the side of the bed. "I don't think so—not yet. But there shall be time for that. Last night was only the first phase of my plan. At the very least, I've managed to persuade him I'm no longer a girl in pigtails." Deep inside, though, Olivia hoped she'd achieved more than that. Now that she'd tasted passion, she craved it even more.

"I'm delighted to see you so happy." Rose sat beside Olivia and wrapped a slender arm around her shoulders. "You deserve everything your heart desires."

Her heart definitely desired James. Other parts of her did as well.

Just then, their lady's maid, Hildy, bustled into the bed-chamber, a tower of fresh bedsheets in hand. "Good afternoon, my ladies. Shall I come back later?"

"No, please stay," said Rose. "It's time Olivia and I wandered downstairs for luncheon."

"An excellent idea," Olivia agreed. "Maybe we can persuade Anabelle and Owen to join us."

"Her Grace is in the drawing room, but the duke is in his study with Mr. Averill."

Olivia's heart nearly leaped out of her chest, and she squeezed Rose's arm. Hard. "Mr. Averill is *here*?"

Hildy placed the new sheets on an ottoman, frowned at the flattened pillows on Rose's reading chair, and began plumping them. "Indeed, my lady. He arrived just as I was heading toward the stairs. Mr. Dennison said he'd escort him to His Grace's study."

Olivia sprang from the bed and went to Hildy's side. "How did he look?"

Hildy eyed Olivia with a mixture of concern and confusion. "Same as he always has, miss—portly, self-important, and somewhat cross with the world."

"Not Dennison. Mr. Averill."

"Oh." The maid's cheeks flushed pink. "I suppose he looked well. Fit. And rather serious."

"Thank you, Hildy," said Rose. "Would you give Olivia and me two minutes, please?"

"Certainly." She dipped a quick curtsy and left, shutting the door behind her.

Olivia turned to Rose, still sitting on the bed. She couldn't make her mouth form the question she wanted to ask, so she asked it with her eyes. They'd always been able to communicate this way. *Could James's visit with Owen possibly mean what I think it means?*

Rose drew a deep breath. "Why else would he be here? He's meeting privately with our brother, the day after he kissed you on Lord Easton's terrace."

"This doesn't seem real." Olivia's legs began to shake; she felt behind her and sank carefully onto the ottoman.

Rose's angelic face broke into a wide smile. "At this very moment, Mr. Averill is downstairs...asking for your hand in marriage. Good heavens. What shall we do?"

Olivia wiped her moist palms on the skirt of her morning dress, which, now that she thought on it, was far too plain a gown in which to accept a marriage proposal. "Let's start by calling Hildy back in. Then I think the three of us should repair to my room so I can change into a prettier gown and have Hildy do something with my hair."

Rose squealed—which was very unlike her—and jumped up to hug Olivia. "I'm so delighted for you."

Olivia blinked away the tears that started to blur her vision. If James's proposal was half as wonderful as she'd dreamed it would be, today was going to be the happiest day of her life.

• • •

"Averill." Huntford waved him into the chair before his desk and leaned back, stretching like he'd been hunched over a ledger for hours. "I was going to visit your office later."

James had been there most of the morning. Flogging himself for his behavior the previous night—a topic he had no intention of broaching with Huntford. But he knew the duke had a business matter to discuss. "I thought I'd save you the trip. I'm on my way to the Lakes." Maybe if he put three hundred miles between him and Olivia, he'd feel less guilty.

"Good God. For how long?"

James shrugged. "Several weeks." Or however long it took Olivia to realize there was no possibility of a future between them. Chances were, a beauty like her would have a beau before the week was out.

Huntford narrowed his eyes. "This isn't like you, leaving town at the drop of a hat. You don't even go out for a pint without charting a course."

"There's not much keeping me in London anymore. And there are a few sites I've been wanting to explore."

Huntford grinned. "Ah. I should have guessed. It's not going to be the same around here without you." He pointed toward the sideboard. "Drink?"

"No," James answered quickly. Guilt squeezed at his throat like a too-tight cravat. The sooner he concluded this meeting and removed himself from Olivia's home—and London—the better. "What was the matter you wished to ask me about?"

"It's sensitive and... complicated." Huntford sighed and tented his fingers. "It involves my sister."

Bloody hell. It was probably too much to hope that the duke was referring to Rose. What if someone had seen James and Olivia together and informed Huntford? He didn't *seem* angry, but the duke was notoriously difficult to read.

Somehow, James managed to choke out, "Which sister?"

"Olivia." Huntford glared over his fingertips at James for what seemed like an eternity. Then he slid open a desk drawer to his right, leaned down, and withdrew a folded, sealed note, which he laid on the desk before him.

James exhaled lightly. Absurd though it was, he felt relief that Huntford had produced a piece of parchment and not, oh, a gun. However, he was not in the clear yet. Inclining his head toward the note, he asked, "What is it?"

Huntford eyed the note distastefully. "It came by messenger yesterday—from my father's solicitor, Neville Whitby."

James blinked. The previous duke had been dead for at least five years, and though he and his friend had never discussed it, James assumed the rumors were true. Huntford's father, heartbroken when his duchess betrayed him, had killed himself with a bullet to the head. In the very study where they now sat.

"I know Whitby. Go on," James encouraged.

"Apparently, my father made an unusual provision in his will. This letter was to be presented to Olivia upon the occasion of her twenty-first birthday."

James shook his head, certain he hadn't heard correctly. "Olivia is twenty-one?"

"Almost twenty-two. Whitby admitted that the letter had slipped his mind."

"Did your father leave any other instructions?"

Huntford snorted. "None. Only that no one, save the solicitor, should be told about the letter until Olivia turned twenty-one. And at that time, it should be given to her."

James pondered the possibilities for several moments. The dark shadows beneath the duke's eyes hinted at his fears. The note could stir up all the grief Olivia endured when her mother deserted her and her father took his own life.

"Is there a separate letter for Rose?" James asked.

"I asked the solicitor if I should expect another when Rose turns twenty-one. Whitby swore that this was the only one."

"Olivia knows nothing of it?"

"No." Huntford's eyes locked on his. "Whitby and I—and now you—are the only ones who know the letter exists. You're the only person I trust enough to tell." The duke stood, stalked to the window, and stared outside. "After all this time. My sisters had finally seemed to come to terms with my father's sudden, violent death. Rose is much improved—although still more reserved than she used to be—and Olivia has shown much more maturity of late."

James resisted the urge to squirm. She'd grown up, all right.

"I'd intended to see her engaged by the end of the season," Huntford continued. "But now...this."

James coughed, grateful that the duke was not facing him and therefore unable to see the sheen of sweat that had broken out on his forehead.

"Perhaps the letter's contents are benign," James said. "Your father could have set up a trust for Olivia."

"I can't imagine he would have done so for Olivia and not for Rose. He adored them both."

"Maybe it's just a bit of family history that he wanted to pass down to his older daughter," James suggested.

"It's unlikely," Huntford said, turning to face him squarely. "My father was not of sound mind in the days just before his death, and I must assume that he penned the note during that time. I'm sure you've heard the gossip about the circumstances of his death. It's all true. When my mother ran off to the Continent with one of her lovers, my father could not bear it. He shot himself." The duke grimaced. "I've never spoken of it with anyone besides my sisters and Belle—before now."

The words *I'm sorry* were on James's lips, but somehow he didn't think his friend wanted his sympathy. What the duke wanted was a solution to today's problem, and the least James could do was help him sort through his options.

"If your father wrote the note in the days leading up to his death, as you suspect, it could be an explanation of sorts."

"That's what I'm afraid of. It could stir up all the pain of that time. And what purpose could it possibly serve, other than to convey the depth of his anguish?"

"It could be an apology."

"I had considered that. But we've already forgiven him. It took me the longest, I'm ashamed to say, but we've all come to terms with it."

James stroked his chin and considered all his friend had shared. "As you've probably already deduced, you have four possible courses of action."

Huntford raised a brow. "First?"

"Carry out the provision of your father's will and give

Olivia the letter. As your solicitor, I would advise you to do so."

The duke scowled. "Next option."

"You could read the letter and then decide whether to give it to Olivia."

"Let me guess, you'd advise against this."

James shot his friend an apologetic smile. "I would. For legal reasons, obviously, but more so because Olivia would likely resent it."

Huntford nodded. "Third option?"

"Destroy the letter. Pretend it never existed, and Olivia need never know."

The duke paced before the window. "It's tempting. Our lives are proceeding so nicely at the moment—why risk ruining that?"

James sighed. "As your friend, I can certainly understand why you'd want to spare your sister any unnecessary suffering, but…"

"But what?" Huntford urged.

"Olivia is a grown woman. Perhaps it's time you treated her as such." James was certain he'd pay for that comment next time they boxed. "Furthermore," he dared, "if you destroy the letter, it can't be undone."

Huntford glowered at the letter as though he couldn't wait to set it on fire. "That's the whole point."

"True. But as the weeks, months, and years go by, you might regret your decision. You might be sorry you never heard what your father wanted to say."

"Damn it, Averill. Sometimes I wish you didn't have quite so much integrity."

Dear Jesus, if his friend only knew.

Eager to change the subject, James said, "There's one

more option I can think of. In difficult situations, it's often the most prudent."

"What's that?"

"Do nothing. Wait. Give yourself time to think it through. In the larger scheme of things, a few weeks or months are unlikely to make a difference—but extra time could bring you clarity."

"Wait," the duke repeated to himself. "I like that."

James relaxed a little. Huntford seemed to have the answer he needed—at least for now—which meant James could be on his way. He was so eager to take his leave that if it weren't extremely bad form, he would have slapped his friend on the back and sprinted for the front door. Rising slowly from his chair, he said, "Well, if there's nothing else you need from me—"

"There is."

James kept his expression neutral, but inside, he unleashed a string of curses. Normally, he would do anything for Huntford, but this situation was different—it involved Olivia. "How can I help?"

Huntford marched to his desk, scooped up the letter, and held it out to James.

James kept his arms pinned to his sides. "I don't understand."

"Take this," the duke said. "Until I decide what to do."

Oh no. No, no, no. "Why don't you lock it in a drawer?"

"Because I'd have the key. I don't trust myself. If I know where it is, I'll be tempted to read it. Or burn it. Neither would be fair to Olivia. Take it"—he shook the letter for emphasis—"and keep it safe."

James held out his palms. "This is a family matter. I shouldn't get involved."

The duke tossed the letter onto his desk and slumped into his chair, defeated. "I apologize. I won't take any more of your time. Thank you for stopping by and for the excellent advice. I'll—"

"Fine." James was certain he would regret this.

Huntford shot him a hopeful look.

"I'll hold on to the letter for a while." James took it and stuffed it into the breast pocket of his jacket. "However, I must return it to you before I leave for Egypt."

The duke closed his eyes briefly, as though deeply relieved. "Thank you."

"You are welcome. Please give my best to Anabelle and ah...your sisters."

Before long, James would be rumbling along the road in his coach, watching London disappear through the rear window. His driver, Ian, claimed he could cover the distance in three days. James had already loaded the coach with the clothes and tools he'd need for a few weeks of exploring in Westmorland and couldn't wait to be on his way.

Huntford stood, walked to James's side, and slapped him on the back. "I'll walk you out."

They made it to the foyer. Dennison was handing James his hat when the door to the drawing room burst open and a blur of pink silk and ribbons spilled forth.

"James! What a lovely surprise."

Well, he supposed he had this coming. "A pleasure to see you, Lady Olivia."

Chapter Three

*Ancient: (1) Relating to a remote time period and the earliest
known civilizations. (2) Very old, as in*
A girl on the marriage mart at the ripe age of two and
twenty was widely considered to be ancient.

At the sight of James, Olivia's breath caught in her
throat—as usual. Each time she saw him, he grew more
attractive. A fanciful notion, and yet the proof stood
before her. James's snug buckskin breeches showed off
his narrow hips and muscular thighs. And his backside
was perfectly formed: taut, well shaped, and...utterly
squeezable.

Recalling that her brother also stood in the foyer, she
reluctantly lifted her gaze from James's trouser area.

Fortunately, he was handsome all over. His sandy
brown hair curled slightly at the ends, begging her to rake
her fingers through it. His full lips, slightly parted, invited
thoughts of kissing.

Soon, she thought, he would be hers—to kiss, to hold,
and to love.

Except... something seemed amiss.

She and Rose had been expecting James to come looking for her in the drawing room after his meeting with Owen. Olivia had practiced several poses—gazing out the window, looking studiously at a book, poring over sheet music at the pianoforte—all so that she would appear mildly yet pleasantly surprised to see James when he sought her out.

But he hadn't.

On the contrary, he had his hat in hand and appeared to be on the verge of... of *leaving*.

Olivia glanced at Owen. Lord knew, he could be intimidating. If he had dissuaded James in any way, balked at the idea of him asking for her hand...

Well, she would require at least a year to forgive him.

In any event, she couldn't let James leave before she had a chance to speak with him.

Before he could take one more step toward the door, she said, "Could I persuade you gentlemen to join Rose and me for tea? We were just about to ring for some."

James opened his mouth to reply, but Owen cut him off. "Thank you, but Averill is in a hurry. I fear I've monopolized too much of his time already."

"Really? For what reason?" she asked rather boldly—even for her.

"A business matter," Owen said. "And it's all resolved, isn't it, Averill?"

"Yes. For now."

Olivia looked from James to Owen and back again. How *dare* they refer to her as a business matter? And why wasn't Averill fighting for her? Fighting for *them*?

Rose placed a gentle hand on Olivia's arm. "We should

let Mr. Averill be on his way." To James, she said, "I hope we shall see you again soon. Perhaps you could join us for dinner tomorrow evening?"

"I'm afraid I cannot." Although James was replying to Rose's invitation, he cast Olivia an apologetic look. "I'm leaving town for a while."

And then she *knew*.

James's visit had nothing to do with her. No proposal was forthcoming. In fact, he'd been about to leave London—without even saying good-bye.

Mortification washed over her, heating her cheeks. Weakly, she asked, "Where?"

"The Lakes," he said vaguely.

Apparently oblivious to her misery, Owen gestured for Dennison to open the door.

"A pleasure to see you, Lady Rose, Lady Olivia." James gave them each a perfunctory bow, and a moment later... he was gone.

Owen headed toward the stairs. "I'm going to spend the afternoon with Anabelle and the baby. I'll see you both at dinner?"

"Of course," Rose answered. When Owen was out of earshot, she slipped her arm around Olivia's shoulder. "I'm so sorry, Liv. Let's go sit and have some tea."

"I just want to go to my room," Olivia said, amazed she hadn't already crumpled into a weeping ball of pink silk. "It was silly of me to assume—"

"No," Rose said emphatically, "it wasn't."

"In any case, I need a little time to think."

"I'll go with you and help you out of your dress."

Olivia shook her head and attempted a reassuring smile. "I can manage."

Rose sighed. "Very well, but I must tell you one thing. You know that I am quite fond of Mr. Averill, but if he hasn't realized by now what a treasure you are, then maybe he doesn't deserve you."

Despite Olivia's desperate struggle to remain outwardly composed, a rebellious tear slid down her cheek. "Maybe he just needs more time to realize what a treasure I am."

A proud smile lit Rose's face. "That's the spirit."

Olivia gave her sister a hug and escaped to the privacy of her room, where she didn't have to pretend to be spirited or strong and could have a good long cry if she wished.

And that was *precisely* what she did.

Several hours later, when it was time for dinner, Olivia pleaded a headache. Anabelle had a tray sent up, but it sat on Olivia's bedside table, untouched. Even the aroma of roast beef and gravy couldn't tempt her.

Her appetite had fled. Just like James.

Good Lord, her melodramatic thoughts were pathetic— even inside her own head.

She'd been a fool to anticipate a proposal, regardless of the timing of his visit with Owen. And she only compounded her idiotic behavior now, crying over him when he clearly hadn't lost a moment's sleep thinking about her. Instead he'd decided to traipse off to the Lakes for a few weeks' worth of fossil-digging, or rock-watching, or whatever he called it.

The painful truth was that he'd never given any indication that he cared for her.

With the possible exception of what she now thought of as The Kiss.

She replayed it over and over in her head, pausing once when Rose came in to check on her and again when Hildy entered to remove the dinner tray. Sleep did not come until the wee hours of the morning, and even then, James invaded her dreams, making her blissfully happy one moment and leaving her utterly distraught the next.

When she awoke late the next morning, she felt slightly improved but still could not bring herself to venture down for breakfast and face her well-meaning sister, brother, and sister-in-law. Fortunately, Hildy arrived with a tea tray, complete with a plate of scones and biscuits.

"Shall I pour for you, my lady?" The maid gave a hopeful smile.

"No, thank you. I'll help myself in a bit."

The maid eyed Olivia doubtfully. After crying for a good part of the night and neglecting to braid her hair before falling into a fitful sleep, she must look a fright.

With a tight smile and a bob of her capped head, the maid left Olivia in peace.

Eventually, she dragged herself out of bed and slipped on her dressing gown. She even managed to swallow a few sips of tea while she sat in her chair and stared out the window overlooking their flower garden.

The tea grew cold, and Olivia lost track of time. She was studying a spiderweb outside the windowpane when a knock at the door demanded her attention. She glanced down and realized she still held her cup and saucer. Brown splotches stained her robe where she'd apparently spilled her tea. Crumbly remnants of a scone littered her lap.

Lord, she was a mess. "Come in."

Both Anabelle and Rose entered, looking like someone had died.

Behind her spectacles, Belle narrowed her gray eyes. "How are you feeling?"

"I'm certain I'll survive," Olivia said. She tried to smile but couldn't summon the energy.

"We've been worried about you." Belle perched on the footstool in front of Olivia's chair. "Has something upset you?"

Olivia glanced at Rose, who shook her head. Olivia hadn't thought Rose would tell Anabelle about The Kiss, but she was relieved to confirm Rose's silence in the matter.

The three women had been close ever since Belle, a talented dressmaker, had been enlisted to make new wardrobes for Olivia and Rose. After Belle married their brother, Olivia and Rose had grown even fonder of her. The three women had few secrets, but kissing James was complicated because he was Owen's best friend and Owen was Belle's husband.

Not only did the whole thing make Olivia's head spin, but it also served as a sad reminder that while Anabelle was living out her fairy-tale romance, Olivia apparently was not destined to do the same.

Belle still gazed expectantly at Olivia. "You can tell me."

"I know. Thank you for your concern. I'm just out of sorts. I shall be fine in a few days."

"A few days?" Belle shot Rose a look of alarm before returning her attention to Olivia. "That's not like you. If there's anything I can do to help, please let me. You must remember that, when all seemed lost, you were largely responsible for bringing Owen and me together. I am forever in your debt."

Olivia wasn't ready to share the full extent of her heartache or humiliation. But her infatuation with James was not exactly a secret. "I suppose I'm sad because James is leaving for Egypt at the end of the summer. I'd hoped to change his mind over the next couple of months, but since he's halfway across England by now"—she sounded bitter and didn't care—"I shan't have the opportunity."

"Oh." Anabelle sat beside her and threw her arms around her. "I'm so sorry, darling. I know how much you cared for him."

Rose took Belle's place on the stool. "It's no wonder you're distressed," she said. "Even as a young girl, you were fond of him."

Olivia knew that Belle and Rose were trying to show sympathy, but they couldn't possibly understand. They used words like *cared for* and *were fond of* when what Olivia felt for James was a thousand times stronger. And it wasn't past tense.

She loved him before. She loved him now.

"Thank you both for your support," Olivia managed. "I'm sorry if my sullen behavior has worried you. I'm sure I'll be myself again eventually." Inside, though, she felt hollow, broken.

"We understand," Belle said. "You must take as much time as you need."

"We will make your apologies at the ball tomorrow night," Rose said, "and at Lady Bramble's soiree the next evening."

"Tell everyone I've taken ill. Or that I've got a horrible case of spots. I'm sure I shall be the subject of much speculation, but I don't give a fig."

"I have an idea," Belle exclaimed. She smoothed a

matted lock of Olivia's hair behind her ear. "You could leave London for a while. Visit one of your great-aunts. I know Aunt Eustace would be delighted to have your company."

"That's true," Rose added. "Her letters always conclude with an invitation for us to visit. Nothing would make her happier."

"I am horrid company at the moment," Olivia said, but the idea of leaving London for the rolling green fields and quaint stone bridges of Oxfordshire tempted her. She could eat dozens of scones and let herself get pleasingly plump. "Let me think on it."

"Is there anything we can get you at the moment?" Belle asked. "A fresh pot of tea or a new book?"

"No. But thank you for everything."

"Owen is worried about you," Belle admitted. "If you don't make an appearance downstairs soon, he'll insist on sending for the doctor. Do you think you could manage to come down for dinner?"

"I'll try."

Belle and Rose each kissed her forehead before leaving her to mull over her options.

Perhaps visiting dear Aunt Eustace was a good idea. She might as well become acclimated to spinsterhood. What better way than to play the part of companion to a sweet, seventy-year-old widow known for her bright blue turbans? At the very least, the visit would allow Olivia to escape London and give her wounds time to heal.

Unless...Olivia sprang out of her chair and paced before the window. The thought of traveling had caused the smallest seed of an idea to take root in her mind and hope to sprout in her heart. Only, she had a different destination in mind.

She simply wasn't ready to give up on James.

Instead of dwelling on the hurt and rejection, she pictured his rakish grin and broad shoulders. Instead of recalling his hasty good-bye, she basked in the memory of his lingering kisses and tender caresses.

But the passionate tangling of their tongues and the feverish way they'd clung to each other—though undeniably wonderful—had not been the most magical part of that night.

That had been when James had reluctantly broken off their kiss and looked at her as though he were seeing her for the first time. And his dark eyes had glowed as though he very much liked what he saw.

He may not have realized it yet, but his appreciative, astonished gaze told her what his words had not—that he *did* care for her. And *not* just as a friend.

Olivia splashed cool water on her face and dragged a brush through her tangled hair. James did not want a simpering, whining miss. He craved adventure and excitement.

Fortunately, adventure and excitement happened to be her specialty.

She was through with hiding in darkened rooms and crying till her eyes were nothing but red, puffy slits. And for the love of God, she was through with scones. She marched to the tea cart, took the remaining pastries, and tossed them out the window to the birds.

She smiled, feeling a little of her old spirit returning.

By the time Rose came to check on her, Olivia had already rung for Hildy and dressed for dinner. Her maid managed to tame Olivia's locks into a simple knot with a few loose tendrils. Rose exclaimed over how well she looked—a little too effusively, in Olivia's opinion. However, she supposed if one ignored her sallow complexion and swollen eyes, one might never know what a wreck she'd been for the past two days.

"I asked Cook to include your favorite—braised ham—on the menu," Rose said. "She insisted on making those pastries you like as well."

Blast. She'd start avoiding sweets tomorrow. "How thoughtful. Thank you."

Rose extended a hand and helped Olivia to her feet. "Shall we join Owen and Anabelle in the drawing room?"

"Yes." Olivia smiled brightly. "May I ask a favor before we go?"

"Anything."

"I thought about your and Belle's suggestion—about visiting Aunt Eustace—and I think a respite from town life is just what I require. I want to leave as soon as possible."

"We can leave in the morning, if you wish."

Olivia shook her head. "You are a dear, and a better sister than I deserve. But I want to go by myself—although I suppose I must at least take Hildy."

Rose narrowed her eyes suspiciously. "Are you just saying that because you don't want me to miss out on the rest of the season? Because I can assure you—"

"That's not it at all. But I've been in a beastly mood, and the last thing I'd want to do is subject you to it for two weeks straight. And honestly, I'd rather be alone with my thoughts." Olivia had other reasons, of course, but the less Rose knew, the better.

Rose looked mildly disappointed, but nodded. "What was the favor you wanted to ask?"

"Help me convince Owen that I should be allowed to go." Olivia worried her lip. Her brother could be very stubborn. It was something of a family trait. "He's been hinting—none too subtly—that it's high time I found a husband. He won't approve of me hiding away in the country."

"Then we must convince him it's necessary to your happiness," Rose said.

Olivia's heart beat faster. "It is."

"I am sure Anabelle can be counted on to help as well," Rose said. "Visiting our aunt *was* her idea."

"I'll write to Aunt Eustace just after dinner and let her know that I should arrive by the end of the week."

Olivia could barely believe her own daring.

But if she'd learned one thing from her mother's desertion and her father's suicide, it was that you never know how much time you'll have with the people you love. She couldn't let James go to Egypt without acknowledging that there was something between them. Especially not after that kiss.

She had an impressive list of adventures to her credit, but this…this plan would put all her other adventures to shame. Equal measures of guilt, hope, and exhilaration glimmered in her chest.

Several counties separated her and James tonight, but they wouldn't for long.

Chapter Four

James sat in the dark, dank, and yet irrepressibly cheery taproom of Haven Bridge's only inn, chatting with his coachman, Ian, and a few villagers who remembered him from the last time he'd visited Uncle Humphrey. How long had it been? Four years? Maybe five. Too long. Uncle Humphrey was the closest thing he had to a father, the man who'd nurtured his love of antiquities and supported him and Ralph the best he could. Coming back to Haven Bridge felt like coming home.

When James had arrived in the small, quaint village three days ago, it had been close to dusk. He'd tossed Ian a few coins and told him to see to the horses, order dinner, and have a few pints. Meanwhile, James had jogged down a pebbled road and eventually up a steep dirt path that wound to the top of a grassy fell. He was surprised that he'd found the spot—his childhood favorite—so easily after all these years, but he'd reached the summit just in time to witness a fiery orange sunset beyond rolling blue mountains. Charming stone walls snaked along lush fields dotted with grazing sheep.

He'd gulped in a lungful of crisp, country air, and as he watched the sun sink into the earth, he'd known that the three-day journey to Haven Bridge was worth it.

Although, after that he'd nearly killed himself trying to walk down the fell and back to the inn in the pitch dark, but it had made for a good story once he was sitting at the taproom later that night.

The next day, James went to visit Uncle Humphrey, hoping the elderly man was still healthy and spry. Though thinner and more stooped than James remembered, he had all his wits about him. He tried to persuade James to stay in his cottage, but James didn't want to impose, so he'd stayed at the inn. He envisioned a summer full of mornings exploring the countryside, afternoons chatting with Uncle Humphrey, and evenings drinking in the taproom.

Life was good—so good, he could almost forget the sealed note that he still carried in the chest pocket of his jacket. What he could not put out of his mind was the hurt and disappointment on Olivia's face the day he'd left London.

He'd only been thinking of her and her best interests when he left. Now she was free to enjoy the attentions of other young bucks and dance and flirt to her heart's content. He swallowed a large gulp of ale, finding it more bitter than usual.

"Where'd you go today, Averill?" Gordon, a miner with a grizzly white beard, lowered himself onto the bench across from James and thunked his half-full glass onto the wooden table.

"A farm east of here, near the river. Ruins all around, and it looks like walls could be buried beneath. What do you know about the place?"

The old man cackled. "Not much. People find things—fragments of metal and polished stone. What do you suppose they're from?"

Averill shrugged. "Hard to say. Could be an old fort or a church."

Gordon stroked his beard. "The land belongs to Sully. That codger wouldn't know a—"

The miner halted midsentence, and the taproom—which had been rumbling with men's cursing and grunts only a moment before—went silent and still.

Then Gordon let out a long, low whistle.

James craned his neck and found the objects of everyone's attention. Two young women—clearly a lady and her maid—glided through the taproom and settled themselves at a table in the corner. Both wore cloaks and bonnets that concealed their features, but they were definitely *not* from Haven Bridge, and that alone was enough to make them an object of curiosity.

The young lady's lithe yet feminine figure drew all eyes—James's included.

"What do you suppose they're doing in here?" Gordon said.

"Well, it *is* an inn," James said dryly. "My guess is they're travelers who need a place to spend the night."

The miner winked. "I knew you were more than a pretty face." He kept his rheumy gaze on the pair of women. "It wasn't smart of them to sit next to Crutcher—he's an ogre even when he's not in his cups. Look, he's already harassing them."

James swiveled around on his bench and watched as Crutcher staggered into the end of the ladies' table, banging it into the wall.

"Sir, I shall have to ask you to return to your seat at once," the young lady said haughtily. Beneath her bravado, however, James detected a note of fear.

Hoping to defuse the situation, he strolled toward Crutcher, who was guffawing as if the woman's request had been the punch line of a bawdy joke.

"Come on, Crutcher," James said. "Join Gordon and me. I'll buy you a drink."

The man squinted at James, sizing him up. His opponents usually underestimated him—and paid sorely for the mistake with a black eye or fat lip.

"I'm not thirsty."

James assumed a casual pose, nudging a pebble on the taproom floor with the toe of his boot, but he spoke firmly. "Come talk to us, then."

"Why in the hell would I want to talk to you when I can talk to these pretty ladies?" Crutcher placed his palms on the women's table and leaned over it, his greasy head inches from theirs. James didn't even want to imagine how foul his breath must smell.

Crutcher opened his mouth to speak, but before he could utter one more offensive word, James grasped the back of his collar, hauled him away from the table, and dragged him toward the front door of the inn. The drunk flailed his arms and kicked a few chairs over on the way out, but at least nothing had been broken. Yet.

Once outside, James thrust Crutcher in front of him. He landed hard on his knees in the dirt. The sun had disappeared behind the hills, and daylight faded fast. Gordon and a half dozen other men spilled out of the inn, eager for a rousing fight.

"You bastard," Crutcher growled as he lumbered to his feet and flexed his fingers.

"Why don't you go home?" James suggested. "Sleep it off, and if you still want to fight me tomorrow, I'll happily oblige." He meant it. What was the sport in sparring with a man too drunk to piss straight?

But Crutcher—all six beefy feet of him—was already lunging toward James, aiming for the knees. James darted to the side, and Crutcher stumbled past him. "Bleedin' coward. Stand tall and fight me."

There was nothing to be done for it. James shrugged off his coat, and when Crutcher launched his fist toward James's head, he was ready. He ducked and Crutcher swung through air. Still crouching, James jabbed his right fist hard into his opponent's gut, just below the ribs.

Crutcher doubled over, gasping for breath.

James stepped back to give him some space. Hopefully that would be the end of that. He glanced up and in the waning light could just make out Gordon's grin—one or two teeth shy of a full set. Behind him and the other tap-room patrons stood the two women who'd started all the commotion.

One of them rushed forward, almost tripping on the hem of her cloak. "James!" she called breathlessly. "Are you all right?"

Good Lord.

It couldn't be.

But beneath the brim of her bonnet were a pair of familiar brown eyes. "Olivia?"

"Yes, it's me," she said, whisking off her bonnet.

A blush stole over her cheeks. "Isn't this an amusing coincidence?"

James stood frozen for several moments before he found his tongue. "It's not entirely amusing. And I suspect it's not a coinci—"

"Look out!" Olivia cried, pointing over James's shoulder. Gordon grabbed her around the waist and yanked her back.

The hairs on the back of James's neck stood on end—a little too late.

He spun on his heel just in time for Crutcher to plow him over. James's feet left the ground and he sailed through the air like he'd been tossed from his horse. His back hit the packed dirt first. A split second later, his skull smacked the ground with a sickening *thud*. Before James could regain his breath, Crutcher landed on top of him and wedged an elbow across his throat.

Air. James needed it—was desperate for a big gulp of it. The world was already growing dark around the edges; dizziness seduced him, and he almost gave in.

"Stop it, you big brute!" Olivia's scolding had no effect on Crutcher, but it sharpened James's focus. He pried Crutcher's elbow away from his throat and, using his legs, rocked his body several times until he gained enough momentum to roll the drunk off him.

Someone grabbed James beneath his arms and hoisted him to his feet. The world tilted and pain spliced through his head.

But he hadn't lost a fight in two decades, and he wasn't about to lose one now.

"Be careful, James." A tremor in Olivia's voice betrayed her fear, but he also heard her confidence. Knew he had to live up to it.

Crutcher circled, testing him with the occasional jab. James deflected them all. At least his reflexes worked on some basic level. He bided his time, letting Crutcher grow more cocky, more careless. Then, just as the bastard drew his arm back for his knockout punch, James landed a solid blow to the face with a lightning-fast right hook. His left fist followed with an uppercut to the jaw.

Crutcher's head snapped back and he fell to the ground like a giant without a beanstalk. Out cold.

For half a minute, no one moved.

Then, everyone moved—except Crutcher.

One of his cronies tried to rouse him with a nudge of his boot heel. When that didn't work, he reluctantly sacrificed the ale in his glass, pouring it onto Crutcher's swelling face.

Most of the onlookers crowded around James. "Well done!" they shouted, slapping him on the back. But he was still dazed, and his head felt too big for his neck to hold.

"Where's Olivia?" he asked.

"Who?"

"The woman's over there," said Gordon, pointing a few yards behind him. "Retrieving your jacket." The crowd of men parted respectfully as Olivia rushed toward James.

"I was terrified for you," she said. "Are you hurt?"

James would have raised a brow, but his head ached too much. "Not mortally."

She giggled nervously. "Oh, well that's good. I believe this is yours." As she thrust his jacket toward him, a folded note fluttered to the ground.

Olivia's letter. Damn it.

She stooped to pick it up and when her fingertips were a mere inch from the note, he dove and snatched it off the ground. The letter secure—if somewhat crushed—in his fist, he pushed himself to his feet and brushed the dirt from his trousers. Again.

Sweet Jesus, that had been close.

Meanwhile, Olivia stood beside him, still holding his jacket and staring at him curiously. "That was a rather dramatic way to pick up a bit of paper," she remarked. "What is it, a writ from the prince regent?"

"Maybe. And I hardly think you are one to lecture on dramatics."

"Point taken." She bit her bottom lip, and something inside him melted a little.

He took his jacket from her, jammed his arms into it, and stuffed Olivia's letter into the chest pocket. He had to be more careful with that bloody note. "What are you doing here?" She opened her mouth to reply, but he cut her off. "Never mind. I don't want to have this conversation right now." He gazed at the circle of inn patrons who'd gathered around them. Crutcher had started hobbling home with the help of his friend, but there were still too many sets of curious eyes and ears. "Gather your maid. We'll go back inside and talk there." As they walked, he asked, "Who else came with you?"

Her cheeks flushed pink. "Our coachman, Terrence. He's seeing to the horses."

Good God. He guided Olivia toward the table where she'd been sitting; her maid trailed closely behind them. No sooner had the three of them sat than the innkeeper's wife set two hearty bowls of shepherd's pie onto the table before the ladies. "I'll be back with some bread and ale," she told them. "Can I get you some stew or a pint, Mr. Averill?"

"I'll take a brandy."

She nodded and scuttled off.

Neither Olivia nor her maid lifted her spoon.

"Please, eat," James said. He had several questions for Olivia, but he wasn't going to ask them in front of her maid. "We'll talk afterward." Huntford couldn't possibly have approved Olivia's jaunt to the Lakes. How the devil had she managed to travel three hundred miles from London without her brother's knowledge?

James had *lots* of questions.

And the most pressing one was what the bloody hell to do with Olivia Sherbourne.

Chapter Five

*Dig: (1) An archaeological site where an excavation is in process.
(2) A cutting, often sarcastic, remark, as in*
Though she undoubtedly deserved it, his thoughtless
dig wounded her to the core.

A mere hour before, Olivia had been so famished that
she'd rashly followed the smell of shepherd's pie into the
inn's taproom instead of ordering it to be sent up to her
room. But now, as James glared at her with disapproving
yet beautiful mossy-green eyes, she could only manage to
choke down a few forkfuls of her dinner.

James was doing a lot of staring and very little talking. Perhaps he was still dazed after being blindsided
by Crutcher, but Olivia got the distinct impression that
he wanted to issue a sound scolding—and was valiantly
attempting to restrain himself until the appropriate time
and place.

Olivia dedicated herself to the task of delaying that
time and place for as long as possible.

No doubt, there would be consequences for her reckless

behavior. But right now, as she sipped her ale and glanced at James from beneath her lashes, she knew the risks had been worth it.

She was three hundred miles away from London. Alone with James—if one discounted Hildy and the dozen or so villagers and travelers in the taproom who eyed them curiously.

"Is that all you're going to eat?" James wore a scowl, but the concern beneath it warmed Olivia's heart.

"Yes." She flashed him her most charming smile. "Are you enjoying Haven Bridge?"

He snorted. "We need to talk."

"Very well." She pushed her plate to the side and folded her hands demurely.

"Not here."

"It's too dark to stroll outside," she said. "What venue did you have in mind, exactly?"

James ground his teeth. "I assume you have a room upstairs?"

"Of course."

In a lower voice he asked, "Which door?"

Olivia flushed. A gentleman asking for directions to her room was shocking—even for her. "The second on the left."

"Go up with Hildy. I'll follow in the next hour or so. When I knock, answer quickly so no one sees me in the hallway outside your room."

Olivia wanted to turn a cartwheel right there on the spot. She was to have a rendezvous with James. Tonight. "I understand." She endeavored to sound cool, as though she did this sort of thing all the time. "Come, Hildy."

As Olivia slid off the bench, James stood. She inclined

her head, determined to exit the taproom gracefully in spite of her wobbly knees.

The moment she and Hildy reached their room, the maid wrung her hands. "It's not proper for Mr. Averill to come knocking in the middle of the night."

"It's only ten o'clock." But she understood Hildy's point, and she shot the maid an apologetic smile. Poor Hildy. Olivia had subjected her to one impropriety after another since they left London three days ago.

"I think you should tell Mr. Averill you'd prefer to meet with him tomorrow. You could go for a walk—and I would accompany you."

"I'll suggest it to James when he arrives, but he seemed rather adamant about wanting to talk."

"The duke would not be pleased," Hildy warned.

That was putting it mildly. If Owen knew what Olivia had done, he'd probably force her to spend the rest of her life in a convent. And she shuddered to think what he'd do to James.

Which was why Owen simply must not learn of her daring adventure.

"Since we have a little time before James arrives, help me change out of this." Olivia eyed her dusty traveling gown with distaste. What did one wear to a late-night tryst?

As though Olivia had uttered the question aloud, Hildy offered, "The white muslin?"

Her maid was, no doubt, hopeful that white would serve as a reminder to all parties that Olivia was an innocent young maiden. Although Olivia was inclined to object for that very reason, she had to agree it was the simplest dress she'd brought and the most appropriate. "Very well."

Hildy had not had time to unpack Olivia's things and immediately began rummaging through her portmanteau. Olivia busied herself as well, washing up and repairing her hair. An hour later, she was ready—sitting in a hard wooden chair, pretending to read a book.

When a knock sounded at the door, Hildy *tsked* and Olivia leaped to her feet.

"Who is it?" she asked.

"Averill." A slight pause. "Who else would it be?"

The rich, deep sound of his voice made her heart beat faster. She opened the door and drank in the sight of his broad shoulders, tapered waist, and long, lean legs. "Would you like to come in?" she whispered.

He propped an arm on the door frame and leaned in to look at her room. Upon spying Hildy, he shook his head. "No." He clasped a hand around her wrist and glanced into the hallway behind him before tugging her forward. "Come with me."

Olivia's mouth went dry, but she turned to give her horrified maid a reassuring smile. "Try to sleep. I'll return shortly."

Before she knew it, James had led her into the corridor. They tripped lightly down the runner covering the old wood floor and ducked into a room two doors down on the right.

James's room. His worn leather bag sat on the floor beside a washstand, and his hat hung on a hook beside it. The faint smell of his shaving soap tickled her nose.

He let go of her wrist, placed a large hand at the small of her back, and propelled her inside. Then he closed the door and turned the key in the lock. He pointed at the bed. "Sit."

As a matter of pride, she ignored the command and sat on the wooden chair near the foot of the bed. James paced in front of her, although the confines of the room only allowed him to take two small strides in one direction before turning around. This seemed to vex him even more.

Olivia waited patiently, hands in her lap and ankles crossed primly.

At last, James halted and raked his hand through his hair like he wanted to pull out a fistful. "What in the *hell* are you doing in Haven Bridge?"

During the long coach ride from London, Olivia had debated how to best answer this question and hadn't come to any clear conclusion—until now.

She had to tell him the truth.

"I couldn't bear the way you left without saying goodbye. It felt like you were running away from me. From us."

"Olivia." His voice was ripe with exasperation. "There *is* no 'us.'"

Ouch. That smarted. "Well of course there is." Before he could contradict her, she added, "And it was powerful enough to drive you out of town."

James closed his eyes. Like he needed a moment to compose himself and his thoughts. "I suppose I deserved that. I handled things badly on the night of the Easton ball."

"You also handled things badly the next day when you visited Owen."

"That may be true. But, Olivia, what would you have had me do? I shouldn't have kissed you, but I did. I can't take it back no matter how much I want to."

Ouch again.

"I'm leaving for Egypt in a couple of months," he

continued. "There can be no future for us. You must realize that."

She shrugged. "I take a different view of things."

"Let me ask a simpler question," James said. "Does Huntford know you're here?"

"I should say not."

James cursed under his breath. "Where does he think you are?"

"With my aunt Eustace in Oxfordshire." Olivia drew in a deep breath. "I made a great show of writing her a letter informing her of my plans to visit but never sent it. I didn't want dear Aunt Eustace to worry when I failed to arrive."

"How very considerate of you." His sarcasm stung. "And how did you convince your coachman and Hildy to go along with your scheme?"

Olivia stared at her hands, wishing her explanations didn't sound so shameful to her own ears. She'd told herself that the ends justified the means, but that didn't prevent her from feeling awful. "When we stopped at an inn the first night, I casually mentioned how eager I was to see Aunt Eustace's charming cottage near the Lakes. The coachman protested at first and said his instructions were to deliver me to Oxfordshire, but I assured him that Owen was aware of the change of plans and that Aunt Eustace was expecting me to arrive in Haven Bridge in a couple days' time."

"So you lied to them."

Must he make her admit it? "Yes."

James resumed his pacing. "How did you know I would be here?"

"I didn't know for certain, but when you said you were

going to the Lakes, I assumed you'd take the opportunity to visit your uncle Humphrey. You once mentioned him at a dinner party. I could tell by the way you described his cluttered study and sharp mind that you were very fond of him—and of Haven Bridge."

James shook his head. "I can't say I recall that conversation."

"It was some time ago," Olivia said.

"And you remembered?" James's forehead wrinkled, and she resisted the urge to smooth away the lines with her fingertip.

She did remember, and she treasured time spent with him—especially the moments where he confided little snippets of himself. "I thought I might like to visit Haven Bridge myself someday."

James sank onto the foot of the bed so that his eyes—which fairly sparked with anger—were level with hers. "Coming here without your brother's knowledge was reckless. You put yourself in peril. If you'd been accosted by highwaymen on the way here, you could have found yourself stranded in the wilderness—or worse."

"The peaceful countryside isn't exactly teeming with thieves. A robbery could just as easily have happened on the way to my aunt Eustace's," Olivia reasoned. She'd never really considered all the things that could go wrong with her plan; she'd been too focused on finding James.

"You are missing the point," James said evenly. "If something *had* happened to you, no one would have even known. Your aunt wasn't expecting you and God knows *I* wasn't."

"I see no purpose in dwelling on all the things that could have gone wrong. Nothing did."

"Have you forgotten that a drunken farm laborer made improper advances toward you? *That* could have ended badly."

She dared a small smile. "But it didn't, thanks to you."

James didn't soften in the least; rather, he looked like he wanted to break something. "First thing in the morning, I shall send word to Huntford informing him of your whereabouts. I suspect he'll come to retrieve you himself, which means he'll have three days of travel in which to ponder various forms of punishment for your ill-advised escapade."

Olivia squirmed on the hard wooden chair. "Perhaps we shouldn't act so hastily—there are other options."

James laughed, a hollow, barking sound. "Such as?"

"Tomorrow, I could write Aunt Eustace, let her know I'm coming, and leave for Oxfordshire the following day. Owen need never know about my detour to Haven Bridge."

"I'm not going to lie to your brother."

"If you want to tell him the whole sordid tale, I cannot stop you." Olivia sighed dramatically. "But do not be surprised when he puts me on the next ship to America."

"It would serve you right."

Now it was Olivia's turn to get up and pace. "And what of you? Do you not bear any responsibility? Not that I would ever dream of implicating you, but one could make the case that you encouraged me."

"I encouraged you?"

"When you kissed me."

"Yes," he snapped dryly, "how could I forget?"

Ouch. Thrice wounded.

"Say what you like, James. But I *know* that kiss meant

something to you. I felt it in the way you held me—like you wanted me all to yourself." She might have added that he looked at her like she was the last marshmallow on the dessert tray, but she saw no need to belabor the point.

He sprang up and grasped her shoulders. "Listen to me. That kiss was a mistake. I will not deny that I got carried away, but I did not expect you to be so…" He shrugged helplessly.

"So *what*?" She had to know.

"So…passionate," he said grudgingly. "Or so skilled at kissing."

Olivia's cheeks heated. The compliment—reluctant though it may have been—more than made up for the barbs he'd delivered earlier. "Thank you. I thought you were quite a good kisser, too."

James's eyes narrowed. "Compared to whom?"

"It's not important. Do go on."

A frown crossed James's handsome face before he continued. "You must realize that we are not at all suited. You are the sister of a duke. I am a solicitor who is leaving for Egypt at summer's end. I do not want or need a wife. The sooner you accept that, the better off we both shall be." With that, he released her arms, strode to the opposite side of the room, and stared out the small window that overlooked the inn's courtyard.

"I would wait for you." Olivia's voice trembled. "Till you returned from Egypt."

"This isn't just about Egypt," James said coolly. "You are my best friend's younger sister. I've never been more cognizant of that fact than I am tonight."

"Why does that sound like a criticism?"

"In coming here, you deceived your family and put

yourself in jeopardy. It was a stupid, selfish, and incredibly immature thing to do."

Until now, Olivia had tried valiantly to imagine she was on a daring and romantic adventure. But James's words rang true. She hated the thought of worrying her family and would never have resorted to this scheme if it wasn't her last chance for happiness. For love. "You may be right—"

"No. I *am* right. From the time you could bat your eyes—which I'd wager was approximately the age of three—you've received everything your heart desired. Ponies, fancy frocks, even jewels. Which explains why it's so difficult for you to accept what I'm saying. And it also explains why we would never suit. I could never make you happy, and you... well, you could never understand me."

His harsh assertion echoed in the ensuing silence.

Olivia's eyes welled and her nose stung, but crying would only confirm his low opinion of her. "I don't think you give me enough credit," she managed. Yes, she'd been blessed with a loving brother and sister. Yes, she'd been born into a life of wealth and privilege. But she knew heartache. She knew the horror and sorrow of finding her father with a bullet hole in his head. She knew the agony of being deserted by her own mother. People she'd thought were her friends had shunned her in her most vulnerable moment.

But not James. He had been the rare friend who stood by Owen—by all of them.

Yes, Olivia understood far more than he knew.

And now, for the first time in—oh, *ever*—she needed to put distance between James and her. "You've given me much to consider," she choked out. "I think I should return to my room."

James's brows rose a fraction of an inch. "Where you will remain all night?"

"Yes." She had neither the energy nor inclination to run off again. Whatever the consequences of her actions, she would face them.

He felt the back of his head and winced. "Sleep is a good idea. I hope I have a clearer head in the morning."

"It still hurts?" Without thinking, she glided to James's side, placed one hand on his shoulder, and probed his crown with her other hand. His hair felt thick and curled slightly around her fingertips as they skimmed over his scalp. At the back of his head she felt an egg-sized lump.

"Ow."

"You're going to have a headache tomorrow."

"I already do."

Some of Olivia's hurt and anger melted away. But not all. "Try to get some sleep."

She turned to leave, but with three long strides he beat her to the door.

"Let me check the corridor," he said. After glancing in both directions, he waved her to follow him and led the way to her room.

She withdrew the key from her pocket and did not look at James as she opened the door. "Thank you for defending me in the taproom earlier. I hope your head feels better soon."

"Don't worry. It's hard." The playfulness in his voice drew her gaze to him, and the heart-stopping smile he flashed made her want to lean into him and press her lips to his.

"Good night," she whispered.

"Lock the door," he instructed. "I'll see you in the morning and decide what to do then."

Olivia nodded, entered her room, and turned the key in the lock. Hildy had left a small lamp burning by the bed, which was turned down. The maid had curled up on a makeshift pallet on the floor, where she slept soundly.

Guilt niggled at Olivia's stomach. Poor Hildy had been tasked with preserving Olivia's reputation—a daunting and unenviable job to say the least. The maid still believed they were going to Aunt Eustace's cottage in Haven Bridge tomorrow. Olivia did not look forward to breaking the news that Aunt Eustace didn't reside in the lovely village after all.

James was right. Olivia was selfish and immature—or, at least, she had behaved that way today. His biting words had stung, but the disappointment she'd seen in his eyes would haunt her for the rest of her days.

As quietly as she could, she shed the white muslin gown and slipped a night rail over her head. Then she tiptoed to her maid's pallet and gently nudged her shoulder.

Hildy propped herself up on an elbow and rubbed at her eyes. "Are you all right, my lady? Is there anything you need?"

"I just wanted to let you know I'm back," Olivia whispered. "Thank you for trying to protect my good name."

The maid blinked groggily. "You're welcome."

"You know, the bed is plenty big for both of us. Climb up and get under the covers—you'll get a better night's sleep."

"I don't mind the floor, my lady."

"I know. But it's not as comfortable as a mattress. Come, hop in. I'll turn down the lamp."

The drowsy maid obeyed, and a minute after her head hit the pillow, she was asleep once more.

Olivia was not so fortunate. James's words sounded in her head for hours. His low opinion of her wounded her like a hundred little cuts. However, what made the pain worse was that, in spite of all he'd told her, she still loved him.

And she had absolutely no idea what to do about it.

Chapter Six

$\mathcal{O}$livia's prediction had come true. James awoke with a headache.

It actually stopped throbbing once he began moving about the sparsely furnished room, dressing, shaving, and pacing. At one point that morning, he'd scrawled out a note to Huntford, informing him of Olivia's whereabouts.

A minute later, he crumpled it in his fist.

He *knew* he should send word to his friend, but he hadn't eaten breakfast yet, and he firmly believed that weighty decisions should never be made on an empty stomach.

So, he packed a few tools in his leather pouch, slung it over his shoulder, and left his room in search of sustenance.

He paused in the corridor outside Olivia's door and listened. Feminine voices murmured, but he couldn't make out the conversation.

While he stood there, frustrated, it occurred to him

that Olivia must be hungry as well. Without much pre-meditation, he knocked on her door.

The murmuring ceased, shuffling ensued, and the door opened a crack. In the space between the door and the frame, Olivia's sultry brown eyes blinked up at him. "Good morning." But her tone belied her words; she greeted him with the enthusiasm one might offer an escort to the guillotine. Her fine brows knit in concern. "How do you feel?"

His injuries from last night's fight were minor, but snippets of the conversation with Olivia in his room rever-berated through his head, proving more bothersome. He'd been too harsh with her, and the truth was, he was in no position to lecture on selfishness and immaturity. "Fine... but famished. Would you like to go for a walk?"

"Very well," she said with unflattering resignation. "I'll get my bonnet and meet you outside."

A few minutes later, they strolled down the village's main street. James welcomed the chilly slap of morn-ing air on his face, but Olivia wrapped her shawl tightly around her shoulders. He wanted her to notice the mist that had drifted off the lake and the purple hue of the hills in the distance. He wanted her to notice the intense green of the pastures dotted with dirty white sheep. The beauty of this place never failed to heal him; surely it could make her feel better, too. But she seemed miserable and broken.

He hated that he'd had a hand in that.

Perhaps this morning he could repair some of the dam-age, maybe even return to the easy camaraderie they'd shared before the kiss on Lady Easton's terrace. He had to try.

Without preamble, Olivia said, "I told Hildy the truth

this morning—that Aunt Eustace doesn't live anywhere near Haven Bridge. She was understandably upset."

"It was brave of you to tell her."

Olivia shot him a dubious look. "It was only a matter of time before she discovered my deception. And I left the chore of telling our coachman to her—not very brave of me. Terrence shall be fit to be tied."

James didn't like seeing her so dejected. He'd never realized how much he'd come to depend upon her cheerful nature and infectious smile.

"Later we will figure out the best course of action," he said. "For now, try to set aside your troubles." He sniffed the air, rich with the smells of yeast, butter, and cinnamon. "Do you smell that?"

She turned up her gently sloped nose and smiled ever so slightly. "Mmm. What is it?"

"Breakfast," he said simply. He pointed at the bakery and offered her his arm. When she placed her hand in the crook of his elbow, he was struck by how right it felt to be walking in step with her. He was much too aware of the gentle pressure of her hand, and when she stumbled, the curve of her breast brushed lightly against his arm. Though accidental and completely innocent, her touch stirred him in places that shouldn't be stirring. Good God.

They walked into the shop and the baker's flour-smudged face broke into a wide smile. "Mr. Averill, I see you've brought me a pretty new customer."

"I have, indeed," said James. "Lady Olivia Sherbourne, meet Mr. Fraser—maker of the best hot cross buns in all of England."

"Everything tastes better here in the Lakes," the baker said modestly, "as you'll soon discover for yourself."

James bought some buns, biscuits, and sweet rolls, confident something in the sack would tempt Olivia. They waved good-bye to Mr. Fraser and walked a little farther down the street to a fruit and vegetable stand. Olivia picked out a couple of ripe peaches, which James paid for and tucked into his leather bag with the rest of their feast.

"I suppose we must go back to the inn," Olivia said.

"Yes, but not right away." James steered her toward the pebbled path that he'd walked over every morning since arriving in Haven Bridge. He'd never taken anyone to his favorite spot on the hill, but he wanted to take Olivia. He couldn't explain why exactly. Except somehow, he knew seeing the dramatic landscape through her eyes would make him appreciate it even more.

She arched a brow at him. "I assumed you'd be eager to send me packing back to London."

"That's not fair," he said.

"No?"

Of course he didn't want to send her away. "It's for your own good."

She sighed. "That is precisely what men say when they want a woman to do their bidding."

James frowned and stopped to face her. "We've already established that you can't stay. But spending the morning here couldn't hurt, and there's a place I'd like to show you—if you're not averse to hiking up a rather steep path." Olivia was utterly incapable of declining such a challenge, and they both knew it.

She retracted the hem of her dress a few inches to reveal a pretty pale blue slipper. "They're not the most appropriate shoes for a vigorous walk, but it hardly matters if they become dirty or worn—I shall have little use for stylish shoes in the convent."

He caught the hint of her smile and his anticipation of their outing increased tenfold. "Excellent." Without thinking, he reached down and laced his fingers through hers, tugging her along the path to his lookout. She squeezed his palm lightly, as if to let him know she was his partner for the next few hours, game for anything he wished to do.

A prospect that was exciting—and dangerous.

The rocky path wound around copses of trees and a dilapidated barn before giving way to a narrow dirt path. They were too short of breath for conversation, but her delighted expression spoke volumes. He'd been right to bring her here. Maybe he could repair some of the damage he'd caused the night before, and he and Olivia could go on being friends.

Thoughts of friendship fled, however, when they were about halfway up the hill. They'd grown warm from exertion and the morning sun, and Olivia shed her shawl, revealing an expanse of creamy skin above her neckline. James tried not to stare, but with each step she took, her breasts bounced slightly, which naturally made him imagine her breasts bare and bouncing above him, her head thrown back in ecstasy as though he and she were—

Christ. What was *wrong* with him?

Olivia harbored feelings for him, but that didn't give him the right to fantasize about her—at least, not like *that*.

But she had a way of creeping into his thoughts at the oddest times. Like when he examined an ancient fertility statue, or when he heard a lively reel, or when he hovered on the brink of sleep in his bed. And since the night he kissed her, he'd had a more difficult time pushing those tantalizing visions from his mind. Her heavy-lidded brown eyes invited him to kiss her, hold her... and more.

James looked up to find Olivia a few yards ahead of him. "You're slowing down," she teased breathlessly. "Can't you keep up?"

He closed the space between them in five large strides; she squealed in mock fear and hurried toward the summit.

Her bonnet dangled down her back, and several tendrils of chestnut hair worked their way loose from her chignon. The tantalizing curls drew his gaze to her nape and the elegant length of her throat.

Damn. He could no longer deny that he desired her; in fact, *desire* seemed far too mild a word, like saying a drowning man "desired" air. But one could have a desire without acting upon it, and James was nothing if not disciplined. This was simply a matter in which his mind must exercise control over his body. He'd always had disdain for men who couldn't hold their baser instincts in check— it was weakness on their part that made them drink spirits in excess, indulge in opium, and squander their fortunes on mistresses.

James would not fall prey to Olivia's womanly charms.

Even if he *did* appreciate them.

They reached the crest of the hill, and he drank in the sight of Olivia as she waded off the trail into a grassy field dotted with bright wildflowers. She collapsed happily, her skirts billowing around her.

James followed, tossing his leather bag to the ground before sinking into the soft grass beside her. He sighed at the glorious view—the vivid green slope of the hill before them, the rolling meadows in the distance, and the winding stone walls. "This is what I wanted you to see," he said simply. "It's my favorite spot in the world."

She turned to face him, her cheeks pinker than usual; whether their heightened color was due to heat or strong emotion, he couldn't say. But he liked the effect.

Her lips parted as though she were about to speak, and her eyes shone as though she were about to cry. She did neither. Instead, she stared at him like she could read his every thought. And if she could, God help him. God help them both.

"What do you think of it?" he asked.

She lay flat on her back and blinked at the bright sky. "Glorious."

James swallowed. Olivia's hair was mostly loose, splayed around her head like a woman who'd just been thoroughly pleasured. Her pale breasts strained against her dress, almost spilling out of the top. With a tug, he could pull down her bodice and expose her nipples, lower his head, and curl his tongue around one until it tightened into a hard little nub. With one swift move, he could flip up her skirts, nestle his head between her legs, and lick at the folds of her sex until she writhed and moaned with pleasure.

Olivia sighed, apparently oblivious to the wicked nature of his musings. She patted the ground beside her in invitation. "You must try this."

Yes, most definitely oblivious.

Nonetheless, he stretched out on the soft earth beside her. Their bodies did not touch, but the inch that separated her arm from his fairly crackled with heat.

"I imagine this must be how the gods and goddesses

feel at the top of Mount Olympus," she said. "It's a little dizzying, isn't it?"

If James felt dizzy, it had nothing to do with Zeus and everything to do with her sweet, citrusy scent. But he simply said, "Mmm."

For a few minutes, neither of them spoke. James turned his head to glance at Olivia's profile. Her eyes were closed, as though she were savoring the warmth of the sun upon her face. He took the opportunity to admire the light smattering of freckles across the bridge of her nose and the thick fringe of her lashes brushing her cheek. Her lower lip tempted him with its fullness; he longed to pull it between his teeth and suck lightly—to taste her as he had that night at the Easton ball. His cock strained against the front of his buckskin breeches and he shifted onto his side, hoping the tall grass might conceal his lust.

Olivia's eyes fluttered open and she, too, rolled onto her side, propping herself up on an elbow. "How did you find this place?"

James shrugged and endeavored not to stare at the swells of her breasts, pressed enticingly together. "I just happened upon it."

"Thank you for sharing it with me."

There was a lot more he'd like to share with her. Lying among the flowers with Olivia, it seemed as though they were miles from anyone else. How easy it would be to forget that she was Huntford's younger sister. And that he was leaving for Egypt in a couple of months.

And that she deserved better than him.

"I'm glad you like it," he said sincerely. "I almost forgot about our breakfast. I promised you the best hot cross buns in England, and I never forget a promise. Come, I'll escort you to the table."

"Table?" She sat up, eyes sparkling.

James stood, took her hand, and helped lift her to her feet. Scooping up his bag, he said, "This way."

He led her to the large, flat rock that overlooked the fell. She easily scrambled onto it and sat with her feet dangling over the edge.

"The view from your dining room is breathtaking." She splayed her palms over the rough stone. "It's pleasantly warm. Almost makes me want to take a nap."

"Not yet," James said. He withdrew a fresh handkerchief from his pocket and laid out the sweets from the bakery as well as the peaches, which he sliced with a knife. He'd thought to bring a canteen of tea, but no cups, and the tea was tepid.

"A picnic!" Olivia exclaimed.

"A primitive one," he said, "but I suppose it qualifies. You must try everything."

Olivia tugged off her gloves before she began sampling. She closed her eyes in ecstasy while savoring the buns. When she bit into the ripe peach, a droplet of juice rolled down her chin, and James checked the urge to lean over and lick it off. She laughed and brushed at it with the back of her hand, blushing prettily.

When they'd eaten all they could, they sat companionably, letting the warm breeze rustle their hair and clothes.

At length, Olivia turned to him. The playful crinkles around her eyes had vanished. "The things you said last night," she began. "You were right about me."

Hell. "I shouldn't have spoken so plainly or harshly, Olivia. I was upset that you'd placed yourself in danger."

She shook her head, and a few stray brown curls waved in the breeze. "One of the things I've always admired about you is that you speak the truth, and you hold nothing back. I think you are incapable of deception."

James thought of the letter from Olivia's father that he'd left in his room at the inn and swallowed. "I had no right to say—"

"It doesn't matter. You made me realize that I've done precious little of value with my life. It's time I changed that."

Good God. What if she really *did* mean to enter a convent? "How can you say that? You've been a devoted sister to Rose. You were the only person she trusted, the only person who was capable of reaching her. And must I remind you that without your assistance, Huntford and Anabelle might never have resolved their differences?"

"They were destined to be together, with or without my interference."

"The point is, your family and friends have often been the beneficiaries of your kind acts."

"They require less and less from me now. I was thinking that I must expand my good deeds beyond the circle of my family and friends, to those who are less fortunate."

"What do you intend to do?" James frowned. Olivia had been gently bred; he didn't like the idea of her visiting prisoners in Newgate or tending to the diseased in filthy hospitals.

"I don't know yet, but I have some ideas. It's time I experienced more of the world and shared my good fortune with others."

He felt like the worst kind of hypocrite. "I hope you're not doing this because of the nonsense I spouted last night," James said. "The blow to my head probably knocked the good sense out of me."

Her lips curved into a faint smile. "No, you were right. And though I cannot deny I wished my adventure would end differently, perhaps this result was for the best."

"Just don't do anything rash. Whatever plans you undertake, discuss them with your brother. I would hate for any misfortune to befall you."

"Thank you." Olivia's eyes brimmed, but she blinked away the tears. "As for my current predicament, I've decided what I must do."

James arched a brow. He'd assumed her fate rested in his hands. He should have known Olivia would have other ideas. "And what is that?"

"I shall leave for Aunt Eustace's this afternoon. The sooner I'm on my way, the better."

"But she's not expecting you."

"I wrote her a letter this morning and asked Hildy to post it."

"And what of your brother?" James asked. "Will you tell him where you've been?"

Olivia stared out at the valley. "I'd rather not. It's cowardly of me, I know, but Owen has a tendency to overreact in matters such as this. Still, I cannot prevent you from telling him, and I understand if you feel you must."

James searched Olivia's face for any sign she was playing coy; he found none. He'd never been particularly good at interpreting tacit meanings, and he knew without a doubt that he'd rather decipher an ancient text than a woman's emotions. But he didn't think Olivia was trying to manipulate him. She looked much too defeated.

"As much as I'd like to spare you Huntford's wrath,

I cannot hide the truth from him. If our positions were reversed, I would expect him to tell me."

Olivia nodded. "You've been friends with Owen for a long time. Your first loyalty is to him—not me."

"Yes," James replied, with more conviction than he felt. He thought of the note to Olivia from her father that Huntford had entrusted to him. He didn't like keeping secrets from her any more than he liked keeping secrets from Huntford. And he seemed to be planted firmly in the middle of their brother-sister relationship.

"Thank you for the lovely breakfast," Olivia said. She stood and brushed off her palms. "Though I could easily spend all day here, I must return to the inn and prepare for the journey to my aunt's house. There's no need for you to escort me down the hill; I can manage the path."

"No," he said quickly. Not because he doubted her ability to handle the terrain. More because he wasn't prepared to say good-bye just yet. "I'll walk you back."

Olivia shrugged as though it mattered little to her either way. As she repaired her hair and replaced her bonnet, he thought it a damnable shame that she couldn't remain as she'd been—laughing, beautiful, and slightly undone. But perhaps it was for the best.

As they made their way down the path, clouds drifted in front of the sun. The breeze picked up and a few fat raindrops splattered on their clothes and skin. When Olivia paused to cover up with her shawl, James tried to hide his dismay.

As the rain fell harder, the pebbled path grew slippery. He caught a glimpse of her thin, delicate slippers and frowned. "Hold on to my arm."

"I shall be fine." It seemed she would be, but when they

were only a few yards from the foot of the hill, her feet skated forward over the rocks and her body fell backward. James leaped behind her and threw his arms around her waist, but he couldn't brace himself or steady her.

She landed on top of him, her soft bottom pressing against his cock, which was already responding in the predictable manner, damn it. She sat up, apparently oblivious to the effect she had on him. His pride would have him think it hard to miss, but maybe she was too embarrassed by the fall to notice the rock-hard length of him beneath her delectable bottom.

He sat up, too, but kept his arms wrapped around her. He found himself reluctant to let her go—and not just for the obvious reason. "Are you all right?"

"Yes. Well, no. I'm rather mortified. I hope I haven't crushed you."

"Hardly."

She rolled off of him with impressive agility, but when she tried to stand, one leg crumpled beneath her. She quickly righted herself and painted a bright smile on her face.

"You *are* hurt." James rose and grasped her shoulders lightly.

"Hmm?" she asked innocently.

"Your leg buckled as though it was injured."

"No, nothing so dire. I fear I'm just clumsy—although that's no surprise to you, is it? I do believe the rain is picking up. Thank goodness we're almost to the inn."

"Would you like to lean on my arm? Or I could carry you."

She froze and shot him a look of mild curiosity, as though she found him a strange and puzzling creature. "I don't think that will be necessary."

James squashed the disappointment that rose in his chest, and they continued down the main street and past the bakery, with Olivia favoring one leg and stubbornly refusing to allow him to help her.

Rain dripped off of the sign hanging outside the inn, and mud puddles had formed on the ground. They stood in the same spot where James had fought Crutcher the night before. It felt like it had been a fortnight ago.

"Here we are," Olivia said with more enthusiasm than seemed necessary. "In case I don't see you before you leave for Egypt, I wish you safe travels. I hope that while you're digging and exploring, you find everything you're looking for." Her voice cracked on the last word.

So. She did still care.

But he didn't dare dwell on that. "I'm going to speak to your coachman and make sure he's adequately prepared for your journey to Oxfordshire."

"That's very kind."

"Good-bye, Olivia." Somehow he forced the words from his mouth.

"Good-bye." She turned and limped into the inn, leaving him standing in the rain, like the fool that he was.

Chapter Seven

> *Preserve: (1) To mummify, keep free from decay, or*
> *protect from destruction. (2) To keep intact, as in*
> She intended to preserve the scrap of her
> self-respect that still remained.

Terrence is worried the roads won't be fit for travel this evening," Hildy said. She deftly unlaced Olivia's rain-dampened dress.

"I have faith he'll deliver us safely to an inn on the way to Aunt Eustace's. Besides, I don't want to stay here another night." She couldn't. Not after the conversation she'd just had with James. She needed to leave before her resolve cracked.

"Very well, I'll tell him to ready the coach." Hildy sighed. "He's accustomed to receiving bad news from me, in any event."

Olivia winced at the slight barb, knowing she deserved it. "Thank you, Hildy. I promise there will be no more deception from me." She tossed aside the damp dress and ducked as her maid slipped a stylish striped traveling gown over her head.

The maid clucked her tongue. "I shall always take your side, no matter what. But Terrence, he's a different story—as much as he adores you, his first allegiance is to the duke."

"I know."

"I'll order a few sandwiches to bring with us and inform Terrence that we'll be ready to leave in half an hour." With one final tug, she secured the laces at the side of Olivia's gown and then hurried into the corridor, shutting the door behind her.

Olivia unpinned her hair and brushed it out before twisting it into a sensible knot at her nape. Then, with some disdain, she eyed the practical pair of walking boots that Hildy had left beside the chair. They were the logical choice, and yet, Olivia could not fathom how she would insert her right foot—which had swelled to roughly twice its normal size—into the confines of a narrow boot. She lifted her hem to peek at her foot, which bulged grotesquely out of her once-pretty blue slipper. She didn't dare remove her shoe, for she'd never get another one on. Instead, she lowered her hem, stuffed the boots into her portmanteau, and limped about the room looking for the stray ribbon or hair comb that may have been forgotten during the packing.

By the time Hildy returned, Olivia was ready and eager to be on her way. She waved Hildy in front of her so that the maid would not notice her injured ankle—she'd only make a fuss and needlessly delay their departure.

As Terrence loaded the coach with their bags, Olivia managed to climb into the cab.

A moment later, the maid poked her head through the coach door and spoke loudly, so as to be heard over the rain pelting the roof. "I'll just retrieve the food the innkeeper's wife prepared," she said. "Then we shall be ready to go." She slammed the cab door shut and darted into the inn, a valiant, yet futile, attempt to dodge the raindrops.

Olivia stared down the narrow, muddy street where she and James had walked together, wishing she were numb—numb to the throbbing pain in her foot and to the torture of knowing that the future she'd let herself imagine would never, ever be. She'd done more than imagine her life with James—she'd believed it to her core. The certainty that she'd one day marry him had been the compass that guided her through decisions large and small. What gown to wear? What would *James* like? What soiree to attend? Where was *James* most likely to be? What book to read? What topic would be of most interest to *James*?

How utterly pathetic.

In hindsight, her eagerness to please him seemed worse than desperate. It was as though she'd forgotten who she, Olivia Sherbourne, was. That she existed quite separately and independently from James Averill.

Anger—at herself, James, and every bloody artifact ever discovered—coursed through her. With clenched fists, she pounded the velvet squabs of the coach. However, they were too soft to provide much satisfaction. So, in a brilliant move, she kicked the bench opposite her with her right foot.

Dear Lord. Her ankle ignited in a fierce and blinding pain that shot up her leg, all the way to her hip. The corners of her vision went black, and she grasped the wall of the coach to keep herself from swooning onto the floor.

Tears stung her eyes. Stupid, stupid, stu—

Bang, bang. The coach's windows rattled from the forceful knock, and the door of the cab sprang open.

Olivia swiped at her eyes. It would never do for Hildy to find her upset—but it wasn't her maid.

There, in the opening, stood James, seemingly impervious to the rain splattering on his shoulders and head. "I was afraid you'd be gone," he said breathlessly.

"I thought we'd already said our good-byes," she said, a bit more sharply than she'd intended.

"I know. But I can't just let you leave for Oxfordshire."

She snorted a little, amazed at his gall. "You're not 'letting me leave.' *I've* made up my mind and I intend to follow through."

Droplets darkened the curls hanging over his forehead and dripped onto his nose. "I've not yet decided whether to inform Huntford of your activities."

"Is that meant to be a threat? Because I've already told you that if you feel it necessary to reveal all to my brother, you may do so without impediment from me."

"I don't understand. Why are you acting this way?"

She couldn't very well tell him that her wretched ankle was throbbing or that her foolish heart was breaking. "Wherever I go, whatever I do, is no concern of yours. Any sway you once held over me is gone. As soon as Hildy returns, we are leaving. With or without your blessing."

"Very well." And with that, he climbed into the coach, closed the door behind him, and deposited himself on the seat opposite her.

"What the bloody hell are you doing?"

James did not so much as raise a brow at her vulgar language. Damn him.

Like a dog trying to dry itself, he shook his head

briskly, sending an arc of droplets flying around him. Olivia recoiled from the chilly spray.

Once, she would have found his disregard for propriety refreshing, even charming. Now it made her want to kick him with her good foot. "What fine manners," she said dryly.

He shrugged. "You started it with 'bloody hell.' "

She huffed but was secretly gratified that he had not missed the remark. "My, how rapidly things seem to have deteriorated."

James crossed his arms over his chest and grinned, making her traitorous heart beat faster. "It's cozy in here," he said. "Nice and dry, too."

"It *was* dry," Olivia corrected. "In any case, now that you have made your point"—though she couldn't say for certain what his point *was*—"you should disembark before anyone notices that we are alone in my coach."

His eyes crinkled and he chuckled as though genuinely amused.

"I'm delighted my distress serves as such a rich source of entertainment."

"Olivia." The way he said her name—so honestly, so intimately—broke through all the buttresses she'd erected around her. "I'm not here to torment you," he said softly.

"No?"

He smiled, and in one fluid motion, hopped off his bench and seated himself on hers. Just that quickly, the temperature in the coach went up ten degrees. The barest inch separated their shoulders; part of her skirt was trapped beneath his thigh. He reached for her hand on the seat between them and squeezed.

Olivia could barely breathe.

"I don't want to distress you," he was saying, as though Olivia could fully comprehend his words while his palm was pressed to hers. "But I'm still grappling with how to best handle this situation. I know I should send word to Huntford. In fact, if I had a lick of good sense, I'd have done so the moment you arrived here last night."

"But you didn't."

"No, and I honestly don't want to," James said. "The problem is, your brother doesn't know where you are."

"Er, not precisely. But he knows I traveled to the northwest."

"At the moment, you're not even in the same county where he thinks you are."

"True." She sighed, disappointed that James felt obliged to point out the obvious. "However, I *am* trying to rectify that. I should arrive at my aunt's by tomorrow night. Assuming I'm ever permitted to actually leave," she added pointedly.

"I've no intention of preventing you from leaving," James said.

"I see." Olivia pondered this a moment. "Then would you mind telling me why you are here?"

"I'm going with you." He released her hand, put his hands behind his head, and stretched out his long, buckskin-clad legs.

Good heavens. "To Aunt Eustace's?"

"Yes, I intend to deliver you safely to her doorstep."

Olivia bristled. "I hardly think I need you to deliver me."

"Yes, well," he drawled, "therein lies the problem— you hardly think."

Of all the—

The door to the coach popped open again. Hildy held

a large basket before her and had climbed halfway into the cab before she realized there had been an invasion of muscle and masculinity. The maid reared back, her eyes wide.

"Allow me," James offered, extending a hand. He helped her board with one hand and took the basket with the other.

Hildy sat on the opposite bench and wrung her hands. "I'm sorry, I didn't realize..." Her gaze flicked from Olivia and James to the door, as though she contemplated making a run for it.

"It's all right, Hildy. Mr. Averill was just leaving."

James shot Olivia a cocky smile. "I think you misunderstand, Lady Olivia." To the maid, he said, "I intend to escort you to Oxfordshire."

"Don't be ridiculous." Olivia seethed. "It will take us the better part of two days. I am sure you'd rather spend that time digging around some druid rock pile."

He leaned back into the squabs. "Not really."

Olivia debated her next move, but it was hard to think clearly when she could feel the heat coming off of James's body. The almost harsh angles of his face were balanced by his full lips and his eyes, the color of soft moss. She would not allow his handsomeness to distract her.

"If you insist on accompanying us, then I suppose you must."

"I must indeed."

Olivia flashed a smile and batted her eyes in her best debutante imitation. "But I see that you don't have a bag. I'm sure you'll want to pack a few items for the trip—a book or journal for passing long hours in the cramped coach, some dry clothes, other necessities..."

James cocked his head. "And you'll be waiting right here for me when I return?"

"Of course," she lied.

"I don't think so."

Blast. "Very well, then." She knocked on the roof; the coach lurched forward. Surely James would come to his senses, halt the coach, and end the charade.

But a half hour later, when a five-mile stretch of muddy, pitted road separated them from Haven Bridge, the truth of the matter sunk in.

She and James would spend the next two days shoulder to shoulder in the intimate confines of her coach. The only bright spot she could find in the situation was that his presence—however infuriating—distracted her from the pain that radiated from her ankle.

This was a bad idea.

Spontaneous decisions such as this were not in James's nature. He believed in preparation, organization, logic. This trip to Oxfordshire flew in the face of all three.

He had nothing but the clothes on his back and the items in his pocket—a few twenty-pound notes and the letter that Olivia's father had left her as part of his last will and testament. He smoothed a hand over the front of his jacket, confirming that the papers were still there.

He'd decided that he must keep the letter on his person. Leaving it in his room at the inn, even for a short period of time, was too risky. Anyone could enter the room and abscond with the letter, and Olivia might never read her father's last message to her.

Knowing the letter was safely stowed in his pocket was some comfort...but not much.

James hadn't had an opportunity to tell his own coachman where he was going or give instructions when to come for him.

He hadn't had a chance to inform Uncle Humphrey of his plans, and the old man would worry when James didn't show for his daily visit.

But if he'd dared to step foot outside of her coach to pack a few items or speak with Ian, he would have returned to find nothing but the deep tracks of her coach's wheels filling up with rain.

And he couldn't let her go like that.

She sat stiffly beside him, sniffing every so often, as though she could barely contain her distaste for his company.

Though he wasn't thrilled about the circumstances either, he had to see that she made it safely to her aunt's. He might have absolved himself of the duty if he'd had the gumption to write a letter to Huntford informing him of his sister's unsanctioned travels...but he hadn't.

To do so would have betrayed Olivia.

Sometime that morning, he'd realized he valued his relationship with her at least as much as his relationship with her brother.

She'd become important to James. In ways he didn't care to examine too deeply.

Clearly she was vexed with him—a state of affairs he found unsettling. He supposed he'd grown comfortably accustomed to being on the receiving end of her adoration. How could he have taken it for granted all those years?

Her maid, on the opposite seat, busied herself with mending. Every few minutes, however, she glanced up at him warily, as though she expected to find that he'd pounced on her mistress while she looked down to knot her thread.

He smiled politely each time the maid looked his way, determined to win her over, even if he couldn't charm his way back into Olivia's good graces.

They'd ridden in heavy, awkward silence for almost two hours. James couldn't bear it any longer. "Is anyone besides me feeling a little peckish?"

Hildy set down her sewing and looked at Olivia. "You haven't eaten since morning."

Olivia flicked a glance at him, and he knew she was thinking of the feast they'd shared on the hilltop.

"I'm not hungry," she said.

Nevertheless, the maid pulled the basket from beneath the bench. "The innkeeper's wife packed us some wonderful sliced chicken sandwiches, apples, and ale. Will you try to eat something?"

"Thank you, no."

Determined to find something to tempt Olivia, Hildy dug farther into the basket. "Oh, there are pastries in here, too. You must keep up your strength, after all."

"For what? It's not as though I'm walking to Aunt Eustace's."

The maid lowered her eyes and replaced the cloth over the basket.

"Oh, Hildy," Olivia pleaded. "Forgive me for being so rude. Certain people"—she glared in James's direction—"seem to bring out the worst in me."

"You'll eat something, then?" the maid asked hopefully.

"Of course."

The smell of freshly baked bread and chicken filled the

coach, and James's mouth watered. Hildy handed him a sandwich. "Here you are, Mr. Averill."

"Are you sure there's enough—for you and the coachman, too?"

"Oh yes," she replied warmly. "How very kind of you to ask."

He and Hildy made small talk as they ate, and soon after, her eyes drooped. She packed the rest of the food away for the driver, leaned against the side of the cab, and promptly fell asleep.

Olivia stared out the window at the gray sky and the rain that continued to fall in sheets.

"I know you don't want me here." James leaned toward her and spoke softly, so as not to wake her maid. "But it was not my intention to make you miserable—only to ensure your safety."

She arched a brow. "Is that so, Mr. Averill? Have you no other motivation?"

James blinked, taken aback by her use of his surname. What other motivation did she suspect? Perhaps she guessed how fiercely attracted he was to her, and that even as they sat there, chaperoned by her maid, he was imagining how he'd like to kiss the soft skin of her neck, just behind her ear.

"What other reason would I have?"

"Hmm, let's see," she said dryly. "Perhaps you don't believe that I'm going to Oxfordshire after all."

Actually, the thought that she wasn't going to visit her aunt Eustace had not occurred to him—and it probably should have. "Where else would you go?"

"I don't know," she said, clearly exasperated by his simple question. "The point is, you don't trust me."

"That's not true. I trust you on the things that count."

"Such as?"

"Well, I know you'd do anything to protect your sister and brother. And you always stand up for what you believe is right."

She studied his face as though she thought he might be mocking her. "Who wouldn't stand up for family?"

Who, indeed? He didn't have half the backbone Olivia did. Even his closest friends didn't know about Ralph, his brother.

"You might be surprised," James said. "What I'm trying to say is that I don't doubt your word. I only knew that if misfortune befell you on your way to Aunt Eustace's, I'd never forgive myself."

Some of Olivia's hard edges seemed to melt, ever so slightly. "That's very gallant of you. But what could possibly happen between here and—"

Bam!

Chapter Eight

The coach bounced violently, sending Olivia into the air and onto the floor. She landed on her bottom—hard enough to jar her teeth—but it was better than landing on her foot. James was at her side, his legs and arms sprawled across the small space.

The maid, who'd slammed into the wall behind her, woke with a cry. "What's happened?"

"Hold on," James warned, though the coach already seemed to be slowing. "We must have hit a rut. Is either of you hurt?" He cupped Olivia's cheeks in his warm hands, as though reassuring himself that she was all right. Her heart, which was already pounding out of her chest, pounded harder in response to his touch.

Olivia nodded. "I'm fine." She turned to Hildy. "Did you bump your head?"

"Not very hard, my lady." But the maid looked too pale for Olivia's liking.

James moved back onto the bench seat and easily

pulled Olivia up beside him. "Stay here. I'm going to check on the coachman."

"Thank you," Olivia said, suddenly very, very glad to have him here.

Before the coach had even come to a complete stop, James slid back the latch and hopped lightly to the sodden ground. He gave her a reassuring wink and shut the door firmly behind him.

Olivia joined Hildy on her bench and gave her a fierce squeeze.

"I've never felt such a jolt. I hope Terrence wasn't hurt," the maid fretted.

"He managed to bring the horses to a stop. That's a good sign." Olivia paused and cocked an ear. "I can hear them talking."

She couldn't make out what the men were saying above the patter of rain on the roof, but she did hear Terrence curse with impressive vigor—and found it oddly reassuring.

A few moments later, James opened the door and popped his head in. "Terrence is fine." Another curse erupted from behind James. "But, as you've no doubt surmised, not particularly happy. One of the coach's wheels dropped into a large pit in the road. It bounced out—thankfully—but the rear axle is cracked. If we keep going, we risk having it snap clean through. We'll have to leave the coach here and get help." He used a tone that brooked no argument.

Olivia ignored it. "We cannot leave the coach on the side of this road. Anyone could ride by and make off with it."

"Not unless they had a couple of extra horses."

Just a day ago, Olivia would have swooned over James's good sense. Now his superior attitude grated on her nerves.

"I'll admit that's unlikely. But the coach is laden with our bags. A thief could make off with all our possessions."

"Not if we carry them," he said.

Olivia wished she'd packed a little lighter. "How far is the nearest village?"

"Terrence thinks we're only two or three miles from Sutterside. Not a bad walk."

Perhaps not—if one had two properly working ankles. "Could we ride the horses?"

James shook his head regretfully. "We don't have saddles."

"We'll be drenched."

"At least *you* have a change of clothes."

Olivia grunted. "I gave you the chance to pack a bag."

A sardonic smile split James's face. "Indeed. And if I'd gone to get it, you'd be the one standing in the rain inspecting the axle instead of me."

She leaned forward and looked out at the gray sky behind James.

"And here I thought you were the adventurous sort," he teased. "Do you have an extra cloak you can throw on? We only have an hour or so of daylight left, so the sooner we're off the better."

Hildy was already collecting items from inside the coach and tying her bonnet more tightly beneath her chin. Olivia hated to admit the truth about her ankle—especially since she'd lied about it on their way to the inn at Haven Bridge—but she had no choice.

"I don't think I can walk to Sutterside," Olivia said casually. "I turned my ankle earlier, during our walk."

Her maid gasped. "My lady, you should have said something!"

"It's nothing too frightful, Hildy, just a tad sore. Still, I believe I shall be better off staying here with the carriage and keeping watch over our bags."

"I see," James said. "And if a highway robber appears, will you fight him off?"

"If I must." But she certainly hoped it wouldn't come to that.

"With what? A parasol?"

"Perhaps Terrence would be so good as to lend me his pistol."

James closed his eyes momentarily, as though praying for patience. Then he lumbered into the cab and sat on the seat across from her. "How bad is it?" he asked. "Really."

Olivia tucked her right foot a little farther beneath the bench. "It will probably be fine by tomorrow, but right now it's . . . tender."

"Tender," he repeated—rather unnecessarily, in her opinion.

"Yes."

"Let me see it."

Prideful, vain creature that she was, she'd been dreading this moment.

Only because if James was to spend the next few years in Egypt, she'd prefer that he *not* remember her as the girl with the elephant foot. "No."

He leaned forward, elbows propped casually on his knees. "I just want to look at it. I won't touch it if it hurts."

She shook her head emphatically and looked to Hildy. No help came from that quarter, as the maid looked nearly as curious as James.

"Why won't you show me?" he asked.

"Modesty."

James burst into laughter. Hildy even chuckled a little. Olivia's excuse may have been a little far-fetched. Still, she longed to take the slipper off her good foot and hurl it at him.

"Fine," she said. "Gawk to your heart's content." Olivia stuck out her right foot and hauled her hem up to her knee.

James and Hildy went dead silent, and for a moment, Olivia wondered if her foot had gotten even worse. Hard to imagine, but maybe it had turned black or was oozing something. She peeked at her outstretched foot and was relieved to find it the same—grotesquely fat, but the same.

"Good God." James held her shin with one hand and cradled her foot in the other. "I'm so sorry, Olivia."

"It's not as though I'm on my deathbed," she quipped, but the truth was she could use a good cry.

"This must hurt like the devil."

It did, as a matter of fact, and talking about it wasn't helping one bit. "A two-mile walk seems out of the question."

He gently placed her foot back on the floor and lowered the hem of her dress. The slight weight of her hem against the top of her foot felt almost as bad as the time Lord Kesley trampled it during a quadrille.

"You definitely cannot walk," James said soberly.

She checked the urge to make a snide remark even though she *had* told him so.

"If it weren't raining and muddy, I might be able to carry you—"

"No," Olivia cried emphatically. After enduring two rejections from him in the past week, her pride simply would not allow it.

"You're right. The ground is too treacherous. We shall have to wait here while Terrence goes for help."

Olivia tilted her head, hoping she'd heard him incorrectly. "*We*?"

"I'm not leaving you alone." James pointed at her ankle and made a face like he smelled a three-day-old fish. "Especially not with your foot like that."

"It's not as though it's going to fall off while you're not looking."

He shrugged like he wouldn't want to make that bet. "Without two good feet, you'd be even more defenseless than usual."

"I'm not nearly as helpless as you might think." She smiled in a thinly veiled threat.

James grinned. "I'm sorry you'll have to endure my company a bit longer."

"Hildy could stay with me," Olivia said hopefully.

"She can if you'd like. But even the pair of you cannot remain here alone. It will be dark by the time Terrence returns. He's unhooking the horses now. I'll inform him of our plans so he can be on his way."

He started for the door, then stopped, his brow wrinkled in concern. "Would your foot feel better if you propped it up on this bench?" Before she could respond, he said, "Let's try." He knelt on the floor and lifted her leg with the same care she was certain he'd have given to an ancient Egyptian princess's mummified leg—though he would no doubt have been more enthralled with the latter. With a traveling blanket that he found beneath his seat, he swaddled her ankle and let it rest on the bench. The throbbing lessened slightly.

"Thank you," she said. "That helps a little."

James nodded and ducked out the door to speak with Terrence. The moment he left, Hildy cleared her throat. "You'll want me to stay with you, then?"

Olivia would have thought the answer obvious. "I think that would be best. Do you have any objection?"

"No, of course not," Hildy said. But she gazed longingly out the window.

"But you would rather walk to Sutterside in the rain than wait here with me in the dry coach?"

"Oh, it sounds awful when you put it like that," Hildy said. "You know I've never been good on long rides."

"You can't have motion sickness—we're not even moving."

"I know, my lady." The maid blushed scarlet. "It's not the movement that's the problem so much as the small space. Now that Mr. Averill is traveling with us, the carriage seems that much smaller. It makes me light-headed."

"Here. We can open the door." Olivia awkwardly leaned over her outstretched leg, undid the latch, and pushed the door open. A damp breeze blew into the cab. "That's better, isn't it?"

Hildy shot a skeptical look at the door. "I suppose."

But just then, another gust slammed the door shut.

Blast. There was no good reason Hildy should suffer on her account—at least no more than she already had. "On second thought, I think you should accompany Terrence to the village. While he sees to the horses and the repairs, perhaps you could secure rooms for us at the inn."

"I could order dinner, too," the maid said eagerly.

"It's all settled, then," Olivia agreed. "Take the cloak from my portmanteau to keep you dry." When Hildy opened her mouth to object, Olivia added, "I can't have you taking a chill."

Hildy smiled gratefully. "You're very kind, my lady." She flung the cloak around her shoulders and scooped up her small bag. "Terrence and I will hurry to the village. He'll return with help in no time at all."

Olivia squeezed the maid's hand. "Be careful, Hildy."

With a bob of her head, she ducked out the door, and Olivia was alone.

For about three blessed seconds.

The door burst open, and Olivia slid to the left so that James didn't have to climb over her leg when he took his seat on the bench opposite hers. Unfortunately, he mistook her meaning and deposited himself—his large, wet self—on the seat directly beside her.

"Hildy and Terrence are heading down the road, horses in tow. They are bound and determined to rescue you as soon as possible. I'm not certain whom they regard as the greater threat—the highway robbers or me."

Olivia tried to ignore the fact that she was alone with James. She'd spent the better part of a decade trying to arrange just this sort of thing, and now that she'd managed it—quite by accident—she wished she were anywhere else.

Because in spite of his determination to leave his family, his friends, and *her* to go dig up mummies, she still cared for him.

The rich, deep sound of his voice melted her insides like butter. One sideways look from his green eyes stole her breath and her good sense.

She was in trouble.

She knew it.

And if the hungry look James cast her way was any indication, he knew it, too.

Chapter Nine

Observation: (1) A scientific notation regarding the details of a site or artifact. (2) A judgment based on one's experience, as in In her observation, James's backside was unparalleled both in firmness and in shape.

*J*ames had no intention of ravishing Olivia.

The problem was that when he was around her, he had a habit of doing all sorts of things he didn't intend.

"There's every possibility a passing carriage could stop and lend us assistance," James said. If he reminded himself of that fact, maybe he'd be less inclined to give in to the temptation to kiss Olivia.

She cast him an indulgent smile. "We've seen exactly one other traveler since leaving Haven Bridge, and that was a farmer in a mule-drawn cart."

"It lacks a certain amount of dignity," he teased. "But with an ankle like that, you can't afford to turn up your nose at a perfectly functional—if rickety—wagon."

"That's true. Thank heaven we're not in Hyde Park. Could you imagine me riding down Rotten Row in the back of a cart with my grossly swollen foot propped on a crate of angry chickens? I can see Miss Starling now, seated on a stylish barouche, gaping at me from beneath her lace-edged parasol with undisguised revulsion." Olivia shuddered. "I suppose I should be grateful that we're in the middle of nowhere. The only witnesses to my shame are the cows, over yonder."

James chuckled. "You've always been able to find the bright side of an unfortunate situation. I admire that about you."

She snapped her head around to look at him, eyes narrowed as though she feared he was mocking her. "Truly?"

"Yes. I admire a great many things about you, Olivia."

She swallowed, working the fine muscles of her neck. "That's kind of you to say."

"It's true. As long as I've known you, you've been full of boundless energy and passion. You've always spoken your mind and been easy to talk to. While you *really* shouldn't have come here without your brother's knowledge—"

"Yes, I believe you've already mentioned that."

"—in some respects, I'm glad you did."

"And why is that?"

"Well, I realize now that I've taken you for granted— your lovely smile, your zest for life, and your unwavering loyalty. I'm sorry that I didn't see it before and that I was blind to the way you felt about me."

But he hadn't really been blind to it. On some level, he'd known that Olivia harbored feelings for him, and he'd abused her devotion by basking in it without acknowledging it. Hell, what red-blooded male *wouldn't* want to be on the receiving end of her adoring glances? Oh, he'd enjoyed the attention plenty. And that made him at least partially culpable for the mess they were in.

"Well," she said slowly, "for my part, I realized about half an hour after arriving in Haven Bridge that I'd made a horrible mistake. But if I hadn't chased after you, I wouldn't have seen the view at the top of your hill or tasted the world's best hot cross buns, and that would have been tragic."

He couldn't have agreed more. And because saying so seemed inadequate, he took her bare hand and kissed the back of it. She gasped slightly but didn't pull away. That was another thing he adored about her—she *never* pulled away.

Her skin tasted of rain, lavender, and *her*. And though he was very, very tempted to trace a path with his lips right up her forearm and beyond, he refrained. "This is just what I mean," he said. "Here you are, stranded in the countryside with an injured foot, and you choose to dwell on the good things instead of the bad."

"I see no advantage in talking about unpleasant matters, but that doesn't mean I don't have regrets."

James squeezed her hand tighter. "What are your regrets?" Suddenly, it was imperative that he know. "Will you tell me?"

Olivia sat quietly for the space of several breaths, and he was beginning to wonder if he'd crossed a line, pushed her too far, when finally she spoke. "I regret that I've led a frivolous life."

"What?"

"It's true. Most of my worries border on the ridiculous— a torn hem, an empty dance card, a nasty bit of gossip."

"I'm no expert," James admitted, "but I think all young women worry about such things."

"No," Olivia said, shaking her head. "Not my closest friends. Before Anabelle married Owen, she struggled to keep her mother alive and put food on the table for her sister. Daphne can treat most illnesses better than our doctor and still finds time to work at the foundling home. And though Rose is two years my junior, she's infinitely wiser. With all the time we spend together, you would have thought some of her serenity might have rubbed off on me." She gave a hollow laugh. "But no. So, you asked me, and now you know. I regret that in my twenty-two years, I've done nothing of any import. I haven't made a difference."

A denial was on his lips, but he bit it back. If he discounted what she said outright, she'd never believe him. So, he waited a few moments and let the patter of the rain on the roof soothe away some of her angst. Then, very softly and deliberately, he said, "You've made a difference to me."

She had.

Who cared that she had few grand accomplishments to her name? He wanted to explain to her that being a good person was more than enough. That loyalty and commitment to family surpassed a whole litany of good deeds or grand adventures.

Olivia laid her head back against the velvet squabs as though she'd been sapped of all her energy. "Everything is so much clearer now."

"How so?" His stomach clenched. She was probably going to say she no longer had a romantic interest in him, that she couldn't imagine why she'd mooned over him for

so long. Of course, that would be for the best, and yet…
selfish bastard that he was, he hated the thought. Olivia's
adoration had been a constant. Knowing that she was in
his corner, no matter what, had made him walk a little
taller, puff his chest out a bit more. She'd been a nuisance
at times, but even then, she'd made him feel like a king.
She'd given him her unwavering devotion.

In return, he'd taken her for granted.

She stared at the ceiling of the cab as though it
were a clear, starry sky. "This trip—no matter how ill-
conceived—has been truly enlightening. For all the years
I was infatuated with you, my one goal was to capture
your attention. *That* was my lofty aspiration. And now that
I've confessed my feelings to you, I realize how shallow
that goal was. Not that you're unworthy, mind you," she
quickly added, "but I can't have all my dreams wrapped
up in someone else. I need to accomplish something for
myself. How can I expect someone as worldly as you to
respect me when I have no real passion of my own?"

Before he could inform her how ludicrous that notion
was, she continued. "Fortunately, I've an idea—for a project of sorts."

"I'm sure it's very noble. But, Olivia, you *have* my
respect. More than you know."

She went on as though she hadn't heard him. "It's nothing so grand, mind you. But this trip reminded me of how
much I love to travel outside of London—how much I
enjoy the countryside. And I started thinking about the
girls at Daphne's foundling home. Last week, when I
accompanied Daphne on her visit, I spoke with several of
the little urchins. Did you know that most of them were
born in London and have never seen the world beyond the

filthy streets of St. Giles? They've never seen cows grazing in beautiful green pastures or gone swimming in clear blue lakes."

"I'm not sure that's a tragedy," James said.

Olivia's face fell, and he wished he could take back his stupid, careless words.

"Perhaps not. However, I still think it would be good for them to see some of the world beyond the walls of the orphanage."

"Oh, I agree," he said quickly. "One can only learn so much from books."

She brightened instantly. "Precisely! I could take small groups of girls on day trips—picnics in the countryside, visits to cathedrals in nearby villages, maybe even a few longer outings for the older girls. What a grand time we would have." Olivia sighed happily.

"I'm sure the girls would be delighted to escape the confines of the classroom," James said. "And the country air would do them good."

"It would indeed. There's a new orphan—an eight-year-old named Molly—who has palsy. She spent the last two years in an institution for the insane before some kind nurse realized she didn't belong there and sent her to the orphanage. She's so grateful to be with the other girls and is already progressing rapidly at learning her tables and letters. But she's so pale. I think it must have been a very long time since she felt the sunshine upon her face."

Olivia's description of the sickly girl reminded him of his brother. It was on the tip of his tongue to say so, but then he remembered.

James didn't talk about Ralph. He never had. Not even to his closest friends.

Oblivious to his musings, Olivia rambled on. "I would need Owen's permission, of course, but I think I could convince him to lend me the use of the coach and a footman or two."

James was about to point out that she hadn't worried about seeking Huntford's permission prior to coming to the Lakes but thought better of it. He didn't want to say anything that would dim the light radiating from her beautiful face. "Your idea sounds splendid to me. Any reservations Huntford may have shall be no match for you."

Olivia grinned. "I can be very persuasive. But sometimes I wish I didn't have to be. It seems I shall be forever at Owen's mercy."

"At least he is fair. And he has never been able to deny you or Rose," James added.

"He's a wonderful brother. I didn't mean to imply otherwise. However, I am an adult." Olivia sat up a bit straighter in her seat. "I don't see why I must beg his permission for every little excursion."

James brushed a hand over the front of his jacket, ensuring that Olivia's letter was still tucked deep within his breast pocket. He could feel the paper beneath the damp fabric. Suddenly, it seemed to weigh as much as the sarsen stones at Stonehenge. Why had Huntford implicated him in what was clearly a family matter? The more time he spent with Olivia, the more he realized the right course of action was to give her the letter.

The problem was, the decision wasn't his to make.

James knew one thing for sure—the moment he saw Huntford, he would hand the letter over to him and demand that he give it to Olivia.

"I've no doubt you'll accomplish whatever you put

your mind to. And I don't mind telling you that I'm a little jealous of those girls for getting to spend idyllic days in the country with you."

Olivia snorted. "I should think you've had quite enough of that. Besides, what appeal could sheep-filled pastures hold when compared with the adventures that await you in Egypt?"

The appeal lay less in the pastures than in the woman who sat beside him. Specifically, it lay in the petal-smooth skin of her cheek, the plumpness of her lips, and the ripe curves of her body.

"As eager as I am to explore Egypt and study its ancient civilizations, England has much to recommend it in the here and now." He squeezed her hand, hoping his meaning was clear.

Olivia did not respond but only gazed out the window. If he was not mistaken, however, a faint blush stole up her cheeks.

"How does your ankle feel now?" he asked.

"Like someone dropped a pianoforte on it."

"You should have told me earlier, you know, so we could have had a doctor look at it."

"I wish Daphne were here," she said. "She'd go pick some herbs, mix up a poultice, and have me frolicking through the fields in no time."

"I'd like to see that. Not the poultice, but the frolicking."

A rumble of thunder in the distance shook the coach, and a look of alarm crossed Olivia's face. She grasped at James's arm and clung to him for a quick, splendid moment.

"Forgive me," she said, clearly embarrassed. "I was just startled."

"Don't apologize." He moved closer and eased an arm around her shoulders. "You've had a tiresome couple of days. Why don't you lean your head on me and rest? I promise not to tease you if you snore."

Olivia eyed him warily but accepted the invitation. Tentatively, she laid her cheek against his shoulder, and the clean scent of her hair filled his head. He lifted a long loose strand from her neck and curled it around his finger, loving the silky feel of it. Gradually, the tension seemed to flow out of her, and her body nestled against him, warm and pliant.

The rain pelted the roof harder and the thunder grew louder and more frequent. A few drops managed to find their way through the top of the door and plunked onto the floor with tiny splashes.

Olivia gave a tired sigh. "What a mess I've gotten us into. How did I bungle things so terribly?"

"The broken axle isn't your fault." He caressed the top of her arm, which, of course, made him want to caress more of her, but he refrained. "And I will tell you this: if I must be stranded in a coach in the middle of a storm, there's no one I'd rather be stranded with."

She turned her face up to his and slowly blinked her beautiful brown eyes. "Truly?"

Damn it. He was going to kiss her.

It would have been impossible not to.

Chapter Ten

*B*last. She was going to kiss James.

Olivia had promised herself she wouldn't, but how could she not?

The spark in his green eyes sent delicious shivers through her limbs, and she melted into him. When he leaned forward, touching his forehead to hers, she was lost. She took shallow breaths, as though the slightest movement might break the tenuous, wonderful spell between them.

"Olivia," he whispered as he lowered his lips to hers.

Though they'd kissed before, this . . . this was different. *This* was the kiss she'd waited for her whole life.

He began gently, as though she were a rare and fragile treasure he couldn't believe he'd had the good fortune to find. His lips brushed lightly over hers—testing and tempting her, promising something more.

She closed her eyes in order to better feel his breath upon her cheek, his fingers in her hair, the solid pressure of his arm behind her. When he parted her lips with his tongue, a sigh escaped her and he swallowed it, pulling her closer and deepening the kiss.

Olivia did not resist him; she couldn't if she tried.

This kiss didn't start out of drunkenness or pity or desperation.

She'd seen the hunger simmering in James's eyes and heard the admiration in his voice. He *wanted* this kiss.

And damn it all, she did, too.

In fact, if lightning were to strike the coach or a flood were to carry it away this very moment, she and James would not have been deterred from this kiss. This breathtaking, knee-buckling, heart-stopping kiss.

He tasted just as she remembered—warm, cinnamony, and male—and she eagerly met every thrust of his tongue, drowning in a heady rush of desire. Though she longed to wriggle closer to him, her right foot was still propped on the opposite bench, making her leg a barrier between them.

Sensing her frustration, he gently lifted both her legs and laid them across his lap. "Much better," he murmured in her ear, sending sweet tremors through her body. "This is madness, Olivia, but I can't help myself."

"Nor can I."

He blazed a trail of kisses down her neck and across her collarbone to the hollow of her throat, where she felt her pulse race wildly. His hair tickled the sensitive skin of her neck; laughing, she lifted his face to hers.

"I dreamed of kissing you many times." Her cheeks warmed at her own boldness. "But my fantasies were always more picturesque."

James shot her a wicked grin, making her heart skip a beat. "How so?" he asked.

"For one thing," she began, "we were usually indoors."

"Why, I'm disappointed at your lack of imagination. Indoors is so ... predictable."

"I may have imagined one or two kisses out of doors," she admitted, "but in those cases, clear, starlit skies were overhead. Not thunderheads."

"Sounds dreadfully boring," James said, a bit distractedly. His heavy-lidded gaze had drifted to the expanse of skin above Olivia's formfitting gown.

"I would not have deemed them boring, but I had no basis for comparison then."

"And now?" With a calloused fingertip, he idly traced her low-cut neckline.

"I'm learning," she said breathlessly, "that there's much more to kissing than I realized."

"You have no idea," he growled, still staring, rather unapologetically in her opinion, at her breasts. Not that she minded.

She twined her arms around his neck and played with the soft curls at his nape. "While kissing has proved to be different than my relatively innocent imaginings, I am learning that reality is better."

A feral gleam lit James's eyes. He leaned in and slanted his mouth across hers, filling her with heat and passion. He swept a hand over her hip and up her belly, lightly brushing the underside of her breast with his thumb. Just when Olivia thought she'd die of anticipation, he cupped her breast, lightly tweaking her nipple through the thin crepe of her dress.

She kissed him harder, determined to make sure he did not stop. He didn't. Instead, he turned his attention to her other breast, making her dizzy with pleasure.

The temperature inside the coach shot upward, clouding the windows with a white mist. Her expertly fitted gown became a source of irritation, as it suddenly seemed to be laced too tightly. Her breath came in shallow rasps, as though air were in short supply. She could remedy the situation easily enough. The responsible course of action would be to stop kissing James.

But since she found that option most unappealing, she proceeded to the second—and slightly less proper— course of action.

Which was to reach down with one hand and loosen the ties at the side of her dress.

"What are you doing?" James's voice was laced with a note of hopefulness that helped to tamp down any embarrassment she should have felt.

"My dress is too tight." She tugged at the shoulders of her gown, causing the neckline to gape. Cool air immediately rushed over the swells of her breasts, which were still covered by her corset and chemise. Well, somewhat covered. "I didn't think you'd object," she said, pleased with the sultry tone she'd managed.

James's eyes darkened till only a thin ring of green remained. His gaze roamed over her, lingering on her bare shoulders, the lacy edge of her chemise, the deep valley between her breasts. Then he bent his head, kissing the skin she'd exposed.

Every touch of his lips, every caress of his fingers, set her on fire, and a sweet pulsing began in her loins.

This was James. *Her* James.

Even better, this was no dream.

Oh, she recognized the recklessness of her behavior. Rose would tell Olivia she deserved better than a romp in a broken-down carriage. Daphne would urge her to safeguard her heart. Anabelle would tell her to be practical—after all, in a couple of months James would be on a ship headed for Egypt.

Olivia *knew* all these things, but she wanted this and recognized it for what it was: a few stolen moments of bliss.

She wasn't going to make love with him—she wasn't a *complete* idiot—but she wanted to learn something of passion, and she wanted to learn it from *him*. Mostly, she just wanted to live the fantasy for a bit longer.

With a boldness she'd always suspected she possessed, Olivia pushed down her corset and chemise, freeing her breasts completely.

"Jesus," James whispered, and the hungry look in his eyes was everything Olivia had hoped for. She reclined against the side of the coach and pulled him forward by the lapels of his jacket.

James needed no further encouragement. He leaned over her, capturing one nipple in his mouth and grazing the other lightly with his palm. His tongue, warm and moist, curled around the tight nub, suckling until her whole body thrummed.

She raked her fingers through his hair, pulling him closer and wishing it were just that easy to keep him there with her. Forever.

He stopped and looked up at her with heavy-lidded eyes. "You're amazing, Olivia."

His words flowed over her like a silk gown. "If you say so."

"We mustn't get carried away, though...er, not any more than we already have."

"I know." Momentarily distracted by the spiral pattern he was tracing on her breast, she paused. When at last his finger reached the taut tip, she sucked in her breath and sighed happily. "Do you think we might enjoy each other's company for a bit longer?"

In answer, he captured her mouth with his and kissed her thoroughly. Maybe Olivia was reading too much into his actions—she'd been known to do that on occasion— but the low growl in his throat and the tender way he cupped her cheek made her think that maybe he wished she belonged to him. In a way, she did—and she always would.

Just not in the way she'd once dreamed.

But she wouldn't let herself think about that right now. Not while James was branding her neck with kisses and running a hand over her hip and down her leg...

Instead, she would lose herself in the moment and do some exploring of her own. She snaked her hands inside his jacket, reveling in the feel of his hard torso beneath his waistcoat. She slid her hands up, over the smooth muscles of his chest, wishing he were not wearing so many layers of clothes.

She pushed his jacket off his shoulders and halfway down his arms, at which point he was forced to stop kissing her in order to shrug it off. He did seem to be rather in a hurry to rid himself of it, which pleased Olivia inordinately. He unceremoniously tossed it aside, and as he did, a folded piece of paper slid onto the floor. She told herself it couldn't be too important. Especially not compared to the prospect of running her hands over his broad shoulders and down his muscled arms.

But a very stubborn and vexing part of her brain recalled seeing that rather official-looking folded paper before. After the fight outside the inn in Haven Bridge. It must be important.

"James," she rasped.

But he apparently thought she'd spoken his name in appreciation of the things he was doing to her—namely, slipping his hand beneath the hem of her gown and chemise and drawing wicked little circles on the sensitive skin behind her knee. In fact, *appreciation* was not a strong enough word. Her limbs felt loose and delightfully lazy, like she'd drunk too much punch at Vauxhall Gardens.

But the letter still lay there on the floor, refusing to be ignored.

She shifted her body to the left, stretched out her arm, and pinched the corner of the paper between two fingers.

James lifted his head and shot her a languorous smile that stole her breath. "I won't let you fall," he said, pulling her firmly back onto the bench. His gaze went to her lips as though he'd kiss her again, but before he could, Olivia waved the letter in front of his face.

The easy smile vanished. As though the coach had been transported to the tundra, James's eyes turned icy and his body stiff. "How did you get that?" His tone stung.

"I picked it up. Off the floor," she said dryly.

He snatched the letter from her, sat up, and quickly stuffed it into the back waistband of his buckskin trousers. "Damn it."

Wincing, Olivia sat up, too. "What's wrong?"

James shook his head slowly, as though their state of half-undress and the personal articles strewn about the cab confounded him. He closed his eyes like he wanted to erase the scene from his mind.

Erase *her* from his mind.

Was she always to be a source of regret for him?

"Here, let me help you," he said, pulling her sleeves onto her shoulders and smoothing the skirt of her gown over her legs. He was in control once more—polite and decorous. Infuriatingly so.

"I can manage," she said, borrowing his chilly tone. While she tucked herself back into her gown and tightened its laces, he shoved his arms into the sleeves of his jacket and moved down the bench a bit, giving her more space.

What the devil had just happened?

"How is your foot feeling?"

Her *foot*? Her lips were swollen from his kisses, her skin tingled from his caresses, and at her very core, she ached with desire. But he inquired after her foot?

"It's fine, I think. No worse than before."

"Excellent." He sat back and looked out the window. "The rain's let up a bit."

Oh no. She was not going to let him pretend that the last half hour—or had it been more?—had never happened. However, she couldn't quite bring herself to discuss their relationship...or lack thereof. She decided on a different tack. "Why do you carry that letter around with you?"

James dragged his hands down his face. "I can't discuss it with you."

"Why not?"

"It's a business matter." His words were clipped, as though he wished to snuff out the conversation.

Well, she wasn't going to be easily snuffed. "It looks like a letter."

He shrugged. "It might be."

"It might be? You don't know? You've been carrying this thing around with you for days."

"Why would you think that?"

"It has fallen out of your jacket on at least two separate occasions. If it's really that important, you might consider taking greater care with it."

"It's important."

"You are confident of that, even though you have no idea what it is."

"I don't want to talk about this, Olivia. It's personal."

"You said it was business before. Now it's personal?"

James leaned his elbows on his knees and held his head in his hands. "Yes."

"I see. The letter—or whatever it is—is of a personal nature. I have no right to ask about it, even if you did have your hand up my skirt a few moments ago."

His head snapped up. "Jesus, Olivia. You make it sound so tawdry."

"Forgive me," she said with mock horror. "Do tell. How would you describe our trysts?"

James heaved a sigh. "I care for you. I respect you."

"You have an odd way of showing it."

"I know. You deserve better, and there are things we need to discuss . . . but I'm not at liberty to do so yet."

"This sounds very mysterious, James." In truth, it sounded like an excuse.

He turned to her, and taking her hands in his, said, "I have not behaved like a gentleman."

"I haven't behaved like a lady."

He smiled weakly. "I haven't been completely forthcoming. When you find out the whole of it, you may want nothing more to do with me. And I certainly wouldn't blame you."

Olivia couldn't imagine wanting James out of her life

any more than she could imagine wanting hot chocolate out of it. Whatever his secret was, it clearly tortured him. The fine lines on his forehead were creased in concern, and shame clouded his beautiful green eyes. She thought she knew all of his secrets, but apparently he had a few more.

"I know you're not perfect," she said. "But that doesn't mean you're not perfect for me."

James raised her hands and pressed his lips, warm and moist, to the backs of them. "Wait and see."

Though rather weary of waiting, Olivia nodded.

There was one matter, however, that simply could not wait.

Chapter Eleven

Unearth: (1) To dig up an artifact buried in the ground.
(2) To reveal something hidden deep, as in
There was no telling what pain the letter's
contents might unearth.

"I'm not certain how to state this delicately," Olivia began, "but I'm afraid I must excuse myself for a few moments."

James shot her a puzzled look. "Why would you—" His eyes widened. "Oh."

She had lent her cloak to Hildy, but no matter. The torrential rain had given way to a light sprinkle. And truth be told, she could use a little cooling off. She scooted toward the door, but unfortunately, James blocked her path.

And he showed no sign of giving way.

"The coachman could return at any time now," he said.

"Or we could wait here another hour," she pointed out.

James scratched his chin, making Olivia recall the sweetly abrasive brush of his jaw along her neck. "You cannot walk on your ankle."

"I did earlier."

"And how did that feel?"

Like a blacksmith had laid her foot on an anvil and lowered his hammer on it. "Fine."

He arched a brow.

"I managed."

"Yes. You always do," he said. "But you might try leaning on other people once in a while."

"And you want me to lean on *you*? For *this*?"

"You don't need to lean. I'll carry you."

Olivia imagined James slinging her over his shoulder, traipsing across a muddy field, and depositing her beside a shrub suitable for her purposes. She could think of few things more horrifying. "I would prefer to do this on my own."

He stared at her for several moments, and Olivia wondered if he would indeed let her pass. Then he exhaled slowly. "Very well. But at the very least you'll need my help getting over the fence."

Good Lord. There was a fence? "Thank you," she said with as much dignity as she could muster.

James opened the door of the coach and backed out of it as though he were afraid to take his eyes off Olivia, even for a second. She slid down the bench toward the door and grasped the side of the coach, bracing herself as she prepared to put weight on her bad ankle. Recalling the stinging pain of walking on it earlier, she hesitated.

James frowned. "Please. Let me carry you."

Though it was hard to deny him anything he asked—especially when his soulful eyes took on that pleading-puppy look—she shook her head. "My ankle is just a little stiff from the hours spent in the coach. It will loosen up."

And with that, she moved toward the door. As she stepped forward, crouched over so as to avoid hitting her head on the ceiling, she carefully balanced on her good foot. When she cautiously tested her right, she had to bite her lip to prevent herself from howling in pain like a wounded animal.

James scowled his disapproval, and before Olivia could protest, he unceremoniously grabbed her beneath her arms and hauled her from the coach. She instinctively wrapped her arms around his neck as her body pressed against his. Secure in his embrace, she relaxed and surrendered to the attraction that instantly ignited between them.

Slowly, she slid down his body. Her breasts, originally at James's eye level, traveled over his muscled chest and down his torso. When her feet—or rather, foot—touched the ground, he made no move to release her. Instead, his arms circled her completely, holding her firmly against him. Olivia was transfixed by his perfect mouth and his hungry expression. The mist that fell from the sky did nothing to cool the heat between them, and the evidence of his desire pressed against her belly. Wanton that she was, she leaned into him, reveling in the feminine power she wielded over him.

Cursing softly, he kissed her forehead and loosened his hold. Olivia smiled to mask her disappointment as he looked up and down the road. "Let's head in that direction," he said, pointing toward a copse of trees in a nearby field.

Of course, *nearby* was a relative term. Yesterday, when she had two perfectly good ankles, she would have labeled the small grove as "nearby." Now it was more like a faraway and distant land.

"Very well." She did not bother refusing his help—not when a formidable-looking, chest-high wooden fence stood between her and her destination. He wrapped an arm around her and walked slowly, stopping after every few steps to make sure she wasn't in excruciating pain.

It *did* hurt, but with James's help she made it to the fence. They paused there, and while Olivia considered the least embarrassing manner of scaling it, James easily swung his legs over the top and landed like a cat on the other side.

Holding out his arms, he said, "Step onto the bottom rail with your good foot and then I'll lift you over."

Olivia eyed him warily. She trusted him to get her over the fence safely. What she doubted was his willingness to allow her to make the rest of the journey on her own. "Fine. But you must promise me that you will remain at the fence."

He turned to look at the trees, a good fifty yards away. "That's a long way for you to walk by yourself."

"You must promise."

Muttering under his breath, James nodded and waved her forward. She'd no sooner climbed onto the lowest rail when he scooped her up, one arm behind her back and the other beneath her knees. He held her so firmly against his chest that she could feel the steady thump of his heart against her shoulder. The mist had turned into more of a sprinkle, and tiny droplets clung to James's lashes, making him look like a younger, beardless version of Poseidon.

"You may put me down now."

He looked at the grove again. "Just a little farther?" He inched his way toward the trees.

"You promised!"

He halted, regret plain on his face, and lowered her gently to the ground, which squished beneath her slippers. "I'll wait right here," he said. "If you need me, just call my name."

"Will you face the road, please?"

With a sigh, James turned and leaned his elbows on the fence.

"Thank you."

Her leg almost buckled with the first step she took, so she began to hop on her good foot. She had to lift the hem of her skirt, and she shuddered to think how ridiculous she must look. But soon she was too exhausted from jumping to dwell on her embarrassment. And even though hopping caused less pain than walking, it still jarred her foot so that she clenched her jaw each time she landed.

Twice, she paused to rest before continuing on. The bottom three inches of her traveling gown were soaked, and her slippers were so muddy they were beyond recognition. When at last she reached the privacy of the little wooded area, she saw to her needs—an awkward affair to say the least—and leaned back against a large tree to catch her breath.

In the last quarter hour the cloudy sky had darkened rapidly; Olivia could barely make out the shape of the coach in the distance. The muscles in her good leg quivered from her exertions and protested at the thought of crossing the field again. She could have crawled if she weren't encumbered by skirts.

There was no help for it. She would have to hop all the way back, in a pitiful imitation of a kangaroo.

She pushed herself away from the tree, took a big

leap forward, and heard a sickening *rip*—the unmistakable rending of fabric. With no small amount of dread, she turned to look behind her. A handkerchief-sized scrap of striped silk stuck to the trunk, which meant it was *not* where it should be—namely, covering her backside.

"Damn." The closest cow, which lay some distance away, shot her a condescending glare and mooed.

Olivia's dress was beyond repair, but really, that was the least of her worries. Her chemise covered her legs somewhat but it was so wet that it was almost transparent.

She resolved to ignore any concerns about modesty for now and concentrate on making her way back to James and the coach. With strength born out of sheer desperation, she clutched the front of her dress to raise her hem... and hopped. She hopped and hopped until James came into sharper focus. She considered calling out to him for help, but she'd come this far—what was a few more yards? He leaned casually against the fence, his broad shoulders narrowing to slim hips and lean, muscular legs. The tails of his jacket covered his bottom, but she knew, even without seeing it, that it was perfectly sculpted and firm.

Letting her thoughts wander in such a pleasant direction distracted her from the painful straining of her muscles and the throbbing in her right foot *until* she hopped onto her hem and lurched forward.

"Oh!"

James turned at the sound of her scream. Probably just in time to see her tumble head over heels into a puddle of foul-smelling mud.

One hoped it was mud.

Blessedly, she hadn't hurt herself further. She was, however, covered in muck from her chest down; a few tendrils of hair had been dipped as well. While James sprinted toward her, looking like some demigod in buckskin breeches, she managed to push herself to a sitting position and scoot her way out of the insidious puddle, which had claimed one of her slippers.

James rushed over and knelt at her side. "What happened?" To his credit, he showed not a hint of disgust at her sludge-covered state.

"While practicing my somersault, I accidentally landed in a pool of mud."

"Are you hurt?"

"No. Though I suspect parts of me will be sore tomorrow."

His gaze slid to the puddle. "What is that blue object floating in the middle?"

"My shoe." She lifted her chin a bit, daring him to mock her.

"Shall I retrieve it for you?"

She shook her head emphatically. "The cows are welcome to it."

His green eyes crinkled at the corners, lifting her spirits in spite of everything.

"I'm going to carry you back to the coach," he said. When she opened her mouth to object, he held up a hand. "We can do this one of two ways. I can carry you like a proper lady, or I can fling you over my shoulder like a sack of grain. Either way, I will carry you. The choice is yours."

"Your jacket shall be ruined." Olivia's bottom lip trembled slightly.

"Do you honestly think I give a damn about my jacket right now?"

"You don't have a change of clothes with you," she reminded him.

"Ah, yes," he said, scooping her up easily. She leaned into him, her head fitting perfectly in the crook of his neck. "I recall your hurry to leave Haven Bridge."

"I'd give anything to be back there now. I wish I could start this day over." She sniffled suspiciously.

"It hasn't been all bad, has it?" He looked into her eyes. "I'd say that parts of the day have been outstanding."

"I suppose," she said with a distinct lack of conviction. Mud had splattered across her cheek, almost blending with her light smattering of freckles. A few strands of hair were plastered to her neck, and her skin was slick with rain. He wanted to tell her how beautiful she was, even now—*especially* now—but he didn't think she'd believe him.

"You'll feel better once we get you out of these clothes," he said. "Er, once we're at the inn, I mean. And you're in your own room."

Good God. When had he turned into a bumbling idiot around her?

She arched a brow at him but said nothing. And she looked miserable.

He carried her toward the coach, treading carefully over the uneven, saturated ground. All he wanted was to get her out of the rain and onto a comfortable seat as quickly as possible. He could kick himself for letting this happen. He should have insisted on staying with her—her stubborn pride be damned.

He managed to get her back to the fence without further injury, thank heaven, but there was no way he could scale the fence while holding her.

"You can put me down," she said.

But she felt so limp and weak in his arms, he doubted her legs would hold her. "Rest a few more minutes," he said soothingly.

"Mmm," she murmured into his chest.

Olivia's eyes fluttered shut, and she seemed to doze off. When his arms grew tired, he leaned against the fence for support. The sky turned dark, and James was just about to rouse her when a cart rumbled slowly down the road toward them.

Help had arrived.

A bearded older man drove the cart, which was drawn by a sturdy pair of mules. Terrence sat beside him, a disapproving scowl on his face. Before the cart had even stopped moving, the coachman jumped down from his seat and rushed to the fence.

He took one look at Olivia's filthy gown and pale face and shot James an accusatory look. "What's happened to her?"

Olivia lifted her head. "I'm quite all right, Terrence. I just slipped in the mud. Mr. Averill didn't want to risk me falling again."

"Why would you be walking at all with your injured ankle is what I'd like to know," the coachman began, but then he waved his hand in exasperation. "Never mind, just hand her to me, then," he said to James. "I'll make her comfortable in the back of the cart before unloading the coach."

Though James hated to let her go, he carefully passed Olivia over the fence. Terrence had thought to bring blankets, so James laid one over the mound of damp straw in the back. When the coachman settled Olivia there, James spread the other blanket over her.

"Thank you for rescuing me, Terrence." Her smile was so sweet and sincere that the coachman's cheeks flushed red. "But what shall we do about the coach? I don't like the thought of leaving it here overnight."

Terrence puffed out his chest. "Don't give it another thought, my lady. I'll stay here with the coach. I've already had a word with the stable master. He's going to bring the horses just after dawn so we can take the coach to the village and get the axle inspected. I suspect we'll be on our way to your aunt Eustace's tomorrow evening."

"If you're to stay in the coach overnight," Olivia said, "you must take this blanket." She whipped it off and thrust it at him.

"I couldn't, Lady Olivia."

"I insist," she said firmly, and tossed it to him.

James helped Terrence load the cart with all the items still in the coach, except for the basket of food, which Olivia was adamant the coachman keep for himself.

"Thank you," he said. "Miss Hildy has your room ready and waiting for you." As an afterthought, he added, "And yours, too, Mr. Averill."

James climbed into the cart beside Olivia. "Excellent. Lady Olivia shall be safe with me."

"Of course she will," the coachman said.

Although the evening had turned dark, James was fairly certain his words were accompanied by a rolling of eyes. He couldn't blame Terrence for doubting him. James shuddered to think what Huntford would make of the situation—if he knew.

The bearded farmer gave his mules a slap of the reins and the cart lurched forward, rolling slowly through the drizzly, moonlit night. Olivia shivered slightly, and James pulled the blanket she sat on up around her shoulders and across her legs. She looked wistful, sad, and dejected.

"I meant what I said earlier," he said.

"Which thing?"

"That I care for you."

"Sometimes you have an odd way of showing it."

"I know." But he would try to do better. Starting now.

Chapter Twelve

Olivia had never been so happy to see an inn.

Her gown—or what remained of it—was soaked through, chilling her to the bone. Bits of straw stuck to the mud on her dress and in her hair. She'd lost one slipper, and the other squeezed her swollen foot so tightly that she'd likely have to cut it off.

Worst of all, her heart was breaking.

Perhaps James was not the man she'd imagined him to be. The man she'd dreamed of would not have turned cold and distant just because she'd asked an innocent question about a letter.

All she wanted was to put on a clean night rail, burrow into a bed, and pull the covers over her head until morning.

James carried her into the inn, and while it stung her pride to be treated like an invalid, she was too weary to argue. He carried her all the way up the narrow staircase and down the hallway to her room without the slightest bit of difficulty. Hildy opened the door, took one look at Olivia, and began fussing like a mother hen. "Oh, my dear. Put her on the bed. No, not on the sheets. Set her on the chair"—as though Olivia were a puppy who'd come in from the yard with dirty paws.

While her maid rummaged through Olivia's portmanteau, James gently placed her on a hard wooden chair and brushed his knuckles over her cheek. "I'll have the innkeeper send up warm water for a bath—and summon a doctor, too."

"The bath sounds heavenly," she said, "but let's wait until morning before sending for the doctor. My ankle will probably feel much better tomorrow."

He shot her a doubtful look but did not argue. Instead, he wagged a finger at her and sternly said, "No walking."

"Blast. That spoils my plans for dancing all evening."

"Lady Olivia!" Hildy scolded. One would think her maid would have grown accustomed to her wicked tongue by now.

James smiled. "I'll leave you, but I'll be in my room if you should need anything."

Hildy ushered him out and closed the door behind him. Then she gingerly peeled off each layer of Olivia's clothing and tossed each article into a sorry heap on the floor. She toweled Olivia's skin dry and helped her slip into a soft, clean robe.

Olivia sighed. "Thank you."

"There's only one small matter we still need to deal with," the maid said.

Ah, yes. The slipper. There was nothing small about it, however, as her grotesquely swollen foot had stretched the shoe well beyond its normal size.

"Let's try the scissors from your sewing kit," Olivia suggested.

Hildy retrieved the scissors, knelt beside Olivia's foot, and carefully began cutting. It was an arduous task for both the maid and Olivia. The fabric was thick and the slightest jarring set Olivia's teeth on edge. After a quarter hour, Olivia had a sheen of perspiration on her brow; she gripped the seat of her chair with both hands.

"Almost done," Hildy said. Then she pried both sides of the slipper apart like a mussel's shell.

Olivia's foot was free. She wiggled her toes—as much as the swelling would allow—and felt the blood rush to them. She wanted to howl from the pain at first, but after a minute the throbbing subsided and she relaxed.

"I hear someone in the hallway," Hildy said. "It must be your bath." She peeked her head outside the door and waved in a pair of maids. One carried a hip bath, while the other bore a stack of linens. They doubled a sheet over and spread it on the floor before placing the tub on top of it.

"The water's heating now, my lady," the ruddy-faced young girl said. "We'll bring it up shortly."

True to their word, they soon returned, carrying two pails each. They mixed the steaming and cooler water, pouring in a little at a time until the temperature was just right. The slight, taller girl produced a bar of soap and left one pail of water beside the tub for rinsing.

Hildy sprinkled a few sprigs of lavender into the water, and the soothing scent filled the room. The water looked and smelled so inviting that Olivia stood and began hobbling toward the bath.

"Careful, now." Hildy rushed to her side. "I'll not have you breaking your neck, too."

Olivia managed to shrug off her robe while holding on to Hildy; then her maid helped her step into the shallow bath. Olivia scrubbed her skin till it was pink, and washed and rinsed her hair. It felt glorious to be clean.

"I'm just going to soak for a bit longer," she told Hildy. She leaned back in the bath, closed her eyes, and let the warm water lull her into a pleasant trance.

"I'm going to see about having dinner sent up for you," Hildy said. "Don't you dare think about getting out of that bath before I return."

"I wouldn't dream of it," Olivia said. "I intend to stay here until I've turned into a prune."

Hildy shot her a skeptical smile.

"You don't trust me?" Olivia placed a hand over her chest, as though wounded.

"We're at an inn, miles away from your aunt Eustace's— where the duke thinks we are. And even though you say Mr. Averill is a gentleman, well...I've seen the way he looks at you."

Suddenly interested, Olivia lifted her head. "How *does* Mr. Averill look at me?"

"Like he's one part smitten and one part mad." Hildy slipped into the hall and, just before she pulled the door closed behind her, ordered, "Stay put!"

Olivia bit back the retort on her lips and sunk lower into the now-tepid water. She *had* gotten all of them into a fine mess.

Her irresponsible decisions had led to James's fight, her turned ankle, and the broken axle on the carriage. It just seemed unfair that now, when she was trying to do the right thing, Fate had conspired against her and left her and James alone in the coach for several hours.

And no matter how hard she *tried* to do the right thing, she would have had to be a saint not to fall prey to charms as potent as his.

At least she was doing her best to correct the situation. With a bit of luck she'd be at her aunt Eustace's before anyone in her family was the wiser. And though she was glad none of them was there to witness her fall from grace—which, ironically, included an actual *fall*—she missed Rose, Anabelle, and Daphne terribly. She even missed Owen, despite the fact that his head might pop off from sheer anger if he knew where she was and what she'd done.

Oh well. There was nothing she could do about it tonight. They should reach Aunt Eustace's tomorrow, or certainly by the day after.

And once Olivia was there, she'd try to figure out what to do with the rest of her life—a life without James.

Hoping to doze until Hildy returned, Olivia closed her eyes, but the memory of James's searing kisses and arousing touch flooded her mind. The passion that had ignited between them was greater than a girl with her limited experience could have imagined.

And she'd done a *lot* of imagining over the years. Although she considered herself a master of the art of fantasizing, all the dreams of her and James had fallen short of the breathtaking reality of them together. There hadn't been silk sheets or romantic candles, but he'd made her feel like a princess—beautiful, important, and worshipped. His touch had made her entire body thrum with pleasure.

Even now, her nipples puckered at the memory. The cooling water lapped at her belly, and a sweet, pulsing ache began at her core. She slipped a hand between her legs and touched herself lightly, then sucked in her breath at the frisson that went through her.

She gripped the sides of the bath and sat straight up. These sensations, new and powerful, were too tied up with the memory of her afternoon with James. She couldn't explore them now—not when she felt so raw, so rejected.

She wanted out of the bath. Now. But she'd promised Hildy she'd stay put, so she reached for a towel and began to rub her hair, small sections at a time. When it was as dry as she could get it, she threw the towel around her shoulders, pulled in her knees, and wrapped her arms around them.

It seemed as though Hildy had been gone for ages, but a quarter of an hour was probably closer to the truth. Still, Olivia was certain that if she spent another five minutes in the tub her feet would transform into a tail and she'd grow scales on her legs.

She would just step out of the tub, slip into her robe, and wait patiently on the chair for Hildy to return. What harm could possibly come of that?

She slowly stood in the center of the hip bath, balancing on her good foot. She couldn't very well hop out of the tub—though she *did* briefly consider it—so she decided that she would have to, at least momentarily, put some weight on her tender foot. Never one to overthink matters, she lifted the swollen and now slightly purple foot over the side of the tub and gingerly rested it on the sheet that covered the floor beneath the tub.

She bit her lip, counted to three in her head, and stepped out of the bath, putting her weight on her bad foot.

Pain shot through her leg, but she'd anticipated that.

What she hadn't expected was that her abused ankle might not support her weight.

Her leg buckled beneath her, and as she tumbled to the floor, the foot that was still in the tub caught on the edge and tipped it over with a loud clatter. Tepid, slightly soapy water sloshed out, soaking the sheet and making an impressive puddle on the floor.

Blast.

Her left hip had borne the brunt of her fall, and it stung so badly that she had to breathe in and out through her nose to keep from crying. Good Lord, she must be the clumsiest person in all of England.

Footsteps thumped down the hall, and a fist pounded the door. "Olivia!" It was James, of course. "Are you all right?" The concern in his voice made her heart trip in her chest.

"I'm fine," she lied.

"I heard a crash. Why does it sound like you're on the floor?"

"I tripped. It was nothing." Her voice cracked on the last word.

"I'm coming in." He rattled the door handle, which was locked.

Coming in? Olivia sat up, her bruised hip forgotten. Where was her towel? "There's no need. Hildy will return shortly."

"You're by *yourself*?" He sounded horrified. "Move away from the door."

Bam. The door rattled in its frame and the wood around the knob splintered. Olivia grabbed the soaked towel and wrapped it around her as best she could, but it barely reached the tops of her thighs.

"James!" she called out. "I don't need rescuing."

"I think you do."

Bam. This time, the door burst open and James shot into the room like a catapult had launched him. His boots landed in the suds that covered the floor and his feet slipped out from under him. His limbs flailed in the air for a second, and he thumped onto the floor beside her, grunting from the impact. He'd left his jacket behind and his shirtsleeves were rolled up, exposing sinewy forearms. His mossy-green eyes were dazed.

Slowly, he pushed himself up and blinked. "You're naked."

Her skin grew hot—in sharp contrast to the chilly wet towel draped across her breasts. But she had her pride, dash it all. She raised her chin and shook out her wet curls. "If I'd been afforded the opportunity, I'd have told you I wasn't receiving."

Jesus. Olivia was sprawled on the floor beside James, and the towel wrapped around her didn't leave much to his imagination. He could see the pebbled tips of her breasts and the sweet curve of her hip outlined beneath the damp cloth. Best of all, her silky, bare legs stretched out. The sweet smells of lavender, soap, and Olivia filled his head. It was almost enough to make him forget why he'd broken down her door. He mentally shook his head.

"The racket I heard from the hallway was on par with a Saturday night tavern brawl. I was . . . worried." Right, that was putting it mildly. He'd imagined her pinned beneath a heavy bureau or sprawled in a pool of blood—and he'd panicked. That panic, pure and fierce, had propelled him right through her door. Now that he could see she was mostly in one piece, he could breathe again. Almost. "How did you end up on the floor?"

"Rather like you did," she said simply. "One moment I was standing, the next..." She waved a slender arm demonstratively.

He cupped her cheek in his hand. "Are you hurt? Besides your ankle, I mean."

She hesitated, as though debating how much to reveal. "My hip is a little tender."

His gaze flicked to her left hip, which she patted with her palm. Though tempted to peel back the towel and inspect her injury for himself, he refrained.

He was refraining from a lot of things, such as kissing her full lips, running his hands over her delectable body, and sweeping her into his arms and carrying her to the bed just a few yards away.

But the door to her room gaped open, barely hanging on its hinges. He skimmed his thumb over the smooth skin of her cheek, then regretfully dropped his hand and pushed himself up onto his haunches.

She pulled the towel more tightly around her. "What are you doing?"

Rather than answer, he carefully scooped her up and stood. She kept one hand on her towel and curled the other around his neck.

"Chair or bed?" he asked.

"Chair," she answered quickly.

He carried her to the simple ladder-back chair and gingerly lowered her onto the seat—for the second time that evening. Her towel caught on his arm, affording him a glimpse of her bottom before she tugged it back into place.

But there was still plenty for him to look at. Her long chestnut tresses lay dark against the pale skin of her shoulders. From his vantage point, he could almost see down the towel into the little gap between her lush breasts. She sat demurely, her legs crossed at the ankles. It would have been a perfectly proper pose if her legs weren't bare—all the way to the tops of her thighs. His cock went hard, and for a moment, he stood there staring at her like an idiot.

Olivia raised a brow and pointed to a rose-colored silk garment on the bed. "Would you bring me my robe?"

"Of course." Damn. He probably should have thought of that.

He strode to the bed, picked up the flimsy robe, and was about to hand it to Olivia when a scream pierced the air.

Olivia and he turned toward the doorway, where Hildy stood, her hands pressed to her cheeks in dismay.

"It's all right," Olivia said soothingly. "Mr. Averill mistakenly thought I was in distress—"

"Yes, how silly of me." James couldn't help rolling his eyes.

"—and attempted to come to my aid."

"The . . . the door," Hildy stammered.

James's face heated. "I'll speak to the innkeeper about getting you a new room. In fact, I think I'll see to that right now." He took two steps toward the door.

"Just a moment, sir." Hildy blocked his path and her steely gaze dropped to his fist, which was full of frothy, pink silk.

"Ah, my apologies," James said, handing the robe to the maid.

"You may guard the doorway," she said icily, "while I help Lady Olivia into this."

James dutifully took his post and tried not to think about Olivia being utterly naked behind him.

"There," Hildy announced a few moments later. "You may turn around, Mr. Averill."

Olivia now wore her robe and one slipper. The maid had also removed the coverlet from the bed and placed it over her mistress—for an extra layer of protection.

All things considered, it wasn't a bad idea.

"I do apologize for the mess and the damage," James said. "I'll take care of it at once."

"Wait, please." The weary maid sat on the edge of the bed.

"What is it, Hildy?" Olivia's voice was laced with concern. "You don't look well."

"I'm fine, my lady. But I spoke with Terrence when I was out and he shared a bit of news that affects us all."

The hairs on the back of James's neck stood on end. "What's happened?" He half expected the maid to say that Huntford had discovered their location and was leading a regiment of the British Army to retrieve them.

"It's the coach," the maid said with despair. "The axle can't be repaired—it will have to be replaced. It's going to take a couple of days, at least."

Chapter Thirteen

*Amulet: (1) A talisman worn by ancient Egyptians
to ward off evil, both during life and in the afterlife.
(2) A trinket or charm thought to bring good fortune, as in*
The day that Olivia had just endured was
proof she needed a powerful amulet—and
perhaps a glass of brandy.

*W*e're going to be stuck here for a couple of *days*?"
cried Olivia.

Across the room, James paled, apparently no more
enthused than she at the prospect of spending two, possibly three, nights at this inn. But his expression was
thoughtful as he righted the tub and plopped the soaked
sheet inside it.

"I agree that the situation is not ideal," he said. "But
at least you'll be able to rest your ankle. First thing in the
morning, I'm going to fetch a doctor so that he can examine your foot and hip."

"Your hip?" exclaimed Hildy. "What's happened to
your hip?"

Olivia shot James a *thank-you-very-much* look, turned to the maid, and said, "Nothing. However, I confess that if I do not eat something soon, I may keel over onto the floor."

The change in subject was sufficient to distract Hildy. "I asked for a tray to be sent up."

"Why don't you take my room for now," offered James. "I could move you and all of your things there."

Olivia wasn't sure she liked being lumped together with her portmanteau as something that required moving. "Thank you. That's very kind."

James shrugged and cast a glance at the splintered door frame behind him. "It's the least I can do."

Olivia couldn't help staring at the broad shoulders that had broken down her door and the tantalizing V of skin exposed by his loosened shirt collar. It was a pity that he hadn't been shirtless when he'd burst into her room.

After the day she'd endured, producing a bare-chested James seemed like the least Fate could have done.

Olivia awoke the next morning in James's bed. Never mind that he wasn't in it. Or that he'd never had the opportunity to actually sleep in the bed. It still tickled her to think of it as *his*.

Hildy drew back the curtains in the small room, letting in far too much light for the early hour.

"I'm glad you're stirring," the maid said, as if Olivia had a choice. "The doctor's on his way up."

James certainly hadn't wasted any time, but she supposed it was best to get the examination over with.

A half hour later, her entire foot was bandaged. She couldn't wiggle a toe if she tried, which was probably a good thing. Sadly, however, there wasn't a slipper in the world that would fit over her bound foot. At least she could endeavor to hide it beneath her gown. Her hip was bruised, but there was nothing to be done for that. The doctor predicted it would be a lovely shade of green by the end of the week.

He had instructed her to stay abed for two days. When Olivia had protested, he agreed that she should be permitted to sit in a chair with her foot propped up. After two days—as long as she did not overexert herself—she could walk using crutches. Of course, she hadn't thought to pack crutches for this little excursion, so the doctor gave her the name and address of a carpenter who could make some for her.

After the doctor left, Hildy helped Olivia dress in a pretty but simple yellow frock, then weaved a white bow through her dark brown curls. She had to admit, the effect was rather charming, and a vast improvement over the torn, muddy dress she'd been wearing the night before.

Hildy helped Olivia sit in a chair and placed a pillow on a stool before carefully propping Olivia's sore foot on top of it. "Would you like to read your book while I see about breakfast?"

Olivia looked wistfully at the crisp, golden morning that beckoned from beyond her window. "No breakfast for me, Hildy. But after you eat something yourself, would you please ask Terrence to order my crutches? Though I've only been confined to my room for half an hour, I feel like a dove trapped in a cage."

"Of course," the maid said sympathetically. She tucked a note containing the carpenter's address in a pocket. "I'll go with him. I can serve as your stand-in for measurement purposes."

Olivia smiled. "Thank you. Just knowing they've been ordered will be a comfort while I'm cooped up here. I wouldn't mind nearly as much if I were someplace I was actually supposed to be—like Aunt Eustace's. Or home."

"Why, Lady Olivia, you almost sound a little homesick," her maid teased. "Just think of this latest trial as another part of your grand adventure." She winked and handed Olivia the book. "The important thing is that we get you well and to your aunt's house as quickly as possible. In the meantime, there's little harm that can come to you here in your room." Hildy threw a cloak around her shoulders as she headed for the door. "I'll return before luncheon. Try to rest till then."

"I shall try," Olivia said resolutely. But truly, she had little choice in the matter.

She'd been staring at her book for three minutes when a knock sounded at the door. She instinctively dropped her injured foot to the floor as if to stand, but caught herself. "Who is it?" she called.

"James." The low timbre of his voice made Olivia's heart trip in her chest. "I am curious to know what the doctor said."

She grabbed the fringed shawl draped on the back of her chair and tossed it over her bandaged foot. Blasted vanity. "Shall I relate the whole of it through the door, or would you like to come in?"

James turned the knob—Olivia hadn't even been certain it was unlocked—and strode into the room, carrying a parcel behind his back. "Am I interrupting anything?"

Olivia sighed. "Not a thing. Hildy's running an errand. I'm trying to figure out how I shall survive being trapped in this room for the next two days."

"Doctor's orders?"

She nodded, and James proffered the flat package wrapped in brown paper.

"Maybe this will help," he said.

As she unwrapped it, he sat on the edge of her bed, looking hopeful—and more handsome than any man had a right to.

The brown paper fell away, revealing several sheets of creamy white vellum and a small bundle of charcoal sticks. Warmth blossomed in her belly. "How thoughtful," she exclaimed. It was the first gift James had ever given her.

He waved a hand at the supplies in her lap. "Might help to pass the time."

"Where did you get these?"

"At a shop in the village. I needed something to occupy me while the doctor examined you, so I went for a walk." An adorable frown crossed his face, and if Olivia didn't know better, she'd think that he'd been worried. About her.

"Thank you." Though the paper and charcoal were simple gifts, she liked them better than jewels. Well, almost.

He leaned forward, elbows on his knees. "Your ankle—is it broken?"

"Sprained. I suppose it serves me right."

She'd only meant to make light of the matter, but James scooped up one of her hands and clasped it firmly in his. "Don't say that. I'm to blame, too, and I'm going to make it up to you."

Goodness. This was sounding more interesting by the minute. "How do you propose to do that?" His slightly rough palm skimmed the back of her hand, sending the most pleasant thrumming sensation shooting through her body.

"I could keep you company—until you grow tired of me."

Olivia tried to imagine growing tired of James... and couldn't. Her confinement suddenly felt less like a punishment and more like a fantasy. James's undivided attention for two days? She couldn't think of anything more appealing.

"Very well." She flashed him a saucy grin. "You may begin entertaining me at once."

James's mind flew to several activities that would be highly entertaining for both of them. He swallowed hard. "What would you like to do?"

She arched a brow suggestively, and that alone was enough to make him hard. Damn.

Standing, he rifled a hand through his hair. "Would you like to test out the charcoal? I could gather a few items for you to sketch. Maybe a pitcher or some fruit—"

"Fruit?"

James shrugged. "Isn't that what people normally sketch?"

"Perhaps, but I don't find apples or oranges particularly... inspiring. As an artist, that is."

"You'd prefer a landscape, then?" He strode to the window, swept aside the threadbare curtain, and took in the inn's mostly barren courtyard. A few scraggly trees bordered the space, but the courtyard's main feature was, unfortunately, mud. "I'm afraid there's not much of a view."

"Says who?" Olivia asked mischievously. He turned

to find her grinning and looking at him like he was a sculpture she was debating whether to purchase. Her gaze roved over his chest, hips, and legs, all the way down to the toes of his boots. She even leaned left in her chair as though she were trying to inspect his ass.

Good God.

He placed his hands on his hips and waited till her eyes found their way back to his. They took the long route. "If you don't want to sketch fruit, I'm sure I could find a flower arrangement. And maybe some interesting fabric to drape behind it?"

"No need," she said, smiling. "I have everything I want right here. Why don't you pull up that chair?"

"You don't mean to..."

"I do. Don't tell me you've never posed for a sketch before." She waved a hand at the chair in the corner. "Let's have you sit in that lovely shaft of light."

He began to balk, but a promise was a promise. Besides, he had no work to do, no place to go. So, he dragged the chair across the wooden floorboards and sank onto the seat. "I don't think I'll make a very good model." The thought of sitting there, watching Olivia watch him, with nothing to distract him but her sultry eyes, inviting mouth, and the tantalizing swells of her breasts sounded like torture. The best kind, perhaps, but still torture.

"Nonsense." She tilted her head to one side and pursed her lips. "Try draping your right arm across the back of the chair."

He opened his mouth to object, but when he saw the big mound of her foot that she'd tried to hide beneath her shawl, he sighed and did as he was bid.

"Now, prop your right ankle on your left knee."

"Like this?"

"That's good...but I think we can do better."

"We can?"

"Pretend you're at your club. How would you sit if you were relaxing there one evening?"

"I don't know. Like this, I suppose." He stretched out his legs and crossed them at the ankles.

Her gaze raked over him once more, slowly. "That will do," she said a little breathlessly. "Yes, I think I can work with this."

She bent her left leg, leaned the stack of paper against it, and lifted a piece of charcoal. "I hope you're comfortable," she said with a grin, "because I expect this will take a while." She sat no more than two yards away, studying him as though she needed to etch everything about him into her memory. If it were anyone but Olivia doing the studying, it would have been an awkward affair, but with her it seemed...natural.

For several minutes neither of them spoke. A warm breeze ruffled his hair and fluttered the edges of Olivia's papers. In the courtyard outside the window, the inn's staff scurried to and fro, calling out greetings, loading wagons, and hitching horses. The bustle one story below provided a stark contrast to the quiet intimacy in the room.

At last, she began to move her hand across the paper in sweeping arcs. The tip of her tongue played at the corner of her mouth as she worked. He itched to tease her about it, but if he did, she might stop. And he didn't want her to change, not even in that little way. Not for him or anyone.

While her attention was focused on her paper, he seized the opportunity to study her. Normally she was like a butterfly, always moving and darting about. But not today. Now she was still enough for James to appreciate her silken skin, her thick lashes, and her tempting curves.

"Let us play a game," she began.

"Are we done with the drawing, then?" Hopeful, he leaned forward.

Waving him back into his pose, she said, "No, we're just getting started. We can play this game from our respective positions."

"Very well. What are the rules?"

Her hand paused in midair and she rolled her eyes. "Must every game have rules?"

He grunted. "Yes. Things would be very random without them."

"Fine. The rules are quite simple. We shall take turns asking one another questions. And we must answer truthfully."

"And if we refuse to answer, shall there be a penalty?"

"But of course." She thoughtfully pressed a finger to her lips. "Anyone who violates the rules shall be required to do one thing of the other person's bidding."

James snorted. Wasn't he already doing Olivia's bidding? "Like what?"

She laughed huskily, stirring something warm and deep inside him. "Use your imagination."

He already was, damn it. "Ladies first." He kept his tone light, but his heart beat faster. If she asked about his childhood or family...

Setting her charcoal on the table at her side, she said, "Have you ever been in love?"

James released a breath. This question he could handle. "Once. Miss Mary Newton. She had beautiful blue eyes that crinkled at the corners whenever she laughed, and she laughed at all my jokes—"

"You don't tell jokes," Olivia interrupted, scowling.

"Maybe not, but Mary thought me quite witty. She found my fascination with antiquities charming. I was nineteen, and so was she. Everyone thought we'd be perfect together."

"But you weren't?"

James recalled the day Mary first met his brother. He'd tried to gently prepare her for Ralph's spastic movements and slurred speech, but upon seeing him, she couldn't mask her revulsion. She'd burst into tears and run out of the house as though Ralph were a beast, hideous and inhuman.

And that was when James knew Mary was not for him.

Olivia leaned forward, awaiting his response.

"No. We were not meant to be."

"Why not? Did she break things off, or did you?"

James shook his head. "You've already had your question. Now it's my turn."

She blew out a breath in frustration, but then held out her arms as if to say, *Do your worst.* "I'm ready."

"I'll need to think about this," he admitted. What to ask the girl who had always been an open book? He knew almost everything about her. Or, at least, he thought he did. "If you could go back in time and undo one thing you've done, what would it be?"

Chapter Fourteen

Olivia pondered James's question. She'd done lots of things she wished she could undo. Three in the last week alone. But if she could undo only one? Of course, she wished she'd done a better job of protecting Rose from the ugliness of her mother's salacious affairs and her father's suicide. But she knew that wasn't what James was really asking.

He wanted to know which of her *own* actions she'd most like to take back.

She shifted in her chair. "I'd like to take the dare."

James rose and walked toward her. Olivia quickly turned the paper—the one that was *supposed* to have the beginnings of a sketch on it—upside down in her lap. He sat on the edge of the bed, an arm's length away from her. She could almost feel his sandy-colored hair between her fingers, the slightly rough skin of his cheeks beneath her palms.

"And here I thought you were courageous," he said.

"I am." She blinked. "I will do your bidding. Whatever you wish."

"If you were *truly* brave, you'd answer the question I posed. For you, a dare is less daunting than the truth."

He was right, blast it all. "I don't like to think about it—this regret of mine. It's…painful. Besides, I fear you'd think me a horrid person. And I couldn't bear that."

James smiled, instantly melting Olivia's insides. "You couldn't tell me anything that would make me think you were a horrid person. But we're all entitled to our secrets." He crossed his arms, causing his jacket to stretch tightly across his broad shoulders. "So, it is to be a dare."

"Yes." Olivia nearly trembled with anticipation. Let it be a kiss or an intimate touch. Something to satisfy the desire that curled in her belly.

But then, she saw something flicker in James's eyes. Disappointment.

"Very well," he said. "Let me think…"

"Wait." Olivia inhaled sharply. "I'll answer the question. Not because I fear what you would have me do, but because you are right. Telling the truth—at least in this instance—is more difficult. But I don't want to keep any secrets. Not from you."

James's green eyes warmed, and he reached out, taking her hand in his. "Don't be afraid. And trust me—I'm hardly in a position to judge anyone."

She inhaled deeply, summoning courage. He nodded encouragingly.

"As you well know, my sister, Rose, is the kindest, gentlest soul you could ever meet. She was at a very vulnerable age when she witnessed, firsthand, my mother's affair.

And when we discovered my father's body lying in a sea of blood in his study."

James squeezed her hand. "I know how close you were to him."

Olivia's throat felt thick and she swallowed once, painfully, before pressing on. "Rose has an inner strength that is unsurpassed, but on the outside...well, she was broken."

"I remember how concerned your brother was for her, and for you."

"Owen tried to protect us as best he could, but Rose simply couldn't bear the pain. She retreated into herself, and for the longest time—almost two years—simply didn't speak. At least not to most people. Once in a while she would whisper, but only to me."

Olivia paused and closed her eyes, bringing the details of the day into focus.

"It was perhaps three years ago. Rose and I were in a crowded milliner's shop on Bond Street. She was looking at ribbons on one end of the counter; I was looking at lace on the other. A pair of pretty, stylish young ladies initiated a conversation with me, and though I didn't know them, I desperately wanted to impress them. We discussed bonnets and gloves for a while, and then they began snickering...at Rose. They'd been watching her, observing how she only gestured and never spoke, even when the shopkeeper asked her a direct question."

"Ah." James nodded sympathetically. "Olivia, you don't have to—"

"Actually, I do." Now that she'd begun telling the story, she needed to finish. Shame welled up inside her and her whole body trembled. "The women mocked Rose. They called her a freak of nature and said anyone as unstable as she surely belonged in Bedlam." She blinked away her tears and looked up at James. "Do you know what I did?"

He swallowed and shook his head.

"I *laughed*." Her belly twisted, the potency of guilt undiluted by time. "I listened to their cruel barbs. Even worse, I pretended not to know my own sister. The sister who's never been anything but kind and loyal to me. I don't think Rose knows of my betrayal and for that I'm grateful. But I know—and I shall have to live with it for the rest of my life."

She gazed into his eyes, afraid of what she'd find there.

But instead of censure and disappointment, she saw warmth. And possibly…affection. "Time to stop flogging yourself," he said. "The depth of your regret shows how much you love your sister. And if Rose did know of the incident, I have no doubt she'd forgive you."

Olivia smiled wanly. "A testament to Rose's generous and forgiving nature."

"Yes. But she couldn't ask for a more loving sister than you." The heat in James's gaze made her pulse skitter. "Thank you for confiding in me."

Olivia sighed. "This was supposed to be a fun game, and I fear I've spoiled it with my maudlin confession."

"Not at all. I believe it's your turn to ask a question. Make it a good one."

"Would you like to kiss me?" The words slipped out of her mouth before she could haul them back.

James chuckled, a deep, rich sound that made her belly quiver. "Is that a question or an invitation?"

Olivia blinked innocently. "A question, of course. A simple one: would you like to kiss me?"

He raised her hand until it was a mere inch from his lips. His breath, warm and moist, played across her sensitive skin. His gaze lifted to her face, melting her with its intensity, as he answered. "I would, in fact, like to kiss you. I would like to do much more than kiss you."

"Such as...?"

"Tsk. That is another question. However, I'll allow it. I'd like to remove the pins from your hair and let your luscious brown curls fall around your shoulders. I'd like to loosen the laces of your dress and slip it off of your body. I'd like to remove your chemise. With my teeth."

Heat rushed to Olivia's face—and other parts of her. "Why don't you, then?"

The seductive gleam in his eyes dimmed slightly, but the longing was still there. "Because you are a lady and I am a gentleman—even if I haven't been acting like one of late. Because if I kissed you, I would never want to stop." He pressed his lips to the back of her hand and closed his eyes briefly before adding, "Because I'm leaving for Egypt in a few weeks and if I were to seduce you right now, I'd be the worst kind of scoundrel."

She set her drawing paper on the floor, tossed her shawl that hid her foot over the back of her chair, and stood on her good foot.

"What are you doing?" James asked, his tone so incredulous one would think she'd slung a leg over the windowsill and was preparing to jump.

Olivia sat beside him on the bed, so close that their knees were almost touching. "I needed to get out of that chair."

James looked at her bandaged foot and frowned. "Let me prop your foot—"

She leaned forward and cut him off. "Kiss me." She was vaguely aware that she was begging but didn't care. "Or I shall kiss you."

He swallowed and opened his mouth, probably to object. She had to do something fast, so she reached up and tugged at the white ribbon in her hair, pulling it inch by inch until it was free. Then she dropped it onto James's lap. While he stared down at the length of silk, she removed a few pins, letting her curls bounce down her back.

"There." She shook her head, loosening the waves. "I've even done some of the work for you."

"Jesus, Olivia." With that, James took her face between his palms and pulled her toward him. Their desire exploded in a kiss that was fierce, hungry, raw. His tongue, hot and insistent, thrust into her mouth, as though he were claiming her for his own. He speared his fingers through her hair and grabbed a fistful like he was afraid she might pull away.

Not likely.

She'd been waiting years for James to unleash the full force of his passion. For her. She'd known it was there, simmering just beneath the surface, like lava waiting to erupt. And now it had.

Every time her tongue tangled with his, he moaned. He breathed heavily, like he was starving for air—and for her. Never had she seen him so stripped of control, and it thrilled her.

He ran his hands down her body, almost clumsy in his haste to possess her. When he roughly cupped her breast through her gown, she leaned into him, sighing as he caressed her through layers of sensuous silk.

When that was no longer enough, he shoved the delicate puffs of her sleeves down her arms and ran a finger all the way around the low neckline of her gown. Then he dipped a hand into her bodice, cupping her breast and grazing her sensitive nipple with his palm.

"Olivia," he gasped. "I want you so badly that I forget who I am and what is right."

"I know who you are," she murmured. "And this feels very right to me."

"That doesn't make it so." As abruptly as their kiss had begun, it ended. James withdrew his hand from her dress and tugged it back into place. "Even if I wasn't leaving London, I wouldn't be right for you."

She sucked in her breath and held it, a vain attempt to dull the stinging in her chest. It was painful enough to think that an expedition had doomed their future together. But now James implied that it was something beyond Egypt, and that possibility hurt tenfold.

She wanted to shake him until he could see things as clearly as she. "How can you say that? I *know* that you are right for me. Why won't you believe me?"

"You think you know everything about me. You don't."

Olivia grabbed two fistfuls of his shirt. "Then enlighten me! I've bared my soul to you today. Why don't you do the same?"

Chapter Fifteen

Pick: (1) A tool with an iron head that is used for loosening soil. (2) To choose, as in
Of all the eligible, handsome gentlemen in London,
she would have to pick the one who was wholly
intent on departing for Egypt.

James could still taste the sweetness of Olivia's mouth, feel the perfect weight of her breast in his hand. His cock, still hard, strained against the front of his trousers.

All of this made it damned difficult to follow the simplest of conversations.

He was trying to do the right thing here, but Olivia didn't seem to appreciate his efforts. She was clutching the front of his shirt like she wanted to throttle him and was gazing up at him expectantly.

Placing his hands over hers, he admitted, "It's hard for me to concentrate when you're so close. Would you repeat the question?"

She closed her eyes briefly as though summoning patience. "I told you my secret. Why won't you tell me yours?"

He was tempted to steer the conversation in another direction or to speak in generalities that would protect his pride and preserve her good opinion of him. But she deserved to know the truth about him.

On two counts.

"Very well." He released her hands and they slid down his torso a few inches before she caught herself and placed them primly in her lap.

"I'm listening," she said. "And don't worry. Nothing you could say would change my good opinion of you."

He stood and began to pace. "That's kind, but also naïve of you to say. What if I confessed I killed someone?"

She smiled serenely. "You haven't. But if you had, I'm sure it would have been in self-defense."

Her confidence in him should have given him hope; instead it made him feel like a fraud. He had the ungentlemanly urge to shock her, to say something to shatter her gilded illusion of him. "What if I seduced a young lady and fathered a child out of wedlock?"

Olivia's mouth fell open and she sat stunned for a few moments before saying, "I've never known you to act dishonorably. But if you once did, I know that you would try to right matters." She gazed up at him then, her brown eyes puzzled. "But you didn't...did you?"

"No. I'm sorry, I..." He walked to the window and stared down at the courtyard. She deserved his honesty. So did Ralph. "It's not that. It's more complicated. This will seem like an odd confession, but I...I have a brother." Just saying the words felt liberating.

"You do?" Olivia's voice was a mix of wonder and joy. "Does Owen know him? Why have you never mentioned him?"

"No one knows about him. I've taken great pains to keep his existence a secret—to deny it, even. And I hate myself for it."

"I don't understand," Olivia said. "Why would you pretend like you don't have a brother?"

That was the crux of it. He had no reason—beyond selfish pride. "Ralph is different."

"How so?" She frowned slightly. "Is he a criminal or . . . insane?"

James shook his head vehemently. "He's friendly and thoughtful and he thinks the world of me."

"That makes two of us." She didn't press him for more but sat patiently, waiting for him to elaborate.

"Ralph was born with palsy. His right arm and leg are weak and atrophied. His speech is slurred. The doctor told my parents he wouldn't survive his first year, but he did. My father wanted to send Ralph away, but my mother wouldn't hear of it. So my father left. Mama and I did our best to care for Ralph."

Olivia gasped. "That's a lot of responsibility for a young lad."

"Don't think I didn't resent my brother. Every time I had to carry him up the stairs or read to him or help Mama bathe him, I was bitter and angry. As if it were Ralph's fault."

"Oh, James." Her voice caught and he turned from the window to face her. Her chestnut tresses shone in the morning light, and she held out a hand, beckoning like an angel who could somehow redeem him. But he resisted her pull. He had to tell her the whole of it, without sparing her—or himself—the worst parts. It would be easier to finish the story if he didn't have to see the disappointment in her eyes, so he turned to the window once more.

"My father sent us money now and then, probably to ease his guilty conscience. Mama scraped together every coin she had to send me to school, even though it meant less for her and Ralph. And when I came home between terms, Ralph would beg me to tell him all about the boys and the professors and my studies. But the thing he loved to do more than anything was to go fishing with me."

"A fine brotherly pastime," she said approvingly.

"One would think. Selfishly, I didn't want to take him, but Mama insisted. She thought the sunshine and fresh air would be good for him. She was never happier than when Ralph and I spent time together. So I took him." He paused, remembering the sweltering day, the mud that squished between their bare toes, and the gnats that hovered relentlessly around their heads. James had been miserable; Ralph thought it was paradise.

"What happened? Did something go wrong?"

"Some older boys found our fishing spot. They taunted Ralph, called him an idiot. They bet he couldn't recite the alphabet. Quizzed him on his sums. Said he was a deformed beast that didn't deserve to walk the earth."

"How awful! What did you do?"

"Nothing. I sat there and listened to it all. Didn't say a word." But even now, over a decade later, he could feel the anger that had bubbled up in him. It was directed at Ralph for being the way he was, at himself for not being anywhere near the kind of brother that Ralph deserved, but mostly at the boys. For being complete and utter asses.

"The more they talked," James continued, "the meaner their barbs grew. Then one of them walked up to Ralph and shoved him off the rock where he was sitting. He fell into the river, fishing pole and all."

"No."

James nodded. "Something inside me turned wild. While my brother flailed in the shallow part of the river, I charged the boy who'd pushed him. When he was on the ground, I straddled him and beat him until blood streamed from his nose. When his friends tried to pull me off of him, I attacked them, too—savagely. I bit and clawed and kicked them till they both writhed on the ground. I might have never stopped if I hadn't heard Ralph calling me, imploring me to forget about them and come help him. Begging me to take him home. So I did. After that, I learned to fight properly, so no one would dare to pick on Ralph again."

"No wonder the memory haunts you. But you don't have to be ashamed of the way you acted. You defended your brother against a trio of bullies. What's so wrong about that?"

"What's wrong is the way I've acted every day since then. I've kept Ralph at arm's length. I told him, my mother, and myself that he was better off staying at home and avoiding other people altogether. So he wouldn't have to be exposed to that kind of ugliness again."

"You were trying to protect him."

"Was I? Or have I really been protecting myself? It's been easier for me this way. Less messy. I didn't bring my school friends around the cottage. Didn't spend much time there—just a monthly visit with my mother and Ralph to give them some money and check on the place." He heaved a sigh and pressed his forehead to the cool windowpane. "Pretending that my gentle, kind brother doesn't exist makes me as horrible as the bullies who taunted him that day. In fact, it makes me a lot like . . . my father."

"No. It doesn't. But if you don't like the way you've treated your brother, why not rectify it?"

"It's not as though I could bring him to a ball, or even my club." But he knew Olivia wasn't suggesting such a thing.

"Let him come to London and stay with you for a week. Introduce him to Owen and Rose and me—anyone you trust. We could go for carriage rides around town, have picnics in the country. Do you think Ralph would like that?"

Yes, he would. "I should ask him."

"Don't wait too long. Summer will be a memory before long."

And James would be gone.

For once, he wished he had more time. With his brother, with Olivia. Ever since the night she'd kissed James on the terrace at the Easton ball, he'd been off-kilter—and he liked the feeling. "Thank you for understanding."

"You're welcome." Olivia smiled, soothing his raw emotions. "Shall we return to our respective sketching and posing positions?"

Not before he told her about her father's letter. "There's one more thing you should know."

"Very well. But why don't you come sit by— Goodness, I can hear Terrence bellowing to the stable hands from up here. He and Hildy must be back from the carpenter's. Do you see them?"

James peered out the window and spotted the coach-man and maid. "Yes." Damn. There went his chance. The maid was probably making her way up the stairs by now, and Olivia was hastily trying to right her dress and her hair.

"I'd better get back into my chair before Hildy finds me thus. She will be glad to see me sketching—such a tame and ladylike pastime."

"True, but if anyone could find a way to make it less so, you could."

She grinned. "I'm sorry we didn't have time to finish our conversation. Could we talk later? Maybe this afternoon?"

"Certainly."

Olivia stood on her good foot.

"Wait." James strode to her side and wrapped an arm around her, marveling at the perfect fit of her body next to his. He helped her to the chair and while she placed her injured foot on the stool, he bent to retrieve her papers from the floor.

Olivia gasped. "I'll take those," she said, trying to snatch the parchment from his hands.

He held the pages just out of her reach and turned the stack over. Then he riffled through the dozen or so sheets he held. All blank.

"What's this?" he teased. "I sat patiently that whole time and you sketched . . . nothing?"

She blushed as he handed her the papers. "I wanted to sketch you, but I"—the tips of her ears turned pink—"I didn't think I could do you justice."

He chuckled. "Anything you draw will be an improvement. It doesn't have to be a perfect likeness, you know. Just make sure you get my strong chin, broad shoulders, muscular—"

"James," she scolded, swatting him with her papers. "Stop at once and pose for me, as you were before." Reaching for her charcoal, she added, "I want to sketch *something* before Hildy returns."

He did as he was told, and Olivia scratched away. Each time she looked up at him, he made a face, which made her giggle. And that made him forget his worries about the expedition and Ralph and the letter from Olivia's father—at least for a while.

Hildy swept into the room, quickly took in the scene, and shrugged. Though it was hardly proper for Olivia to be alone in the room with him, all sorts of rules had been overlooked the last few days. At least everyone was fully dressed.

"The carpenter said he'd get to work on the crutches right away and that they should be finished later today. He asked that I come back to test them, so Terrence is taking me this evening after dinner."

"Tonight? That's wonderful!" cried Olivia. "Thank you."

James stood and said, "Since you can't go out, perhaps I could have a dinner tray sent up and join you? And you could finish my sketch."

"Mr. Averill brought me the supplies, Hildy," she explained. "Wasn't that lovely of him?"

"Indeed!" The maid scurried toward Olivia. "Let me see how it's coming along."

She clutched the papers to her chest. "Er, not until I'm finished."

James shot Olivia a knowing look as he walked toward the door. "I'll see you for dinner, at, say, seven?"

"Perfect."

James thought so, too.

Chapter Sixteen

*L*ater that evening, James followed the mouthwatering smells of roast beef, vegetables, and freshly baked bread down the corridor to Olivia's room, but he hesitated when he reached her door.

He felt inside his jacket and checked that her letter was tucked securely in his pocket. Owen might never forgive him for what he was about to do, but it was the right thing. And not just from a legal standpoint. Olivia was a grown woman, and what she did with her father's letter should be her choice.

Determined to see his decision through, James knocked on the door.

Hildy welcomed him in, sweeping her arm toward a small round table set with linens, china, and a vase full of wildflowers. "Everything is ready for you and Lady Olivia to dine."

Olivia was seated already and wearing a gown that wouldn't have been out of place at a London ball. Golden silk skimmed her shoulders and dipped to a low V in the front, baring the ripe swells of her breasts. Her hair was piled high on top of her head, except for several rogue curls that framed her face.

James swallowed hard. She was gorgeous, and the way she smiled at him made him feel like he could scale a pyramid. There was so much he admired about her. She wore her heart on her sleeve. She let the people around her know what they meant to her.

She lived life like every damned day mattered.

And when James was with her, he realized it *did*.

"Come, join me," she said.

Unable to speak, he smiled and gave a polite nod to Hildy as he seated himself across from Olivia.

"Isn't it lovely?" In the glow of a single flickering candle, she beamed.

"Indeed."

Hildy cleared her throat. "Terrence and I will dine downstairs before making our way to the carpenter's. But just because you'll have your crutches does not mean you may use them tomorrow. The doctor said you must rest for *two* days."

Olivia's expression turned calculating. "Well, I think the morning of the second day would certainly quali—"

"No," he and Hildy said in unison.

"Fine." Her shoulders slumped, but the trace of a smile lit her face. "I shan't argue with you because Hildy has been spoiling me. Look, she even found us this lovely bottle of wine."

The maid blushed as she scooped up her shawl and satchel. "I wanted your dinner to be special. You've had a trying couple of days."

"My own fault," Olivia admitted. "But thank you for helping me make the best of it."

"Enjoy yourselves," Hildy said, heading for the door. "We've a bit of a ride to the carpenter's but should return by nine-thirty or so."

The maid walked out, leaving him and Olivia alone. After a brief, cozy silence, he said, "You look beautiful. I didn't realize tonight was supposed to be formal—and I didn't think to bring my evening jacket."

"I shall try to overlook your state of underdress," she teased, "if you promise not to notice that I am wearing only one slipper."

"Agreed." He poured the wine, then reached out and squeezed her hand. "Earlier, I mentioned there was something I needed to tell you. You see—"

"Wait. We should have a toast," she said, raising her glass. She paused a moment to think, eyes alight with mischief. "To this evening. May it be full of surprises that delight us now...and live fondly in our memories...forever."

He lifted his glass and though he nodded his assent, he doubted the revelation he had for her—about her father's letter—was the kind of surprise she had in mind.

"We have no staff to serve us," she said, "but I confess I prefer it this way. We can pretend that no one exists but us."

"Allow me." He removed the lids from her plate and his own and set them aside. "I'm happy to play the role of footman tonight. Whatever you need, all you have to do is ask."

"My mind is positively swimming with possibilities, but do you know what I'd most like?"

"You must tell me. I live to serve."

"I'd like to know what it is about Egypt that fascinates

you—so much so that you'd leave behind the comforts of London and your family and friends to explore there."

"It's complicated. I don't know if I can put it into words."

"Will you try, please? I truly want to understand."

No one had ever asked him this before, but he could tell that his answer mattered to her, so he resolved to try his best to explain. "Your brother and Foxburn assume I'm going to Egypt because I want to escape the strictures of society—especially cravats."

"And are they are mistaken?"

He grinned. "Not entirely. I plan to leave most of my cravats at home. But it's more than that."

She swallowed a bite of asparagus and smiled encouragingly.

"When I was about twelve years old, I read about a tomb in the ancient pyramids and was fascinated by the Egyptians' concept of the afterlife. I wanted to believe that there was a world beyond this, and I asked my mother how it would be for Ralph. Would he be able-bodied and strong? Would he be able to express himself like the rest of us—clearly and with little effort?"

Olivia put down her fork. "What did she say?"

"She cried. And then she asked me what I thought. I said that if a pharaoh could have soldiers and slaves and cats in the afterlife that the least Ralph could have was his good health."

She sighed softly. "That seems perfectly reasonable to me, and very sweet. Do you think the Egyptians had it right, then? That the things that are important to us while we are alive are the things we will need after we pass on?"

"In a way. But the things that are important aren't wealth or servants."

"What is?"

"The love we have for our family and friends. I think that is the thing that will ultimately endure."

Her eyes brimmed. "I hope so. I miss Papa, but I like to think of him loving me and Rose and Owen from afar."

Jesus, this was the perfect opening. "Olivia, I—"

"But I don't want to talk about that now." She dabbed at her eyes with her napkin. "Tell me how your passion for Egypt grew."

Sensing she needed time to compose herself, he said, "I read everything I could about the civilization. After Napoleon's Egyptian expedition, there were volumes written on the subject—tomb maps, drawings, and paintings. But I became frustrated when the books didn't contain the answers to all of my questions. I wanted to know how the pyramids were built and what life was like for those not lucky enough to be born pharaohs. I decided that I wanted to discover the answers myself, digging in the sand of the Egyptian desert, rather than search for them in the dusty pages of a book."

"So it's a desire to understand ancient Egyptians that has led you to explore."

He thought about that for a moment. "I'm intrigued by other ancient civilizations, too, by the possibility of discovering common threads between us and those who lived thousands of years ago. There's a French linguist who's been able to decipher some of the hieroglyphics found in the tombs. If we could just read the messages they left behind, we might understand."

"We might learn they're not so different from us."

"Yes," he said gratefully. "I like to imagine we're connected by our humanity—our need to love and be loved." Good God, he was babbling like an idiot.

Olivia sighed. "That's beautiful. I never knew."

"Never knew what?"

"That you're such a romantic."

"I'm not," he said firmly. "I'm a realist."

She shot him a knowing smile. "Of course you are."

"All that aside, the civilization accomplished so much. And the land and people are both foreign and exotic. I can't wait to walk the narrow streets of Cairo, ride over miles of sandstone and desert, and see the pyramids and the Sphinx with my own eyes."

Olivia sat back and nodded to herself. "I believe I understand," she murmured.

"You do?" His explanation hadn't felt adequate, but he shouldn't be surprised that she had managed to glean something from his clumsy ramblings. She'd always met him more than halfway.

"I've been quite content living here in my safe, comfortable, familiar world. I've never felt the need to travel to distant lands. But you're so passionate about it that you may have just changed my mind."

"I wasn't trying to—"

"I know. I'm just happy that I finally understand. And it will make tonight all the more exciting."

"It will?"

She set her napkin on the table and grinned. "Absolutely. Finish your dinner, and then all will be revealed."

He let his gaze wander over the sweet curve of her neck and the tantalizing swells of her breasts, shamelessly hopeful that all sorts of things would be revealed.

Olivia took a large sip of wine. James looked especially handsome tonight. His sinewy strength and rugged charm were the same as always, but there was also something different about him. Something that, in all the years she had known and loved him, she had never seen in him before—vulnerability.

For once, he'd stopped being Averill—dashing solicitor, renowned pugilist, and intrepid explorer—and was just James. James, who worried about his family and questioned his future, just like other mere mortals.

And that openness—the honesty she'd seen in his beautiful green eyes—had made her knees go weak. Even though she was sitting. She could never have survived the conversation standing.

But the night was just beginning.

Brimming with anticipation, she said, "I thought we would do a little more sketching tonight—if you have no objection."

"None at all. Shall I fetch your supplies? Move our chairs to our respective positions?"

"Not yet. We're going to do things a bit differently this time."

His fork stopped halfway to his mouth. "Differently?"

She nodded. "We're reversing roles. I shall be the model, and you shall be the artist."

"No."

She lifted the hem of the table linens and reached beneath for the large satchel she'd placed there, then set it in her lap. As though she hadn't heard him, she said, "I'll just need your help setting up."

"Olivia, I don't draw."

"Move your chair close to the window, as it was before, then help me to it."

"I'm the farthest thing from an artist there is. I could

try to describe you in words. I could use all sorts of numbers and measurements to try to capture your essence. Drawing is out of the question."

She blinked slowly, then let the full force of her displeasure wash over him. "James, we both know that I am more than words or numbers. And if you think I'm about to let you near me with a measuring tape, you are sorely mistaken. Besides, you haven't even tried drawing. How can you call yourself an archaeologist if you don't have a little journal that you whip out of your pocket and draw sketches of your findings in?"

"I record my observations," he said firmly. "I don't draw pictures."

Olivia straightened her spine. "I am not some dusty, lifeless artifact buried along the banks of the Nile. I'm the girl you've known for a decade and the woman whom you've recently kissed. And you're going to draw me."

James stared at her for several seconds. "Very well. But you've been warned. The results won't be pretty."

Goodness. She hadn't anticipated any resistance at this early phase. The challenging part was still to come.

As he rearranged the furniture as she requested, she admired the subtle flexing of his muscles beneath his jacket. A sigh might have escaped her.

He looked up. "Did you say something?"

"Hmm? No. This looks perfect. Now, if you wouldn't mind helping me walk to the chair by the win— Oh!"

James scooped up her and her bag and held her close to his chest. His hard, warm wall of a chest.

She wrapped an arm around his neck because she thought it might help him if she shifted some of her weight. It had nothing to do with wanting to feel the downy curls at his nape or the corded muscles of his neck.

He didn't move but simply stood there, holding her and gazing into her eyes like there was something he wanted to tell her. Something tender and moving.

Ridiculousness, of course. But this was the same fantasy she'd been having since she was approximately twelve years old. No wonder she saw things in the depths of his green eyes that weren't really there.

And then his gaze flicked to her mouth, lingering there.

Her heart hammered in her chest, because there was *no* mistaking that look. He wanted to kiss her.

Coincidentally, she wanted to kiss him, too.

He seemed slightly breathless, which Olivia chose to believe was a consequence of his desperate longing for her and not of the effort he exerted in order to hold her.

Though neither of them spoke, Olivia could feel the frantic beating of his heart.

His lips parted, and without thinking she raised a finger and began to trace them, savoring every sensuous curve and testing the fullness of the lower one.

James made a strangled sound, closed his eyes for a moment, and nipped at her finger, capturing the tip between his teeth.

She breathed in sharply but didn't pull away as he took more of her finger in his mouth—so warm and wicked— and sucked on it until her nipples tightened and her body tingled from head to toe.

When he released her finger, she cradled his face in her hands and pressed her lips to his, sighing at the sweet, familiar taste of him.

He kissed her too, but not with the same unchecked

power as before. This time, he seemed to hold back, giving only as much as she gave, resisting his desire and the natural escalation of passion that occurred whenever they touched.

And even though that was just as well, she ached for more.

The kiss cooled to a low simmer before she reluctantly ended it. James nuzzled his forehead to hers and breathed her name so sweetly that if she dwelt on it she could easily be reduced to tears.

With a breeziness that was all show, she said, "Pleasant though that distraction was, you are delaying the surprise. And I still require your help with a couple of things. First of all, you may set me in the chair." Maybe then she'd have a prayer of being able to think straight.

He placed her upon the wooden seat of the chair but kept his arms around her for a moment more, as though he were reluctant to let her go. "What else can I do?"

"Take the coverlet from the bed and hold it up in front of me—like a curtain."

His forehead wrinkled adorably. "I don't understand."

Ignoring his real question, she said, "You just hold one end and let the rest hang—"

"No, I mean why would you want me to do that?"

"Ah. *That* is part of the surprise. Hold the blanket above your eye level. There is to be no peeking."

He stoically did as she asked, with only the slightest bit of mumbling under his breath. Once the coverlet hung between them, she took a deep breath and began her transformation.

First, she eased her arms out of the little puff sleeves of her dress. She'd asked Hildy to leave the laces on her dress a bit looser this evening. Even so, she had to perform impressive contortions to free her arms. After accomplishing that much, she tucked the sleeves into the bodice of her gown so that they were invisible. Already she felt daring and bold.

She glanced up to make sure James wasn't cheating. Satisfied, she went to work on her hair. She undid a few pins in the back, letting most of her curls fall past her bare shoulders. Then she opened the satchel and began rummaging through it, causing some of the items inside to clink.

James shuffled his feet. "What in God's name are you doing?"

"Patience," she cooed. "It will be worth the wait." Unless she ended up looking foolish and silly, but there was no sense in dwelling on that very distinct possibility.

At last she found the crown she had fashioned by winding a gold silk ribbon around a pointed tiara and carefully placed it on her head. Next came her exotic necklace, which was actually just a golden chain with several earrings and feathers hanging off of it, but when she'd squinted at it in the looking glass that afternoon, it had *almost* looked exotic. She clipped long, dangling earrings to her lobes and added one last item of jewelry—a large cuff bracelet that just fit onto her upper arm.

She had only one more detail to attend to. She retrieved a bit of kohl and a handheld mirror from her satchel. Though her hands were shaky, she managed to apply a thin line of kohl to each lid and beneath each eye.

There.

She checked her reflection. This was as close to Cleopatra as she could get—at least under the circumstances. She'd scrounged through her trunks all day just to come up with this makeshift costume, hoping it would elicit one of James's slow, secretive smiles, the kind that heated her blood and left her curiously breathless.

She wanted this night with him—an evening to remember always. James was the only man she'd ever love, and she wanted one night of passion with him, even if it meant she was giving up the chance for marriage to a respectable gentleman. She knew the risks involved, but she'd risked so much already. And fortunately, they were miles away from London and the censuring looks of the *ton*.

James was worth any risk. Olivia had dreamed of him for ten long years, and if she didn't reach out and seize this chance to be with him—tonight—all her dreams would slip through her fingers as surely as Sahara Desert sand.

"Are you almost done?"

"Why, are your arms getting tired?" But her teasing was a delay tactic. What if he thought her ridiculous and tawdry? He was so passionate about ancient Egypt, and she didn't want him to think that she was trivializing it by boiling it all down to one famous queen. She just wanted him to see her in a different light. Not as his best friend's little sister or as a damsel who required rescuing . . . but as a woman. And—God willing—as a desirable one.

She shoved the satchel under her chair, threw her shoulders back, and took a deep breath. "You may lower the blanket."

His arms dropped to his sides, and the coverlet pooled at his feet. He opened his mouth as if he were about to say something, and then froze. And blinked twice.

As his gaze roved over her, Olivia's heart pounded in her chest. But she held her chin high as she awaited his reaction—some sign of what he thought.

"You look so..."

She raised a brow.

"...so...I don't know." He dropped to his knees and searched her face as though the proper adjective might be found there.

"Beautiful?" she offered helpfully. And hopefully.

"God, yes."

So he *was* pleased. And the hungry look on his face said he was more than a little affected. A flood of relief emboldened her further. "Exotic and seductive?"

"Olivia." He said her name like a warning.

Which she ignored.

She leaned forward, giving him an unobscured view of her décolletage, and said, "Do you like it?"

His eyes dropped to the gold necklace glinting on the swells of her breasts. "What man wouldn't?"

"I don't care what other men think. This is just for you."

"Olivia," he said again, his voice ragged, "I'm trying very, very hard to resist you. But you're making it nigh impossible."

Good, then her plan had worked. The nervousness she'd felt earlier evaporated. Never more sure of what she wanted, she scooted forward on the chair and wrapped her arms around his neck, pulling him closer. "Right now, you have two choices."

"I'm listening."

"You can go get some paper and draw me..."

"Or?"

"You can ravish me."

Chapter Seventeen

*The Stone Age: (1) A prehistoric period during
which stone tools were widely used.
(2) A distant time period, as in*
Olivia's love for James dated roughly back
to the Stone Age.

James's jaw dropped. *Ravish?* "You shouldn't say
things like that, Olivia."

"I'm certain Cleopatra asked for what she wanted.
Why shouldn't I?"

"There's nothing wrong with asking for what you
want, but—"

"Well, then, I want this." She took his face in her hands
and kissed him like she really *was* Cleopatra. And with
all the skill and confidence of the renowned queen, she
brought him to his knees.

She melded her mouth to his, exploring with her
tongue, then pulled gently on his lower lip with her teeth.
He moaned into her mouth and for a few moments surrendered to desire—and to her.

When she broke off the kiss, he was panting like he'd fought three rounds at his boxing club.

"So what is it going to be?" she whispered. "Would you rather sketch me . . . or ravish me?"

Dear God. "It's not a question of what I'd rather do," he admitted. "It's a question of what's right."

"The way I feel about you *is* right. It has to be." Her brown eyes pleaded for understanding.

He wanted to tell her that he understood perfectly, because he loved her, too. It would be such a relief to bare his soul to her. But there was the small matter of his expedition, and even though she'd once said she'd wait for him, the trip was fraught with danger. A quarter of the men on the last large expedition hadn't returned alive. Besides, he hadn't told her about her father's letter—yet.

"I'm not worthy of such devotion."

"I know." She gave him a saucy smile and ran a fingertip up and down his neck. "But you shall always have it."

"Olivia, I care about you greatly." He could tell her that much. "But I think it would be best if I went to the other chair, picked up the paper and charcoal, and tried my hand at drawing."

With a forlorn sigh, she released him. That probably should have been his first hint that she had more surprises planned.

He stood and Olivia's eyes flicked to the bulge at the front of his trousers. She raised a brow and pursed her lips seductively, God help him.

After retreating to the chair opposite her, he picked up the sketching supplies and waited as Olivia settled herself.

"How is this?" She turned sideways on her seat and looked seductively over one shoulder.

He fumbled the charcoal he was holding. "Very nice." He looked down at the blank paper and drew the lines of the window frame behind her. A fine rectangle with straight sides and right angles—no luscious or distracting curves. But when he glanced up to check the proportions of the ledge, Olivia had moved. "Is something amiss?" he asked.

"The pose felt a bit stiff and unnatural. Let's try something different."

"If you insist."

"I think we must." With that, she began to unlace the tie at the side of her dress.

"Don't do that."

"Trust me. This will be a vast improvement." Holding the front of the gown to her chest, she let the sides fall away, exposing inches and inches of creamy smooth skin from her shoulders down her spine, all the way to the small of her back. Then she wriggled her bottom like a mischievous mermaid preparing to sun herself on a rock. "How's this?"

Jesus. "Shouldn't you be wearing a corset underneath your dress? Or a chemise? *Something?*"

"Lady Olivia most certainly should. But I'm Cleopatra. Remember?"

He shifted in his seat in an effort to ease his painful erection. No luck. "Fine. But I must ask you to be still." Her seductive pose was distracting him from the task at hand—namely, drawing the parallel floorboards beneath her chair.

"Try to imagine that I'm reclining on a plush chaise," she said huskily. "It's a pity we don't have one."

James grunted and tried to concentrate on the paper in

front of him. So far, he had blocked in the window and the floor. Next, he would sketch the small framed landscape hanging on the wall.

Anything but Olivia.

"How can you possibly draw me when you won't even look at me?"

"I *am* looking at you," he lied.

"Perhaps the costume is too much."

He glanced up and watched her remove the gold crown from her head and the cuff from her arm. "So we are done with drawing?" he asked hopefully.

"No." The sharp look that accompanied the word made it considerably more emphatic. "We are not." With that, she sat up straight and reached behind her neck—presumably to undo her necklace. As she lifted her arms, the front of her gown dropped to her waist.

Exposing rosy-tipped breasts that begged to be touched... and kissed.

The paper in his lap floated to the floor and his heart began to beat triple time.

Oh, he was *definitely* looking now.

She took her time unfastening the necklace, then dropped it into the satchel beside her. She made no move to cover herself but looked directly at him as she gracefully gathered up her hair and twisted it into a pile on her head. "Do you like this?"

"God, yes." His voice was little more than a croak.

"Or is it better like this?" She let her heavy tresses tumble down around her shoulders, pouted prettily, and arched her back.

Where in the name of God had she learned how to do that?

Nothing she did should surprise him—and yet, she constantly did.

She seemed to be waiting for a response, but damned if he knew what the question was. So he said the thing that was on his mind. "You are a lovely and exotic Cleopatra, but I think you are even more irresistible as yourself."

She blinked. "Do you mean it? The part about me being irresistible?"

"Absolutely." In fact, it was impossible to resist her for another second.

In two strides he stood before her, scooped her into his arms, and laid her crosswise on the bed. Crawling over her, he whispered, "Are you sure, Olivia?"

"I've been dreaming of this moment for a decade. I don't wish to apply undue pressure, but you might try to make it worth the wait."

"I shall do my best." He would do anything to give her pleasure. But though the thought of losing himself in her was very, very tempting, he wouldn't risk getting her with child. Not when he was about to leave England. Not while there was so much unspoken between them.

So he would have to content himself with making this a night she would remember—always.

Olivia had known the moment James surrendered—she'd seen it in his eyes. And even though he didn't love her with the same abandon she loved him, she knew in her bones that this night would be one of knee-melting, eye-opening pleasure. And she couldn't wait.

James laid her back upon the bed and shifted his hips on top of hers. Under his weight, she sunk into the mattress, comfortably captive and more than willing to give herself over to him and to passion. As their mouths melded, he dragged the front of her gown below her waist and cupped her bare breast in his hand, teasing her taut nipple with his palm.

"So damned beautiful," he murmured, his breath warm and moist against her neck. "I adore everything about you, Olivia. Tonight, you're mine."

"Yes," she said, thrilling at his words and tingling from his touch. "And you are mine." She pushed his jacket off his shoulders until he took the hint and obliged her by shrugging off the garment and letting it fall to the floor. He wore no waistcoat; only a thin cotton shirt separated his skin from hers, and she longed to feel his chest, warm and hard, pressed to hers.

Grabbing two fistfuls of his shirt, she pulled the hem free and slipped her hands beneath, skimming her fingers over the subtle, masculine contours of his torso. A light sprinkling of hair tickled her palms, and though she'd imagined running her hands over his chest many, many times, the reality was tenfold better. Perhaps a hundred-fold. "This has to go." She clutched the front of his shirt and gave it a firm tug. "Now."

Groaning, James reluctantly lifted his head from her neck where he'd left a trail of searing kisses. But as he sat up and hauled his shirt over his head, he smiled down at her with such tenderness and passion and honesty that if she didn't know better, she'd think it was... well, it looked like the stuff her dreams were made of.

The sight of his bare chest made her want to pounce on him and she was about to do just that when he said, "Your gown needs to go, too. Everything does."

Heat crept up her chest and neck, not from embarrassment, but from desire. "Very well. But if you insist on sketching me in the nude," she teased, "you mustn't let anyone else see it."

He growled. "Don't worry. I'm not good at sharing."

Sighing happily at his words, she reached for the gold silk bunched at her waist.

He placed his large, warm hands over hers, stopping her. "Let me."

She reached up and traced a line from his ear to his jaw. "Very well, Mr. Averill. I shall leave it up to you."

A delicious gleam lit his green eyes as he slid off the bed and stood before her. With heart-stopping deliberateness, he slipped the silk over her hips and down her thighs, inch by inch. She delighted in the sharp intake of his breath when he realized she wore nothing beneath her gown. She might have worn stockings if not for the bandage on her right foot. It seemed silly to wear just one, so she'd left her legs bare, and now she was glad.

She leaned back on her elbows and didn't attempt to cover herself as his appreciative gaze swept over her. She drank in the sight of him as well, wondering at the flat planes of his belly and the breadth of his shoulders.

He crawled onto the bed beside her, pulled her close, and kissed her with an intensity that awed her. She reveled in the feel of his skin against hers—the intimacy of it could almost make her weep. With each thrust of his tongue and each stroke of her skin he seemed to be telling her that he wanted her...and possibly even cared for her. Of course she'd dreamed of more than that, but this was enough for now.

And even though he couldn't—or wouldn't—tell her exactly what was in his heart, she would tell him what was in hers. If she didn't, she would surely regret it for the rest of her days. She needed to seize this opportunity to tell him what he meant to her.

It would be ever so much easier to speak coherently if James weren't touching her everywhere—squeezing her bottom, suckling her breasts, and rocking sweetly against the juncture of her thighs. A lovely, hypnotic pulsing had begun in her core, leaving her hungry and breathless. But she fought back the desire, just for a moment, and broke off their passionate kiss. "James," she whispered.

"Yes, love?"

Her heart squeezed. "There's something I must tell you."

"You don't need to say anything. Just feel."

"I am, believe me. But I realized that even though I told you I loved you, I never told you why."

"It doesn't matter. Your love is a gift. I'd never question the source of it."

"Allow me to enlighten you anyway. It's not your physique—though I confess to being particularly fond of your chest. And it's not your boxing prowess or even your sharp mind. It's your integrity."

"Olivia—"

"Please, let me finish. You are loyal and honorable. Everyone turns to you for advice—not just because you are clever and smart, but because you always know the right thing to do. And you do it. I respect that. I just wanted you to know."

James went very still, gazing deep into her eyes for several moments before he spoke. "You give me too much credit."

"No." She sat up and reached for him, cradling his

cheek in her hand. "It's true." And then, because the mood had turned rather serious, she skimmed her hand down the side of his neck and splayed her hand over the middle of his chest. "Now that I have you where I want you, I intend to take full advantage. Consider yourself warned."

The hint of a smile returned to his face. "I will."

Satisfied that she'd said her piece, she leaned forward and pressed her lips to the warm skin at the hollow of his neck, inhaling the familiar, heady scent of him. Then she kissed a path toward one flat nipple, teasing it with her tongue till it was as erect as hers. All the while, her hands skimmed over his lean body, narrow hips, and taut backside. Heaven help her.

"That's enough," he growled, pressing her back against the mattress. He turned gentle, kissing her lips softly, like she really was some princess he'd happened upon in the woods. His muscles seemed to quiver from the restraint he exercised, but he stoked her desire slowly and skillfully— drawing the sensation out of each playful nip of his teeth and each exquisite touch of his hands.

He deepened their kiss as he ran a hand over her hip and down her thigh. When he eased his hand between her legs and stroked the soft skin at the tops of her thighs, she opened herself to him, trembling with anticipation.

"You're shaking." His forehead wrinkled in concern. "Are you cold? Nervous?"

"No. It's just that I've wanted this for so long. I can't believe I'm really here with you."

"It's more real than you know," he said wickedly. And with that, he began to touch her, tenderly parting the slick, sensitive folds at her entrance and exploring until he found the spot and the amount of pressure that gave her the most pleasure. Desire coiled inside her, making her belly quiver. Sensing she was on the edge of something big, she dug her fingers into James's sinewy shoulders and called out his name.

He stopped stroking—which was not at *all* what she'd wanted—and smiled at her, smoothing a few tendrils away from her face. "That's my Olivia. So beautiful, so full of passion."

Yes. She *had* been full of passion. But now he was talking, and even though his words were very sweet— *Oh my.* In one fluid motion, James had slid off the bed and knelt beside it. He pulled her toward him and pressed her knees apart so that his head was level with...well, her nether parts. And she was fairly certain she knew what he intended to do.

Good Lord in heaven. She was right.

He bent his head, his wavy brown hair tickling the insides of her thighs. And since she couldn't possibly just lie back while something so momentous was happening, she sat up and watched, committing every tender touch, every sweet sensation to memory. His fingers kneaded her bottom while his tongue brought her to new heights. And because it had felt very good when James had done it, she caressed her own breasts, increasing her pleasure even more.

He glanced up and watched, then moaned against her, creating vibrations that started a sweet, heady thrumming in her core. It hurtled toward her with a thundering intensity—almost as powerful as her love for James. And then she shattered into a million little blissful bits.

James sprawled on the bed beside Olivia and sprinkled her forehead with kisses, letting her catch her breath.

He needed time to catch his, too. She was everything a man could want in a lover—smart, funny, beautiful, and loyal. And she loved him.

She rolled toward him, her brown eyes shining with love, her cheeks flushed with passion. "I have always loved the way I feel when I'm with you—alive and free and safe—but this...this was something new."

His chest swelled a little at that. "I'm honored I was the one to introduce you to pleasure."

"It couldn't have been anyone but you, James."

Though flattered by her words, he felt the need to set the record straight. "Your body would have responded to the touch of any lover with a modicum of skill."

"My heart wouldn't have. There's no one else I trust like you."

Guilt nearly strangled him, but he managed to choke out, "Speaking of trust, there's something you should know." The timing wasn't exactly fortuitous for a confession, but he couldn't let her go on thinking he was some paragon of virtue.

But her wicked fingertips were trailing down his chest and over his belly, tracing the waistband of his trousers. "We can talk later," she said. "For now, we must finish what we started."

He closed his eyes against the temptation. "No. We have taken enough chances for today. Let's get you dressed and presentable before Hildy returns."

"She won't return for another hour at least. And I think it very unfair that you would deny me the opportunity to give you pleasure." The tips of her fingers dipped inside his waistband and brushed the head of his cock.

He groaned. What she was saying made sense, in a

twisted way. Or was he only choosing to believe that it did because her nimble fingers were now unbuttoning his trousers?

"You shouldn't be doing that," he warned. But they both knew his heart wasn't in it.

"Try to stop me." She rolled on top of him then, kissing the flat planes of his belly and drifting lower and lower until he realized she meant to take him in her mouth. And she did. With little preamble and no hesitation, she held the base of his cock and licked the tip, testing the taste and feel of him before guiding the shaft into her mouth.

Thought became impossible; light danced at the corner of his eyes. He moaned and called out Olivia's name, but she was relentless—stroking and sucking until he thought he'd die from the exquisite torture of it. He denied himself release as long as he could—and then some. But when the unmistakable, unstoppable rush of pleasure began, he lifted Olivia up and they clung to each other like they had just washed up together on a beach, happy and exhausted.

Olivia nestled in the crook of his shoulder, sighing as though she was on the verge of sleep. When he excused himself for a moment, she grasped his arm, reluctant to give up her pillow for even a short time. However, she was grateful when he returned with a damp cloth for them to clean up with and the coverlet to keep her warm.

"We shouldn't linger too long," he said.

"I know. But it feels so heavenly lying here with you. Let's enjoy a few minutes more before real life intrudes again."

He rested his chin on the top of her head and inhaled

her citrusy, feminine scent. "I don't suppose a few minutes would hurt."

But the waning light and Olivia's steady breathing lulled him into a trancelike state. His limbs grew pleasantly heavy and he drifted off to sleep, blissfully unaware of the ramifications of one brief, if not-so-innocent, nap.

Chapter Eighteen

A ruckus in the corridor outside Olivia's room roused her slightly, but she snuggled closer to James. He'd draped an arm across her hips in his sleep, and she found the weight and warmth of his body sweetly comforting. She glanced up at his full lips, slightly parted, and his dark lashes, wishing to preserve this moment in her mind forever.

But the commotion in the hallway grew louder till it seemed to be directly outside her door. The tiny hairs on the back of her neck stood on end.

"James," she whispered urgently.

His eyes fluttered open and he gave her a lazy, heart-melting smile. "Yes, beautiful?"

"Do you hear that?"

Bam.

Instantly alert, he sprang off the bed, pulled the coverlet up to Olivia's chin, and grabbed his trousers. The pounding on the door continued, along with a great deal of grunting.

"Damn." He shot her an apologetic look. "They're going to break down the door if I don't open it."

Her stomach dropped. At least she was far from London. No one knew her here, save Hildy and Terrence. They must have returned early. She sat up, tucked the coverlet beneath her arms, and nodded bravely.

"Just stay there." James had pulled on his trousers and was almost to the door when the wood around it began to splinter.

"Wait!" he shouted, but a second later the door burst open, slamming against the wall with a sickening thud. James moved in front of the doorway, shielding her from the intruder—at least momentarily. She caught a glimpse of broad shoulders and a dark head that were terrifyingly familiar.

"Huntford?" James's voice was full of disbelief.

Oh no. Owen. Dread flooded her veins. Somehow her brother had tracked them down. And the look on his face said he was going to kill James.

"You scheming, devious bastard!" Owen threw a punch that collided with James's jaw. He staggered back from the force of it, and Olivia's gaze met her brother's.

"Owen," she said. "Stop, please! I'll explain everything."

Her brother's face contorted with rage and his fists clenched as he looked around the room. He eyed the intimate dinner table, James's discarded shirt, and her gown puddled on the floor. "No need to explain," he spat. "I can put the pieces together. Averill, you're a dead man."

James stood tall and faced Owen squarely. "You have every right to be angry."

" 'Angry' doesn't *begin* to describe my rage."

"Let's settle this elsewhere. You're upsetting Olivia."

"Don't speak her name!" Owen threw James against the wall and landed a blow to his gut.

"No!" Olivia cried. James's arms hung at his sides. He wasn't even trying to defend himself, much less fight back. She wrapped the blanket around her torso and leaped out of the bed. When her foot hit the floor, blinding pain shot through her leg, but she ignored it, determined to end the madness.

James glanced sideways at her. "Your ankle. Stay back. I'll be fine."

"Oh no, you won't," Owen retorted, punching him once more in the ribs.

Olivia pulled at Owen's arm, but he continued his assault and didn't stop until James slumped to the floor, moaning and gasping for air. She understood why James didn't want to hurt his best friend, but why hadn't he even deflected the blows?

At last Owen stepped back and blinked at James, who had blood trickling from his nose. Her brother looked dazed, as if he'd been the one who'd been bludgeoned about the head. "Dear Jesus," he said, sinking into a chair.

Olivia dropped to her knees beside James and took his face in her hands. "I'm sorry. This is all my fault."

"No." He sat up, using the wall for support. "I deserved this—and more. Grab one of your gowns and, if you can manage it, go to my room to dress. Stay there until I've had a chance to talk with your brother."

"I'm not leaving you alone with him." There was no telling what Owen might do without a witness in the room.

Owen closed the door—or, more precisely, propped it up in front of the door frame—and dragged his chair over to where James and Olivia sat. He didn't look at her, but in a voice devoid of emotion said, "Put on your gown. I need to deal with him."

"He didn't know that I would follow him to the Lakes," she said.

"But when he discovered that you had, he saw no harm in sharing a bed with you?"

Olivia winced at her brother's cold and callous tone. But she knew it was only to mask the disappointment and hurt he felt. She'd lied to him and ignored every rule of propriety.

"I'll do as you ask. But please listen to the whole story before you condemn James. He's only here because he was trying to protect me."

Owen snorted.

Her insides in knots, she picked up her gown and hobbled to the far corner of the room. Owen's back was to her, but she listened carefully, hanging on every word.

"I trusted you," Owen said simply.

"I know," James replied. "I'm sorry."

"Does she know about the letter?"

Letter? Olivia froze, straining to hear James's response.

"No, but—"

"Did you read it?"

"No!"

"I assume you know how this is going to end."

"Of course. I will marry her."

A lump the size of an egg settled in her throat.

"Because you got caught," Owen spat. "I wanted better for my sister."

"I know," James said raggedly. "She deserves better."

Regret and frustration swirled in her head. Her brother

and James sat there, discussing her future as though it were already decided. And she knew in her heart that it was. Fate—coupled with her poor judgment—had intervened to make her greatest wish come true.

Only she'd never, *ever* wished for it to happen this way.

She hastily tied the laces of her gown and limped toward her brother. "To what letter are you referring?"

"Why are you walking like that? What's wrong with your leg?"

"What letter?" she repeated. To James, she said, "Is it the same one that keeps falling out of your jacket?"

"I wanted to tell you—" James began.

Owen cut him off. "It's nothing. Never mind. You have bigger worries."

"It's from your father," James said. "He wrote it to you."

"Damn it, James!"

She felt as though the air had been sucked from her lungs. "Papa? But…how?"

Olivia had never been the swooning type, but now a low buzzing began in her ears and she swayed on her feet. James called out her name and stood, but Owen pinned him to the wall with one hand. Why didn't Owen want her to have the letter? And why had James kept it hidden from her?

She staggered toward the foot of the bed where James's jacket lay in an untidy ball and dug into his pocket. There it was. Her letter…from Papa.

One of the hardest things about losing him had been the suddenness of it. Countless times since his death, she'd wished for the chance to speak with him again, to hear his warm, gravelly voice and see the affection in his eyes. No one had been closer to Papa than she, and no one had felt the loss more keenly.

But he'd written her a letter—a letter that Owen *and* James had withheld from her.

Oblivious to the pain in her ankle, she whirled toward the door.

"Stop," Owen commanded.

But she yanked on the door, till the whole thing came crashing into the room, barely missing her brother's head. She darted down the corridor into James's room, slammed the door behind her, and locked it. She had to read the letter, and no one—not James nor Owen nor the devil himself—was going to stop her.

As she collapsed onto James's bed, she tried not to dwell on the fact that he'd been keeping this secret from her. She tried not to think about their current dilemma and the humiliating way in which her fairy-tale evening had ended. And she especially tried not to think about the desolate look on James's face when he'd said, *"I will marry her."*

Of course she'd dreamed of marrying James, but not like this. She'd wanted to be his heart's desire—not obligation.

Her eyes burned, her nose stung, and her ankle throbbed. A knock rattled the door in its frame.

"Olivia, let me in." Owen's muffled voice came from the hallway. More calmly, he added, "Please. You shouldn't be alone when you read the letter."

He was probably right. Papa hadn't been well in the days leading up to his death—anything he'd written then could be disturbing. But she needed to read it without Owen hovering about.

"I don't wish for company, thank you." She needed time and space to absorb Papa's message. And even though she would have dearly loved to have Rose or Anabelle or Daphne to lean on, this was something she had to do alone.

"Do you think you might wait a bit, then?" Owen asked. "You're overwrought at the moment."

She sniffled. "Perhaps I am. But I'm not as delicate as you seem to think."

"I did what I thought was in your best interest. I shouldn't have kept the letter from you."

Yes, well, he was not the only one who'd made a bad decision. She'd made several in chasing James across England. "I was wrong, too," she admitted. "I'm sorry for all the trouble I've caused, but you don't need to protect me anymore."

"What if I want to?"

Her throat clogged with emotion. "It's time for me to stand on my own."

"Very well." His voice was tinged with resignation— and perhaps respect. "But I shall be right here if you need me."

Taking a deep breath, she turned the letter over; with trembling hands she broke the seal. Her eyes blurred at the sight of Papa's familiar, uneven handwriting. She could almost hear his deep, gentle voice as she read the words.

My Dearest, Beloved Olivia,
    I hope that by the time you open this letter, sufficient time has passed that you are able to think of me without anger or disgust, but perhaps I ask too much

of you. I wish that I had been a better father to you and Owen and Rose, but I am confident that the three of you turned out wonderfully in spite of your parents' many flaws.

You may wonder why I chose to write to you and not your older brother or younger sister, and I shall tell you. Owen is quick to anger and slow to forgive. I do not fault him for it—he only wants what is best for you and your sister. Rose is wise beyond her years but so fragile. You, Olivia, are the strongest of the three and the glue that holds our family together. You are the one who makes your big brother laugh and who protects your younger sister. You are the one whom I trust with the information I'm about to impart.

You see, your mother is not the only one who was unfaithful during our marriage. I was too. Rebecca—I suppose you could call her my mistress— worked at the bookshop that I frequented in town. Though not half as beautiful as your mother, Rebecca had a sweet, easy smile and sharp mind that immediately drew me to her. For several months we met in secret, but then one evening when I came to her, she turned me away, saying she no longer wished to see me.

I tried to respect her wishes, but desperate to know how she fared, I spied upon her as she walked to the bookshop one morning…and discovered that she was with child. Still, she refused to see me. Shortly after that, she left town and did not return until summer, when I happened to see her in the park, carrying a small bundle close to her breast—a little girl, only a few months old. She let me look at her and said her name was Sophia. Sophia Rolfe. I never saw them again, for I'd reconciled with your mother. I sent Rebecca a generous sum each year for the next eighteen years so that they would not want for anything. I realize now that money was not enough.

I recently learned that Rebecca took ill and died. I considered writing to Sophia and telling her who I was, but I feared she would not welcome the news that I am her father, and I had no wish to complicate her life. That is the excuse that I told myself, at any rate.

I fear, my dear Olivia, that I have thoroughly shocked you by this point in my letter, and I regret any pain that this knowledge causes you. It is my hope—and I realize this is asking a great deal of you—that you will find it in your heart to forgive me. Perhaps you will one day pay Sophia a visit and make sure that she is well settled. Maybe you will tell her that you are her half sister, maybe not. I've enclosed the last address I had for Rebecca as well as a crude sketch of her carrying Sophia. I made it from memory—after seeing them that day at the park.

I shall leave it up to you to decide whether to share this information with Owen and Rose. I don't want to cause any of you more distress, but I could not go to my grave without somehow acknowledging Sophia as my daughter.

As for the rest of you, I honestly believe that you are better off without me. However, I wish I could be there, if only to see the beautiful, kindhearted, gener-

ous young woman you've become. Know that whatever you decide to do with this information, I am proud of you and love you.

Give my love to Owen and Rose as well.

Papa

Olivia stared at her father's handwriting, looking for some clue—any inconsistency that might prove the letter was a cruel hoax—but found none. The letter had been written by Papa's own hand.

She let it slip through her fingers and backed away from it, scooting toward the head of the bed. She wished she had never seen it, that she could turn back time and remain blissfully unaware of its existence. She pressed her back against the wooden headboard and glared warily at the paper.

"Olivia? Are you all right?" She'd forgotten Owen stood outside the door, and the concern in his voice only made it harder not to cry.

"Yes." She didn't trust herself to say any more than that. How dare Papa do this to her? Why did he have to burden her with this knowledge? He was supposed to be the ever-faithful, loving husband and gentleman. Not some libertine who took up with a random shopgirl.

"Will you let me in?"

"No." She eyed the letter with disgust. How she'd enjoy shredding it to bits and tossing the pieces to the wind. She couldn't let Owen read it. She didn't want him to feel as awful as she did. Besides, she needed time to think about Papa's revelation—without interference from her well-intentioned but overbearing brother.

"I'm sorry about the letter. I truly am. But even if you

won't discuss the contents with me, we still have the serious matter of the highly improper circumstances in which I found you." Though he was on the other side of the door, she could just imagine his dark brows slashing downward in disapproval.

She snatched the letter from where it lay on the bed, unceremoniously folded it, and stuffed it into her bodice. Then she limped to the door and yanked it open. "I doubt I am the only one who's engaged in such scandalous behavior."

That silenced him for a moment. "At least I had the good sense not to get caught," he muttered. Then, making a face, he said, "What is that dark stuff on your eyes?"

"It's nothing. Owen, about tonight. We didn't—"

"Stop." He held up a palm. "I don't want to hear the specifics. One thing is for sure—this was beyond a stolen kiss on a terrace. You've been traipsing across the countryside, unchaperoned, for days—and you're not even in the same county that you said you'd be in. If not for the note from Terrence, I'd have never known where you were. I know what I saw tonight, and you know what the consequences must be. So does Averill."

Olivia waved her brother into the room and shuffled to a chair.

"What's wrong with your leg?" he asked again, taking a seat on the edge of the bed opposite her.

"I'll tell you all about it later. Where's James?"

"In the other room, washing the blood off his face."

Olivia winced but was glad for a few more moments alone with Owen. However unlikely it was that she'd change his mind, she had to try. "I know that I disappointed you and that you are acting out of concern for me."

"Precisely."

"You are worried about my reputation."

"Damn it, Olivia, I'm worried about a lot of things."

"Consider this. No one saw James and me together but you. You would never gossip about it—"

"That's not the point."

"Of course it is. It's only a scandal if people know. And no one knows."

"You don't think the innkeeper and his wife and all the guests will know about it before the taproom shuts down tonight?"

"Well, if you hadn't kicked in the door—"

"Don't," he snapped. "You brought this on yourself."

"Yes. That's just it. This was my fault. And if you make James marry me, everything will be ruined."

Owen raked his hands through his hair. "I thought you were fond of James."

"I am. But I must admit I'm disappointed that he kept the letter from me."

He wearily dragged a hand down his face. "I asked him to hold on to it for me. He was doing me a favor."

Olivia hung her head.

"Listen, we can talk about the letter later," Owen said. "Can you honestly tell me that marriage to James would make you miserable?"

She sighed. "No. I love him. But I don't want to marry him this way."

"What do you mean 'this way'? What difference do the circumstances make? You'll be married."

"He's leaving on an archaeological expedition at summer's end."

"No. He's not."

"Yes. He must." She leaned forward, suddenly desperate to make her brother understand. "I *cannot* be the reason he doesn't go. He'll resent me for the rest of his days."

"After tonight he's lucky that he *has* any more days. Maybe that knowledge will help him come to terms with his missed opportunity to explore Egypt."

"It's more than that, Owen." She sniffed back the tears that threatened. "I don't want a husband who doesn't want me. I don't want a cold and empty marriage like our parents'. I want a love like yours and Anabelle's."

At the mention of his lovely wife, the creases around Owen's eyes softened. "I understand that you're upset. You've had a trying day. But let me make one thing very, very clear. Averill *will* marry you. What you and Averill make of that marriage...well, that's up to you. And at the risk of sounding unfeeling, I don't really care. All I know is that as soon as I can arrange it, the two of you will be standing in front of the vicar exchanging your vows."

"Please—"

"Don't oppose me on this, Olivia," he said, quietly but firmly. "You will not win—you'll only succeed in exhausting us both."

At that, all the fight went out of her. Well, almost. "Very well, I will marry James. But only if you allow him to go on his expedition afterward."

"That's no way to begin a marriage."

She agreed, and just the thought of saying good-bye to him for two years made her heart ache. She could well imagine the whispers of the *ton* when they learned that she'd been deserted by her husband shortly after the wedding. But she could not be the reason James's dream was shattered. "This is not a typical engagement, and it won't be a typical marriage. I want James to go."

Owen stared at her intently for the space of several heartbeats. "Fine. Once you're married, I won't interfere. I won't prevent him from going. But I will think less of him if he does."

The future she'd dreamed of—marriage to James—was about to happen. And it felt all wrong.

"Now, if you won't tell me about our father's letter," Owen said, "at least tell me what happened to your foot."

It seemed ridiculous to talk about something as mundane as her foot while her mind grappled with the fact that her brother had discovered her and James naked in bed *and* that she had a half sister roaming around England somewhere. But Owen would not be satisfied until he heard the whole story. "It happened a couple of days ago. I was—"

"Pardon the interruption." James stood in the doorway, fully clothed and quite respectable-looking, if one discounted the bruise that was already forming beneath his left eye. He cleared his throat and looked past Owen, right at Olivia, his green eyes full of sadness and resignation. "Olivia," he began, "may I have a word?"

She wanted to shake him. Less than an hour ago they'd laughed and kissed and talked—and brought each other indescribable pleasure. And now they stood across the room from each other like casual acquaintances at an awkward dinner party. The distant, vacant look on his face nearly broke her heart.

"Of course. Owen, would you give us a moment, please?"

He snorted. "Whatever Averill has to say to you, he can say in front of me."

"But—" she protested.

"It's fine. Your brother should hear this, too." James walked toward her and stood stiffly before her chair. "I want you to know that while I know I have not acted honorably, I respect and admire you greatly. I'm deeply sorry that I took advantage of you—"

"You didn't. I—"

"No. I did not behave like a gentleman." His eyes begged her to let him finish. "I can't undo what I've done, but I can try to make it right."

As he lowered himself to one knee, Owen muttered something unintelligible and turned his back to them. And in her head, Olivia was screaming, *No, no, no! Please don't do it like this.* Even though he was obviously sincere, it felt like a mockery of her fantasy, in which he made a heartfelt proposal, proclaiming his love for her and sweeping her off her feet.

James reached for her hand and held it like he was greeting his dear grandmama. "You would be doing me a great honor," he said, "if you would agree to become my wife."

He gazed up at her expectantly, as if they were both actors and he was waiting for her to recite her line. There was no passion in his proposal, no happiness. This was a defeated man doing his duty—nothing more.

"Maybe we should all get a good night's sleep," Olivia said. "We can discuss this more tomorrow."

James's shoulders slumped; he released her hand and began to rise.

"Stay there," Owen ordered James. To Olivia, he said, "That was a perfectly good proposal, and I want to hear you accept it."

"Very well," she said, to no one in particular, because apparently what she said and thought didn't carry much weight. "I accept."

Owen raised his brows as James stood, cringing as though a rib were broken or bruised. "It wasn't the most moving proposal I've ever seen." Owen shot a look Olivia's way. "Nor the most graceful acceptance. But I suppose they'll have to do."

A shuffling noise sounded from the hall, followed by a gasp. "Lady Olivia?"

Gads. She'd almost forgotten about Hildy. "I'm in here," Olivia called out.

The maid appeared in the doorway, triumphantly holding a crutch in each hand. "Look what I've— Oh my. Good evening, Your Grace." Her cheeks blossomed red as she curtsied before Owen, crutches and all.

Olivia idly wondered if anyone else—perhaps the coachman or the innkeeper—would wander into the room before the night was over. And she couldn't *wait* for it to be over.

"Thank you, Hildy. Why don't you go to our room? I'll join you there shortly and explain everything." All too happy to be dismissed, the maid scurried away.

With no small amount of exasperation, Owen said, "I have yet to receive an explanation for your injury, but at this point I think it can wait until the morning. Though it goes against my better judgment, before we all retire to our *separate* rooms, I shall give the pair of you two minutes alone—no more. I'll be standing in the hallway."

Thank God Owen had shown this bit of compassion. Olivia desperately needed some sign from James that things were going to be all right between them, that he didn't view marriage to her as the equivalent of a life sentence in the Old Bailey.

Owen shot them both a stern warning look before striding out the door.

Olivia sprang to her feet in spite of her now-throbbing ankle and threw her arms around James's neck. "Are you hurt?"

He gently extracted himself from her embrace and moved a respectable distance away. "I'll be sore for a day or two. It's nothing."

"I never meant for this to happen. I'm so sorry."

"I'm sorry, too."

"Maybe there's a way—" she began.

"No, I gave Owen my word. We may as well resign ourselves to the fact. I will do my best to make you happy."

"I know you will." But she couldn't imagine being happy when James so clearly wasn't.

"Did you read the letter from your father?"

At the reminder of the letter he'd kept from her, she looked away. "I did. I have a lot to think about."

"If there's anything I can do…"

"I don't think so."

"Then I should let you rest. Things will seem better in the morning."

And then, with a sad smile, he left.

There was no kiss, passionate or otherwise, no affectionate glance or word, no humor or charm. Just a vague hope that things would seem better tomorrow.

Perhaps it was true, for they couldn't possibly get any worse.

Chapter Nineteen

Restore: (1) The act of cleaning an artifact in an
attempt to return it to its original condition.
(2) To bring back to good form, as in
He'd betrayed her trust in him, and now he'd do
any damned thing in his power to restore it.

*J*ames chafed at taking orders from anyone. And ever
since Huntford had burst into Olivia's room the night
before, he'd been issuing commands, telling James what
to do and when to do it. The hell of the thing was, Huntford was letting him off easy, and James knew it.

So, when he was summoned to the inn's private dining
room for breakfast at nine o'clock, he did not question it,
even it if did rankle him. Olivia and Huntford were waiting there, and neither one looked like they'd gotten much
sleep. He probably had circles under his eyes, too, but
they were eclipsed by the huge bruise that had already
appeared on his cheek.

The mood was somber, and James supposed they were
mourning the death of his and Huntford's friendship.

James felt like a whole chunk of his history—as well as his future—was suddenly gone. He'd experienced a similar void after losing his dog, a lovable mixed breed named Hermes, a few years back. But this was worse. This was James's fault. And if Huntford shot him blistering looks for decades to come, it was no less than James deserved.

"Good morning," he said, before making a polite bow to Olivia. He noticed her new crutches leaning in the corner.

"Good morning." She pushed a piece of ham around with her fork.

"Fill a plate." Huntford pointed to the table behind him, laden with platters of eggs, toast, ham, and fruit. "Then we'll talk."

James poured himself coffee and sat next to Olivia, drawing a scathing glare from her brother. "What would you like to discuss?"

Huntford set down his fork. "I've decided that the marriage shall take place in Haven Bridge, where there will be far less gossip than there would be in town. We can say that it was your infirm uncle's wish to see you wed and that you happily indulged him."

"That's quite a story," James said. The irony of it was that Uncle Humphrey probably *would* derive great pleasure from attending the ceremony. Turning to Olivia, he said, "Would a small wedding in Haven Bridge suit you?"

Huntford crossed his arms impatiently; James ignored him.

"Yes," she said softly. "I suppose the location is not so very important to me."

"Excellent," said the duke. "I'll take—"

"Wait," James said. The sight of Olivia so impassion-ate about her own wedding was unsettling. "If location does not matter to you, what *does*?"

"I'd like to have my sister and close friends here, but we're so far from home."

"Yes, we are," Huntford cut in. "That's the beauty of it."

"Perhaps we can arrange for them to come," James offered.

Olivia brightened a little, but then her brother said, "The less people who are here to witness it, the better. *I*, of course, will be there to see the union take place with my own eyes. Later this morning, I shall escort you both back to Haven Bridge and see that Olivia is settled in the inn there. Averill, you'll stay with your uncle—or any-where you like, so long as it's not the same inn. I plan to spend the afternoon meeting with the local vicar and arranging for the banns to be read."

James cast a glance at Olivia. Her face was almost as pale as the simple white gown she wore—a striking dif-ference from the lush gold confection she'd slipped out of last night. His blood heated at the memory of her boldly unlacing her dress for him and exposing delectable, silky skin. Good God. He shook his head and pulled him-self together, grateful that her brother couldn't read his thoughts.

Huntford was still talking. "I have business to attend to, not to mention my wife and daughter, so I'll leave this evening for London. But never fear, I'll return to Haven Bridge in three weeks' time, before the happy nuptials take place."

"It seems as though you've planned everything," Olivia said.

"Not quite. For obvious reasons, I hesitate to leave you in the same village with one another when you have only your maid as her chaperone, but I don't see how to avoid it. In any case, your fate is already sealed. You might as well use the time to plan your wedding—and your future."

Olivia glanced at James, and he saw the wariness in her eyes. The adoration, the trust that had been there last night were gone. In keeping the letter from her, he'd crushed her lofty opinion of him. Where she'd once thought he was the model of integrity, she now doubted his intentions. And who could blame her?

Three weeks until the wedding. That's how long he had to try to make things up to Olivia.

That's how long he had to help her regain her sparkle.

Later that afternoon, James was back among the picturesque hills of Haven Bridge. He retrieved his belongings from the inn, said good-bye to Olivia under the watchful eye of her brother, and rode his horse to Uncle Humphrey's cottage. He rapped on the door. There was no answer, so he tested the handle, found it unlocked, and walked in. "Uncle, are you here?"

He wended his way around unwieldy stacks of books and two sleeping cats, and followed the rather loud snores coming from the study.

In his sleep, Uncle Humphrey looked older and frailer. In his waking hours he wielded a sharp wit and intelligence that made it easy to forget that he was close to eighty years old. Not so now. One of the cats stirred, stretched, and leaped onto Humphrey's leg, prodding him awake. He blinked several times, looked up at James, and said, "Wondered where you'd been," as though it were perfectly normal to wake up and find someone had walked into your house unannounced. "What happened to your face?"

He touched his fingers to his bruised cheek. "I took a punch."

"You?" Humphrey's white eyebrows furrowed together in disbelief. "You're not usually on the receiving end."

"I deserved it."

"Oh." Humphrey nodded thoughtfully. "How is she?"

"Who?"

"The girl. The one you chased after."

"I didn't *chase* after Lady Olivia. I was endeavoring to escort her safely to her aunt's house."

"I see." But he said it in a way that suggested he knew very well the reasons his nephew had left Haven Bridge at the drop of a hat. And he was probably right, damn it.

"We're engaged," James said flatly.

"What's this? Felicitations, my boy! I believe the news calls for a drink. Pour us each a bit of Scotch, will you?"

"Of course." James walked to his uncle's sideboard. "But I'm not sure it's cause for celebration. Her brother, the duke, is forcing us to marry."

"Ah. Well, a betrothal is special regardless of the circumstances surrounding it."

James splashed the Scotch into a couple of glasses and handed one to his uncle.

Humphrey pet the cat, which had settled itself between his hip and the arm of the chair, then shifted to his right to give his whiskered friend more space. He sipped his drink in silence for a minute before asking the question that had plagued James ever since last night—maybe even before. "What does this mean for your expedition?"

If anyone could understand his dilemma, it was Uncle Humphrey. He shared James's passion for antiquities and exploring and was, quite possibly, even more enthused about the trip than James was.

"I still want to go."

"Does Lady Olivia have any objection?"

"I haven't had the chance to discuss it with her. But I can't imagine she'd be thrilled at the prospect of me leaving the country days after we marry."

He glanced at Humphrey, hoping for a lecture on how he'd be a fool to even consider passing up this once-in-a-lifetime opportunity to explore the ruins of an ancient civilization with a skilled and respected team.

"You have a difficult decision to make."

"What would you do?"

Humphrey took a long, wheezing breath and closed his eyes. He sat like that for maybe a minute—long enough that James wondered if he'd resumed his nap. But then he coughed, opened his eyes, and said, "Take her on a picnic."

James shook his head. Maybe Humphrey wasn't quite as sharp as he'd once been after all. "No, I meant about the expedition. Would you stay or go?"

"I can't answer that. I'm not in your shoes. But I remember that whenever your aunt Dorothy and I needed to work through a particular problem, we would pack a lunch and take a long walk and spend some time together. You could gain some clarity, some perspective. The worst that could happen is that you'll have spent the day with a pretty girl."

James stroked his chin. This wasn't exactly the sort

of wisdom he'd been seeking, but he supposed a picnic couldn't hurt.

"She *is* pretty, isn't she?" Humphrey's cloudy eyes sparkled with mirth.

"Very. Almost as pretty as Aunt Dorothy."

"Ah. Then you're a lucky man, indeed."

Maybe Humphrey was right. He remembered the impromptu breakfast he'd shared with Olivia in his favorite spot atop the hill, before she'd injured her ankle. Though it afforded the best view in all of Haven Bridge, it definitely wasn't accessible on crutches.

As if he'd read James's mind, Humphrey said, "Take a couple of horses to the northwest corner of my property, where the river runs into the woods. There's something almost magical about that place."

"Magical? As in sprites and fairies?"

Humphrey ignored the question. "I haven't been there in years, but I've always suspected it's sacred ground. Promise me you'll visit it. With your pretty fiancée."

James shrugged. He had approximately three weeks to fill before the wedding. "Certainly." Belatedly, he remembered the small matter of him needing lodging. "I have another favor to ask, Uncle. Would you mind if I stayed here with you for the next few weeks?"

"Not at all. Provided you pour me some more Scotch." He held up his glass and gave a crooked grin.

James obliged his uncle, removed a stack of books from the chair opposite him, and sat. "Tell me more about the land by the river."

Olivia was once again installed in a room at the Fife & Frog in Haven Bridge. Owen had departed the night before, and though he'd refrained from lecturing her one last time, she'd seen the disappointment in his eyes, and it stung tenfold worse than his anger.

She shuffled about her room on her crutches, like a bird fluttering in a too-small cage. She could cross the room in four long strides, but her arms ached from exertion. Hildy pointed out that Olivia wouldn't be so sore if she remained in one spot for more than, oh, ten minutes, but she could not help her restlessness.

In an obvious attempt to distract her, Hildy rifled through the contents of Olivia's trunk. "We need to find a suitable dress for you to be wed in. Perhaps the rose silk?"

Olivia shrugged. "It'll do." If this were the engagement of her dreams, her sister-in-law, Anabelle, would lovingly craft a gorgeous gown. Daphne would alternately tease Olivia and offer her risqué wedding night advice. How she missed them, not to mention Rose and her quiet, solid support.

"It's simple and elegant," Hildy said cheerfully. "And I'll pile curls on top of your head and wind ribbon through your hair, just the way you like."

A knock at the door startled both of them. Hildy dropped the dress and scurried to the door. "Mr. Averill. Good morning."

He stood in the doorway looking breathtakingly handsome in a russet-colored jacket, buckskin breeches, and boots. His brown hair was charmingly windblown, and the warmth in his green eyes made her heart skip a beat.

And yet, everything was awkward and distant between them. It might have been the stilted proposal—not his fault, but highly awkward nonetheless. Or, it might have been the matter of Papa's letter.

James knew how close she'd been to her father and how deeply his death had affected her. Yet, after all she and James had shared—cozy conversations, stirring kisses, and more—he'd hidden the letter from her. Owen had explained everything, how their father's solicitor had delivered the letter and how Owen had hesitated to give it to Olivia. He'd tried to absolve James of blame, saying that he was only trying to be a good friend.

But she'd thought *their* relationship was important, too. She wondered if she'd forever play second fiddle to Owen where James was concerned.

"I apologize for calling so early," he said. "But it looks like it will be a glorious day, and I wondered, Lady Olivia, if you'd like to join me for a picnic."

Olivia arched a brow and cast a pointed look at the crutches she held. Though she longed to escape her room, the very thought of traversing rutted dirt paths made her arms hurt. "I'm afraid I wouldn't make it very far."

"There wouldn't be much walking required of you. I've brought along an extra horse, and we can ride to our destination—a little spot on my uncle Humphrey's land. I've never been myself, but he says the river is so clear and cool that you won't be able to resist dipping your toes in it."

"I'd only be able to dip one set of toes." She was aware she sounded like a sullen fourteen-year-old, but this was about protecting her heart, which had suffered just about all the ache it could take. Tempting though the picnic was, she couldn't let herself get too close to James. The more time they spent together, the more painful it would be when he departed for Egypt.

"I stopped by the bakery for hot cross buns . . ."

Not the buns. Oh, he was good—very good. She sighed. "I suppose the fresh air and sunshine would be welcome."

"Even if the company would not?" James's contrite smile said that he knew he was not in her good graces... but that he'd like to be.

"I didn't mean to imply such a thing. Hildy, you'll join us, won't you?"

"Er, I'm not one for riding, my lady. Could I walk alongside you?"

James shook his head. "It's probably three or four miles over fields. Too far."

How convenient. "Well, since we are now engaged, I don't suppose it matters. Hildy, would you please fetch my bonnet and parasol?"

A few minutes later, James was hoisting her onto a docile brown mare with white markings. "How does the saddle feel? Are you comfortable?"

"Quite." She'd forgotten how much she loved the view from atop a horse, and the feeling of freedom that came from riding. She couldn't wait to get into an open field and see how fast the mare could run.

James tied her crutches to the back of his saddle and deftly swung himself onto his chestnut gelding.

He led the way up the village's main street, past the tiny shops and the village square. The road wound around a well-kept cemetery and, farther up the hill, a quaint church. The church in which they could very possibly be married.

As her mare trotted by it, Olivia's gaze lingered on the stone walls, arched door, and yellow wildflowers that surrounded the brick path leading to the steps. The picturesque scene was not so different from her fantasies.

James did not seem to notice the church. His eyes focused on the rolling green mountains, the deep silver lake, and the cloudless azure sky. The warm breeze tousled his hair and the sun streaked it gold, leaving Olivia rather breathless. After a mile or so, he stopped and pointed across a field of tall grass. "We're headed west, toward the tree line. We can keep to this pace if you'd like, or—"

Before he could finish his sentence, Olivia grinned and urged the mare into a gallop. The wind whipped at her bonnet, pushing it off her head and freeing long tendrils from confining pins.

James rode several lengths behind her. Though he surely could have overtaken her at any time, he gave her space and let her savor the rush of thundering over miles of grass and watching the trees rise up to meet her.

A long, winding stream bordered the edge of the woods, and she pulled back on the reins, catching her breath as the mare meandered along the water's edge. James joined her there and slid off his horse, encouraging him to drink. Looking up at Olivia, he said, "You seemed like your usual self just then. I liked it."

She arched a brow. It might have been the exhilarating ride, the warm breeze, or the lush scenery. Whatever the cause, her heart *did* feel lighter.

James walked along the stream, leading both horses toward the shade of the trees, then surveyed their surroundings. "Uncle Humphrey was right—this is a beautiful spot. Let me spread out a quilt, and I'll help you down."

He untied their supplies from the backs of their saddles and handed a lacy blue and white parasol to her. She opened it, and from her perch atop the mare admired the view as James set up the picnic.

His muscles flexed beneath his jacket as he unrolled the large quilt and snapped it in the air before letting it float to the ground, half in the sun, half in the shade. He propped her crutches against a tree trunk and set a bag in the shade. Olivia hoped the bag held the hot cross buns—the mere thought of them made her mouth water.

He approached then, holding his arms out to her. She slid off her sidesaddle and wrapped one arm around his neck as he easily caught her. He slipped an arm beneath her knees and walked toward the blanket. After he set her down in the shade on the soft cotton quilt, she closed the parasol, put it aside, and removed her bonnet. The day was warm, and she was thinking that it wouldn't bother her one bit if James were to remove his jacket. Or shirt, for that matter.

He tended to the horses, watering them and feeding them a few apples before tying them to a low bough several yards away. He paused at the edge of the stream to wash his hands and shook them dry, then joined her on the blanket, sprawling his long, muscular legs in front of him.

They began their meal with wine that he poured from a canteen into rustic tin cups, and it tasted better than anything she'd sipped from a crystal glass.

"For the first course," he said, "we can dine on sandwiches or sweet buns. Name your preference."

At last, an easy decision. "Sweet buns."

There were four, and after Olivia ate two—which were every bit as heavenly as she'd remembered—she decided to forgo the other offerings, at least for the time being. As James refilled her cup with wine, he said, "I think we should talk."

Olivia looked into the green eyes that she'd once trusted...and still adored. "I agree. What would you like to start with?"

"Your father's letter."

"I'm not discussing the contents with you," she said.

"I understand. I won't push you to reveal what he said if you don't want to. However, I don't think we should keep secrets from each other."

Ah. *Now* he didn't want to have secrets. She bit back the remark, closed her eyes, and listened to the soothing gurgling of the river.

"I planned to tell you about the letter that night—the night Huntford found us. I was about to, but you looked so...so...beautiful. You can be damned distracting. I don't expect you to believe me, and maybe it doesn't make a difference anyway, but I thought you should know."

Olivia gazed at his slumped shoulders and haunted face. Yes, she believed him. Besides, she was still glowing on the inside from the fact that she'd distracted him with her beauty.

"I should have told you about the letter before—I wanted to—but I didn't want to betray your brother either. I should never have gotten involved in your family's business anyway. I'm sorry."

"Is that why you visited my brother the day after the Easton ball? To discuss the letter with him?"

James nodded slowly.

"Do you want to know how foolish I am?"

"You're not foolish."

"I thought you'd come to ask Owen for my hand in marriage."

"Oh, Olivia. I'm sorry," he said again.

"I think it is I who should be sorry. I never should have kissed you on the terrace. That's what started this whole series of unfortunate events—from your fight, to my sprained ankle, to the coach's broken axle, to my fall from grace. All of it could have been avoided. If I'd only refrained from kissing you."

James lay on his side and propped himself on an elbow. "I'm not sorry you kissed me. And I distinctly recall kissing you back. And liking it."

She tried not to look into his seductive eyes—truly, she did—but she'd never been able to resist their pull, more powerful than the tide. Something warm stirred in her belly, and it almost melted her resolve to keep her distance. Almost.

"We've both made mistakes, and now we must live with the consequences. But there's no need for you to miss out on exploring the Egyptian ruins, not when you've waited so long for this opportunity. I want you to go." She managed to utter the words without the slightest tremor in her voice. It was imperative that he believe she was perfectly fine with sending him off shortly after their wedding and living in solitude for two years.

He sat up then. "Are you certain? The *ton* will think it odd."

"That's not a good reason to give up your dreams. You have the chance to go on an adventure that comes along only once in a lifetime. Why would you bow to convention?"

"I wouldn't want you to be an object of ridicule. I care for you."

Olivia swallowed the knot that formed in her throat. He cared for her but made no mention of love. Summoning all her acting skills and every ounce of courage she possessed, she said, "I care for you, too. And that won't change just because you spend a couple of years away. We can begin our life together when you return."

"You are very generous, Olivia."

She shrugged as if it were a trifling matter. "It's not as though I'm accustomed to married life. Little would change for me, I suspect. I could move into your house, where I'd be close to my brother and sister and could visit any time I liked. I'd spend the rest of my time doing a bit of decorating and getting to know your staff."

"I don't have a large staff—just a housekeeper, cook, and maid."

"I can hire additional people if it seems necessary." She congratulated herself on sounding so matter-of-fact while discussing these sorts of mundane details while, inside, her heart was breaking. "I can take care of things at home while you're away—I can even visit your mother and brother."

"No, I'd rather you didn't."

"Very well," she said coolly, pretending that his curt reply didn't sting in the least.

"I don't know what to say. After the events of the last few days, I never imagined that you would encourage me to leave on my expedition as planned." His face broke into a cautious smile, and she knew she was doing the right thing.

"I see no reason why our marriage should change your plans. Lots of husbands and wives spend time apart."

He gazed out at the sparkling summer day, a thoughtful look on his handsome face. After several moments of silence, he turned to her. "I want you to know how much this means to me. Thank you."

Tentatively, he reached out and cupped her cheek, then leaned in and pressed his lips to hers. He kissed her so tenderly, so sweetly, that it almost hurt. Her body begged for more—his tongue in her mouth, his hands on her skin, his body melded to hers—but they both kept their passion in check. She savored the cinnamon taste of him, the warm breeze that tickled the curls on the back of her neck, and the simple fact that, for now at least, they were together.

He abruptly ended the kiss and looked up at the leaves rustling above them. "If you'll excuse me for a few moments, I'm going to take a short walk, stretch my legs. Do you need anything before I go?"

She briefly touched a finger to her lips, still tingling from their kiss, and shook her head. "Feel free to explore. I shall be fine." She could use a moment to collect herself as well.

James shot her a grateful smile, scooped up his bag, and strode toward the narrowest part of the stream, which he crossed in one long jump and followed on the other side. Olivia watched him as he walked away, and when she could no longer see him, she lay back on the quilt and sobbed.

Chapter Twenty

One chaste kiss with Olivia had left James as hard as a rock. He'd wanted to reach under her skirts and touch her till she moaned with pleasure. He'd wanted to strip off her clothes and lay wildflowers on her belly. He'd wanted to bury himself in her and make her his, once and for all, forever.

But if he was going to Egypt, he could not seduce her. No matter that they would soon be husband and wife. He could not risk getting her with child.

So he'd scooped up his bag, which contained a few basic digging tools, and walked away, hoping to cool off. He followed the winding river, staying close, in case Olivia should need him.

He stopped at a bend where the bank sloped gradually to the water, shrugged off his jacket, and rolled up his sleeves. The lazy current meandered over rocks and branches, too weak to sweep away anything more than a few leaves and twigs. He leaned over the stream and splashed water on his face, letting cool droplets trickle down his neck.

He hadn't expected Olivia to encourage him to leave on his expedition at summer's end. Most new brides would petulantly demand their husbands' time and attention. But she was giving him a gift.

As the truth of that struck him, his gaze automatically scanned the landscape and rested on the wall of hard-packed earth in front of him. Several rocks jutted from the claylike embankment, and something about their arrangement struck him as odd. They seemed too uniformly spaced to have been randomly deposited by the stream, so he rummaged through his bag, located a small pick, and began to break away at the soil.

The digging wasn't strenuous, and the steady thump of metal sinking into the clay provided a welcome distraction. He concentrated on a one-yard span of embankment, methodically chipping no more than a few square inches of dirt at a time. Before long, dust covered his hands and sweat glistened on his arms. Though he found nothing more than a collection of stones the size of his fist, the way they lined up suggested that they may have been a boundary of some kind.

He checked the position of the sun in the sky—he'd been known to lose track of time while digging—and packed his things in his bag. While washing up in the stream, he was already making plans to return to the spot and continue his digging. His head was full of questions about the stones and who might have once inhabited this idyllic spot by the river.

Oddly enough, he couldn't wait to share his discovery— meager though it was—with Olivia.

He hurried back toward the tree where he'd left her. From yards away, he spotted the quilt lying in the shade.

With no one on it.

His heart hammered and he picked up the pace, jogging as he scanned the surrounding area looking for her. Surely a pink dress trimmed in white would stand out against the green backdrop. And then it did.

He drew up short when he saw her. She sat on a large flat rock with her skirt hiked up to her knees, toes dangling in the water. Leaning forward, looking into the stream, she offered him an enticing view of her breasts above the rounded collar of her gown. Her crutches lay on the grass behind her, abandoned.

She didn't see him at first, and he didn't want to startle her by shouting. But then she looked up, smiled, and waved, warming something deep inside him.

He joined her on the rock, took off his boots, and sank his feet into the chilly water next to hers.

"Isn't it heavenly?" she asked. "I feel cooler all over."

"Your bandage is gone."

Raising her chin, she said, "I took it off. It doesn't hurt... well, as long as I don't walk on it."

"I hope you weren't bored while I was gone."

She arched a brow. "I'm capable of amusing myself."

He nodded, wondering if she was implying she was capable of amusing herself for two whole years while he was in Egypt.

"I began digging at a spot a little farther downstream."

Her eyes rounded. "Did you find anything?"

"Not yet. But it might be promising."

"Don't let me keep you from it. I'm content to remain here if you'd like to return."

"No," he said quickly. "I'd rather spend the afternoon here with you... talking."

"Very well." She smiled encouragingly. "What would you like to discuss?"

"I've been thinking that I should write to my mother and brother," he surprised himself by saying, "to inform them of our engagement."

"That's a lovely idea." Brown eyes alight, she said, "Do you think they'd be able to attend our wedding? I'm eager to meet them."

"I don't think so." The day would be full of drama as it was. James didn't want to place Ralph in the middle of it. He didn't want his brother to feel like some kind of pariah. Besides, it was too far and difficult for him to travel.

"I understand," she said evenly.

"My family situation is complicated," James admitted. "You are fortunate to have such a close relationship with your brother and sister."

"Perhaps. Although at times I find my brother's involvement in my life to be extremely *in*convenient," she said pointedly. "I don't pretend to know the challenges you've faced in having a younger brother with physical limitations. But I do know that family is family and it's a bond that can never be broken."

She was right. And no matter what excuses he made, their wedding would be an excellent opportunity to introduce his brother to Olivia and Huntford, at least. "Family is family," he repeated. "Thank you for reminding me of that. I shall write to my mother and Ralph this evening and encourage them to come to Haven Bridge."

"Truly?" She swirled her feet in the water, clearly delighted. He found himself delighted by her happiness—and possibly the view of her bare legs.

"Do you think your sister will come?" he asked.

Her gaze snapped to his. "Hmm?"

"Lady Rose. Do you think she'll attend the wedding?"

"Oh, I hope so. Owen can be such a bear, though. I wouldn't be surprised if he banned her, Anabelle, and Daphne from attending just to spite me."

"Something tells me that nothing could keep them away."

"We're fortunate to have been blessed with siblings. I don't know what I'd do without mine." Her voice cracked a little on the last word, and she looked as though she might cry.

He placed a hand over hers, on the rock between them. "What's wrong?"

She sniffled and took a moment to compose herself before responding. "I wish I could leave Haven Bridge— just for a few days."

His gut clenched. "What? Why?"

"To return to London. There's something I need to take care of . . . someone I need to see."

He wanted to ask her *who*, but if she'd wanted him to know, she would have already said. "You could write to your brother and ask him."

"No, he'd never agree to let me leave this village before the wedding, and after all I've put him through, I don't blame him."

"Perhaps if he knew the reason?"

"I can't tell him—or anyone. Not yet."

"I see." Clearly she wasn't ready to trust James with her secret, whatever it was. And why should she? He tamped down his disappointment. "Would a letter suffice?"

"It's something that would best be accomplished in person," she said thoughtfully, "but I suppose a letter might be better than nothing."

"It sounds as though both of us have letters to write this evening," he said. "But for now, I have a suggestion."

"I'm listening."

"I propose that we eat the sandwiches I packed and rest a little before it's time to ride back to the inn."

A smile chased the seriousness from her face. "That sounds wonderful."

She turned to reach for her crutches, but he stood and swept her into his arms and whirled her around. She clung to his shoulders as he walked her to the quilt and set her down. After she adjusted her skirts and took off her bonnet, he handed her a sandwich.

"Are you going to return here tomorrow to explore some more?" she asked.

"I am."

"Do you think you might bring me with you again? I promise not to distract you. And I would be happy to bring our picnic."

Warmth bloomed in his chest. "I'd welcome your company tomorrow, with or without sandwiches. And though I am sure I'll find your presence a distraction, it will be the best possible kind."

Olivia poured wine into each of their tin cups and raised hers. "To new discoveries," she said.

James touched his cup to hers and drank, thinking that where his beautiful fiancée was concerned, there was much he longed to discover.

At the inn that evening, Olivia tried composing a letter to Sophia. Again. She'd started three times before, but all she had to show for those attempts were the crumpled papers littering her desktop. So before she began anew, she thought for several minutes, and then she wrote.

Dear Miss Rolfe,

You do not know me, but my late father was a friend of your mother's. I understand that she passed away several years ago, and I am most sorry for your loss.

I was recently made aware of a connection between us, and while I would prefer to elaborate in person, I am not currently at liberty to travel to visit you. You see, my older brother discovered me in a compromising position with his good friend and I find myself rather hastily engaged. I am currently in the small village of Haven Bridge in the Lakes and must remain here until my nuptials some three weeks hence.

If, by some chance, you are able to travel here before then, I should dearly love to make your acquaintance as well as impart further information, which I am certain you will find interesting. I am staying at the Fife & Frog inn.

I have also enclosed a lovely little sketch of your mother holding you when you were but a babe. I never had the pleasure of meeting your mother, but it is evident by the way she looks at you in the drawing that you were the center of her world.

Thank you for your kind consideration of my request to meet me in Haven Bridge before the summer's end. If you are unable to do so—and I certainly understand there are any number of reasons why you

*might be unable to join me—I shall seek you out upon
my return to London.*

*Sincerely yours,
Olivia Sherbourne*

There. She'd debated whether to include the bit about the scandal but figured that Sophia would find out the sordid truth sooner or later. Perhaps word had somehow spread to London and her half sister had already heard the stories about the notorious Lady Olivia.

Olivia smirked to herself, for the thought didn't trouble her nearly as much as it should have. And with that, she folded the letter and the sketch and carefully placed them in an envelope to go to London on the next mail coach.

The following day was even hotter than the day before. Once again, she and James rode to the spot beneath the tree, but Olivia was curious to see whatever it was that had captured James's attention. "May I watch you dig?"

He blinked in surprise. "Of course. If you don't mind being in the sun."

"I shan't wilt."

"Very well. It's downstream a bit."

A little farther on, Olivia spotted an old cottage in the woods, barely visible through the thick foliage. "Look," she said, pointing. "A little house. Do you suppose anyone lives there?"

"Stay here." James swung his leg over his horse and hopped lightly to the ground. "I'll investigate."

He returned less than a minute later. "Nothing but a shack. I'm guessing it's been deserted for years. Probably an old woodcutter's cottage. I'll ask Uncle Humphrey about it."

Olivia would have loved to see it for herself if walking weren't such a chore at the moment. Perhaps she'd have the opportunity on a future picnic.

"We're almost there," James said. "We'll set up camp at that next bend."

"Set up camp," she repeated, arching a brow. "Does this qualify as an expedition, then?"

He turned to her and frowned as though the mere suggestion were an insult. "Hardly. It's just a pleasant afternoon outing."

"Is that all?"

"With a beautiful woman," he added.

Olivia beamed. "While I appreciate the compliment, I must disagree with your conclusion. There are two of us exploring, and we have a specific destination in mind. You yourself said that we shall set up a camp, and I have brought provisions. I assume that you brought tools?"

"Of course."

"Well, then, what more could we possibly need in order for this outing to count as an expedition?"

His beautiful mouth slowly curled into a heart-melting smile. "Nothing. I assume you are willing to work. All the members of an expedition have duties, you know—responsibilities to the larger team."

"I'm more than willing to do my part." As long as it didn't require walking. And wouldn't soil her dress overmuch. Oh dear.

"Let's go."

They stopped near a bend in the stream, where the bank was waist-high and a wide, sandy area at the bottom sloped gently toward the water. From atop her horse, Olivia saw a dozen or so rocks lined up on the pebbly sand. "Is that what you found yesterday?" She'd been hoping for something more interesting, and preferably sparkling.

James dismounted and helped her do the same. She balanced herself beside the mare while he retrieved her crutches. "Yes," he said, his enthusiasm far out of proportion to the discovery, in Olivia's admittedly inexpert opinion. "They were jutting from the embankment, spaced just as I've arranged them there."

He handed her the crutches and she slipped them under her arms. "Are we going to look for more today?"

"Yes. But there's no telling what else we'll find. Sometimes the unexpected discoveries are the sweetest."

She fed the horses some carrots while James spread the quilt on the grassy embankment.

"If you're going to work down there"—she nodded toward the sand—"then I should, too."

Smiling broadly, he hopped off the embankment and spread the quilt by the stream, doubling it over so that it would fit. He waved her closer, took her crutches and laid them on the grass, then held his arms out to her.

She resisted the temptation to launch herself at him but did sink into his arms, sighing as her body pressed against the hard wall of his chest and slid down his taut abdomen. He prolonged the embrace, lowering her just an inch at a time, and his heart beat nearly as fast as hers. When at last her slippers touched the sand, she looked up at him—or, more precisely, his mouth—and parted her lips in invitation.

He bent his head and kissed her. A kiss that was soft,

sweet...and frustrating in the extreme. She leaned into him, letting her hips brush against the front of his trousers, and was gratified to know that he wasn't unaffected by her. When she bumped lightly into him, he groaned, cupped her cheek, and broke off the kiss.

"This is not the sort of thing we normally do on expeditions," he said.

"I should hope not." And yet she hoped for more.

James hopped onto the embankment to retrieve their bags and her parasol, and then, much to Olivia's delight, he removed his jacket. When he returned, he went straight to work, digging from left to right, slowly exposing more of the same smooth, evenly spaced stones that he'd unearthed the day before. He worked quickly but so carefully that if a teacup had been buried between two of the stones, she had no doubt he'd remove it quite intact.

Mesmerized by his brisk, efficient movements—not to mention his firm, beautifully sculpted backside— Olivia fantasized about their future. He was going away for a couple of years, but he'd come back to her. And then they'd start their life together. Perhaps he didn't love her now, but there was a chance that someday he would— even if he hadn't chosen to marry her of his own free will.

And while she could entertain herself all day thus, admiring the view of his thin shirt clinging to his muscled shoulders and back, she thought she might at least create the *illusion* that she was doing something useful. So, she withdrew a journal and a pencil, opened to a clean page, and wrote the date at the top. Then she began to sketch the stones that James unearthed. Thankfully, they were the smooth and uniformly shaped kind of stones that didn't require any sort of artistic skill to sketch.

She included labels to indicate the approximate distance between each of the rocks and made notes about the quality of the soil of the embankment and the texture of the sand below it.

She was so absorbed in her drawing that she was startled by the shadow that suddenly crossed her page. James stood over her, a thoughtful expression on his face. "What do you have there?"

Resisting the urge to snap the journal closed, she said, "It's my contribution to the expedition—a drawing. A crude one to be sure, but a drawing." And she handed the book to him, bravely offering up her meager efforts for his review.

He gazed at the pages crowded with her notes for several seconds, then looked at her, his expression unreadable. "Where did you learn to do this?"

"Where did I learn to draw an oval?" she asked. It was a far cry from Gainsborough.

"To sketch like this. It's remarkably accurate. You've represented the relative size and position of the stones, all seventeen of them."

"Yes, well, thank heaven that I wasn't required to count above twenty," she teased. "My accuracy tends to decline significantly after that number."

"I'm being serious, Olivia. This kind of drawing is just what I needed. You've even included notes about the soil and the sand." He shook his head in amazement, like she was some sort of stone-drawing prodigy. She had to admit it felt nice to be appreciated, to do something that James respected.

"I just jotted down a few bits of information I thought you'd want to remember, like the time of day and where the sun was in the sky, and the approximate distance from the site to the tree line." She *had* been rather proud of thinking to include that little detail. Perhaps she was better at sketching than she gave herself credit for. James's stare alternated between the journal page and her, like he couldn't decide which he was more enthralled with.

"It's perfect. May I borrow it? I'd love to show it to Humphrey. Your drawing would allow him to explore the far corners of his land from the comfort of his cat-hair-covered armchair. I'm certain he'll have some theories as to the use of the stones."

Inordinately pleased that he liked her rudimentary scribbles enough to share them with his uncle, she magnanimously said, "The journal is yours."

"Thank you, Olivia."

A thought occurred to her then, and bubbled out before she could stop it. "Is it possible I could join you on the expedition? That is, I realize I have little to offer in the way of—"

"No." James spoke firmly, even if his eyes showed regret. "Egypt is dangerous, and there will be no women in the group."

"Some woman has to be the first—it may as well be me."

"You are accustomed to soft mattresses and silk sheets. I can't imagine you among the scorpions and rabid camels."

He had a point there, but she would not be deterred. "I would give up every luxury to travel with you, to be at your side. And I know you'd protect me."

James ran a hand through his hair, let out a breath, and gazed into her eyes intently. "From this moment forward, I will *always* protect you. With my own life, if need be."

A delicious shiver ran through her.

"But the expedition is no place for you. Several members of the last group were lost to disease and drought—"

"James! I had no idea the trip was so fraught with peril. I shall worry about you desperately." Her heart was already pounding with dread.

He reached for her hand and smoothed the back of it with his thumb. "I am strong, and I've learned from the experiences of the teams who've gone before me. I'll be prepared. But I wouldn't subject you to such risks."

"I...I understand." But it still stung. "I'm afraid you shall not be able to prevent me from worrying about you."

"I shall be fine," he said so confidently, she almost believed him.

"You do seem rather invincible."

He arched a brow. "I am. And while Egypt is out of the question for you, there is plenty of exploring and digging to be done around here—if you'd like to pass the time with me."

"Of course I would." She would savor every day that remained with him. "And I'll be happy to add drawings of any other sites we explore around here."

God help her if he discovered an artifact with a remotely complicated shape. Anything more complex than a blob, and she'd be done for.

"That would be wonderful," James said, beaming at her like he meant it. He knelt beside her and placed the journal on the quilt.

Then he took off his shirt.

Surely, the heat had addled her head. This bare-chested

James was just a fantasy—one she'd imagined hundreds of times over the last decade.

But this was more vivid—more breathtakingly real—than any fantasy she'd had. Which was truly saying something.

The skin on his shoulders and chest was a little lighter than on his neck, and a fine sheen of perspiration made him glisten like Apollo. His nipples were flat and darker than her own, like the skin of a ripened peach. His broad shoulders tapered to a rippled abdomen and slim hips.

Olivia dug through her bag for her fan and waved it. Vigorously. When she finally trusted herself to speak, she said, "Ah, I think you are confused. This is not your dressing room, and I am not your valet."

He chuckled. "Thank the Lord for that." He mopped the front of his chest with his wadded shirt, then tossed it onto the bank above them.

She fanned herself harder. "What, precisely, are you doing?"

In one easy motion, he pulled off a boot and propped it near the riverbank. "Going for a swim." He took off the other boot and grinned. "You should join me."

"A . . . a swim?" she sputtered.

"More like a wade, I suppose."

"We're hardly twelve anymore," she said. As if either of them needed reminding. The proof stood before her. He was six feet of male. Chiseled, tanned male.

"You'd rather roast on the shore than take a refreshing dip?"

No. No, she wouldn't. But in order to protect her vulnerable heart, she was trying to keep some barriers between her and James. Barriers like clothes.

As though he'd read her thoughts, he said, "You can keep all or some of your clothes on if you'd like. Or not."

She considered stripping naked just to see if he would react as casually as he'd have her believe. But even *she* wasn't that daring.

"I thought this was an official expedition. Is swimming allowed?"

"Absolutely. And encouraged."

She was dreadfully hot. Her curls were wilted, and her cotton dress clung to her like a second skin. From a few feet away, the cool, clear water beckoned. "I'm quite comfortable here," she lied.

He shrugged, as if he didn't know the subtle movement would flex every muscle in his shoulders and chest, thereby causing her mouth to water. Damn him. "Suit yourself. You can stay there and admire the view."

"I presume you're referring to the rolling hills and the cloudless sky." She waved the fan with renewed vigor as he waded several yards into the river, then leaped in, dunking his head beneath the water. He emerged splashing, spraying cool droplets in sparkling arcs around him. His hair slicked away from his face, he looked even more virile and perhaps a little dangerous. Dear Lord, the heat was affecting her ability to think clearly.

"You wouldn't believe how good this feels," he called out, leaning back, floating, and closing his eyes like he was in ecstasy. His wet shoulders glistened in the sun and his impressive biceps were just visible above the waterline.

How she'd love to be in the river with him, his slick body next to hers, the water gently lapping at their chests.

She shifted her backside, numb from sitting for so long, and pretended the gritty sand in her shoe didn't bother her in the least. Sweat trickled between her breasts. "What does the bottom feel like?"

He opened his eyes and shot her a puzzled look. "The bottom?"

"Of the river." She smiled innocently, as if she could possibly be referring to anything else.

He seemed to think about that for a moment. "Just hard-packed sand and a few smooth stones."

"Nothing slimy?"

"Not unless you count the eels."

She shuddered. "That's not funny."

"If you join me, I promise to protect you from anything slimy. Where's your sense of adventure?"

Oh, it was alive and well. And it had gotten her into enough trouble already. "If you must know, I've been try- ing to suppress it."

"And have you been successful?"

"Quite." Granted, it had only been a few days. And she felt James chipping away at her willpower like so much soil beneath his pick.

"We're alone here, Olivia. In a few short weeks, we're going to be married. Don't be so obstinate."

She huffed. "I'm *not* being obstinate."

He floated closer, then took a few steps toward the shore till the water was knee level. His trousers molded to him, revealing every delicious inch of his hips, thighs, and, er, male parts. God help her.

"Then join me. I can't have you fainting from the heat."

She was about to swoon, that much was true—but not from the heat. As he continued striding toward her, she had the highly improper thought that she'd like to lick the rivulets of water running down his chest.

At last he stood over her, half naked and wholly captivating. He held out his hand to her, and a few blissfully cold drops plopped onto her arm.

She tossed aside her fan, disgusted with its ineffectiveness, and discarded her bonnet.

A girl could only resist so much wickedness, blast it all. She was going for a swim.

Chapter Twenty-One

Deity: (1) A god or supreme being, such as Hathor, the
Egyptian goddess of joy, motherhood, and love.
(2) One revered as supremely good, as in
He emerged from the river naked—and completely
unaware that he resembled a virile water deity.

James had seen the moment Olivia capitulated. When
a few water droplets landed on her skin, something in
her beautiful brown eyes gave in to the pure pleasure of it.

Now that he'd convinced her to go for a dip with him in
the river, he found himself intrigued by the possibilities.
She removed her slippers and set them next to her fan and
bonnet. He sent up a heartfelt prayer that the pile of discarded articles of clothing would grow.

And it seemed someone in heaven was listening.

Olivia hiked her gown up to her knees, reached beneath
the skirt, and rolled off her silk stockings. Into the pile
they went. James's mouth went dry.

She reached up for the hand he'd extended and stood—
on one foot—facing him. "Given the circumstances,"

she said, "the most prudent thing for me to do is remove my gown. If I wore it into the river, it would take hours to dry."

"I couldn't agree more. Taking off the gown is the prudent course of action." He grinned.

Rolling her eyes, she hopped and turned at the same time, presenting her back to him.

Worried she'd lose her balance, he grasped her elbows. "Can I do something to help?" Though he was honestly trying to act the part of a gentleman, he didn't blame Olivia for shooting him a skeptical glance over her shoulder.

"No, thank you."

There was nothing for him to do but watch as she unbuttoned her gown, slipped the sleeves off her delectable shoulders, and shimmied out of the dress. She still wore her chemise and her stays over it, but she was already working on the laces at the front. A few moments later she tossed her stays onto the discard pile and faced him once more, her lush form leaving him drunk with desire.

He tugged at the frilly strap of her chemise and arched a brow. "Are you sure you don't want to remove this, too?"

She arched a brow right back at him. "Are you sure you wouldn't like to remove your trousers?"

"Actually, I would." He reached for his waistband, but Olivia grabbed his wrists.

"Never mind. Help me into the river before I lose my resolve."

He scooped her into his arms, surprised at how much lighter she felt without all the usual clothes and trappings. Her skin felt hot against his wet chest, and a few tendrils of hair dangled from her neck, tickling his shoulder. The closer they got to the water, the tighter she clung to him—like she wanted to avoid getting wet as long as possible. But after he'd taken a couple steps into the river, her feet—and luscious bottom—dipped below the water's surface, and she jumped.

She sucked in her breath and dug her fingers into his shoulders. "It's chilly."

"Give it a minute and try to relax." He loosened his hold on her, letting the water bear some of her weight, and sunk lower into the river until soon they were both submerged up to their chests.

Olivia sighed and let her head fall back, exposing inches and inches of creamy neck that practically begged to be kissed. "This . . . feels divine."

It did. He could think of several things that would feel even *more* divine, but for now, the cool water and the gentle pressure of her body against his were enough. She kept one arm coiled around his neck and swirled the other in the water, letting the weak current curl around her.

"It's been years since I've done anything like this. I'd forgotten what I was missing." She lay back, stretching so that she was almost horizontal in the water. Her chemise floated around her hips, giving him an excellent view of lithe, supple legs. Her full breasts thrust toward the sky, their taut peaks visible through the transparent cotton of her chemise. Her chestnut curls floated in the water around her head, giving her the look of a very naughty water nymph.

Dear Jesus. James swallowed hard. If he didn't put some space between them, their swim would turn into something else entirely. He took a step back, and though Olivia's eyes were closed, she immediately sensed he'd moved, lifted her head, and clasped her arms around his neck. As if that wasn't torture enough, she wrapped her legs around his waist. "Where are you going?"

"Nowhere. You seemed so relaxed. I thought you might like me to get out of your way."

"But I don't want to touch the bottom of the river, remember? There's the matter of my injured foot, and I'm not exactly an expert swimmer, and—"

"You're afraid you might encounter something slimy."

"Yes." She smiled guiltily and flexed her thighs more tightly, pressing against the front of his trousers and nearly driving him mad.

One of the straps of her chemise fell off her shoulder, and his gaze dropped to her smooth, almost pearlescent skin. Despite the cold water, his cock was hard and undeniably ready for action. "Olivia, I..." He swallowed.

He wanted to tell her that he cared for her. And *not* just because she had her legs wrapped around him. He loved that she wanted to meet his brother and that earlier that morning she'd surreptitiously pressed a few wildflowers into her journal. He loved that she'd do anything for her family and that she was stubborn enough to hop through a cow field on one foot in the rain.

He just loved...being with her.

And he wanted to make her his. Now.

He looked into her brown eyes, dark with desire, and felt his heart squeeze in his chest. "There's something I need to say."

"Yes?" She wriggled closer, till their breath mingled in the air between them, and stared at his mouth. Like she wanted him to kiss her. With a cool fingertip, she traced little circles on his nape.

"Well, the thing is…"

She pressed warm lips to the side of his neck and sucked lightly, then greedily ran her hands down his back and up his sides till he thought his knees would buckle. He knew he should stop her and tell her what he felt for her. But other parts of his body were in charge at the moment. There was no reining them in.

So he slid his hands beneath her bottom and guided her closer, letting her feel his arousal and the perfect fit of their bodies.

With a soft moan, she rubbed against his cock.

All the passion they'd been denying suddenly burst free, their self-control shattering like a dam that had been patched one too many times. She speared her fingers through his damp hair and thrust her tongue between his teeth. He slipped a hand inside her chemise, caressed her breast, and continued to rock against her, driving them both into a breathless, dizzy, desperate frenzy.

Being with her felt so right. Holding her tightly, he walked to the shore and gently lowered her to the quilt. Her chemise was plastered to her legs and torso, and the slight summer breeze made her shiver. Before he could suggest removing the soaked garment, she did it, pulling it over her head in one smooth motion. She tossed it onto the discard pile and leaned back on her elbows with a knowing, wicked smile.

Dear God, he was in trouble.

And he wouldn't have it any other way.

He didn't take his eyes off her as he fumbled with the front of his trousers. Her damp hair dark against her shoulder, the flush on her cheeks, the perfect globes of her breasts, and her long, smooth legs made his heart beat out of control. If he lived to be ninety, he'd forever remember the way she looked at him, full of anticipation, trust, and love.

At last he shed his trousers and lay next to her on the quilt. Skin to skin, they explored each other, reveling in each small sigh and moan. She sat astride him and traced the contours of his chest, pausing to lick his nipples like a cat lapping up milk. When she began to trail kisses down his abdomen, he stopped her and rolled her onto her back.

"My turn." He touched between her legs and parted her slick folds with his fingers, watching her intently to see what pleased her. When she closed her eyes and arched her back, he lowered his head and tasted her, teasing her with his tongue until she came apart and cried out in ecstasy.

While they each caught their breath, they lay side by side on the shore. Just beyond their feet, the water trickled past, lapping softly at the rocks. The sun winked overhead, warming their bodies. It should have been a relaxing, tranquil scene, but James was so aroused that nature's beauty was quite wasted on him.

"It feels so wicked and wanton to be lying naked out of doors," Olivia said. "I confess I like it." She leaned over him and plundered his mouth, letting her bare breasts brush against his chest. As she hungrily kissed him, she reached down and stroked his cock, moaning softly into his mouth as though touching him pleased her as much as it did him.

Which he very much doubted. There was nothing tentative or shy about the way she touched him. Or about the way she did *anything*.

Olivia had always been the kind of woman who knew what she wanted, and James was very, very lucky that for some unknown reason, she wanted him.

The problem was that if she continued kissing and touching him with such delightful abandon, their love-making would be over before it had begun in earnest.

So, he took both of her wrists and with one hand pinned them on the ground above her head. He closed his eyes and focused on breathing evenly for five seconds, hoping to regain some semblance of control.

When he opened his eyes, Olivia shot him a wicked smile. "I haven't hurt you, have I?"

"No, beautiful. You've enchanted me."

"Well, that was shockingly easy."

"I mean it, Olivia."

"I know. I feel the same way. I want to be with you. Right now."

James's blood thrummed in his veins and his pulse pounded in his ears. He positioned himself between her legs and kissed the sweet column of her neck as he slowly eased himself into her. She inhaled deeply as her body stretched to accommodate him.

"I'm sorry," he gasped, hating the thought of hurting her.

"Don't be." She cradled his face in her hands. "This is what I've wanted, what I've dreamed of for so long."

He didn't check the raw, powerful, hot desire he felt. Olivia wouldn't let him, anyway. Seductive, sensual, and sweet—she was his.

He rocked against her, slowly at first, letting her get used to him. But when she thrust her hips and wrapped her legs around him, he let instinct take over. He pumped harder, losing himself in her tight heat, in the sweet smell of her neck, and in the salty taste of her skin.

God, she felt good.

He wished he could have made the moment last all day. Hell, he would have been happy if he'd managed to last more than a few minutes. But he couldn't. He came fast and hard, saying her name over and over.

She wrapped her arms around him and buried her face in his shoulder as he caught his breath. In all his life, he'd never been so content. So happy. Though he would have liked to remain just so all day, he realized it might not be the most comfortable position for Olivia. And he could already feel the sun burning his ass.

So he carefully withdrew and propped himself on an elbow beside her.

She looked gorgeous. Her hair was a mass of damp, wild curls and her lips were swollen from their kisses. But there, on her cheek, was the unmistakable, shiny track of a freshly shed tear.

Alarm shot through him. "What's wrong?"

"Nothing—that is, I don't know. I was just overcome by all sorts of feelings." She swiped at the tear, and James instinctively reached for his handkerchief before recalling that he was, in fact, naked.

"I'm sorry," he said again.

"What are you apologizing for?" He got the impression that he'd somehow made things worse.

"For upsetting you. Here, let me get something to cover you." The quilt wasn't large enough to wrap around her, so he picked up her dress from the heap of clothes and draped it over her.

Sniffling, she sat up and clutched the gown to her breasts. "Thank you."

And then, because she was squinting from the sun's glare, he retrieved her parasol, opened it, and held it out to her.

She looked up at him, blinked, then burst into laughter.

"What?" he asked, glancing from side to side.

"It's very kind of you"—she hiccupped midlaugh—"but it's just that I've never"—*snort*—

"Never *what*?"

She wiped the tears from her eyes. "Seen a naked man hold a lace-edged parasol."

"Right. Here you go." He handed her the parasol, thinking it was fortunate that he wasn't insecure about his body—and how he adored the sound of her laughter.

He grabbed his trousers and wrung them out over the river before putting the clammy, stiff things back on. It was time for Olivia and him to have a serious conversation about their future—a feat that would probably best be accomplished while he wore at least *some* clothes.

They'd made love, and that changed everything. There could be a babe. And if there was, he shouldn't be in Egypt when the child was born. Like ancient ruins in a sandstorm, his life's dream was crumbling.

"Would you like a drink?"

"Maybe in a bit." She tilted her head. "I realize that I'm the one who's a watering pot, but it seems like you have something on your mind."

"I would like to talk. You see, I've made a decision about the expedition."

"Oh?"

"I'm not going."

Her brows knitted. "Of course you are."

Why would she contradict him? "No, I'm not. I'm staying here in England, with you."

"That's ridiculous, James. This expedition is your dream. You'd be a fool to give up the chance to go."

He agreed with her on some level. How he wished he didn't have to choose. "You deserve a husband who'll stay by your side."

"Well, naturally, you'd feel obliged to tell me that after we...after we did what we did. You're being a gentleman."

"No, damn it. I'm not."

"You must admit that your timing is suspect."

"Why does the timing matter? I've realized my place is with you."

"Was that before or after I'd removed my gown?"

"After, I think."

She nodded emphatically as if to say, *That's what I thought.*

Olivia inhaled deeply. *I've realized my place is with you.* It wasn't quite a declaration of love, but it was close. These were the words she'd longed to hear, and yet the timing was all wrong. She'd loved him for ten long, exasperating years. He could have chosen any time during that decade to return her affections. Year seven would have been perfectly acceptable. Or year nine. But it was only *after* they'd been caught in bed together, forced into an engagement, and made love to each other that his feelings had caught up with hers.

Now, when she'd realized that she didn't want to be the reason he stayed.

James's sense of honor was making him do this. If he knew how much she'd miss him or how worried she'd be for his safety, he'd give up his spot on the expedition. He'd stoically set aside his own ambitions and remain at her side—for her sake. He'd say that he didn't care about the expedition, that she had saved him from two years of bad food and primitive living conditions.

So, if she truly wanted him to go to Egypt, she had to convince him that she was indifferent, when she was anything but.

She focused on the task at hand and tried not to look directly at James's bare chest, because that had the same effect on her decision-making abilities as gulping down three glasses of wine. She also endeavored to ignore the fact that she was naked. The way James's sultry gaze roved over her arms and legs suggested that he was having difficulty ignoring her lack of clothing as well. She felt a flush creep up her neck. As he stroked the back of her hand, her whole arm tingled.

"I thought this was what you wanted."

She shrugged. "I think I've grown up in the last couple of weeks. I've learned that I can't tie up all my hopes and dreams in one person. I need to rely on myself and be comfortable in my own skin."

A small, wicked smile lit his face. "I *love* the way you look in your own skin."

Heavens. Was he listening to her at all?

"I won't pretend I don't care for you," she said, "because I do. I just think that, given the way we became engaged, it might actually be a good thing for us to spend some time apart. You could go on your expedition and explore to your heart's content. I could spend some time with my family and get to know yours. We'll both have time to adjust to the idea of being married. After all, we'll be spending the rest of our lives together."

"You need time to adjust?"

"Naturally. I've never had a husband before."

"I've never had a wife before either. But I think we'll be good together."

A lump the size of one of James's blasted stones settled in her throat, and her eyes began to burn. *This is the time to be strong, Olivia. Strong and convincing.* She pulled her hand away. "I would have never guessed you were so sentimental, James. You know, one of the things I've always admired about you is your analytical, logical nature."

"I thought it infuriated you."

"Perhaps it frustrated me, occasionally, but I respect the way you make decisions so thoughtfully, without giving in to emotions or impulse."

"But you're one of the most impulsive people I know."

"Precisely! That's why I require a husband who is steady, one who stays the course."

"What are you trying to say, Olivia?"

"That you've been planning this trip to Egypt for months—nay, years—and you shouldn't let an impromptu wedding affect those plans. Go on your expedition. Explore like you've always wanted."

He stared at her as though he couldn't believe his ears. "There could be a babe."

Dear Lord, she'd forgotten about that. She did some quick calculations. "I don't think so." She kept her voice light. "But I'll know for certain within the week."

"I see." He raked his fingers through his hair and clasped his hands behind his neck. Olivia had to look away because the sight of his flexed arms was making her light-headed. "If you were with child," he said, "I'd never leave you."

Sweet. Except she supposed that implied the opposite: that if she wasn't pregnant, he *would* leave. "All I'm suggesting is that while we may not have had a choice in getting engaged, we do when it comes to the rest of our lives."

"You are correct. It *is* up to us." His green eyes simmered as he pushed a stray lock of hair behind her ear. "I know what I'd like to do right this minute."

She swallowed. He might not love her with the same ferocity that she loved him, but there was no denying the heat between them. The hungry, yet surprisingly tender, look on his face melted her like so much chocolate. "What might that be?"

Slowly, he peeled her dress away from her body. As his gaze roved over her, he drew in a breath. "I confess I want to do all sorts of wicked things with you. But first, I thought you might like another dip in the river to cool off, followed by lunch. What do you say?"

His smile made her whole body thrum, and when his eyes strayed to her breasts and lower, she felt like a ripe peach that he was about to pluck from a tree. "That sounds...heavenly."

He scooped her up easily and carried her back into the river, where the water tickled first her toes, and then her bottom, and then her breasts. She straddled him and traced the line of his jaw, reveling in the rough feel of his stubble beneath her fingertip. He kissed her sweetly and ran his big hands over her back as the cool, gentle current soothed the slight soreness between her legs. An insistent pulsing began there, and she pulled him closer, clawing at his back and tugging on his hair.

"Jesus, Olivia." He bent his head, drew her nipple into his mouth, and suckled her till she was writhing from the sheer pleasure of it. And when he slipped his hand between them and touched her, she was lost.

"I want you," she breathed. "Please." She rubbed herself against him, pleased to find him aroused, for in spite of her bravado, she really had very little idea of how these things worked. She did know, however, that his trousers presented an impediment and set about rectifying that small matter. She tugged on the front of them until something gave, and James laughed into her mouth—a sound so delicious she wanted to eat him up.

"I think you just fed one of my buttons to the fishes."

"Shhh. I don't want to think about the fishes right now. Just help me."

His eyelids were heavy and his smile knee-melting as he obliged her, unbuttoning the placket at the front of his trousers until she could finally hold his shaft, smooth and oh so rigid against his belly.

"Can we do it like this?"

He muttered something that might have been a curse, a prayer of thanks, or both. "We can. Are you sure you're ready, so soon after we...?"

Dear God, she was ready. She may not be able to tell him that she still loved him desperately or that she hated the thought of spending the first two years of her marriage without him beside her. But she could love him with her body. She could create a memory that they'd both tuck away and save for the nights when a thousand miles separated them. "I'm ready."

His hand on her hip, he guided her lower, until he was poised to enter her. "We'll take it slowly this time."

She may have pouted in response, because he chuckled and said, "Trust me."

She should have known she could trust him.

He filled her, then let her take the lead, setting the pace and rhythm. The sun shone on their heads and the water kissed their skin as she moved on top of him, pushing up, then taking him deeper, over and over until her legs were locked around him and she was whimpering for the same kind of release she'd had before.

"Easy, love." Squeezing her bottom in both hands, he thrust fast and hard, increasing the friction between them until the sweet pulsing was shooting through her limbs and thundering in her ears. Being with James was nothing like she'd imagined. Because never in her life could she have imagined something so raw and powerful and wonderful. She arched her back and cried out as she surrendered to the rush that overcame her, pleasure pounding through her bones before slowly fading into something quiet and healing.

His handsome face creased with concentration, James touched his forehead to hers. Breathlessly, he said, "Hold on."

Olivia rallied what little strength she had left, and when he began to move inside her again, he met her thrust for thrust. She drew his lower lip into her mouth and raked her fingers over his chest and down his abdomen. He gasped, and every muscle in his body tensed as he called out her name—and came inside her, again.

Chapter Twenty-Two

An hour later, James and Olivia dozed, stark naked, beneath the shade of a large oak. He had moved the blanket there, wrung out their clothes, and left them in the sun to dry. They'd sipped wine from tin cups and devoured the bread and cheese they'd brought, along with a couple of juicy apples.

Sated and full, they'd lain on their backs and stared at the green canopy above them. James laced his fingers through hers, kissed the back of her hand, and pressed it to his chest, then drifted off to sleep.

Olivia must have done the same.

When she awoke, he was dressed and packing his tools in his bag. Her hair was matted to the side of her face and she feared she'd drooled a little on the quilt. Suddenly self-conscious, she sat up and drew her knees to her chest.

"Good morning, beautiful," he said, without the slightest hint of irony. How she loved him for that.

"It's the afternoon. And I'm sure I look like a hoyden."

"An adorable hoyden." He picked up her chemise, snapped it in the air to rid it of grass and pollen, and tossed it to her.

She quickly slid it over her head, sighing as the sun-soaked linen warmed her skin. While James retrieved the rest of her clothes, she raked her fingers through her tangled curls. It would be a miracle if she could coax them into any semblance of a respectable knot, but it was difficult to care. Especially when the afternoon had been so lovely and so...enlightening.

Her clothes felt tight and confining after a few hours of uninhibited bliss, but she supposed they were necessary before she and James rode back into Haven Bridge. After she'd dressed and repaired her hair the best she could, she slipped her crutches under her arms and followed James toward the horses.

"Wait." He halted midstride, his forehead furrowed. "I think I'll collect a sample of soil from the riverbank, something I can take back to Humphrey, along with your drawing. Would you excuse me just a moment?"

"I'll come with you."

He helped her walk the short distance to the river, and Olivia watched from the embankment while James hopped lightly to the sand. He slung his bag off his shoulder, withdrew a small drawstring pouch, and crouched beside the stones he'd unearthed earlier. He'd just scooped a handful of soil into the pouch and was tying the string when something in the bank behind him glinted in the sun. She blinked to be sure she wasn't seeing things. Sure enough, there amid the dirt, a speck of metal winked.

"James, I think you just uncovered something."

He looked down where he'd been digging. "Another rock?"

"No. It's shiny." She shuffled to the edge of the grass and pointed. "There."

He crouched again and brushed his fingers over the newly exposed soil. "Ah, I've got it." He stood, faced her, and opened his palm to reveal a small clump of soil. Gingerly, he pushed the dirt away to reveal a small metal ring.

"Incredible," he whispered, moving closer so that she could see.

"Oh," she said, striving to sound equally awed, even though it was hard to appreciate the band while it was caked with mud.

James rubbed the ring clean against the sleeve of his jacket, carefully rinsed it in the river, and dried it. His voice low with wonder, he said, "I think it's gold, Olivia. And likely very, very old."

His face was alight with excitement, and she could almost see his mind spinning, playing out the possible histories of the ring, imagining who might have worn it. And in that moment, she truly understood this passion of his. It wasn't about achieving fame or fortune so much as touching a piece of the past. "Would you like to give me the journal? I can add some more notes and indicate where—"

"No." He jumped up onto the grass and held out the ring. "Let's see if it fits."

Now the gold sparkled in his palm, looking like it could have come straight from a fancy jeweler's on Bond Street. Olivia hesitated a moment, then swallowed and held out her right hand—since wearing any sort of band on the left before her wedding might be inviting bad luck. Even so, her traitorous fingers trembled.

James's own hand was steady and his smile broad as he slid the ring on. "It's perfect," he breathed, smoothing his thumbs over the back of her hand while they admired the ring together. "It's yours, Olivia. I want you to have it."

"Shouldn't you give it to Uncle Humphrey? This is his land."

"He'd want you to have it. I'm sure."

"But . . . but you haven't even properly studied it yet. We don't have any idea whom it belonged to. Maybe some poor picnicker dropped it and will return looking for it."

James laughed. "A mere seven hundred years too late."

The hairs on the back of her neck prickled. How strange to be wearing something that might have been crafted in the Middle Ages. "It's that old?"

"Quite possibly. Humphrey has been telling me stories, and he's long believed that there was once a church or monastery somewhere along the river, dating back to the twelfth century."

Heavens. "All the more reason why I can't keep it." She tried to slip it off, but it wouldn't slide past her knuckle. James pressed her hand between his palms.

"If you hadn't seen it, it would have been washed away with the next heavy rain and deposited on the bottom of the river, not to be found for another seven hundred years—if ever." She opened her mouth to object, but he shook his head, raised her hand to his lips, and kissed it softly. Almost reverently. "Of all the people who have walked on this ground, I think you were meant to find it. You. And of all the days you could have found it, I think you were meant to find it today, which, in my mind at least, was pretty special."

Something warm and tingly stirred in her belly. It

almost sounded as though her logical, scientific, number-loving fiancé believed in fate. "It *was* special."

"Then it's settled. The ring is yours. I'll still purchase you a wedding band," he added, "but you and I will know that this ring symbolizes our wonderful afternoon by the river."

"And *in* the river," she added mischievously. "Don't forget about that."

His mouth curled into a wicked grin. "As if I could."

James cradled her face and kissed her like they were in front of a church.

It might have been the very best moment of her life—if she didn't know that her happiness would come to an abrupt halt when he left for Egypt in a few short weeks.

"Uncle Humphrey, I'd like you to meet my fiancée, Lady Olivia." James sidestepped a cat that darted from the room, and Olivia bumped into an odd sculpture on a low table, steadying it just before it tipped over.

"At last." Humphrey gripped the arms of his chair in order to hoist himself out of it, but Olivia stopped him. "Please, don't get up. It's a pleasure to meet you, Mr. Crompton." She smiled and bobbed her head.

"Pshaw, we're to be family. You must call me Uncle Humphrey." The man's rheumy but kind eyes focused on Olivia, crinkling at the corners. "I've been asking James to bring you around for days. I know this place isn't exactly Carlton House, but I haven't forgotten how to play the part of host. I think we can round up some tea, can't we, James?"

Before he could respond, Olivia smoothly removed a stack of books from an ottoman, set them on the floor, and sat across from Humphrey. "Thank you, but I did not come for tea, only conversation. And though I've never been to Carlton House, I suspect that even if I had, I'd prefer your cottage, with books and curiosities in every corner."

The old man nodded his approval. "How is your ankle? What happened to your crutches?"

James snorted. "An excellent question, Uncle. She should be—"

"I have decided to use them for kindling," Olivia interrupted. "And my ankle is much improved, thank you."

"Glad to hear it. No bride should have to walk down the aisle with crutches if she can avoid it."

"Agreed," she said, happy to have found an ally in James's uncle. "And how are you feeling?"

He dismissed her question with the wave of a gnarled hand. "I tire easily. What else would you expect of a man my age? But I shall be at the church on the day you and James marry. I wouldn't miss it for the world."

"I'm glad to hear it."

James held up the bouquet of wildflowers that Olivia had picked on her way to the cottage. "Uncle, these are from Olivia. I'm going to see if I can find a vase for them."

"Go on, then, but don't use the African clay vessel— it's from the fifteenth century, and it leaks. Oh, and don't use the Greek vase with the Orpheus painting either. The cats already broke the matching one."

James rolled his eyes and wandered toward the back of the cottage. "I'll find something."

"Excellent," pronounced Humphrey, watching James walk away. "Now we may speak freely. I must have a look at this ring. May I?" He held out his hand.

"Of course. By all rights, it's yours."

He chuckled. "I have no need for it, and you found it."

Olivia tugged at the ring, but it wouldn't budge. "My finger must be a bit swollen," she said apologetically.

"No matter, let me see."

She stood before him and extended her hand, feeling rather awkward as he grabbed the magnifying glass on the table beside him and peered through the lens at the ring. "It's very plain."

"But beautiful in its simplicity." Olivia felt the need to defend it.

"Oh, quite." Humphrey's eyes never left the gold band. "It has a slight bevel around the edges. Any inscription?"

Olivia frowned. She hadn't removed the ring since the day they'd discovered it—almost a week ago. "I don't know. There could be something on the inside."

The old man's eyebrows shot up his wrinkled forehead. "I'm surprised James didn't check."

"Speaking of James," Olivia said, glancing toward the door where he'd left, "I know that he inherited his love of antiquities and exploring from you. May I ask you something of a personal nature?"

Humphrey set down his magnifying glass and laced his fingers together. "Certainly, my dear. Ask away."

"Have you ever been on a large expedition?"

"No." A wistful expression settled over his lined face. "I wanted to, though. I yearned for the adventure, the thrill of uncovering the secrets of the past."

"What prevented you from going?"

"Responsibilities kept me here for many years. After that, my health prevented me from travel. So I must content myself with books and other men's accounts of their discoveries. I regret not going when I was young and able, but it's hardly a tragedy." Except, the pained expression on his face suggested it was.

Olivia had suspected as much, but even so, her heart sank. "James is considering giving up his spot on the expedition, and I don't want him to. This is his dream and the opportunity of a lifetime. He must go to Egypt."

"It's generous of you to give him your blessing and encouragement. But whether or not he goes is his decision." He tented his fingers and shook his head thoughtfully. "I certainly don't envy him, having to choose."

"What will it be like for him? Is it very dangerous?"

"It can be. The area where he's traveling is far from England's civilized shores. Other groups have suffered from the lack of food and water, diseases, and horrible, swarming insects." Humphrey must have seen the alarm she felt, because he quickly added, "But James's team will be well prepared, and he's a far cry from your typical pampered Englishman. He can defend himself against anyone."

That *was* some comfort. "Would you help me?" Impulsively, she reached out and clasped Humphrey's hand. "Would you reason with him? Convince him to go? I can see how sad you are that you never had the chance, and I don't want him to feel that way. I don't want him to squander this opportunity because of me."

"Young lady, if there is one thing I've learned in all my seventy-some years, it's that logic is no match for love."

She shook her head. "I don't think love is a part of this equation. Did James tell you that my brother is forcing us to marry?"

The old man quirked a brow. "It makes little difference."

Oh, but it did. To her, at least. "He didn't have a choice."

"We *always* have choices, my dear."

"Yes," she said thoughtfully. "Yes, we do." Looking into Humphrey's kind old eyes, she added, "Please, promise me that you'll encourage him to go—no matter what. I know that, in his heart, he still longs to go. He belongs on that expedition."

Humphrey opened his mouth to respond, but James strode into the room.

"Here we are." He proudly presented the flowers, which he'd stuffed into a pitcher. Water dripped down the sides and several of the flower stems bent at odd angles. He looked about the room for a flat, available surface on which to place the arrangement.

"Shall I set that on the mantel?" Olivia took the flowers and attempted repairs before placing the pitcher out of the reach of the cats. She hoped Humphrey realized that she didn't wish to continue the conversation about the trip in front of James.

"Lady Olivia, I must compliment you on your excellent drawings. I feel as though I'm there with you at the river. Such an idyllic spot, isn't it?"

A flush crawled up her neck as she nodded mutely. She and James had found it idyllic, indeed.

"Will you be returning there today?" Humphrey asked.

James flashed her a knowing smile. "There's much more to explore."

Heavens. If she had any hope of encouraging James to leave her, she needed to stop spending so much time with him. "Actually, I need to return to the inn. I'm woefully behind on my correspondence." It was true—she was always behind on her correspondence.

"Allow me to walk you back," James offered.

"There's no need. Stay and enjoy your uncle's company." Turning to Humphrey, she said, "Thank you for sharing your insight and wisdom, sir. It's easy to see why you are James's favorite uncle."

"And it's easy to see why he chose you as his fiancée," he said, with a slight emphasis on the word *chose*.

"I look forward to seeing you again soon." Olivia reached for one of his hands and gave it an affectionate squeeze.

But as she started to pull away, he gripped her fingers surprisingly hard, keeping her there. His eyes were glassy and his mouth opened slightly, as though he were in a daze.

James moved to her side. "Are you all right, Uncle Humphrey?"

"What? Oh yes, I just had a feeling—I get them sometimes, you know." He looked up at Olivia like he knew all her secrets, and in a tremulous voice said, "It's the ring. You were meant to have it. It's important that you know that."

"I understand," she lied, because it seemed like what the old man needed to hear.

"Very good." He released her, laid his head against the chair, and closed his eyes like he was weary to the bone.

James smiled and raised a finger to his lips, then walked her toward the front door of the cottage. He leaned in as though he wanted to kiss her, but Olivia pretended not to notice. "Your uncle is a treasure. Thank you for the introduction."

"Are you sure I can't convince you to go to the river with me?"

She shook her head and started out the door. "I have some correspondence to tend to."

"I believe you mentioned that. Is something troubling you?"

"Of course not." She didn't look at him. "I've just been neglecting certain things, and while I've greatly, ah, enjoyed our afternoons at the river, I cannot squander every day there."

The hurt look that crossed his face made her want to throw her arms around him, but she couldn't give in to weakness. She was doing this for him.

He recovered quickly and smiled. "I do realize that I cannot demand your undivided attention *all* the time. Even if I wish I could."

"I appreciate your understanding."

He frowned. "You *would* tell me if anything was amiss, wouldn't you?"

"I would. In fact, there is something you should know." Blast, this was difficult. "You were concerned last week that after our, ah…."

"Lovemaking?"

"Yes. That I might be…"

"With child?" Something akin to hopefulness flashed in his eyes.

She nodded. "I'm not. I wanted to put your fears to rest."

"They weren't exactly fears, Olivia. I—" He looked like he wanted to say more, but clamped his lips shut.

"I've been thinking," she continued, "that it would be prudent to postpone any further…lovemaking…until after we are wed." And until after he returned from Egypt.

"I don't mind waiting, Olivia. It will only be another

week or so." Indeed, Owen would be returning to Haven Bridge with the marriage license any day now. "But we can still spend time together, can't we?"

How she longed to say yes, that she would happily spend every waking and nonwaking moment with him from now till eternity, doing anything he liked from digging, to drawing, to making love. "I don't think we should. It's bad luck for the bride to see her groom before the wedding."

"Superstitious tripe."

"I see no reason to tempt Fate."

He reached out, as though he intended to pull her close, kiss her till she was warm and pliable, and put an end to this nonsense. She stepped back.

His brow furrowed. "Did something happen? Uncle Humphrey didn't say something to make you uncomfortable, did he?"

"No," she said quickly. "Not at all. I'm sure most brides feel a bit anxious in the days leading up to their nuptials." It was remarkable how the lies came faster and easier now.

"Very well." He rubbed the back of his neck. "But you'll go back to being the Olivia I know right after the wedding, I hope."

"I'm certain I shall." She waved and set off down the walk, without looking back—so James wouldn't see her cry.

Chapter Twenty-Three

*Hieroglyphs: (1) Early Egyptian picture symbols,
dating to the fourth millennium BC.
(2) Indecipherable handwriting, as in*
Olivia's hastily scrawled letter was approximately
as legible as hieroglyphs.

Olivia had thought she'd return to the inn, ponder what Humphrey had told her, and consider how best to persuade James to go to Egypt. But the moment that she opened the door, Hildy pulled her into their room and glanced nervously into the hallway before closing the door. "A young woman was here, looking for you, my lady."

Olivia sucked in a breath. She'd all but given up on the hope that Sophia would respond to her letter. In retrospect, Olivia's invitation to meet her in this remote village had seemed silly at best and presumptuous at worst. "Who was it?"

"A Miss Sophia Rolfe."

Her heart beat faster. Her half sister *was* here. "Was she alone?"

"She was, indeed. I told her that you were out. She said that she's taken a room here for the night and would wait for you downstairs in the taproom."

Olivia removed her bonnet and handed it to the maid. "How did she look?"

Hildy tilted her head thoughtfully. "Her manners are fine, but her dress has seen better days. I don't believe she moves in the same circles as you and Lady Rose. Do you know her?"

"I know *of* her, but we've never met."

"That's very odd." Hildy frowned. "Why would she seek you out?"

"I wrote to her. We have more in common than you might suspect." Olivia checked her reflection in the looking glass above the washstand, took a deep breath, and smoothed her clammy hands down the front of her skirt. Now that the time had come to meet Sophia face-to-face, it occurred to her that she should have given some thought to the matter of how best to break the news to her. "This meeting will probably take a while."

"Shall I go with you?"

"No, thank you, Hildy." When the maid began to wring her hands, Olivia gave her wrist an affectionate squeeze. "There's no need to worry."

"You've already done a bit of walking today. Why don't I fetch Miss Rolfe and have some dinner sent up here for the two of you?"

"I shan't leave the inn." And before her maid could protest further, Olivia gave a little wave and made her escape.

The taproom was not crowded, and she had no difficulty spotting Sophia. She sat alone at a corner table, dark curls peeking from beneath her straw chip bonnet. Her head was bent over a book and the glass of ale in front of her appeared untouched. Olivia approached and cleared her throat gently. "Miss Rolfe?"

Blue eyes, startling pale, looked up at her and then blinked. "Yes. You must be Lady Olivia. Please, join me."

She slid into the chair across from Sophia and, having decided as she walked downstairs that the best course of action would be to reveal the truth quickly rather than unnecessarily drawing things out, began to launch into her explanation. "Thank you for coming. I'm sure you are curious to know exactly why I've—"

Dear God. She stopped, her throat tight and her thoughts scrambled.

Sophia's serene expression—from her kind eyes to her patient mouth—were the very picture of Papa.

"Are you all right?" Fine dark brows knitted in concern.

Olivia looked away until she was relatively sure she wouldn't burst into tears. "Yes, I apologize. I just wasn't expecting…"

Sophia opened the front cover of her book and placed the sketch of her mother holding her on the table between them. Her lower lip trembling, she asked, "Where did you get this?"

Olivia swallowed. "From your father."

Sophia sat up straighter, a flicker of anger crossing her face. "You know him?"

She nodded. "I'm afraid he died a few years ago. But yes, I knew him. He was my father also."

Fingertips pressed to her temples, Sophia said, "But your father was…"

"The Duke of Huntford."

"No. That cannot be. My mother said that my father was a customer at the bookshop."

"Perhaps he was."

"Surely she would have mentioned it if he were a duke."

"Unless the duke was married."

Sophia covered her mouth with her hand and then let it fall to her lap. "How old are you?"

"Twenty-two."

"I am twenty-three. So we are … ?"

"Sisters." Half sisters to be more precise, but it was hardly the time to split hairs.

"Forgive me, I … I need a moment to … make sense of this."

"Of course," Olivia murmured, thinking that they could both use more than a moment.

"How did you come to possess this sketch?"

"It is a very long story, and I will tell you everything that I know, which may be frustratingly little. However, first I think I shall speak to the innkeeper and request that our dinner be served in the private dining room."

And so, fortified by a hearty meal and a few glasses of wine, Olivia shared the raw and terrible truth about their father's suicide, the note he'd left for Olivia, and what little she knew about his affair with Sophia's mother.

Sophia explained that upon her mother's death, she'd received a rather substantial sum that her father had provided for her care and upbringing and that her mother had been too stubborn to spend. Sophia had poured most of the money into improving the bookshop, which was her mother's legacy and Sophia's livelihood.

It was impossible not to like Sophia, even if she did have striking good looks, an enviable slender figure, and an abundance of intelligence. She listened to everything calmly and, in turn, shared the few details that she had gleaned from her mother. Slowly, they began to put the pieces of their lives together.

Sophia ate the last bite of pie—how on earth was she so thin?—and set down her fork. "Tell me about your brother and sister."

"They are your brother and sister as well. If you are able to stay for a few days, you shall meet them. Rose is quiet and wise, like an old soul in a young woman's body. Owen is fiercely protective. But since marrying Anabelle, he is less apt to brood and growl."

"In your letter you mentioned that Owen discovered you in a compromising position?"

"Yes, he broke down a door."

"That must have been terrifying."

"There are certain things a sister does not wish her brother to see—things I imagine he was not particularly pleased to see either."

"And now you and—James, is it?—must marry. Do you find the situation distressing?"

Olivia was grateful that Sophia didn't assume that she'd hoped to be caught. Of course, she could understand how one might draw that conclusion, especially since she'd chased him to the Lakes. But still, a bit of sisterly loyalty was bolstering.

"For years, I've dreamed of marrying James. Now that it's about to happen, I wish I could stop it."

"You do not love him, then?"

Olivia paused, debating how much she should reveal to this relative stranger—even if she was family. But her need to confide in someone won out. "I love him more than I ever thought possible."

"Then why don't you wish to marry?" Sophia's nostrils flared slightly. "Is it his station? Does he lack the necessary wealth?"

"No! I don't care about either of those things." Relief flashed in Sophia's pale eyes. "But I don't want him to marry me out of a sense of duty, and I don't want him to stay in England with me while he wishes he were participating in digs in Egypt. When he's older and looking back on his life, I don't want to be his biggest regret. He deserves this chance to chase his dream. Everyone does."

"Ah. I see. I don't suppose you could convince Owen to postpone the wedding until after James returns from his expedition?"

"No. I believe the only circumstance that would prompt him to call off the wedding would be James's death, or mine." Olivia fingered the stem of her empty wine glass. "James is equally determined to marry quickly—in his eyes, honor demands it."

"That's all well and good, but you should have some say in the matter, too."

"Owen would say that I forfeited that right on the night I climbed into bed with James. I am stuck."

"Unless..."

Olivia's ears perked up. "Unless what?"

"Unless you did not show up to the wedding."

"I could never leave James at the altar. That seems, I don't know...drastic. And cruel."

"Perhaps. But if he truly believed that you didn't want to marry him, he might feel free to go on his expedition. My point is, there are always choices."

Interesting. Uncle Humphrey had said something similar.

"And each choice has its own consequences," Olivia said, more to herself than to Sophia.

Her half sister was correct. Olivia had always taken charge of her own fate, and though that tendency often got her into trouble, at least she was making her own decisions. She stood and paced the length of the small, private dining room. "*If* I were to run away before my wedding," she began slowly, "the timing would have to be perfect. I'd need a window of several hours—preferably more—in which I could get a head start."

"Agreed. You'd have to leave early one evening and travel throughout the night." Sophia's cool, matter-of-fact manner was both impressive and slightly frightening.

"I'd need a safe, secret place to hide out," Olivia continued. "James would almost certainly come looking for me, as would Owen."

Sophia tapped a slender finger on the wood table as she considered this. "That is problematic—especially where your fiancé is concerned. If he were to travel all over the countryside looking for you, he'd miss out on the expedition anyway."

"True, and that would be a tragedy twice over. I'll have to make him believe that I don't wish to marry him." She looked down at the ancient ring he'd given her and then added, "I'm not certain I'm that accomplished an actress."

"If you doubt your ability to convince him in person, you could leave a note."

"That seems a bit cowardly."

"Yes. But you'd be doing it for him."

Olivia nodded. "I would. The other advantage of leaving a note is that I could assure my family that I was safe. I should hate to worry them needlessly." It was a hare-brained plot to be sure, but it wouldn't be the first one she'd undertaken. Nor, most likely, would it be the last.

"I'll need to think it over, but thank you for offering your perspective. After the shock I've given you today, I should be comforting you. Instead, you are counseling me."

"I simply think we women deserve to have a choice when it comes to deciding our futures, and I am willing to help you in any way that I can."

"You're very kind, Sophia. Fortunately, I don't need to make a decision tonight."

"Indeed. It's been a long day and we—"

The door to the dining room burst open, allowing the noise from the taproom to pour in, and both women gasped as Owen's broad shoulders angled through the doorway.

Her brother really did have the most uncanny timing.

"I have it," he said, whipping a folded paper from his breast pocket and slapping it against his palm.

"Good evening to you, too," Olivia said. "I presume 'it' would be the special license?"

"It would. You will marry three days hence." Her stomach dropped to the floor. Three days.

Owen's gaze landed on Sophia and he narrowed his eyes as though something about her was familiar. "Have we met?"

Sophia turned to Olivia, who gathered her own wits and said, "My brother seems to have forgotten his manners. Allow me to introduce him—Owen Sherbourne, the Duke of Huntford."

Owen bowed and looked expectantly at Olivia. Sophia clutched the arm of her chair in a death grip.

Ah, well, there was no use in prolonging the inevitable.

"Owen, allow me to present Miss Sophia Rolfe. Our sister."

Chapter Twenty-Four

The next evening, James walked into the inn's taproom, eased onto the stool next to Huntford's, and leaned an elbow on the bar. The duke stared straight ahead, but his jaw twitched—he knew James was there. The handful of farmers and tradesmen chatting at the tables behind them were some comfort. If the duke murdered James, at least there would be witnesses.

"Welcome back to Haven Bridge, Huntford." James nodded at the innkeeper, who poured him a glass of ale.

"It wouldn't be my first choice of destinations, but I'll admit the village has a certain charm. I expect that the arrival of my family will double the population."

"Are many of them coming, then?"

The duke shrugged. "I had to let two cottages down the road in order to accommodate everyone. They should arrive tomorrow. I informed them that the wedding's happening Sunday morning, whether they are here or not—and I'm not bluffing."

James stroked his chin. "My mother is planning to arrive tomorrow also." Hopefully Ralph would make the trip as well.

"Anabelle is cross with me," Huntford continued. "She says that Olivia must have a proper wedding dress and that she is the only one who could possibly create it. She's probably sewing in the coach as we speak."

"That's very thoughtful of her." Anabelle was not your average duchess.

Huntford's eyes softened. "She'd do anything for Olivia."

"As would I."

The duke looked sideways at him.

"I mean it," James said. "I'll admit that a month ago, marriage was the farthest thing from my mind. But the more time I spend with Olivia, the more I realize what a fortunate man I am. There's something else you should know."

Huntford's glare warned he was in no mood for news of the bad variety.

"I've canceled my trip to Egypt." James had regretfully written a letter to the expedition's organizer that afternoon, so there'd be time to offer the spot on the team to someone else. It hadn't been a hard decision, choosing between Olivia and the expedition—he knew it was the correct course of action. But he was still adjusting to the idea that a chapter of his life had come to a close before it had even begun.

"Good." Huntford nodded approvingly. "You made the right decision, even if Olivia doesn't realize it. Who knows? Maybe there'll be time for that kind of travel... later on."

"Absolutely," said James, with all the confidence he

didn't feel. They both knew that this had been his one chance. His shot at adventure had slipped away.

Huntford grunted, and they sat in silence for a few moments, as though the few sentences they'd spoken had used up their store of words for the time being. And yet, things were easier between them. Not quite like they'd been before, but Huntford was thawing.

At last, the duke said, "I see your eye has healed. Mostly." He took a large gulp of ale and clunked his glass on the bar. "I should have hit you harder."

James snorted. "If you had, you'd be attending a funeral instead of a wedding."

Huntford arched a brow. "Exactly." After draining his glass, he said, "Olivia's ankle seems to have improved."

"Yes." But James was concerned that something besides her ankle plagued her. She'd seemed distant when last he'd seen her, and he suspected something more than pre-wedding nerves was to blame. "How does she seem to be faring?"

"As well as can be expected. It's a shock of course."

James nodded, even though he rather thought the shock of their sudden engagement should have worn off by now, especially after the afternoons they'd spent together at the river.

Owen rubbed the stubble along his jaw. "She seems to be coming to terms with it better than I, but then, she's had a little more time to adjust to the idea."

"Of marrying me?"

"No. That we have another sister."

James almost choked on his ale. "What?"

"Ah. She didn't tell you. I suppose she considered it a family matter."

But he and Olivia were going to be a family—at least the start of one. "Another Sherbourne sister?"

"Aye. And she's here."

Good God. No wonder Olivia had been acting so strangely. "Does this have anything to do with your father's letter?"

"It does. Buy us another round of drinks, and I'll tell you everything."

James listened as Huntford shared what he knew about the letter and his newfound half sister. He imagined Olivia reading the letter for the first time. Family was everything to her, and her father's revelation must have shaken her world. "I need to see her," James said. "I need to talk to her."

"I invited her and Sophia to join us for dinner—Hildy said they declined."

"Isn't that odd?"

"They're probably discussing womanly topics," the duke said. "Getting to know one another."

But James wasn't at all sure. He checked his pocket watch. "I should return to Humphrey's cottage. His elderly housekeeper could use some assistance with tidying the main rooms in preparation for my family's visit. We're losing the battle to books and cats."

"Your family? Who's visiting besides your mother?"

"Hopefully my brother—Ralph."

"Wait. You have a brother? Why haven't you ever mentioned him?"

"Ralph has palsy, and I'm afraid I haven't been a very good brother to him. But that's about to change."

Huntford nodded thoughtfully. "I look forward to meeting him."

"And I can't wait to introduce him to you." He slid off his stool. "When you see Olivia, would you tell her that I'd like a few moments of her time tomorrow?"

"I can tell her," Huntford said noncommittally. "But brides have strange ideas about seeing their groom before the wedding. After Sunday, you'll have plenty of time together."

"Right." James wondered if he could scale the wall outside of Olivia's window.

"One more thing, Averill."

James looked him in the eye.

"Don't even think about attempting a midnight visit to my sister's room."

Damn it. "The thought never crossed my mind."

The next morning, Owen moved Olivia and Sophia out of the inn and into one of the cottages that he had let. She was to share a room with Sophia, since she hadn't met anyone else yet. Owen, Anabelle, and their sweet daughter, Elizabeth, would take the second bedroom. The third was for Olivia's sister Rose, and Anabelle's sister, Daphne. Her husband, Benjamin, was unable to make the trip. The other cottage was for Aunt Eustace and a few other great-aunts who'd heard about the wedding and insisted on making the trip in spite of their gout, digestive ailments, and other assorted complaints.

It would be cozy, to be sure, and Olivia was warmed by the outpouring of familial support, but guilt gnawed at her insides. They were all coming to witness her wedding.

A wedding that she'd recently decided wasn't going to take place.

The coachman placed Sophia's and Olivia's bags

in their room, and the kindly woman whom Owen had hired to act as housekeeper opened a window to let in the breeze. "Just let me know if there's anything you need, my dears," she said. "Luncheon will be ready in an hour or so."

As she scurried out, Olivia sank onto the edge of the bed; Sophia closed the door and sat on the chair opposite her.

"We must work quickly," Olivia said. "The rest of the family will arrive shortly and then we shan't have a moment's peace. They'll ask you endless questions—I hope you are prepared for that—but I know they'll be as fond of you as Owen and I are."

Indeed, once Owen overcame the shock of discovering that he had another sister, he immediately took Sophia under his wing. He hadn't completely come to terms with the fact that Papa had been unfaithful—it was so much easier to place all the blame on the mother who'd left them. But even though Sophia was living proof of their father's infidelity, it was nigh impossible to dislike her. Her forthright manner and the grace with which she'd accepted the news about her father—and them—had quickly won over both Olivia and Owen.

And now, Sophia was Olivia's biggest ally in her attempt to ensure James went on his expedition.

"I expect a slew of questions, and I'm sure I'll have many for them as well." Sophia tugged off her worn gloves. Olivia made a mental note to purchase new ones for her. "This will work to our advantage, however. If there's one thing that could distract the family from your wedding preparations, it's the revelation that you have a half sister. If I didn't know that you were intent on preventing the wedding from happening, I'd feel badly for causing a stir."

"Nonsense. We are delighted to finally know you and regret that our meeting is long overdue. But you make an excellent point. Having you here shall take the focus off me and hopefully provide an opportunity for me to slip away shortly after dinner. If I make it to Sutterside by nightfall, I can be on the mail coach first thing in the morning."

"Are you sure you don't want to tell me your destination? If something unexpected or unfortunate were to happen, it seems *someone* should know where you are."

Funny, Olivia recalled James saying something very similar to her. "No, the less you are implicated, the better. I am asking too much of you as it is."

"They're going to give chase as soon as they realize you're missing."

"Undoubtedly. But I only need to elude them for a week—long enough for James to believe that I don't wish to marry him and come to the conclusion that he should leave on his expedition. Uncle Humphrey will do his part to convince him. Once I know James is gone, I'll return to London and face the wrath of my brother."

Sophia shuddered. "He won't be pleased."

"I know. I regret the worry I'll cause him and Rose. I hope my note will allay some of their fears. And for their sakes, I hope my summer escapades don't end up as fodder for the gossip rags."

"Again, my presence may deflect some of the gossip away from you."

"Oh, I am sorry." Olivia reached out and patted Sophia's hand. "I wish you didn't have to be subjected to any ugliness. The scandal sheets can be so cruel."

Sophia shrugged. "I rather look forward to it. Now, you should prepare a small bag to take with you. You'll need money, a change of clothes, and a few necessities."

"Yes. And I still need to compose the note." That was going to be the most difficult part of the whole thing—convincing James that she didn't want to marry him so that he'd truly feel free to leave on his expedition.

"Perhaps I should leave you for a bit, give you time to gather your thoughts. I was thinking I'd go for a walk anyway."

Olivia stood and impulsively hugged her sister. "Thank you, Sophia. I am so grateful that you made the trip here. You have every reason to be bitter and resentful about the way Papa treated you and your mother, and yet you are not."

"I do not think that would do any of us any good. I may not have been raised as a duke's daughter, but I can hardly complain. And I must confess I've always wished for siblings. I did not expect to get them at the age of twenty-three, but I suppose it's better late than never." She hugged Olivia back, then firmly pointed her in the direction of the escritoire below the window. "Good luck writing your note."

As Olivia was reaching for the desk drawer, she happened to glance out the window. James was striding up the walk, his handsome face lined with determination. Heart pounding, she stepped aside and pressed her back to the wall.

"What is it?" Sophia asked.

"James is here. I can't see him." She could already feel her resolve cracking.

Sophia quickly drew the curtains. "I'll tell him you're resting."

"I haven't even told him about you yet," Olivia said guiltily. "I wanted to meet you first. But perhaps Owen has."

"I'll introduce myself. Do not worry." The door knocker clanked, and Sophia shot Olivia a reassuring smile. "Pack your bag. Write the letter. I'll take care of this."

Olivia pressed her ear to the closed bedroom door and let James's deep, rich voice seep under her skin. She couldn't make out the words of his and Sophia's conversation, but she heard his disappointment when he learned that Olivia wouldn't see him. When the front door closed, she ran to the window and peeked from behind the edge of a curtain. Hands on his hips and head hanging low, he walked away from the cottage. Upon reaching his horse, which was tethered to the picket fence by the lane, he squinted up at the house toward the very window where she stood.

Confident the curtain hid her, she remained there, very still, as he mounted his gelding and rode away.

If her plan worked as intended, it would be the last time she saw him—for at least two years.

She sat down at the escritoire and pondered the best—and most convincing—way to say good-bye.

Chapter Twenty-Five

Sacrifice: (1) The act of killing a person or animal as an offering to a divine being. (2) To give up something for the benefit of another, as in
He would sacrifice anything to make Olivia happy—and to make her his.

As James rode away from the cottage where Olivia was staying, his confusion escalated. *What the hell is going on?*

He might not be particularly skilled at interpreting social cues and emotions, but he *knew* Olivia had not been resting.

He knew it in his bones.

Which meant that she was avoiding him out of anger or fear or . . . something.

This evening he *would* see her and right matters, so that when they said their vows in the church tomorrow, there would be no hesitation, no regret.

When he arrived at Uncle Humphrey's, a coach was parked outside and a servant unloaded a couple of bags—his mother's and Ralph's.

James hadn't realized until that very minute how much he'd missed them. No one knew him like they did. They knew that his fear of heights had kept him from climbing trees and that he'd struggled with every single damned French lesson. They knew the ache of being abandoned by a husband and father who couldn't accept his younger son's physical limitations. They knew the comfort and ease of midwinter dinners at the kitchen table in front of a warm stove.

James bounded up the walk and into the cottage. "Mother?" he called.

"James!" She appeared in the small entryway and threw her soft arms around him. "My goodness," she said, wiping a tear, "you're more handsome than ever."

"And you are prettier than ever," he said, meaning it. Her green eyes twinkled, and if her hair was a bit more gray than brown, it suited her.

"Where's Ralph?"

"H-here." His brother's jaw and neck had grown thicker over the last few months. Ralph limped toward him, and James met him halfway, wrapping him in a fierce hug.

"Whoa," said Ralph, laughing, "c-can't breathe."

James gave him a brotherly slap on the shoulder and raised a brow. "If I didn't know better, I'd think you'd been sparring."

Ralph shrugged but flushed at the compliment. "I've b-been going for w-walks." He spoke slowly, with obvious concentration. "Trying to do ch-chores around the house."

"He's a great help," their mother chimed. "He carried firewood last winter."

"Aye, I can carry w-wood. Just don't ask me to carry t-tea." As he held out a shaky hand to demonstrate the challenge hot liquids presented, his entire face split into a grin that melted James's heart and lifted his spirits.

"It's been too long," James admitted. "And I can't wait for everyone to meet you both."

"Everyone?" their mother said incredulously. "We weren't expecting many people would be able to attend, given the . . . ah . . ."

"Scandalous circumstances?" he teased.

It was her turn to blush.

"What is going on in there?" Humphrey called from his study. "If there's some sort of reunion taking place, move it in here so that I can witness the bloody thing from my chair."

Mother raised her brows. "My brother is as feisty as ever, I see. He seemed so peaceful when he was sleeping."

"It's deceiving," James agreed. "Let's relocate to the study and see if we can find a seat amid Humphrey's collections of statuettes, books, and cats. There is much I need to tell you both."

His mother linked an arm with each of her sons. "We cannot wait to meet Lady Olivia."

"You'll adore her," James said. "It's impossible not to."

Olivia had just finished writing her letter when two coaches pulled up to the cottage.

As her family started to pour out, she didn't even attempt to hold back her tears.

They'd come so far, just to be present and support her on what should have been the happiest day of her life. She hoped they'd forgive her when they realized they'd traveled all the way to the Lakes for naught.

She flew down the stairs directly into Rose's arms.

Laughing, her sister said, "I think this must be the longest we've ever been separated... but I suppose I must get used to it now that you are to be married. I'm so happy for you, Liv!"

Anabelle and Daphne joined in the hug, each offering their own congratulations and good wishes.

"Never fear," said Anabelle. "Even with short notice"—she shot Olivia a mildly scolding look through her spectacles—"I've managed to create a gorgeous gown for you."

"It *is* stunning," agreed Daphne. "I confess to being slightly jealous." Golden curls framed her rosy cheeks as she smiled. The very idea that she was jealous of Olivia for any reason was absurd.

"How is Benjamin?" Olivia asked. "I hope he's been feeling better of late."

Daphne's eyes turned dreamy. "He has indeed. He wanted to come, but he's undergoing a new treatment for his leg. The regimen lasts several weeks, and I didn't think he should stop midway through."

"I feel badly for taking you away from him."

"Oh, he shall be fine. And I wouldn't miss your wedding for anything."

Feeling smaller than a piece of lint, Olivia turned to Anabelle. "Where is Lizzie? It has been a month since I held her—I hope she hasn't forgotten her aunt Liv."

"You're not very forgettable," said Anabelle sweetly. "And she is with Owen. Ah, here they are now."

The babe looked like a doll cradled in the crook of his arm. "Have you told them about Sophia yet?"

Olivia rolled her eyes at her brother's typical lack of tact—it's not as though they'd had time for a proper conversation. "No. She's gone for a walk."

"Who's Sophia?" Rose asked.

"Our sister."

The women gasped, and Olivia ushered them into the sitting room. "Come make yourselves comfortable and I'll ask Mrs. Simpson to bring us tea. Then *Owen and I*"—she pinned her brother with a glare—"will tell you everything."

Olivia explained about their father's note and watched a whole range of emotions flick over Rose's face: hurt that Papa had written only to Olivia; shock that the father she'd worshipped had been unfaithful; and finally, an eagerness to meet Sophia and welcome her into the family.

It was fortunate that Sophia had been on a walk when the rest of their clan arrived; it gave everyone a few minutes to come to terms with the news—or at least start to. The note had given Olivia more time to adjust, to rewrite in her head the brief family history that she'd always believed to be true. Now she saw the rest of them engaging in the same struggle. Sophia had probably planned to be away from the cottage when they arrived, for this very reason. In the short time Olivia had known her, her newly discovered sister had shown thoughtfulness and sensitivity, even though the situation was certainly more difficult for her than it was for the rest of them. Olivia was saying as much when Sophia walked through the door, her cheeks flushed from her walk.

"Good afternoon," she said a little breathlessly. "I hope I'm not interrupting. I'd be happy to return a bit later, if you'd like."

"Not at all." Rose walked over to her and clasped her hands. "Olivia just told us everything about…well, everything…and I couldn't be more delighted to meet you. In fact, I'd say our meeting is long overdue. I'm sorry for that."

"There's no need to apologize," Sophia said kindly. "We've all been in the dark, it seems. The last thing I want is to cause turmoil for your family."

Rose shook her head, her auburn locks bouncing vehemently. "You aren't, and besides, this is your family, too. Whatever comes, we will weather it together."

The whole room burst into a flurry of hugs and tears and exclamations of agreement. Rather predictably, Owen took the opportunity to slip away, claiming he was going to put Lizzie down for a nap.

When the initial excitement faded, tea was served in the cozy sitting room, and the women settled in, eager to know everything about Sophia from her childhood, to her bookshop, to her current life in London. Under different circumstances, Olivia would have happily chatted with the women throughout dinner and into the wee hours of the morning. As it was, however, she was acutely aware of the clock on the mantel ticking away. And though she hated the thought of leaving them so soon after their reunion, timing was of the utmost importance if her plan was to succeed. And, for James's sake, it simply had to.

When Daphne offered to refill Olivia's teacup, she shook her head. "Would it be terribly rude of me to excuse myself? I find I'm insanely jealous of my little niece napping upstairs."

"Oh, of course not," said Daphne. "You need your rest. Tomorrow is a momentous day."

"Are you feeling all right?" Rose asked, her perceptive gaze flitting over Olivia.

"Indeed." She tried to keep her voice light. "I've had

a few late nights recently, and I fear they've caught up with me."

"Understandable," said Sophia. "Why don't you go lie down? I'll check on you before dinner, but if you're sleeping soundly, I won't disturb you. We can send up a tray later."

God bless Sophia. "Thank you—that sounds perfect."

"Just a moment," Anabelle said in a tone that brooked no argument. "You must try on your wedding gown so that I can make any last-minute alterations that might be needed. It shouldn't require more than a quarter of an hour."

Oh no. Trying on the wedding gown and putting Anabelle to more trouble on her behalf was surely more than she could endure. But there was no way to refuse her sister-in-law—especially when she was in bossy seamstress mode. Olivia looked helplessly at Sophia, who gave her a subtle but encouraging nod.

"I cannot wait to see your creation," Olivia lied.

Anabelle beamed. "Let us go, then. We shan't let the rest of them see you in it until you're walking down the aisle."

A few minutes later, her sister-in-law walked into Olivia's bedchamber, a shimmering blue confection draped across her arms. As Anabelle helped slip it over Olivia's head, a sob escaped her, but not for the reason that Anabelle assumed.

Her sister-in-law lifted her spectacles and dabbed at her own eyes. "Yours and James's is a great love, and your wedding deserves a great gown." She sighed, then circled Olivia, checking the dress from every angle.

Olivia was grateful that the room didn't have a full-length mirror. If she could see herself in the gown, she'd probably crumple to the floor. Was she doing the right thing? She desperately wished there were some other way to ensure James went on his expedition, but time was in short supply. Running away was her last resort, and it simply had to work.

Luckily, her sister-in-law was too concerned with fixing the gather at the back of the dress to notice Olivia's distress. Anabelle murmured to herself, pinned the silk in a few places, and eventually helped her out of the gown.

"What's this?" Anabelle caught Olivia's hand and examined the ring.

"James and I found it near the river where he was digging. He thinks it's very old."

"It's beautiful—a splendid wedding band."

A lump lodged in Olivia's throat. "I'm fond of it." Needing to change the subject, she said, "I hope the alterations won't require too much more of your time."

"I only need to make a tuck here and there." Anabelle smiled brightly. "And it is a labor of love. I'm so happy for you. I know that this wasn't the way you'd planned to become engaged, but don't let that dampen your joy. Clearly, you and James were meant to be together."

"I'm not certain about that. I don't believe James realized we were destined for one another until Owen blackened his eye."

Anabelle winced. "When it comes to protecting you, Owen can be…overzealous. But James would have gotten around to proposing, black eye or no."

Olivia sighed. She'd never know what James would have done. "Thank you for the gown. I've never worn anything so lovely. And thank you for not being cross with me after I...lied. I'm sorry I made you think I was going to Aunt Eustace's."

"You had your reasons. And I of all people know that sometimes we behave badly for a good cause."

Olivia arched a brow. "Yes, well, my reason was slightly more self-serving. You were saving your mother. I was chasing after a man."

Anabelle laughed. "And it worked. Well done." Her gray eyes twinkling, she scooped up the gown and pointed at the bed. "Everything will seem better after your nap. Sweet dreams of blue silk and your handsome solicitor."

Olivia dutifully walked toward the bed, even though she had no intention of napping. Anabelle swept out of the room but then popped her head back through the doorway. "I almost forgot to mention, Rose and Daphne are arranging a wedding breakfast."

Oh dear. "That's not necessary. In fact, I—"

"Nothing grand, just a small family gathering. Owen has requested that the menu include hot cross buns from a bakery in the village. You see? Even your ornery brother is getting into the celebratory spirit. Now rest."

Olivia listened beside the door, and when Anabelle's footsteps faded, she locked it. Heart hammering, she put on her plainest gown and stuffed a small portmanteau with one spare gown and shift, a warm shawl, and a blanket. She slid a small pouch of coins deep into the pocket of her dress and added a larger pouch to the portmanteau, leaving room for the supplies she'd need to purchase.

After reading the letter she'd written one more time, she sealed it and placed it on her pillow. All that was left to do was sit there, waiting for the right moment to make her escape.

And to think of all the spectacular ways in which her plan could fail.

The sound of the doorknob rattling made her leap to her feet. "Who is it?" she whispered.

"Just me, Sophia."

Exhaling in relief, Olivia unlocked the door and let her in.

Sophia quickly shut it. "Do you have everything you need?"

"I think so."

Sophia frowned. "I don't like the idea of you being on the road alone at this time of the evening."

"I'll be in Sutterside before nightfall and on the mail coach early tomorrow morning." More lies.

"Very well. Dinner will be served in a quarter of an hour. I'll tell everyone you are sound asleep. Wait another quarter of an hour before you go down. While Mrs. Simpson is busy serving in the dining room, you should be able to slip out the front door."

"Good, the conversation is always lively at our family dinners. No one will hear me above the chatter." But Olivia had already decided that she'd toss her portmanteau out the bedroom window into the flower bed below as a precaution. If someone caught her leaving the cottage, she could claim she was sneaking out for a pre-wedding rendezvous with James. Unfortunately, the opposite was true.

"I'll linger downstairs as long as I can after dinner," Sophia said, "to give you as great a head start as possible."

"Thank you for your help." Olivia squeezed her hand. "You mustn't go to great lengths to cover for me. Just act as though you are as surprised as anyone. The letter should explain everything."

"Be careful, Olivia. If there's one thing that I've already learned about this family, it's that they adore each other—and you, in particular. I understand why you feel the need to do this, but don't put yourself in jeopardy. Now that I've finally met you, I should hate for anything to happen to you."

Olivia swallowed and gave her half sister a wobbly smile. "As soon as James is on his way to Egypt, I shall come out of hiding, and I promise you that I shall lead the safest, most boring existence of any woman in England."

"I wish you luck." Sophia hugged her and kissed her cheek, then quietly slipped out of the room.

Olivia locked the door just in case Rose, Anabelle, or Daphne decided to peek in on her before making their way downstairs for dinner. She sat on the bed, holding her breath and praying that Fate gave her a little help tonight.

She was going to need it.

Chapter Twenty-Six

$\mathcal{J}$ ames rapped on the front door of the cottage, determined to see Olivia in spite of any ridiculous superstitions that forbade it. He wanted to tell her that he'd canceled his trip and hoped that the news would make her happy. He'd missed her smile, like one missed the sun after a week of rain.

A small, gray-haired woman answered the door, and when he introduced himself as the groom-to-be, she was all too happy to usher him into the crowded sitting room. Huntford sat next to his wife, who was sewing a mound of blue silk on her lap. The duchess's sister, Daphne, cooed at the swaddled baby in her arms. Lady Rose and Miss Rolfe stared thoughtfully at the chess pieces on the table between them.

Only Olivia was missing.

Once the others saw him, the room erupted in a chorus of exclamations.

"Averill," Huntford said. "Finally, someone to join me in a glass of port."

The women welcomed him more effusively, inviting him to sit and congratulating him on his impending nuptials.

"It's wonderful to see you all," he said. "I don't wish to disturb the family gathering, but I'd like to visit with Olivia briefly. Is she here?"

"She's resting," Miss Rolfe said quickly. The skin on the back of his neck prickled. Olivia had been "resting" when he called that morning as well. He couldn't imagine Olivia—the girl who was constantly moving—taking two naps in one day. Something was definitely wrong.

"Is she feeling well?"

"I think so," Anabelle said. She surreptitiously swept the blue silk off her lap and covered it with a pillow on the settee. "I was with her before dinner. It's been an eventful few days for her, however, and she wants to be well rested for tomorrow."

"I understand." He twisted the brim of his hat. "I just can't shake the feeling that something is...wrong."

"Wrong?" Daphne looked up, her blue eyes full of concern. "In what way?"

"I'm not certain, but I haven't seen her in a while, and the last time she seemed troubled and distant." Lord, he felt like a fool, standing before her family and discussing... feelings. But he had to see Olivia.

"Her unease is understandable," Miss Rolfe said. "I fear my presence has been an added strain during an already hectic time."

"You mustn't think that, Sophia. Olivia wanted you here. Indeed, we're all glad to have the opportunity to meet you and spend time with you." Rose frowned slightly at the chessboard between them. "Especially since you're the best chess opponent I've had in years."

"Would you care to join us?" Anabelle asked. "Owen would be glad for your company—as would we all."

"Thank you. Perhaps Olivia will wake and put in an appearance." Too agitated to sit, James paced the length of the small sitting room. Short of charging upstairs, there was little else he could do. If he knew which room was Olivia's, he could come back in the middle of the night, scale a trellis or some damned thing, and enter her window. But knowing his luck, he'd end up in Huntford's room.

"I'll tell you what," Lady Rose said kindly. "I'll go upstairs and peek in on Olivia. If she's stirring, I'll let her know you're here."

Miss Rolfe stood abruptly, jarring the chessboard. "Why don't you let me check on her?"

Lady Rose waved her back into her chair. "My legs could use a stretch. Besides, a short break will give me time to contemplate my next move." To James she said, "Perhaps I'll be able to put your mind at ease."

"You are most kind." He let out a breath and hoped against hope that Olivia would soon walk down the stairs. But the gnawing feeling in his gut wouldn't go away.

Lady Rose swept gracefully from the room. He continued pacing while Huntford watched him, a bloody amused look on his face.

A frightened cry from upstairs drew gasps from everyone, and James bolted, taking the steps two at a time. "Lady Rose?"

She met him in the corridor, her face a mask of shock and confusion.

"What is it? Where's Olivia?"

"She's not here."

His stomach dropped. "I don't understand."

"This was on her pillow." She handed him a folded piece of paper, his name penned across the front.

Huntford bounded up the steps. "What's going on?" he demanded.

"You mustn't lose your temper," Rose warned.

The duke growled. "Too late."

James moved between them. "Olivia wasn't in her room. She left this on her bed." He held up the note, and when Huntford tried to snatch it from his hand, he quickly moved it out of his reach. "It's addressed to me."

He walked into her bedchamber and stood by the window where there was more light and at least a shred of privacy, then slipped his finger under the seal.

Dear James,

I pray that you will one day forgive me for leaving this way, and for what I must now say: I cannot marry you.

You were right from the start. When you told me at the Easton ball that what I felt for you was infatuation, you were correct. I professed to love you without having the faintest understanding of the emotion. When you left for Haven Bridge, I impulsively followed you, creating trouble for both of us—trouble that you neither asked for nor deserved. Now I must set things right, not just for your own sake, but for mine as well.

When Owen first decreed that we should marry, I did not think there was any alternative. Admittedly, I

*did not object overmuch. I fear I was very much smit-
ten by your good looks, charm, and kindness—but we
both know that love requires something deeper, more
lasting.*

*Of course, I am still fond of you, and I always shall
be. I also respect you greatly, which is why I would
not subject you to a marriage—nay, to a life—without
love. You should not be forced to marry. You have a
dream to pursue and that is what you must do.*

*I realize that my brother will not be pleased with
me, and I am sorry to disappoint him once again.
While I have no wish to create more trouble for him or
my family, I'm afraid I must. Even Owen—powerful
and determined though he may be—cannot make
a marriage happen without a bride. And so, I have
run away.*

*Please assure my family that the location to which
I'm traveling is safe. I have suitable lodgings at my
destination and will not want for anything while I am
gone. I would urge them not to waste their time looking for me, but I suspect they will search nevertheless.
While I truly appreciate their concern, they should
know that their efforts will be in vain.*

*I do not plan to live in exile forever (unless my
family should deem it necessary). I will return to our
home in London after you have left on your expedition to Egypt, for I am fairly certain that even Owen
cannot orchestrate a wedding while you are on
another continent. In any event, once you are away,
I will return to my family, beg their forgiveness, and
willingly, if not gladly, face the consequences of
my actions.*

Please tell my family that I regret they traveled so great a distance, all for naught. I am blessed beyond measure to have their love and support, and I hope to one day make up for the trouble I've caused. Please tell Anabelle that the gown she made for me is the most exquisite thing I have ever seen, and she should be the one to wear it—not I. Please tell Sophia that I am delighted to know her and look forward to many sisterly visits and chats when we are back in London. Finally, please tell Owen that I love him and that I borrowed one of his horses. I shall take excellent care of her.

I hope that this news does not come as too great a shock. Indeed, I suspect and pray that once you have had time to adjust to the idea that we shall not marry, you will find you are relieved. Enjoy your time in Egypt, for exploring is what you were meant to do.

Sincerely yours,
Olivia

James shook his head, barely able to comprehend the words on the page.

Huntford jammed his hands on his hips, impatient. "What does it say, Averill?"

He tossed the letter onto the bed. Olivia may have written it, but he didn't believe a word. "Read it if you'd like. I'm going after her."

Huntford grabbed the note and scanned it. "Damn it. Where could she be headed?"

Rose worried her hands. "What about Aunt Eustace's? Olivia knows that Aunt Eustace was coming here for the wedding...maybe she means to hide out at her house?"

James was already moving toward the door. "Anabelle said she saw Olivia just before dinner. That was, what, three hours ago at the most? She can't have gotten far, even on horseback."

"She's an excellent rider," Rose called out as he jogged down the corridor and the stairs. Owen was using a stable about a mile up the road, not far from the inn where James and Olivia had stayed. His own horse was tethered to the fence out front of the cottage and he quickly untied the reins and launched himself into the saddle. He rode hard, ignoring the curious stares of village folk out for an evening stroll. When he burst into the stable, a lad with a freckled, dirt-covered face emerged from a back stall and waved his cap. "Good evening, sir."

"Have you seen a lady?" James panted. "A pretty young woman with brown hair?"

"Pa saddled a horse for her, just before he went home for dinner."

James was already leading his horse back outside. "Which direction did she ride?"

He jabbed a thumb at the air. "South, toward Sutterside. She asked Pa about the mail coach."

"Did she say anything else?"

"No, sir. But she gave Pa and me each a coin." He flipped his in the air. "Nice lady."

"She is." James dug in his pocket for a coin and tossed it to the boy, who snatched it out of the air with one hand. "Her brother, the Duke of Huntford, should arrive here in a few minutes. Tell him that I'm heading south and that I'll find Lady Olivia."

The lad bobbed his head. "Yessir!"

James launched himself back onto his horse and charged down the road, kicking up dirt behind him.

The sun sunk behind the hills, and the evening light faded fast. What in God's name was Olivia thinking, traveling alone at night?

Obviously, she was desperate to escape marriage to him, and that stung—worse than Huntford's right hook. The things she'd written in her letter didn't match his memories. Where was the woman who'd lain with him by the river and laughed when he'd tickled her belly with wildflowers? How could that *not* have been love?

Other questions echoed in his head, repeating themselves in time to the rhythmic pounding of his horse's hooves on the ground. But the answers weren't going to come from a letter, and they most certainly weren't going to come from inside his head. Only when he looked into Olivia's eyes would he know the truth.

And he prayed that truth wouldn't devastate him.

For now, his mission was to find her and make sure she was safe. He told himself that with only a three-hour lead, Olivia couldn't have traveled far…and that in the sleepy countryside, no trouble would befall her.

Unfortunately, trouble did seem to have a way of finding her, or vice versa.

By the time James reached Sutterside, darkness had fallen. He jumped off his horse, handed the reins to a stable boy, and asked him a few questions, but the boy hadn't seen a woman riding a gray mare. James strode into the inn—the very same one where Huntford had found him and Olivia—and saw the innkeeper behind the bar of the taproom.

The portly man scowled when James approached. Perhaps his displeasure had something to do with the two splintered doors that had coincided with his stay.

"What'll you be havin', Mr. Averill?" He sighed. "Not a room, I'm hoping."

"Just information, good sir. Have you seen Lady Olivia Sherbourne?"

"I have not." The innkeeper busied himself rubbing an invisible spot off of the bar.

"That is a shame," James said dryly, "for I would have compensated you handsomely for any helpful information you might have had."

The man looked up and raised a wiry brow, as though insulted. "Then it's a shame I don't have any."

"We only want to make sure she's safe," James said thoughtfully.

"We?"

"Did I mention that Lady Olivia's brother, the Duke of Huntford, will likely walk through that door within a quarter of an hour? You remember the duke—big, dark, brooding fellow, with a violent temper? But if you don't know anything..."

"Wait. My wife spoke with her."

James's pulse quickened. "Get her. Now."

The innkeeper left and returned a few minutes later, pushing his wife forward as she dragged her feet. "Tell him, Sally."

She eyed James suspiciously, her lips clamped.

Clearly, her loyalties lay with Olivia—and the fairer sex in general. He tried a softer tack. "I understand my fiancée was here. It's important that I find her. It's not safe for a young lady to travel these roads alone, especially at night. Please. Tell me what you know."

The woman raised her chin. "Lady Olivia didn't reveal her plans to me, but it was clear that she didn't wish to be found. I'm sure that a kind lady like her has her reasons."

"She doesn't want to marry me," James admitted. Saying the words out loud was like pulling the bandage off an oozing wound.

"But you're forcing her to," the innkeeper's wife spat.

"No one can force Olivia to do something she doesn't want to. But I *am* hoping to convince her." He sighed. "All of that is irrelevant. She's three hundred miles from home and could be in grave danger. Is she here?"

The woman deflated, her shoulders slumping. "No. She left a couple of hours ago."

James nodded encouragingly. "And what did she say? Do you know where she was headed?"

"She asked when the mail coach would be going through Mapleton. I told her early tomorrow morning."

"Mapleton...the village just south of here?"

"Yes, she asked about the inn there. And then she inquired about the villages farther south. She was in a hurry, like she wanted to go as far as possible before nightfall."

James was already itching to get back on his horse and go after her. "Is there anything else you can tell me? Anything else I should know?"

The woman shook her head. "I gave her some food to take with her."

"Thank you—you've been very helpful." He dug into his pocket and slapped a few coins onto the bar.

The innkeeper's wife eyed them, then pushed them away. "Keep your money."

But James was already heading toward the door, praying that Olivia wouldn't be foolish or desperate enough to ride at night. The darkness would slow his pursuit, but with any luck, he would reach Mapleton well before morning and stop her from getting on the mail coach.

However, his gut told him that it wouldn't be that simple.

It never was with Olivia.

Chapter Twenty-Seven

*Oasis: (1) A fertile, green place in the desert,
usually having water. (2) A refuge, as in*
She'd forever think of the idyllic spot by
the river as their private oasis.

Olivia had never jumped off of a moving cart before, and her heart beat triple time at the thought. She scooted all the way to the back and let her feet dangle over the edge, but the ground below was farther away than she'd imagined and seemed to slide by at an alarmingly fast rate. Which would have been daunting even if she *hadn't* recently turned her ankle.

She took a deep breath and summoned her courage. So far, everything had gone according to plan. Upon reaching Sutterside a couple of hours ago, she'd gone directly to the bakery, where she'd purchased three loaves of bread. From there, she'd found a fruit stand where she was able to add peaches, apples, and ripe berries to her bag. At the inn, she'd bought some dried meat, cheese, and a bottle of wine.

Most importantly, she'd spoken to the innkeeper's wife, confident that James and Owen would somehow charm or otherwise convince the woman to reveal what Olivia had told her.

Of course, she had no intention of heading south or taking the mail coach. They'd be able to track her much too easily. No, she was headed to the last place anyone would think to look for her—back to Haven Bridge.

She'd left Owen's horse behind at Sutterside, hoping James and her brother would be too busy pursuing her to realize that she'd abandoned the horse for other means of travel. It had been easy to find a farmer traveling north. Olivia had smudged her face, clothes, and portmanteau with some road dirt and covered her head with a dark shawl. She approached the farmer in the village square as he finished unloading grain from his cart. When he said he was going north, she requested a ride—and the utmost discretion regarding his passenger—in exchange for a few coins. He'd shrugged his shoulders and agreed.

He'd offered her a seat on the bench beside him, but she declined, saying she preferred to ride in the back and rest.

In truth, her plan required her to jump off the back of this jostling cart shortly before reaching Haven Bridge. She couldn't risk having someone see her in the village, and she didn't wish to respond to the farmer's questions. If he did happen to mention his odd passenger to someone, all he'd be able to say is that she'd disappeared somewhere between Sutterside and Haven Bridge.

The cart rumbled over a bump, jarring Olivia's teeth. Night had fallen, and the time was right. She craned her neck to look up and down the road; no one else was in sight. She dragged her heavy bag to her side and, knowing it would be the point of no return, shoved it over the edge. It bounced inelegantly and produced a little puff of dust. The farmer didn't notice.

Now it was her turn.

One, two, three . . . *jump*.

She fell forward, landed on her hands and knees, and rolled several yards, her skirts twisting around her legs. She stayed down for a few seconds, catching her breath and making sure that she was still in one piece before untangling herself and scurrying to retrieve her portmanteau. What if the wine bottle had broken? Her extra clothing and her food would be ruined.

When she spotted the bag, she began walking faster, and when she finally gripped the soft leather handles, she said a little prayer of thanks. The contents of her bag were critical to the success of her plan, and a peek inside revealed that while the contents had been jostled, the wine bottle had survived the fall.

It was tempting to stay on the road rather than brave the tall grass—home to countless insects, no doubt—and the uneven ground that lay beside the main road. But she couldn't risk being seen by someone who would tip off James and Owen. Besides, a woman walking alone at night would make an easy target. So she opted for the brush and the rocky terrain that might help to keep her hidden.

Glad that she'd worn her ugliest, sturdiest boots, she trudged through the grass and lugged her bag up a slight embankment. At the top, she found a narrow path where the vegetation had been trampled by other travelers. She fervently hoped she didn't happen upon any of them on her walk back to Haven Bridge.

She treaded cautiously over the matted grass, certain that a snake would slither across her toes. But since the sun had set and the sky grew darker by the minute, she couldn't really tell what creatures lurked in the wild—a blessing, she supposed.

With every step she took, her bag became heavier. When the muscles in one arm began to ache, she switched it to the other. After a half hour, her shoulders burned and her arms were numb, but she didn't dare stop. She had a great distance to go before this night was over.

Her ears perked at a clopping in the distance, and she crouched low, keeping still. The noise grew louder and before long she spotted movement on the otherwise deserted road. A horse galloping, too fast in the darkness, its rider leaning forward like he was on a mission. Olivia held her breath and watched as the man rushed by.

Though the moonlight was dim, she recognized him. She would have recognized him anywhere. The breadth of his shoulders, his lean hips, his athletic grace. James.

He'd come after her, as she'd known he would.

Oh, she'd hoped the letter would dissuade him, but deep in her heart she'd known he wouldn't give up easily. The most gut-wrenching part of writing the letter was imagining him reading it and knowing the hurt and betrayal he must have felt.

She wanted to call out to him, to tell him she loved him and that she didn't mean a word of that stupid, horrid letter. She wanted to tell him that she'd marry him anytime and anyplace, so long as they could be together.

But that would mean the death of his dream, and so she kept quiet, kept still. She waited until the pounding of the hooves faded into silence.

And then she dropped her head to her knees and cried.

"What have we here?"

The deep, sinister voice made her leap to her feet and stagger back. A stranger, large and imposing, grabbed her already sore arm so tightly that she cried out.

"Quiet." He shook her with a force that knocked her teeth together.

Her heart thundered in her chest as his insolent gaze crawled over her, taking in her dark clothes and stuffed bag. "Running away? Did no one warn you about evil men who prey on girls like you?"

Oh, James had warned her—one time or twenty. "Let me go."

He chuckled, and the hollow sound sent chills over her skin. "What's in the bag?"

"Clothes. Not your size."

"We'll see." He picked it up, the whites of his eyes growing larger. "What heavy gowns you have."

"Slippers, too," she said, amazed she could be flippant and petrified at the same time.

Still squeezing her arm with one hand, he bent down, yanking her with him, and opened her portmanteau. He flipped it over, spilled everything onto the ground, and began rummaging through it. When he came across the bottle of wine, he arched a slick brow and set it aside. Inevitably, he also found her pouch of coins, which he held to his ear and shook, smiling at the clinking it produced. He shoved the pouch into his pocket and jerked her to standing again.

"A lady of means. Why, it's my lucky day." He leaned forward, his reeking breath invading her nostrils. "Give me your jewelry."

"I don't have any with me." It was the truth. Where she was going, she had no need of jewels.

"None? I find that hard to believe." He grabbed her chin and turned her head to the side, checking her ears. Then he looked lower, scowling at her unadorned neck. "Let's see your hands," he demanded.

She held out her shaking hands, belatedly remembering the ring. The gold ring James had given her, from the river.

"Give it to me," the robber spat.

"No." She hadn't cared about the wine or the money, but this was different. "It's my wedding band," she lied. "And not worth very much." She reached into her pocket and produced the last of her coins. "You can have these instead. Just take the money and leave me, please." Her voice quivered.

The brute greedily added the coins to his pocket and shook her again. "I want the ring."

"I don't know if I can take it off," she said truthfully. "If you let go of my arm, I'll try."

He narrowed his eyes but did as she asked, watching her like he was afraid she'd bolt any second.

She twisted and pulled on the ring, but it wouldn't come off.

"Let me see," he said impatiently. He grabbed her hand and tried to wrench it off, pulling so hard she thought he'd either scrape her skin off or break her finger.

The more he pulled, the more her finger swelled, throbbing like she'd slammed it in a door.

"Please," she cried out. "It's not going to come off until my finger does."

His sinister laugh pierced the air as he reached into his

boot and brandished a knife; moonlight glinted off the blade. "If that's the way you want it." He lunged for her hand again, and she spun away, just out of his reach.

"Wait. Give me another minute. I'm sure I can loosen it." Only, she wasn't sure at all. And though she would have liked to think the thief was bluffing about cutting off her finger, she didn't want to take the chance he wasn't. She spit into her hand and worked the saliva around the ring. It moved a little.

"I grow weary of waiting, you cheeky chit. I'll have that ring. Now."

He grabbed her from behind, wrapping an arm around her waist, then pressed the blade, cool and razor sharp, against her cheek.

Blood pounded in her ears; her knees wobbled. She kept twisting the ring—it was almost over her knuckle. But the sick feeling in her belly was telling her that even if she managed to remove it, he wasn't going to let her go. He was having far too much fun torturing her.

His rancid breath wafted over her face. "You're a feisty one." Then the point of his knife pricked her skin, unleashing her rage.

She screamed and jammed her elbow into his gut, loosening his hold just enough so that she could turn and dig her heel into the top of his foot. He yelped and his knife dropped to the ground. She dove for it, snatching it before he could. Her ring popped off her finger and flew through the air.

Panting and shaking with fear, she gripped the hilt of the knife with both hands and waved it with a lot more bravado than she felt.

Undaunted, the robber hulked toward her. "You little—"

The unmistakable rhythm of galloping hooves thundered toward them. "Help!" she screamed.

"Bitch." Her attacker grabbed the wine and stumbled into the taller grass. She could just make out his silhouette mounting a swaybacked horse and charging off across the field, away from her and the rider coming down the road.

Her knees did give out then. She dropped the knife and collapsed to the ground, shivering in spite of the balmy night. The rider still galloped down the road, toward her, at full speed. She doubted he'd heard her, and now that the robber had fled, she was grateful she hadn't been discovered. She peered through the reeds as the man passed her on horseback, a blur of black on gray. Owen. He charged past her, oblivious to everything but his goal—finding her.

Without even meaning to, her brother had saved her. If she survived this ordeal, she would never again complain about his tendency to be overprotective. In fact, she rather adored him for it. As she watched him disappear into the darkness, her heart squeezed in her chest.

And that was more than enough sentimentality for one night. Still wobbly, and worried that the robber would return, she grabbed the knife and carefully wrapped it in a shawl before placing it in the bottom of the portmanteau. She crawled around, gathering all the other items and shoving them in, too. She spent more time than she should have feeling around in the grass for the ring, but quickly realized the futility of it. It broke her heart to leave behind that little piece of James, but she couldn't waste any more time. So, heedless of what rocks or other obstacles might lay in the path, she ran.

Fueled by fear and love and anger, she ignored the branches that scraped the back of her hands and the weight of her bag slamming into her thigh. She ignored the stitch in her side and the quivering of her exhausted muscles.

When at last she saw the lights of the inn at Haven Bridge, she sank to her knees, leaned to the side of the path, and retched.

Once the spasms ceased, she sat back and rested her head on her knees. Her heart gradually slowed to normal. The night breeze cooled her neck, damp with sweat.

She had to press on.

By her calculations, which were not so much calculations as a sort of highly fallible intuition, the abandoned cabin on Uncle Humphrey's land was about four miles away.

The cabin was the perfect place for her to hide out. No one would suspect that she'd doubled back and hidden right under their noses. And Lord knew that *no one* would believe she'd tolerate such primitive living conditions. She could scarcely believe it herself.

But she was willing to endure a week or so of discomfort if it meant James could leave for Egypt unencumbered by guilt—or a wife he hadn't asked for.

She pushed herself to her feet and brushed off her hands. There would be plenty of time for self-pity once she reached the cabin. In fact, there'd be little else for her to do but sleep...and think.

It occurred to her that the last leg of her journey would have been much more enjoyable if she'd had a horse. Or a coach with plush velvet squabs. But she was not the spoiled, pampered, squeamish Olivia of old.

So, she hefted the bag onto her shoulder and suppressed a groan. She could travel faster if her load was lighter, but she didn't dare leave any of her supplies behind. She would need them all. At least she didn't have to worry about the wine bottle any longer.

The village was even more peaceful than usual. She could just make out the lake in the distance, shimmering in the moonlight. She hadn't seen or heard anyone on the main road for some time, and before long, she'd leave it behind for paths that were even less traveled. She'd walk up the path where she'd turned her ankle—at least it wasn't raining—and past the spot where she and James had eaten hot cross buns on the rocks.

It would be slow going, but with a modicum of luck, she'd reach the little dilapidated cabin—her safe haven—by dawn.

Chapter Twenty-Eight

$\mathcal{O}$livia awoke later than usual to thirst scraping her throat and hunger gnawing at her belly. Her head pounded and the sunlight streaming through the cabin's only window sharpened the pain. She threw off the shawl that served as her coverlet and rolled off of her crude pallet—a blanket she'd doubled over.

One of the wooden floorboards was broken and some were warped, but the floor was relatively clean, thanks to a few leafy branches that she'd turned into a makeshift broom. She could have worked wonders with a scrub brush and a bucket of soapy water, but at least the cobwebs were gone.

She shielded her eyes as she felt along the ledge of the window, then grasped the handle of the knife she'd taken from the highway robber. Carefully, she carved a tally mark in the wall beside her.

Seven nights.

She'd survived a week alone in the woods.

Closing her eyes, she whispered a prayer. James would board a ship today and begin his journey to Egypt. Though her chest ached from grief, she sighed with satisfaction.

Her plan was working. She had only to manage one more night of solitude.

But it wasn't going to be easy. She reached for her portmanteau—which was also her pillow—and looked inside. Her supplies were terrifyingly low. She'd run out of bread and fruit a couple of days ago. All that was left was a bit of dried meat.

She stood slowly, steadying herself with a hand on the wall. When the dizziness faded, she staggered to the cabin door and opened it, flooding the small room with light.

Though she hadn't seen a single soul for a week, she still feared being spotted by someone passing through Uncle Humphrey's land, so she scanned the horizon for any movement. Nothing but birds flitting from tree to tree and leaves trembling in the warm breeze. Blinking in the sunlight, she stepped outside and took a gulp of fresh air.

The greatest challenge of the last week had been neither thirst nor hunger. Oh, she would have gladly traded her favorite pair of earrings for tea and a scone, but what plagued her the most was boredom. Inside the cabin, the hours blurred together so that she could scarcely tell the difference between morning, midday, and evening.

Fortunately, she'd found a pastime of sorts—digging. She didn't have proper tools, but sticks weren't in short supply. After she'd whittled the end of a branch to a point, it worked almost as well as the pick James carried in his supply bag. Over the past few days she'd spent hours along the riverbank, painstakingly uncovering interesting little artifacts. Most of them were the same rounded stones

James had found. But between the rocks she'd also discovered bits of metal, tarnished with age. Perhaps she'd draw them in her journal before giving them to Uncle Humphrey. She hoped they'd make him smile.

Today would be her last day of isolation, and though there was not much she'd miss about the cabin, she realized, with no small amount of surprise, that she *would* miss exploring and digging by the river.

She grabbed her makeshift pick and tin cup, then walked along the little path she always traveled to the river. Upon hearing the gurgle of the water over rocks, she ran to the river's edge, leaned over, and filled her cup. Greedily, she drank, emptying the cup before dipping it into the river again.

The water ran down her throat, crisp and cool, slaking her thirst and easing the pounding in her head. She lay in the grass, remembering the glorious afternoons she'd spent there with James. That was the unique torture of this place—memories of him surrounded her.

With a sigh, she sat up and walked farther along the river, soaking in the beauty of the mist-covered mountains and peaceful pastures. She was just about to hop onto the sand beside the riverbank to dig when an odd chill stole over her skin.

She froze, and the hairs on the back of her neck stood on end, as though someone were watching her.

Dropping her things, she ran toward the security of the woods. Heedless of the branches and thorns that assaulted her, she darted toward the old cabin and ran inside. Her hands trembled as she slid the lock into place.

As her heart pounded violently, she told herself that her nervousness was due to lack of food and companionship.

She sank onto her pallet and pulled her knees to her chest. For several minutes, she barely breathed as she listened for the sound of footsteps in the brush or the rattle of the rickety door in its frame.

But it turned out that no one had followed her, and she needn't have worried.

She was quite, quite alone.

James had been to London and back looking for Olivia. But she'd vanished like a fairy into the forest. Gone.

Though she'd stopped at the inn in Sutterside, she'd never stayed there. And while she'd asked a couple of people about the mail coach, no one seemed to have actually *seen* her on one. He did find the horse she'd taken when she left Haven Bridge. And a farmer close by said he'd sold fruit to a young woman with a large bag.

Olivia's trail had grown cold after that. He'd visited her aunt Eustace's house and, on Rose's suggestion, their cousin Amelia in London, but neither one had seen Olivia. Everyone was desperately worried about her. Especially him.

She'd been gone for seven nights, and when he thought of all the danger that could have befallen her, it made him insane.

But after interrogating three different serving women at three different inns along the highway today, he realized he needed a new strategy.

And he needed something to go on.

So he was going back to where the trail had started to retrieve the only real clue he had—Olivia's letter.

He'd left it at the cottage where her family was staying, and it occurred to him that they might have some new information as well. So he reluctantly returned to Haven Bridge—without Olivia.

He was a few miles outside the village when he noticed a scuffle going on, well off the side of the road, to his right and up a small hill. Urging his horse forward, he rode up the incline to investigate.

An elderly man holding a basket of vegetables cowered as a larger man in a torn, filthy jacket circled him, wielding a knife.

They both turned in surprise as James approached and dismounted. He eyed the man with the knife. "This is hardly a fair fight. You have a dagger, while your opponent is armed with a few potatoes and carrots."

"This is no fight," the old man croaked, as if James could not deduce what was going on. "He tried to steal my vegetables!"

The robber sneered at James, his yellow teeth gleaming against the backdrop of his grimy face. "Spare me your lectures. You know what they say about thieves and honor. I don't give a damn about fairness. I want an advantage." His gaze flicked over James's empty hands. "And right now, it looks like I have it."

The robber turned his attention to James and took three steps toward him.

James didn't budge. The farmer, wild-eyed and trembling behind the robber, reached for a potato and cocked his arm as if to hurl the spud at his attacker. James shook his head and waved him off. "I'll handle things from here."

The old man hobbled quickly down the hill toward the road, losing a couple of carrots on the way.

"Your valuables," the thief demanded, waggling his fingers at James. "Let's have them."

James's fists clenched involuntarily; he stretched his fingers and smiled. "You've terrorized enough people for one day. Pack up your things and go far away. Don't come back. Ever."

"Maybe I will take a nice long ride—on that horse of yours. But first I'll have your blunt and your valuables."

"I wouldn't even give you a halfpenny."

"Brave talk for a fellow facing the tip of my blade." He admired the sharp point. "There's no ladies around to impress, you know."

"And do you prey on helpless women, too?"

"Well, now. I could tell you that I don't, but it'd be a lie." He cackled at his own twisted wit.

The skin between James's shoulder blades prickled. "Have you seen a young woman traveling alone here in the past week?"

"Maybe. What's it worth to you?"

James's patience snapped. He took one stride forward, grabbed the hand with the knife, and twisted it behind the thief's back. "What did you do to her?" A lethal mix of rage and dread coursed through his veins, and his self-control teetered on the edge of a cliff. "Think carefully before you answer, because I'll jump at any damned excuse to break your neck."

The robber struggled to twist himself free, but James tightened his grip until the thief's fingers turned blue and the knife dropped to the ground.

"Where is the lady?" If he'd hurt Olivia, he was dead. Stone cold.

"It was a week ago I saw her. All I took from her was a bottle of wine."

"Lying bastard." James spun the thief around and

slammed a fist into his chin. He staggered back, landed on his ass in the dirt, and immediately began scuttling backward.

"What did you do to her?"

"Nothing!" The robber struggled to stand, blood trickling out of the corner of his mouth.

James shoved him in the chest, easily knocking him back to the ground. "I want to know exactly what happened. Where is she now?"

"How the hell should I know? I looked through her bag—there was nothing worth taking. Just some clothes and food."

"Food?" It seemed a curious item to pack, unless... "What else?" James growled through his clenched teeth.

"A small pouch of coins. Hardly anything."

"And you took them."

"I left her the food." The thief scooted away until James grabbed him by the front of his jacket and hauled him to his feet.

"If I find out that you laid a hand on her, harmed her in any way—"

"I didn't, I swear! She pulled a knife on me. I had to run for my life."

"You should have run farther."

Before the robber could reply, James landed a solid blow to his nose. His eyes rolled back in his head and he dropped to the dirt like someone had chopped him down with an ax.

He wasn't dead, but close.

Oddly enough, the encounter gave James newfound hope. If Olivia had truly managed to escape the thief—

and if any woman could, it was she—then perhaps her trail was not as cold as he feared.

Why had she brought food with her? She may have wanted to travel without stopping for meals, or . . . perhaps she planned to hide out indefinitely. But where?

He checked the thief's pockets and found a gold watch and a few coins, but nothing that could be traced back to Olivia.

At least he knew she had been on this path, presumably traveling on foot, just seven days ago. He would walk it, looking for clues, on his way back to Haven Bridge.

He took his horse by the reins, leading him down the narrow, grassy trail, unsure of what he hoped to find. Maybe a scrap of fabric had ripped off the hem of her dress or she'd dropped a hairpin or some other bauble. He was desperate to find any little thing that might confirm she'd been there and hadn't vanished from the face of the earth.

And then, something bright gold winked amid the weeds and brush along the side of the path. He blinked, and it was gone. He took a few steps forward and dropped to his knees, parting the tall grass and searching for the glint of gold.

There it was.

The ring they'd found together at the river. He recognized the smooth, ancient metal, the beveled edge, the delicate size. Olivia's ring.

His mind spun madly. Why would her ring have been carelessly tossed in the brush?

He couldn't imagine her discarding it—regardless of what she'd written in her letter, he *knew* that the afternoons they'd spent by the river meant something. And those memories were all wrapped up in this ring. No, she wouldn't have willingly gotten rid of it.

But what if there had been a struggle? The robber could have demanded she take it off or tried to wrestle it from her. And if she'd resisted at all—just the foolishly brave sort of thing that Olivia would do—the ring might have gone flying into the grass, lost. Until he stumbled upon it.

Dread chilled his insides. He prayed that Olivia had fled from the thief as fast as her legs could carry her and that somehow, somewhere, she was safe. But his discovery of the ring shook his faith. Like a punch to the temple that comes out of nowhere, it left him stunned and reeling.

Dear God, he loved her.

He loved her with an intensity that frightened him. He should have realized it before now, but he'd been distracted. His expedition, her father's letter, the fight with Huntford, and his guilt over the way he'd treated his brother had kept him from seeing what he should have seen all along.

She was the center of his world, the only thing that really mattered.

The possibility that something terrible might have happened to her shook him to his core. His life was nothing without her. He'd give up a pharaoh's riches to have her by his side. And he prayed he had the chance to tell her that.

He brushed the ring across his lips before sliding it deep into his pocket.

He thought of the thief lying unconscious several yards behind him. Certainly there was more to the story than the robber had revealed. Part of James wanted to revive him with a splash of water and demand the rest of the facts; part of him wanted to revive him just so he could pummel him all over again.

The only thing James knew for sure was that the pieces of the puzzle were not fitting together. He needed to analyze Olivia's letter again, find out what Huntford had learned—if anything—and devise a new plan.

He simply had to find Olivia. And he had the awful, sickening feeling that time was his enemy.

The sights and sounds around him came into sharp focus—the weeds rustling in the breeze, the shadow of a hawk circling overhead, the frantic drumming of his heart in his chest. He pulled his horse alongside him, jumped into the saddle, and took off, hoping Haven Bridge would hold some answers.

Chapter Twenty-Nine

*Strata: (1) Layers of earth that correspond
to different historical periods. (2) Levels of social
hierarchy or class, as in*
The daughter of a duke and a mere solicitor
may be in completely different social strata
but still be perfectly matched.

Through the window of the cabin, Olivia watched the sky turn pink. It would be dark soon, her self-imposed week of seclusion almost over.

She would spend one more night there, and in the morning use what little of her strength remained to walk to Uncle Humphrey's cottage. She wondered if James's kind old uncle would even recognize her.

Her normally bouncy curls were limp and tired. Her dress, covered in dirt and dust, hung on her like a sack. She could scarcely imagine how pale and drawn her face must look.

And so, partly because she had no wish to give Uncle Humphrey a stroke, and partly because she desperately longed to be clean again, she decided that on this, her last night, she'd risk a quick swim in the river.

She found the small cake of lavender soap she'd packed, unwrapped it, and inhaled its sweet scent. She gathered the tin cup, too, and the shawl that would have to serve as a towel. When the sky turned a smoky shade of purple, she ventured out of the cabin.

The small indulgence of bathing in the river wasn't going to ease the heartache of losing James—she doubted anything could—but at least she might feel human again.

She traipsed along the trail to the river, dropped her things on the grassy bank, and drank several cups of water. Nothing but pastures, mountains, and gorgeous sky surrounded her, and still, she hesitated. Stripping naked out of doors was daring, even for her. It had been different when James had been with her. She'd been too distracted by the heat in his green eyes and the feel of his hands on her to be embarrassed or ashamed.

So much had changed since then.

But after a week of tears, boredom, and hunger, she was determined to enjoy this small pleasure. She took a deep breath and hauled her dress and chemise over her head in one swoop, relieved to be free of the soiled garments. Her skin tingled in the humid evening air, and as she released her hair from its braid, the long strands tickled the small of her back.

She hopped down the embankment and sat on a smooth rock at the water's edge. The rock, still warm from the sun, heated her bottom while she dipped her toes into the cool, gurgling river. Her nipples tightened in anticipation as she eased herself into the chilly water.

Without James to carry her, she couldn't be squeamish

about letting her feet sink into the soft bed of the river. She grabbed the soap, dunked her head beneath the water's surface, and came up gasping, cold droplets running down her neck. After lathering the soap between her palms, she worked it through her hair, then leaned back and let the gentle current rinse the suds away. Next, she scrubbed every inch of her body, from the tip of her nose to the spaces between her toes.

When at last she was done, she stepped from the river, skin pink and glowing in the moonlight, and rubbed herself dry with her soft shawl.

Darkness had fallen quickly, but she was reluctant to return to the cabin—and even more reluctant to don the dirty clothes she'd worn before.

But maybe she didn't have to.

She scooped up her dress and chemise and, holding them at arm's length, walked back to the river. It would only take a few more minutes to wash them, and if she hung them out overnight, they'd be mostly dry by morning; she could face Uncle Humphrey and her family wearing clean clothes.

She'd left her other, equally dirty, gown back in the cabin, so she had nothing to wear while she washed the clothes. Still, it wasn't as though she had any company, save for a random deer or fox, and it wasn't as though they wore breeches or jackets either.

So, whistling a melancholy ballad, she plopped herself down on the warm, smooth rock and went about washing her gown—her first ever attempt at playing the part of laundry maid.

Oddly enough, she found that the mindless work of swirling, soaping, rinsing, and wringing was rather soothing. It even took her mind off of James—a little bit.

• • •

James burst into Uncle Humphrey's cottage and strode into the study, where Humphrey, not surprisingly, snored in his chair. Ralph limped into the room behind him, a crooked smile lighting his youthful face. "Welcome back."

"You're still here." James hugged him, holding on a little longer than usual. "I thought you and Mother might have decided to return home. I glad you didn't." He led Ralph back into the small foyer so they wouldn't disturb Humphrey.

"M-Mother turned in early tonight. Should I wake her?"

"No, let her rest."

"She's been worried about you," Ralph admitted. "I told her you would be all right."

"Of course I am. Olivia is the one who is in danger."

"Wh-where is she?"

"I haven't the slightest idea." James dragged a hand through his hair. "A couple times I thought I was close to finding her, but I wasn't. The only clue I have is this." He dug deep into his pocket, withdrew the ring, and held it out for Ralph to see. "It's hers. I found it on a path that runs parallel to the main road just outside the village."

Ralph looked at the ring soberly, as if he understood that it represented all of James's hopes—and his worst fears. "M-maybe it was loose and fell off while she was walking," he ventured hopefully.

"Perhaps," James replied. But he knew that the ring had fit snugly. He sank onto a bench in the cramped hallway and patted the space beside him; Ralph joined him.

They sat in silence for a minute, each lost in thought as James turned the gold band over and over between his finger and thumb. "We found it a couple of weeks ago while I was digging on the northwest corner of Humphrey's property. Olivia was the one who spotted it in the soil. I knew she was destined to have it."

Ralph shook his head as though he hadn't heard correctly. "B-by the river? I was walking there earlier today."

"That far? You really are getting stronger," James said proudly.

Normally, Ralph would have beamed at the compliment, but he frowned like he hadn't heard it. "It's odd you should m-mention that place. I thought I saw someone walking near the tree line this morning, but they d-disappeared into the woods before I could tell for certain."

Good God. The cabin was nearby. What if she'd—

James grasped Ralph by the shoulders. "Could it have been Olivia?"

"The p-person was far away. I j-just assumed it was a boy poaching." He closed his eyes as though he were envisioning the scene. "B-but yes," he said confidently. "It could have been her."

Suddenly, all the clues made sense. She'd packed clothes and food and wine. She'd never gotten on the mail coach.

What if, this whole time, Olivia had been hiding on Humphrey's land, almost in plain sight? What if she'd spent the better part of a week trying to survive alone, in a primitive cabin in the woods?

"It could have been her," James repeated. "I'm going to find out."

Ralph's brows knit together. "There's n-nothing around there. What would she d-do for food?"

"If she's hiding in the woods, I imagine she's getting by on very little. Olivia can be quite stubborn."

"N-not unlike someone else I know." Ralph smiled as he jabbed James in the chest with one finger. "G-go see if your fiancée wishes to be rescued."

James was already halfway to the door. "She probably doesn't. But I'm going anyway."

"Wait. T-take some cake with you, just in case." Ralph pointed to the kitchen. "She could be starving, and a little food might help your chances of winning her over."

For a younger brother, Ralph was rather wise. James scrounged around the small, cluttered kitchen and found some cakes, apples, and bread. He filled his flask with wine and stuffed the supplies into a bag.

As James prepared to leave, Ralph stifled a yawn. "Get some sleep," he ordered. "I'll see you in the morning."

"I hope you have some good news then."

James clasped his brother's shoulder. "So do I."

Minutes later, he was riding at breakneck speed in the darkness. Foolish, but he didn't give a damn. He bent low over his horse and urged him on, trusting him to remember the way. Before long, a ribbon of water shimmered in the moonlight, and as it drew closer, he pulled up on the reins and dismounted.

He followed the familiar turns of the river, pausing at a couple of choice spots to look for footprints on the bank. Nothing. He passed the site where he'd uncovered the stones while Olivia had sat beside him, sketching. The rocks were lined up like soldiers, just as he'd left them, but there were more. Someone else had been digging along their riverbank.

The old cabin wasn't far from here. He had only to search for the path that led into the woods. If he remembered correctly, it was about fifty yards southeast of—

Good God.

He drew up short and placed a quieting hand on his horse's neck.

Ahead of him, he could just make out the silhouette of a woman perched on a rock like an elusive water nymph. Her damp hair veiled her face, and she whistled softly as she twisted fabric over the river, wringing the water from it.

He hoped it was Olivia—and he hoped it wasn't. He needed to know that she was safe and well. But he hated the thought of her spending a week on her own, completely deprived of most necessities, let alone her usual luxuries.

And the truth was that it hurt like hell to know that she'd willingly endure this sort of hardship and misery to avoid a future with him.

He didn't dare call out to the woman for fear she'd flee into the forest. Instead, he walked quietly along the river. With every step, his heart beat faster, as if it, too, recognized her swift, sure movements and the quizzical way she angled her head.

As he drew closer, a cloud that had shrouded the moon skirted away, illuminating Olivia just enough for him to see that she was, thank God, in one piece and unharmed.

She was also completely naked.

Desire pumped through him, and his cock hardened, even though his brain knew there were more pressing matters to attend to.

His horse whinnied, and Olivia's head snapped around. In a blink, she was off and running. She dropped the garment she'd been washing and ran toward the woods, straight toward the cabin.

He gave chase, but by the time he reached the cabin, she'd already slammed the door. It was so dark beneath the foliage that he couldn't see more than a foot in front of him.

"Olivia," he called out. "Please, let me in. It's me, James."

A little cry came from behind the rickety door. "James? Is it really you?"

He swallowed and pressed his forehead lightly against the warped wood. "It is. Who else would know that you once hopped all the way across a cow field on one foot in the rain, and that you are a much better artist than you let on, and that you're too squeamish to let your feet touch the bottom of the river?"

The door creaked open, just a crack. "I'm not squeamish about that anymore. However, if I see one more spider in here, I may very well lose my mind."

Ah, this was still his Olivia. Relief flooded his veins. "I'm sorry I frightened you just now. I'm sorry about everything. Can we talk?"

She hesitated, then nodded. "Give me a moment to put down my weapon and make myself presentable."

Good God. "A weapon?"

"A knife," she called from the dark interior. "A little souvenir from my travels." When she returned to the door, she admitted him into the dark room. She'd wrapped a blanket around her and tucked it under her arms—arms that looked too thin.

He wanted to pull her close and feel her heart beat against his chest. He wanted to taste the sweetness of her skin and breathe in the intoxicating scent of her hair. But for now, he only brushed his knuckles gently against her cheek. "Are you all right?"

She sighed. "Yes."

"Why?" he asked simply. She knew what he meant.

"I wanted you to go." Her voice was hoarse and raw. "On your expedition. You *should* have gone. Why didn't you?"

"I can't believe you're asking me that. Did you honestly think that I'd sail off to another continent without knowing where you were? Without knowing that you were safe?"

"Yes," she said harshly. "I told you in my letter that I would be safe, and you can plainly see that I am. Why didn't you take me at my word?"

"Why? Maybe I didn't want to believe your damned letter. Not the part where you implied that the time we spent together meant nothing. Not the part where you told me I should leave you. And most definitely not the part where you said you didn't love me after all."

Silence stretched between them, and James wished to God he could see her face more clearly, or better yet, read what was in her heart.

"I wanted you to be happy," she whispered at last. "I realized how selfishly I'd behaved when I chased after you. I expected you to give up your dream so that you could stay here and fulfill mine. And then Owen caught us and the choice was taken away from both of us."

"I'll admit it felt that way at first. But the more time I spent with you, the more I realized we were meant to be." He clasped her hands between his, praying she'd understand. "Every mishap, every conversation, every kiss brought me closer to you. I love you, Olivia."

"Oh, James." She looked up at the ceiling of the shack like she was trying to keep her tears from brimming over.

"I love you, too. But I really wanted you to go—to realize your dream."

"Come here," he said, opening his arms.

She took two halting steps toward him, then buried her face in his chest, sobbing into his shirt.

He ran his hands over her back and curled his fists into her damp hair, assuring himself that she really *was* here with him and reveling in the rightness of holding her again.

"Olivia," he said softly, "it means the world to me that you went to such lengths just to convince me to go. You're the most generous person I know. But I gave up my spot on the expedition before you ran away."

"I wish you hadn't."

"I thought you'd be happy that we would begin our marriage together."

"But I keep thinking about poor old Uncle Humphrey."

"What does Humphrey have to do with any of this?"

"He never got to go on an expedition, never got to explore the world beyond the pages of his books. And when he talks about the opportunities he missed...well, his eyes look sad and haunted."

"That's because he drinks too much and spends far too much time in the company of his cats."

"I think it's because he never followed his dream. And I couldn't bear it if one day, years from now, I saw the same haunted look in your eyes. I want you to be happy—truly happy."

He tipped her chin up and smoothed the pad of his thumb along her jaw. "Well, the first thing that would make me happy is getting out of this miserable cabin." He swept her into his arms, kicked the door back, and angled her body through the opening. She nestled her head in the crook of his shoulder, and for the first time in a week, James exhaled.

He let out all the worry and fear and uncertainty and felt that empty space fill with love and hope and goodness.

He carried her to their spot by the river and set her on her feet before shrugging out of his jacket and laying it on the ground. "It's not much of a blanket, but less itchy than sitting on the grass."

She laughed as she sat, tucking her legs beneath her. "Grass does not bother me. In fact, after this week, little does."

"Except for spiders."

"Of course."

Recalling the stones by the river, he asked, "Were you, perchance, digging during your stay here?"

"I might have done a little exploring of my own." She grinned. "I found a bit of metal that looks like it might have been a cross—and more stones, too."

He arched a brow. "You sound like an antiquarian."

She shrugged her thin shoulders. "I needed something to fill my days. I have to admit it was … pleasant."

"And maybe a little exciting?"

"Yes." She nuzzled his neck, and his pulse leaped in response.

He beckoned his horse with the cluck of his tongue and untied the bag from his saddle. "I brought a few provisions."

Olivia's head perked up instantly. "You have food?"

"I do." He handed her the bread and chuckled as she ate every last crumb. He gave her everything he'd brought, including the flask of wine.

While she ate, he retrieved the dress and chemise she'd been washing. He wrung them out once more before spreading each garment on a rock to dry.

As she licked a drop of apple juice from the back of her hand, she lay back and gazed happily at the sky. "That was the best meal I have ever had—especially the cake," she sighed.

James sprawled beside her. "That was actually Ralph's idea. He was walking around here this morning and thought he saw someone. And I wondered if it might have been you. I hoped."

"Ah. I had a feeling I wasn't alone this morning. I am glad to know it was your brother, and not the robber who I— Well, never mind."

"You needn't worry about him anymore."

"How is your brother? And your mother?"

"They are fine. But right now, I want to talk about us."

Olivia blinked and turned toward him. "I've made a mess of things, have I not?"

"No. I don't think this"—he pressed his palm to hers—"qualifies as a mess at all."

"Well, what would you call it?"

"I'd call it love. You braved a week in the wilderness in the hopes that I'd travel to Egypt. I scoured half of the English countryside searching for you because I can't imagine a future without you in it."

Hope curled in her belly, warm and sweet. "Then I suppose it's a very good thing that you found me."

"I love you, Olivia. More than a museum full of ancient artifacts and a desert full of unearthed relics."

She quirked a brow at him. "High praise, indeed."

More soberly, she added, "And I love you. More than a wardrobe full of exquisite gowns and a bakery full of hot cross buns. And I'm not saying that just because of your chest"—she ran her hand over the smooth broadcloth of his shirt—"although that *might* have something to do with it."

James leaned in and touched his forehead to hers. "I was so worried about you." The anguish in his voice nearly brought her to tears. "I thought—"

"Shhh." She smoothed a fingertip over his full bottom lip. "I'm here. I'm fine. And I'm going to prove it to you."

With that, she pressed him down onto his back, leaned over him, and touched her lips to his. For the briefest of moments, they were frozen just so. Only the two of them existed, their breath mingling in the warm summer air.

This was what she had always wanted. The kind of love that could survive secrets and mistakes of huge proportions. The kind of love that took a hopeless situation and made it seem...well, right.

Desire flared and the kiss deepened. James groaned as he tugged at the blanket she'd wrapped around her. It fell away, leaving her completely bared to him. Greedily, he caressed her breasts, hips, and bottom, setting her on fire.

She pulled at his clothes, too, and soon the warm, hard planes of his chest and torso grazed her nipples, tantalizing and teasing them to aching points.

He slipped a hand between her legs and touched her entrance. She was wet already, and trembling with need. "James," she breathed, "I lied in my letter. I've never stopped loving you. It's always been you. It always will be."

He rolled on top of her, slid his hands beneath her bottom, and looked at her with a tenderness that left her breathless. "You've given my life meaning, Olivia. I was searching all over the place trying to find something... something that really mattered. You were right here, all along."

She wrapped her legs around his hips, drawing him close. He looked into her eyes as he entered her slowly, their bodies joining perfectly.

They moved together, rocking until they were panting, hot, and desperate for release.

"Don't ever leave me again, Olivia," he begged, cradling her head in his hand.

Her heart squeezed in her chest, and the pulsing between her legs spiraled. "I won't. I pro—"

The word died on her lips as an unstoppable wave of pleasure surged through her. She arched her back, pulling James along with her.

He said her name as he came; he said it like a prayer.

And when the sweet tremors subsided at last, he rolled onto his side and gave her a grin that melted her insides like chocolate. Again.

He took a long curl that lay on her shoulder and wound it around his finger. "Tomorrow we will deal with our families and their questions and wedding plans. Tonight is just about you and me. And I can't imagine anything more perfect."

Olivia sighed happily, but it wasn't *quite* perfect.

Luckily, she had an inkling of how to make it so.

Chapter Thirty

$\mathcal{J}$ ames hoped he was repeating the words correctly.

Each time he looked at Olivia, radiant and beautiful in a pale blue silk gown, he forgot where he was—namely, the tiny church in Haven Bridge, at his own wedding.

He dragged his eyes away from his lovely bride to Huntford, sitting in the first pew and swiping suspiciously at his eyes. The duke had been so relieved when Olivia was found that he'd agreed to her request to delay the wedding for two more weeks.

Anabelle may have had something to do with that. She said that Olivia needed to regain some weight before she wore the wedding gown that she had created for her. And she simply refused to alter it again.

The extra fortnight also allowed some of the relatives who'd left Haven Bridge after the first wedding attempt to return. Foxburn accompanied Daphne this time, and the earl looked more relaxed than James had ever seen him. He still wore a wry grin—the kind that mocked James for being a lovesick sap. Which he was. Of course, Foxburn was equally smitten with his own lovely wife and James would remind him of that fact at the first opportunity.

Olivia's sister, Rose, and half sister, Sophia, sat beside each other. They looked happy and...relieved. Perhaps they knew better than anyone how stubborn their sister could be.

James's mother and brother were sitting in the front pew behind him. Ralph wore a smart jacket and cravat and beamed proudly. His mother dabbed at her eyes. She'd casually worked the subject of grandchildren into the conversation no less than three times in the past two weeks.

Uncle Humphrey was sandwiched between two of Olivia's great-aunts. He'd cut back on the brandy for the last several days and vowed that he'd be fit enough to haul himself out of his chair and attend the wedding. Sure enough, he had, and some of the older ladies had even declared him to be utterly charming.

"Mr. Averill?"

James jerked his gaze to the vicar's face and shot him an apologetic smile. "I take this woman to be my wife..."

An hour later, he and the wedding guests were milling about the lawn behind one of the cottages Huntford had rented, enjoying a small but elegant breakfast that Olivia's family had arranged.

Olivia and Daphne sat beside Ralph, and the three were deep in conversation about their plans to arrange outings for the children at the foundling home. Olivia had suggested enlisting Ralph's help with the project, and he was delighted to be involved.

"Autumn will be the perfect time for a picnic in the

countryside," Daphne said. "We can have the girls bring journals and write notes about the plant life and animals they observe. I must brush up on the Latin names so that the girls will have the correct nomenclature."

Olivia rolled her eyes in mock exasperation. "The whole point of the outing is to get their noses out of books for a few hours. It shall be an afternoon *without* Latin!"

"But we must make the most of this learning opportunity." Daphne turned to Ralph, looking for support.

"P-perhaps the girls could collect a few s-specimens and look up their names when they're back at the foundling home. An activity for a rainy d-day."

Olivia stood and kissed Ralph squarely on the cheek. "You are both diplomatic and brilliant—just like your brother."

She cast James wicked glances as she flitted between the guests, thanking them for coming and graciously accepting their good wishes. Her cheeks were no longer hollow and her stunning gown revealed that her lush curves had returned. With her hair piled on top of her head and her flowing dress, she resembled a classic Greek beauty.

Best of all, she had a lovely twinkle in her eyes that could mean either that she was very happy or up to something.

He suspected both.

She walked to a table, grabbed a silver fork, and tinged it against her champagne glass. "Ladies and gentlemen, may I please have your attention." She cast a heart-stopping smile in his direction. "Especially yours, Mr. Averill."

The small crowd chuckled, and he inclined his head politely, wondering what the hell his beautiful wife had in store for him.

"I realize it's not customary for the bride to give a speech, but it comes as no shock to most that I'm not a customary sort of person. I want to first apologize to those of you who went out of your way to attend our wedding not once, but twice. I am truly sorry for the unnecessary effort and worry I caused you.

"The reason I fled was not because my feelings for James wavered. On the contrary, I knew that I loved him beyond anything, and I thought that if I convinced him I didn't want this marriage, he'd be free to pursue his dream of going on an archaeological expedition."

James shook his head, unsure why she'd revisit the matter. *She* was his dream, above all else. He opened his mouth to tell her so, but she held up a hand and continued.

"James was willing to give up that adventure so we could be together. Only, it occurred to me that perhaps he didn't have to choose."

He sidled up to her, leaned toward her ear, and whispered, "I thought we'd settled this, Olivia. Can we discuss it later, please?"

Ignoring him, she went on. "So, with a little help from Uncle Humphrey, I've arranged for us to have a wedding trip...to Egypt."

He blinked. "What?"

"We'll meet the team in Cairo. It won't be as long as the expedition you had planned," she said excitedly. "Just six months. I thought that might be enough time for us to do a fair amount of digging and sketching."

"But...I don't—"

"We leave tomorrow." She squeezed his hand and looked up at him, eyes shining. "Isn't it wonderful?"

Their family and friends clapped and cheered.

He felt like he was on the stage of some strangely realistic theater performance. "That's very sweet, Olivia," he said softly, "but I can't imagine that your brother is going to—"

"I've already spoken with him about it. I had thought we should take a year to travel, but he convinced me to return within six months." She leaned in closer and whispered, "I don't know which of us—you or me—he's going to miss more. He's forgiven you, you know, even if he won't admit it."

James shook his head. "So, we are going to Egypt?"

"Tomorrow," she repeated. "Uncle Humphrey wrote to one of his colleagues, and together they made the arrangements. Humphrey tells me our living conditions won't be as luxurious as my bedchamber in St. James Square, but on the other hand, they're sure to be more comfortable than a deserted cabin."

Egypt. He'd convinced himself he didn't want to go. And the truth was that as long as Olivia was by his side, he didn't give a damn where he was. But he couldn't deny the excitement that he felt at the prospect of an adventure—with her.

He swooped her into his arms and spun her around, heedless of the pruny expressions on the faces of her great-aunts. "You couldn't have given me a better wedding gift," he said, setting her feet on the ground again. "Thank you."

"You are most welcome, my dear husband."

Husband. He liked the sound of that.

"I have an announcement as well." Humphrey coughed and wiped his brow with a handkerchief. He stood shakily, and James rushed to his side to support him.

"What is it, Uncle? You shouldn't strain yourself."

"Nonsense. It's high time I did." Addressing the entire gathering, he said, "James is like the son I never had. And now he has a beautiful bride who already feels like a daughter to me. They've reminded me of what it was like to be young and in love. In fact, I don't believe I've ever seen a couple more in love."

"Thank you, Uncle."

Humphrey nodded. "I have a gift for both of you. It's not riches or jewels, but it is special nonetheless. I want you to have the land by the river. It's yours to explore and enjoy to your heart's content."

Olivia gasped. "Uncle Humphrey, we couldn't."

"Of course you could. And if you must know, I have an ulterior motive. I'm hoping you—and someday your children—will visit me here in Haven Bridge."

James shook his hand and embraced him at the same time. "We would visit you regardless, you know."

"This way I'll be sure."

"You've been like a father to me. That's the best gift of all."

Humphrey nodded and swiped at his face. "Damn insect flew into my eye."

With a chuckle, James helped him settle back into his chair. Then he went to Olivia and scooped up her hand in his. "Though it's not nearly as grand, I have something for you as well."

"You do?"

"Yes." He swallowed, then dropped to one knee, hoping he didn't bumble this. Olivia had always wanted a romantic proposal, and by God, she deserved one.

Even if it was a little late.

"Olivia, I'm not adept with words unless they pertain

to contracts and the like. Legal matters do not pose a problem for me"—Good Lord, this wasn't starting out well—"but feelings are a different matter entirely." He swallowed and she nodded, giving him the courage to continue. "You burst into my life like a hummingbird, zipping here and there, demanding more from me. Challenging everything I thought I knew about myself and making me realize that the greatest treasures do not come from the past but from the present. From the friends and family who have shared in our lives and made them richer. With you, life will always be an adventure, and every chapter will be sweeter than the last. I am the luckiest man alive to have you as my wife."

Olivia blinked like she was holding back tears and several women sighed. Huntford grunted.

"Oh, I almost forgot." James dug into his pocket, pulled out the ring, and held it out to her.

Olivia clapped her hands over her chest. "But that's my— How did you find it?"

He shrugged. "I suppose Fate has a way of taking care of these things." He took her hand and began to slip the ring onto her finger.

"Just a minute," Uncle Humphrey cried. "Before you put that on, let me see it." He shuffled over, unceremoniously plucked the ring from James's fingers, and squinted at it. "Eustace, let me borrow your lorgnette."

Aunt Eustace handed it over, and everyone watched as Humphrey examined the gold band through the lenses. His eyes focused, then grew wide.

"What is it?" Olivia asked.

"There's an inscription on the inside," Humphrey said. "Look."

Olivia held the ring close to her face. "'*Amor vincit omnia*.' My Latin is not up to snuff, but I think it means—"

"Love conquers all," said James, rising to his feet. He put the ring on her finger and pressed a kiss to the back of her hand.

"Yes," she breathed. "It certainly has."

As everyone cheered and clapped, he leaned close to her ear. "Do you still have the Cleopatra costume?"

She raised a brow. "I might."

"Be sure to pack it."

"As you wish." Her eyes were full of promise—and love.

"On second thought"—he nipped lightly at her lobe—"I think you should wear it tonight."

She gave him a sultry smile. "I can't wait."

Jesus. He was already counting the minutes.

Don't miss the next scandalously sexy
Honeycote Novel from award-winning
author Anne Barton!

Lady Rose Sherbourne has always been
the quiet sister, the very voice of reason.
She knows she must wed a respectable
gentleman—and her first love is anything
but. Too bad her heart has a rebellious
streak a mile wide...

See the next page for a preview of

One Wild Winter's Eve.

Prologue

Summer 1815

*E*ven nice, obedient girls needed to escape now and then.

Lady Rose Sherbourne left shortly after breakfast. A warm breeze whipped tendrils of hair against her cheek, and the heels of her boots sank into the deliciously soft grass, still glistening with dew.

Each step across the vast lawn took her farther from Huntford Manor, its imposing grandeur, and its paralyzing memories.

Better yet, each step took her closer to Charles.

She glanced over her shoulder at the house, assuring herself that no one had seen her slip away. Her visits with the stable master—like so many other things—were best kept secret.

But the truth was, there was nothing improper about her relationship with Charles. Not really.

Perhaps the sight of his tanned forearms, large hands, and easy grin made her breath hitch in her throat. There wasn't a seventeen-year-old girl in all of England who'd be unaffected by his strength and quiet confidence. But her visits with Charles were not about flirtation. They were about preserving her sanity.

Some days, when she could feel it hanging by the very thinnest of threads, she fled to the stables and watched him work. The even strokes of his brush over a horse's coat, the rhythmic flexing of his shoulders as he pitched hay soothed her frayed edges. With him, she could forget who she was and what she'd seen. She could simply bask in the moment, and if she wasn't completely happy, well, she was close.

She sighed. Yes, the very best thing about Charles was the way he made her feel...normal.

As he tended to an injured horse or poured water into the troughs, he'd talk to her, his deep, expressive voice washing over her and healing her soul. While she perched on an upside-down pail, he'd tell funny stories, without seeming to find it odd that their conversation was completely one-sided.

Without minding that she never spoke.

Upon realizing that she was mute, some invariably analyzed her. *When, precisely, had she stopped talking? Could she make any sounds at all? What doctors had she seen and what treatment did they prescribe?* Others took her silence as a personal challenge, saying all manner of outrageous things in order to provoke a response—one that never came.

But Charles didn't treat her as an object of curiosity. He simply accepted her.

In her satchel, she carried a couple of books for him, carrots for Prometheus, and a small jar of milk for Romeo. She'd missed them terribly the past two days, too busy with dress fittings and ball preparations to steal away for a few hours. And so this morning she'd seized the opportunity to spend time with them, in spite of the gray clouds gathering in the western morning sky.

As she walked into the stable, the familiar smells of horses and hay tickled her nose. She looked around for Charles's shock of blond hair, topped by the brown cap which was always slightly askew. He wasn't there, and yet his presence filled the place. His overcoat hung from a peg beside the door, and a pair of work gloves lay on the ledge of an empty stall beside an open, face-down book. She glanced at the spine and smiled at his choice of reading material: *Annals of Agriculture and Other Useful Arts*.

One morning, over a game of chess, he'd shared that he dreamed of owning land. Selfishly, she hoped he wouldn't leave Huntford Manor anytime soon. She withdrew the volumes of mythology and Grimm's fairy tales from her bag and placed them beside his book.

The half dozen stalls to her right were occupied by Thoroughbreds—the very best a duke's money could buy. In a smaller stall to her left was Prometheus, a faithful old draft horse of questionable breeding. His back dipped and his tongue tended to hang from his mouth. Rose was willing to wager that Charles had brushed the horse's brown mane that morning, and yet it had already matted sweetly around his face. His ears perked up when he saw her, and she dug into her satchel for the carrots. He slurped them from her hand, then snorted haughtily, gloating for the benefit of the Thoroughbreds.

Rose wished she could ask Prometheus where Charles was. And where Romeo was, for that matter. The fluffy gray cat was usually first to greet her, twisting around her ankles, shamelessly crying for attention and treats. She peeked into the empty stall beside Prometheus—the one Romeo had usurped shortly after Rose found him—and checked the dry trough where the cat liked to nap. Empty. Only one thing was sure to bring her fickle friend out of hiding. She poured his milk into a tin bowl and waited.

"Lady Rose?"

She turned as Peter, a boy of ten or so, shot her a friendly grin. The freckle-faced stable hand practically worshipped Charles. "Are you looking for Mr. Holland?"

She nodded.

"He went searching for Romeo."

Rose tilted her head in a silent question.

"The cat wandered off a day or two ago and hasn't been round since."

Oh dear. Rose frowned.

"Don't worry, Mr. Holland will find him."

She walked to the back door of the stable and gazed at the thick woods that lay beyond. Peter came to stand beside her and pointed to a dirt path that led through a clump of trees and disappeared in the brush. "He went that way—not long ago."

Rose gave the boy a grateful smile and headed down the trail.

A sudden gust of wind plastered the skirt of her green morning dress to her legs, and she glanced at the darkening sky. Romeo had seemed well enough during her last visit, but what if he'd gotten sick? Or ventured into the woods and foolishly tangled with a snake or fox? She picked up her pace, ignoring a rumble of thunder so low she could feel it in her belly.

She followed the path as it meandered around the trunks of towering elms and twisting oaks, looking for Charles or Romeo. Once, she would have called out to them, her words floating through the forest. Now she was as silent as the hare that trembled in the hollow log near her feet. She'd forgotten the sound of her own voice.

And sometimes feared she'd never hear it again.

A familiar but unwelcome thudding began in her chest. She mustn't dwell on her troubles, mustn't dwell on the past. She walked faster, as if putting distance between her and her worries were just that easy. Low-hanging branches grabbed at her hair, and thorny underbrush scratched at her ankles. The woods blurred past her, muddy green. Her ragged breathing echoed in her ears, and the pungent smells of damp soil and leaves closed in around her, almost suffocating in their intensity. She picked up the front of her skirt and ran, looking down and dodging the stones and sticks in her way.

The toe of her boot caught on a gnarled root. Her satchel sailed through the air and the ground rose up to meet her.

Until a pair of strong arms caught and steadied her.

"Rose?"

Blinking, she looked up at Charles. He searched her face, his expression a mixture of concern and wonder.

"What's happened? Are you hurt?"

His hands easily encircled her arms above her gloves, his palms warm against her bare skin. His light brown eyes crinkled at the corners, letting her know he was happy to see her.

Was she well? She took a deep breath and felt the tension in her body uncoil. The forest came back into focus and her breathing slowed. Her heart still beat fast, but for possibly different reasons. She nodded.

Charles looked at her arms where he clasped them, frowned, and released her quickly, as if his hands had betrayed him. "Forgive me." He raked his fingers through his sun-streaked hair before retrieving his cap from the ground and stuffing it into the back pocket of his trousers. Then he scooped up her satchel and led her toward a small clearing several yards away.

"I was worried about Romeo," he said. "But I found him. The only problem is, I don't think we can call him Romeo anymore. Look."

He pointed at a nest of leaves on the ground, protected by a log on one side and a large rock on another. The cat rested there, sprawled on his—no, *her*—side, two tiny black kittens nursing under her watchful, weary gaze.

Bubbly with delight, Rose clasped her hands beneath her chin and knelt for a closer look.

The babes climbed and tumbled over one another, greedy for their mother's milk and attention. But as Romeo licked the back of one's head, her leg twitched and lifted. Another kitten.

Charles's brow creased. "You might not want to watch this, Rose. It's, ah, messy. Let's return to the stable. I'll do a few chores, and then you can beat me in chess."

She shook her head firmly. *Nothing* could drag her away.

Sighing, Charles sank on his haunches beside her, so close that his thigh brushed the skirt of her gown. "This could take a while, but I don't think she's in much pain."

Rose watched transfixed as the third kitten's hind paws

emerged first, followed by a rounded belly and pointed face. It resembled a bat wrapped in cobwebs, eerily still.

Romeo stretched, and her foot sent the newest kitten rolling like a black-and-gray mummy. It landed several inches from the leafy nest, and Rose's fingers itched to nestle it beside its mother's warm body. She took off her gloves.

"Patience," Charles whispered. "It's best if we let Romeo take care of this herself."

However, the gray cat was distracted and tired. Rose didn't blame her one bit, but after a minute passed, she shot Charles a pleading look. The newborn kitten, trapped in a thin film, looked so lifeless compared to its fuzzy siblings.

She reached out, unsure how to help but knowing she had to try.

"Wait. The less we handle the kitten the better." Using a handkerchief pulled from his pocket, he carefully broke the membrane and wiped the kitten's face.

Though its body unfurled slightly, it didn't move. Didn't breathe.

Charles's mouth was pressed in a thin line, and Rose wanted to scream at Romeo. *Take care of this one. It needs you.*

"If it doesn't start breathing soon, it's not going to survive." He swept the kitten into his handkerchief, laid flat on his palm. "Come on, little one."

Tears gathered in Rose's eyes. The creature looked so small, so helpless, with its eyes closed tight and its chest motionless. She leaned over Charles's hand, wishing she could somehow breathe life into the kitten.

Desperate, she lifted a corner of the handkerchief and

rubbed it over the kitten's chest. The fur there turned soft as down, but her patient remained in a precarious twilight—not quite alive, not quite dead. Several drops of crimson stained the crisp white cotton handkerchief. That couldn't be good. Tears rolled down her cheeks, and because she didn't know what else to do, what else to try, she rubbed the kitten's chest harder.

Charles reached for her wrist, stilling her. "I'm sorry, Rose."

No. This kitten was like her. Fragile and broken, but *not* dead.

She closed her eyes and made one last, fervent wish.

Overhead, thunder cracked, sending birds fluttering. Raindrops pattered on the canopy of leaves, searching for a path through the dense foliage. Several plunked on her head, streaked down her forehead, and mingled with her tears. But Charles's warm strength flowed through her, and she willed it to flow through the kitten as well.

"Rose. Look, he's moving!"

Unbelieving, she opened her eyes. The kitten yawned and stretched its paws, writhing on Charles's hand.

He gazed at her with wonder. "You did it. I should never have doubted you."

His words made her glow on the inside, but then his face dimmed.

"We still have a problem, though. It shouldn't be bleeding this much." He pointed at the kitten's belly. "See where the cord ripped? We need something to tie around it. I don't suppose you have anything in your bag?"

Frowning, she shook her head. She had string at the house, of course, but by the time she ran there and back, it could well be too late.

Where to find string or thread? She flipped over the edge of her gown, hastily yanked a thread from the hem, and held it up for Charles to see.

"It's perfect. Your fingers are better suited for this than mine. I'll hold him while you tie the strand tightly around the cord. Don't worry, you won't hurt him. Or her," he added with a heart-stopping smile. "We'll have plenty of time to figure that out later."

Her hands trembled so badly that the thread missed its mark and she tied a knot in the air.

But Charles spoke softly, his breath warm near her ear. "Take your time. This one's a fighter. You're almost there."

The rain fell harder, plopping on the backs of her hands as she worked. Charles held his cap over the kitten to shelter it, and Rose remained focused on the task before her. She pressed on, ignoring the thunder, the blood, and, most daunting of all, her self-doubt.

At last, she pulled the strands tight and looked at Charles triumphantly.

"Well done." The approval in his voice and in his eyes made her belly flip—in a strange and pleasant way.

She held up the ends of the thread, each several inches long.

"Here, hold our patient. I've got a knife." In one smooth motion, he snapped open a pocketknife and cut the extra lengths off the thread. "Let's return him to Romeo and his siblings. See if he can hold his own."

Gingerly, Rose placed the kitten in the nest, just under its mother's chin. It huddled close to her neck, nuzzling against her fur and soaking up her warmth.

Romeo remained vexingly aloof.

"He won't take no for an answer," predicted Charles. "Just you watch."

Refusing to be ignored, the kitten crawled its way on top of its mother's head and slid down her nose. At last, she began to lick its fur.

"Thank God!" Charles jumped up, lifting Rose and spinning her till she was breathless and dizzy. Lowering her slowly to the ground, he added, "He's going to be fine."

The kitten *would* be fine. And maybe—just maybe—she would be too.

Because standing there in the rain, with Charles's hands firmly on the curve of her hips, she felt strong enough to face anything. Even her past.

His chest rose and fell as rapidly as hers did—faster than it should. His amber eyes turned a rich chestnut, and his gaze dropped to her mouth. Like he wanted to kiss her.

There was a long list of reasons why she shouldn't let him.

She was a lady; he was a stable master.

She was gently bred; he bred horses.

She was expected to marry a gentleman; he came from a long line of servants.

And yet, in spite of all that, she placed her hands on his chest and lifted her chin, inviting him to kiss her. It was, perhaps, the most daring and reckless thing she'd ever done.

Charles was worth it.

"Rose…I…" He wrapped his hands around her wrists, his face clouding with regret. "This is…tempting. But there's a line we cannot cross. If we did…if *I* did… there'd be no going back to how things were."

Maybe she wanted to cross the line. Jump right over it. She gripped the lapels of his jacket, willing him to understand.

"I'm fond of you, but sometimes...I don't know what you expect of me, what you want from me."

I want you to heal me, to make me whole, to make me feel alive. I want you to kiss me.

She held her breath as he searched her face. With a sigh, he looked away, and she knew that for once, her silence had disappointed him. *She'd* disappointed him.

He released her and took two steps backward. "If ever you need a friend, you may depend on me. But I think it's best if you don't visit the stables for a while."

She gasped, reached for his arm, and opened her mouth.

He froze, expectant.

And all the things she wanted to say to him, all the feelings she wanted to confess, died somewhere between her heart and her throat. She pressed her lips together.

He nodded, as though he should have known better than to hope for more. "Good-bye, Lady Rose."

Fall in Love with Forever Romance

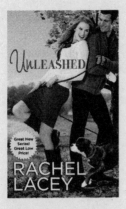

UNLEASHED
by Rachel Lacey

Cara has one rule: Don't get attached. It's served her well with the dogs she's fostered and the children she's nannied. But one smile from her sexy neighbor has her thinking some rules are made to be broken. Fans of Jill Shalvis will fall in love with this sassy, sexy debut!

MADE FOR YOU
by Lauren Layne

She's met her match... she just doesn't know it yet. Fans of Jennifer Probst and Rachel Van Dyken will fall head over heels for the second book in the Best Mistake series.

Fall in Love with Forever Romance

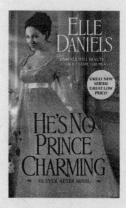

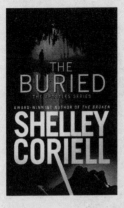

THE WICKED WAYS OF ALEXANDER KIDD
by Paula Quinn

The newest sinfully sexy Scottish romance in *New York Times* bestselling author Paula Quinn's Highland Heirs series, about the niece of a Highland chief who stows away on a pirate ship, desperate for adventure, and the pirate captain whose wicked ways inflame an irresistible desire...

VISIT US ONLINE AT

WWW.HACHETTEBOOKGROUP.COM

FEATURES:

**OPENBOOK BROWSE AND
SEARCH EXCERPTS**
•
AUDIOBOOK EXCERPTS AND PODCASTS
•
AUTHOR ARTICLES AND INTERVIEWS
•
**BESTSELLER AND PUBLISHING
GROUP NEWS**
•
SIGN UP FOR E-NEWSLETTERS
•
**AUTHOR APPEARANCES AND TOUR
INFORMATION**
•
SOCIAL MEDIA FEEDS AND WIDGETS
•
DOWNLOAD FREE APPS

BOOKMARK HACHETTE BOOK GROUP
@ WWW.HACHETTEBOOKGROUP.COM